THE WAR IN THE DARK

NICK SETCHFIELD

THE WAR IN THE DARK

TITAN BOOKS

The War in the Dark
Print edition ISBN: 9781785657092
E-book edition ISBN: 9781785657108

Published by Titan Books
A division of Titan Publishing Group Ltd
144 Southwark Street, London SE1 0UP

First edition: July 2018
1 2 3 4 5 6 7 8 9 10

A CIP catalogue record for this title is available from the British Library.

Printed and bound by CPI Group (UK) Ltd, Croydon, CR0 4YY

For Dad

SEMPER OCCULTUS
'ALWAYS SECRET'

Motto of the British Secret Intelligence Service

1

OCTOBER 1963

Christopher Winter had never put a bullet in the head of a priest before. The idea felt faintly blasphemous.

He smiled in the half-light. It was the kind of morbid little thought that came to him on these occasions. Sometimes it felt like a ghost trace of conscience. He let it go.

He was a tall man in his forties, lean as fuse wire, his black curls cropped close to the skull, military fashion. His face was nearly as unexceptional as he needed it to be. Only his eyes betrayed him, startlingly green in the London dusk. The lids were hooded, as if trying to conceal the remarkable irises.

It was almost evening. Clouds the colour of ash occupied the sky. Winter waited in the doorway of Kingsland Edwardian Butchers, inhaling a ripe tang of meat and sawdust as he watched the Portobello Road.

Tables filled the street. There were stalls of silverware and bric-a-brac, lamps and decanters, apples

and pocket-watches. A sudden gust scattered a sheaf of antique maps. They blew into the gutter, their edges claimed by petrol spills.

No sign of Hatherly, his echo man. Not that Winter was meant to see him, of course. Hatherly was entrusted to be invisible, only revealing his presence if things turned ugly. Once a child's nanny had caught a ricochet and lay pooling bright, innocent blood on a marble floor in Mayfair. Hatherly had broken cover and taken a bullet in the sternum for his trouble, shot by the same Soviet sniper that had just eliminated a defector. *An operational failure*, the memorandum had stated. The girl had died two days later.

Winter wanted to spot him, just as a matter of professional pride. It was good practice.

He let his Woodbine flare and die. The streetlamps were on now, their sodium glow exposing a fine rain. Winter buttoned his houndstooth coat and retrieved a pair of driving gloves from its pockets. The lambskin strained over his lean fingers and prominent knuckles. He could feel the dull weight of his Webley & Scott .25 against his heart.

It was time to kill Father Costigan.

As he walked he lit another cigarette and recalled Faulkner's briefing. The SIS had kept tabs on Costigan for a while now. Given his position his communist sympathies naturally attracted attention. It wasn't unusual for such men to fall hard for leftist rhetoric – priests often fancied themselves as social reformers – but it was always

noted, and never favourably. No one wanted Marxism disseminated under cover of whist drives and evensong.

And then his name had surfaced in Soviet radio traffic. The British monitoring station in Vienna had snagged it, flashed it home. The clergyman was trading secrets with the enemy. Just how the priest of a shabby little church in Notting Hill had access to the finer particulars of British intelligence was a detail Faulkner had chosen not to share.

Winter had no idea what information was bleeding to Moscow. He knew only what he needed to: Costigan had leaked material of national importance. That was enough. His superiors knew more, of course, but secrets built the hierarchy, polished the mirror-maze.

The Church of St John of the Cross stood on the corner, squat and soot-stained. A scruffy noticeboard carried faded flyers for weekly choir practice and the Christmas jumble sale. There was a stone Christ crucified in the doorway, captured in an agony of granite. Winter nearly stubbed his cigarette out on the effigy but he hesitated. He wasn't an especially good man but he tried to keep his soul as clean as he could. He tossed the Woodbine to the pavement and let it expire among the weeds.

Winter stepped through the porch and into the creamy gloom of the nave. The pews were lit by candles, illuminating the stained-glass window that dominated the interior. There was a striking scent of decay. Something mouldering, halfway between damp and dust.

Winter's training was triggered as he entered the church,

approaching his target: he found himself scrutinising every potential point of concealment and escape, appraising the geometry of threat, just as he had been taught.

His senses bristled. This was a place of worship in the heart of his own country but there was something here that uneased him, something that refused to be measured and evaluated.

A motion caught his eye. He glanced up at the ceiling. For a moment the shadows themselves seemed to swarm across the rafters.

He stepped deeper into the church, past the pews with their threadbare hassocks and dilapidated hymn books. An eyeless bust of St John of the Cross faced him across the nave. The statuette's blind gaze felt strangely reproachful. Once again something shapeless crawled at the very edge of his vision. He tilted his head and saw nothing.

It was colder now, as if London's chill had entered the church in his wake. He kept walking, taking care to soften his steps on the flagstones. He passed the font. There was a dull bronze smear on the chipped porcelain. It looked very much like blood.

He hoped Hatherly was close.

'Onward, Christian soldier,' said a voice, behind him. The words were gentle, warm and threatening, like a razor dipped in honey.

Winter turned. A figure stood at the entrance to the church, haloed by the glow of the porch light. He was a portly man in a black cassock, jowls bulging over the rim of his dog collar. He wore wire-framed spectacles. The

moon-shaped lenses shone with reflected candlelight, obscuring the eyes.

'Father Costigan?'

'Of course.'

Not that Winter needed to ask. He knew precisely who this man was. Only an hour ago he had studied a black-and-white photograph in a crisp manila folder, noted every liver spot, registered every mole. Asking the man to confirm his identity was a formality, part of the ritual.

The priest began to walk towards him, past the dimly lit pews. His steps were easy, unhurried. 'I don't know your name,' he said, 'but I can guess why you're here.'

Winter wouldn't draw the gun. Not yet. It would look like he was flinching.

'Clearly I've betrayed Queen and country,' smiled the priest, softly mocking the words. 'Time for my divine punishment, in the name of national interest. You people do love your biblical judgements.'

Winter's voice was even. 'Kneel on the floor and place your hands at your temples.'

The priest smirked as he drew level with Winter. The man smelt of must and abandoned rooms. 'And what about your punishment?'

Costigan's eyes were revealed now. They looked like bags of blood, weighing upon the lids. The priest met Winter's gaze and matched it.

'Just look at you. I've rarely met a soul so in need of redemption. I can almost taste it. What in God's name have you done in your life?'

'Father Costigan. Please. We can do this with dignity. Kneel on the floor and place your hands at your temples.'

Again there was a ripple of shadow at the periphery of Winter's vision. He kept his gaze locked upon the priest. 'I won't ask again.'

Costigan held the moment, contemptuous. And then he turned and walked to the lectern that stood to the side of the nave. A mahogany eagle roosted upon it, its beak carved in a snarl. Costigan picked up a Bible, bound in oxblood leather.

'By the book, I see. Well, this is my book.'

He wet a thumb and leafed through the pages. And then he paused, with a smile.

'And I beheld, and heard an angel flying through the midst of heaven, saying with a loud voice, Woe, woe, woe, to the inhabiters of the earth by reason of the other voices of the trumpet of the three angels, which are yet to sound!'

The priest's voice was commanding, full of religious theatre. The words filled the empty church.

'Revelation chapter eight, verse thirteen. The King James Bible. Though some say there's a mistranslation and it's actually an eagle that's flying through the midst of heaven. The eagle is, after all, the enemy of the serpent. Are you my enemy, young man?'

Winter was thrown by the priest's reaction. In his experience men usually anticipated the bullet in a number of ways, none of them especially dignified. There was terror, there was pleading and sometimes there was a

16

frantic attempt to charm. This was something new. Costigan was gliding above this confrontation. He had an arrogance that seemed utterly unafraid.

'We can go in the back,' said Winter, flatly.

The priest laughed.

'Yes, we wouldn't want to stain the house of God. Dear Mrs Gilligan works miracles with the duster but blood is so troublesome.'

He closed the Bible, left the lectern and walked back to Winter.

'Tell me,' he said. 'You clearly believe in judgement. Do you really think you won't be judged for killing me? In a holy place like this, no less?'

'You have betrayed your country.'

'My country!' the priest spat. 'This kingdom of rain? Don't be so stupid. And tell me, just what secrets do you imagine I've traded?'

'Not my job to know.'

Costigan leaned close, his lips curling. His breath smelt faintly of tar. 'My secrets will burn the flesh from this world.'

It was time to end this. Winter reached inside his overcoat. The pistol felt reassuring in his hand, heavy and familiar. He ignored the sweat on its lattice grip and removed a silencer from an outside pocket. In a quick, deft movement he screwed the tube to the head of the barrel, twisting it into place. It clicked, locked.

'On your knees.'

The priest threw a hand towards him. It held a knife,

17

plucked from the cassock. The blade flashed and found Winter's arm, puncturing his coat and piercing the flesh. There was a hot flare of pain but Winter kept the gun tight in his fist. He smashed it against Costigan's hand. The knife tumbled to the flagstones.

The priest's fingers curled around Winter's forearm. He had remarkable strength. The hand closed, choking a fresh spasm of pain from the wounded arm.

The gun jerked upwards. Winter's finger squeezed. A bullet fired with a cordite stench. It struck the stained-glass window, splintering a cherub.

The priest's nails dug into Winter's wrist, pricking the skin, claiming blood. Winter forced the trembling gun higher, closer to Costigan's face. Another bullet fired. This one sailed into the rafters, scattering dust, useless as the last.

Costigan's other hand reached for Winter's face. The broad palm pressed against his mouth, the nails targeting his eyes. Again the power in the man was astonishing. He seemed possessed by a feral energy.

Winter locked his fist around the priest's arm and pushed back. As he did so he looked into Costigan's eyes. Something moved in the pupils. Something that didn't entirely belong to a man. Something that was one with the church's shadows.

The priest's hand moved closer. Winter stared at the greasy flesh. It was bulging, translucent. The skin itself seemed to strain, as if struggling to contain something.

'Christ,' he breathed.

The hand was bulbous now. Swollen, it cracked and tore. A shoal of insects burst from the ruptured flesh. Flies, lice, silverfish.

The creatures poured onto Winter. Instinctively he shut his eyes and bolted his mouth, though he wanted to cry out, even scream. He staggered backwards into a pew, shaking the flood of insects from his face even as he sensed them scurry into his hair.

Finally he forced his eyes open and stared at Father Costigan. The priest's expression was savage now, his face streaked with gobs of bile. He had removed his glasses. The man's eyes were orbs of pure blood. Tiny albino spiders prised themselves out of the tear ducts, their pale legs curling over the lids.

Winter raised and steadied his gun. He aimed for the head.

'I am beyond flesh,' Costigan said, defiantly. 'Flesh shall burn.'

Winter pulled the trigger. A bullet tore through Costigan's skull, shredding bone. The priest fell.

Winter stepped forward, kicking insects from his shoes. Hearing only his own fractured breathing he pulled a pencil and a notebook from his pocket, turned his wrist to expose his watch and noted the exact time. His pencil tremored in his hand. His writing was a brisk scratch.

It was then that he smelt smoke. The corpse was burning: flames spread from the cassock and began to consume the body. They leapt from the priest and sought the pews, feasting on the old wood. The lectern, too,

caught fire, the carved eagle succumbing to the rage of unnatural flame. Hymn numbers burned and blackened.

Winter's eyes prickled at the smoke. His lungs began to rebel at the charred air. Turning to go, he glanced at the stained-glass window, seeing the London night through the headless, bullet-smashed image of a cherub. There was a star in the sky, pin-bright.

Winter left the church. He wanted to run but he walked, as calmly and as casually as he could, for all that he was dripping insects. And then, when he had paced the length of the street, he turned into an alley, dropped to his knees and vomited.

He crouched there for a while in the cool dark, his head resting against the rim of a steel bin. His arm pulsed with pain from the knife wound and the sleeve of his shirt felt tacky with blood.

He tried to process what he had just seen. The whole experience had the gauzy feeling of a waking dream. All he knew was that he had encountered something extraordinary. Something that had just rewritten the rules of his world.

He gathered himself, rose to his feet and began to walk back to Portobello. It was raining now, a determined rain that drummed the pavement and turned traffic lights into fairground blurs of colour. *This kingdom of rain…* Winter heard a fire engine in the distance.

He passed the junction of Chepstow Villas, past its intersection with Westbourne Grove. As he did so he saw a familiar figure across the street, sheltered by a tree.

Hatherly. His echo man. Thank God.

Winter quickened his pace. He had no idea how he would explain any of it. He was just grateful for his colleague's presence. That was all that he needed right now. That and a whisky mac in the cosy fug of The Old Star and Crown.

He nodded as he crossed the road, dodging a black cab and a cyclist.

'Hatherly, I…'

The man almost had the face of Hatherly.

Almost.

Winter peered through the shadows of the branches that played across the silent figure. Momentarily familiar, the man's features had shifted like water, resolving into the face of a stranger.

'I'm sorry,' said Winter. 'I assumed you were somebody else.'

The man walked away, barely registering the encounter. Winter watched him cross into Westbourne Grove.

For a moment he had seemed to have no face at all.

2

A white light, sharp and urgent.

It was there at the edge of his perception, inescapable. His eyelids flinched, quivered, resisting its brilliance. He sensed himself moving out of a deep, consuming darkness. The light was summoning him.

Winter opened his eyes. His pupils shrank, instinctively contracting. The electric glare was blinding.

He began to see the room.

There was a tall lamp to his left, its spindly aluminium frame bent into a crouch. The bulb was close and bullyingly hot. He could feel his pores tingling with sweat as the wattage burned.

He looked down at his arms. They lay on the padded rests of a chair. One had a bandage over the knife wound, a rust-coloured smear of blood soiling the gauze. The other was bare, the shirtsleeve rolled to the elbow. There was a fresh bruise below the wrist and a puncture mark where a sizeable needle had clearly entered his bloodstream. Both arms throbbed.

'So just how do you account for what happened?'

demanded a voice, insistent but weary.

Still muzzy, Winter focused beyond the light. A figure solidified: a stocky, bearded man in a three-piece worsted suit, his hair a silver thatch. Sir Crispin Faulkner, head of SIS. Next to him was a man he didn't know. He had a dispassionate gaze and wore a doctor's coat. There was a fat hypodermic in his hand. It held a viscous amber liquid.

So they had drugged him. Sodium thiopental or some kind of hypnotic benzodiazapene, he imagined. Truth serum. Potent. Effective. Standard practice. Not normally applied to one's own side. It would certainly explain the lurch of nausea he was now experiencing. His body and his memory were reconnecting.

This was no debrief, he realised. It was an interrogation.

Winter reached for words. 'I… I cannot account for it, sir.'

There was a third man in the hot, boxy room. A friendlier presence, for all that his face was grim with concern. Winter saw the paisley bow-tie, the familiar watery eyes. Malcolm.

'It could always be some kind of psychotropic agent,' said Malcolm Hands, stepping from the shadows. He rested an arm on a filing cabinet. 'Hallucinogen of some sort. Airborne dispersal or contact activation. Skin on skin, that kind of thing. I've heard that the CIA are making remarkable progress in the field.'

'I doubt it's the Americans,' said Faulkner, curtly.

'Well, I've no idea where the Soviets are with the technology.'

'You bloody should. We should be on top of all of this.'

There was a scratch of a match. Malcolm lit a Capstan and offered the packet to Winter. 'Cigarette?'

'God, yes.'

Winter borrowed the matches and lit a cigarette. He took a quick, hungry drag and let the smoke disperse through his nostrils. The bitter vapour troubled his throat and he coughed. There was still a furtive taste of chemicals on his tongue.

'I don't care what the Americans or the Reds have,' he said. 'There's no hallucinogen in the world halfway powerful enough to do that. I know what I saw in that church.'

'Do you?' asked Faulkner.

Winter buried a mutinous comeback. He took a moment to steady his thoughts. 'Sir, it was real. Whatever I saw, it was real. I am not lying to you. And I am not losing my mind.'

'The psychiatric officer will assess that,' said Faulkner, briskly. 'Now consider yourself relieved of active duty, pending his findings. When we finally find your blasted echo man we'll be sure to let you know.'

Faulkner gathered a wad of paper, jammed it inside a manila folder and took his leave of the room, trailing an irritable pall. The quiet man in the doctor's coat locked his syringe in a silver case and followed him.

'I'll be outside,' said Malcolm, softly.

Winter nodded, extinguishing the Capstan. He

rolled his cuffs down, taking care not to snag the shirt on the bloodied bandage. He raised himself up and, unsteady for a second, grasped the chair for support. The room tilted around him. Then he regained his bearings and collected his jacket. It had been neatly folded and placed on the desk. They were nothing if not considerate.

Winter straightened his tie, closed the door and stepped into the corridor. It was as dismal as all the other passages in the building, part of the decaying connective tissue of 54 Broadway. It could have been a drab, dusty corner of some neglected public school. And sometimes that was exactly what the service felt like. A crumbling fiefdom, breeding the charcoal-suited officers of empire while the world raced on outside.

Winter had no idea what time it was. His watch had been removed. It was probably in his jacket pocket. As he hunted for it he peered through the window. Sunlight made a greasy haze of the glass. Was it morning? He saw neat rows of dark cars, their bonnets gleaming like ranks of beetles in the autumn light.

He found his watch and buckled the cracked leather strap. Almost midday. He had the feeling that time had been taken from him. How long had he been in that room? He could barely remember entering it.

Malcolm stood at the end of the corridor, admiring a painting. It was a gloomy portrait of an Elizabethan, mounted in an ornate gilded frame. The man in the picture had a hard, unreadable gaze and a trim satyr's

beard. A white ruff circled his throat.

'Interesting man, Sir Francis Walsingham,' said Malcolm, indicating the portrait with a languid jab of his cigarette. 'Elizabeth's favourite. The first spymaster. Set up a network that reached as far to the east as Turkey. He understood the value of intelligence, that chap. We're all his children, you know.'

'I remember,' said Winter, joining him beside the painting. 'You showed me this picture on my first day here. You told me we were the New Elizabethans. I tried not to laugh.'

'Did I really? It sounds like me.' Malcolm smiled and the skin wrinkled around his wan grey eyes. 'Precious little sense of history these days. But the wars we fight are still his wars, for all the new names we give them. Do we really imagine this is the first Cold War? We've been fighting them for centuries.'

Winter regarded the brushwork. There were tiny cracks where the paint was flaking. 'You told me something else he said. "Knowledge is never too dear."'

'I'm touched, Christopher. You have an excellent memory.'

'You're a bloody good teacher, Malcolm. When you're sober.'

Malcolm's eyes narrowed and his voice fell by a register. 'Here's another one of the old boy's little sayings. "See and keep silent." Not the worst words to live by.'

He leaned closer, though they were quite alone in the passageway.

'Tea dance at nine,' he said, with a quick, tight smile. 'Don't be late, dear heart.'

And then he turned in the direction of the fire doors, his heels ringing on the hardwood floor.

Winter stared after him, intrigued. Typical Malcolm.

The Fairbridge Hotel had taken a bomb in the war. A V-2 had torn out of a starless sky in 1944 and punched through the roof, piercing five elegant storeys and killing over three hundred people. The building's jagged, scaffolded remains still stood derelict in Knightsbridge, waiting for someone to give its ghosts a future.

Winter entered the penthouse ballroom. Rainwater ran between the broken tiles, pooling in dark corners of the dance floor. An elegant bronze of a female dancer lay toppled, her severed head flung amid the rubble. There was a charred Art Deco bas relief, decorated with pelicans, and a large mirrored door, blackened and blistered by the heat of the blast.

The roof was gone, of course. Shards of masonry framed the night sky like a jawful of smashed teeth. Winter looked down. The bomb had left a hell of a hole. The innards of the hotel lay exposed: a spine of lift cages and great steel struts that still held its shattered grandeur together.

There was the sound of a piano. Someone was artlessly picking out a tune with a single finger, like a child. The strings were clearly damaged. It made the melody even

sadder. Winter took a moment to place it. 'A Nightingale Sang In Berkeley Square'. One of his mother's favourites.

'How do the words go?' asked Malcolm Hands, ending the tune in a discordant ripple of chords. 'Something about angels dining at the Ritz... Your mother liked it, didn't she?'

'She did. I told you that?'

Malcolm nodded. 'Funny the things that lodge in the memory.'

He struck a key, and struck it again, repeatedly. 'This song makes me think of Phillipa. 1942. April. Early morning. We were on Primrose Hill, still dressed to the nines, still rather sloshed. She looked at the city and she turned to me and said, "I think the war's over." I asked her what she meant. She smiled – she was pretty – and she said, "Because I think I just heard a nightingale sing in Berkeley Square." Two months later she was dead. Aerial bomb. Just like this place.'

Malcolm struck the key again. This time he let it resonate. 'Yes, funny the things that stick in the mind.'

He looked at Winter. 'Now Von Braun's working for the Americans on their precious rockets. Sometimes I wonder if there are any true sides anymore. Maybe we just take turns being friends and enemies with everyone. Stops it getting boring, I suppose.'

It was nine o'clock. The Fairbridge was a shared secret between them, an occasional private meeting place beyond the eyes of the service. Sometimes you needed spaces like that. A refuge. A chance to breathe, to confide.

The two men were close – or as close as their choice of career allowed them. They had begun almost as mentor and pupil. Now they enjoyed something that felt close to real friendship. And still, Winter realised, there was much about Malcolm's life that he didn't know. He had never mentioned a Phillipa before.

Winter edged past the crater in the floor, moving around the stiff-backed chairs. Some of the tables still had champagne glasses upon them. Their once immaculate tablecloths were filthy with soot. 'Any sign of Hatherly?'

'Not a word. I've sent Haynes in as a priority. He'll find him.'

'It should be me.'

'You're relieved of duty, remember. We wouldn't want to undermine Sir Crispin, now would we? I doubt he'd take it terribly well.'

'I don't need psychiatric assessment, Malcolm.' The words felt hot on his tongue.

'I know you don't. That's why we're meeting here. There's a lot I need to tell you. Take a look…'

Malcolm gestured upwards, through the rent in the roof. Winter saw only the London sky, deep blue and full of stars…

'What am I looking at?'

'I believe it's called the future, though I could be mistaken. Go on, take a really good look. You might see them. Their orbit occasionally takes them over London.'

'I don't know what I'm looking at.'

'Telstar 1,' smiled Malcolm. 'Telstar 2. Our

30

communications satellites. The clever twins, up there giving the Sputnik boys a run for their money. Sometimes I imagine I can see them winking, but it's probably only Venus.'

Winter knew of the Telstar project, of course. The first satellite had launched the summer before last, its successor earlier this year. They were a bright hope for Britain. A sliver of tomorrow. God knew the war still clung to this country like silt. What was the phrase Harold Wilson had used in that speech the other week? The white heat of technology? You could feel it beginning to burn these days.

'We have placed new stars in the sky,' said Malcolm, grandly. 'In 1572 Dr John Dee saw a new star. That winter it lit up the skies of Europe. People feared it, naturally. They'd always believed that the heavens had been fixed at the point of creation. They'd studied them, mapped them, pinned them down in their charts. This was something new. This meant the universe could change. It could alter. All things were not eternal. It must have been a bloody terrifying prospect for the poor bastards.'

Malcolm paused, his pale eyes more alive than Winter had ever seen them. 'Now here we are. The New Elizabethans. We're not afraid of the skies anymore. Perhaps we should be.'

'Malcolm,' pressed Winter, impatient for a straight answer. 'Why am I here?'

Malcolm took a breath. 'The world is more than we know, Christopher. And less than we hope.'

Winter let his frustration show. 'What does that even mean?' he snapped.

'It means that the true Cold War has been fought for millennia. The oldest war we know. The war we fight at the edges of the light. The war in the dark.'

Winter heard the words but took a moment to make any sense of them. If not for his experience in Notting Hill he might have imagined Malcolm was suffering some kind of breakdown.

'What did I encounter in that church?'

'A demon,' said Malcolm, bluntly. 'We caught one in Kursk, once, back in the forties. They're an absolute bugger to interrogate. All available intelligence suggests they're a lower order of unearthly being. Powerful, amoral, frequently feral. They don't tend to take sides as such. They're players and chancers. Very much out for themselves. An absolute nuisance, really.'

'How long have we known about them?'

'I can show you files dating back to the court of Elizabeth. Accounts of these beasts that would freeze your heart. John Dee was one of us, you know. Not just a scholar and an alchemist but a spy and an agent of Walsingham. We've always been engaged in this war, Christopher. Always.'

Winter paused to process this. He half heard the hum of Knightsbridge traffic through the torn roof. It seemed to belong to a whole other world. 'So what was Costigan trading?'

Malcolm's tongue wet his lips. 'Runes, as far as we can

ascertain. Occult symbols and signifiers. We've seen them before. Intercepted some in '59 in Krasnoyarsk. We've had codebreakers on them. Turing's mob. No luck.'

Malcolm pulled a metal flask from his jacket pocket. He twisted the cap and took an anxious swig. There was an aroma of whisky. Winter declined the offer of a sip.

'Whatever these symbols are, whatever they mean, they are clearly important. So important that the Russians want them very badly indeed. I know men who believe these secrets may be more powerful than the atom bomb.'

'How is that possible?'

'Oh, I've stopped thinking in terms of the possible. It gets you nowhere.'

Malcolm pocketed the flask. 'There's not really that much difference between spycraft and magecraft, you know. It's all symbols and enchantments. Crack a code, cast a spell. We're all walking in the shadow realms, Christopher.'

Winter considered Malcolm's words. He needed to make some kind of practical sense of all this.

'So Costigan was trading with the Russians?'

Malcolm shook his head. 'That's what we thought at first, when we fished his name from the Soviet chatter. Turns out there's a third party. A man in Vienna, rather well connected. No politics. That's who the priest was trading with.'

'That's not how I was briefed. I was told Costigan had Soviet principles.'

Malcolm snorted. 'Do you think these creatures have

any kind of principles? Look, it's messy. You didn't need the details.'

'Who's in on all this?'

Malcolm wiped his mouth, mopping a smear of whisky from his lips. 'I can't tell you. I'm not meant to tell you any of this. But you've just become involved, haven't you? And once you're involved there's no easy way out.'

The older man stepped close to him. In a gesture that was almost fatherly he smoothed the collar of Winter's overcoat.

'Go home to Joyce. Make sure she's safe.'

Winter found himself bristling in spite of the kindness in Malcolm's voice. 'Joyce? She's never been a part of this!'

'They won't care,' said Malcolm. And then, more gently, 'I'll do what I can.'

And with a small, weak smile he walked away. His body was quickly claimed by the shadows of the ballroom.

Winter stood there in silence, aware of how cold he felt in this broken place. Other, sharper instincts kicked in: was he alone? His eyes examined the darkness. He tilted an ear and heard a drip of water, pinging on an overturned table in the far corner. The only scent was the lingering trace of Malcolm's whisky. Yes, he imagined he was quite alone – unless they were very, very good.

He raised his head, looking through the ragged remains of the roof.

There were new stars above London.

3

The corpse of Carl Hatherly was waiting in the car. It was propped up in the passenger seat, gazing blindly through the windscreen. The dead eyes were almost accusatory.

Winter sighed. The sight of his colleague's body rattled him. It also made him feel weary.

He had parked his Ford Zephyr in a quiet alley at the rear of a hotel, close to a loading bay. As he approached the vehicle he saw that the door had been jimmied, and expertly so. He noted the telltale scratch of wire on the chrome of the lock. The car had only been there half an hour. They had known he was coming.

He scanned the alley and quietly unlocked the driver's door. There was a clatter of metal on tarmac and he froze. Just a fox, bothering a bin. The animal pattered into the shadows and the street was silent again. Winter eased himself into the driver's seat, glaring into the alleyway. His fingers tattooed a rhythm on the wheel. And then he turned to examine the body.

There was a hole in the exact centre of Hatherly's

forehead. The melted flesh formed a tiny, blood-ringed whorl around the wound. It was a neat, unshowy job. Precise. Efficient. Professional.

Winter caught himself. Christ. He was actually critiquing this kill.

He closed the eyes of his echo man, almost tenderly. And then he lifted the cold, bloodless hand, shuddering at the fish-scale texture of the skin. There was a vicious imprint in the flesh. Hatherly's wrists had been scored by cord. He had been bound before he died.

Winter knew this for what it was, of course. A piece of theatre. A warning. A totem.

Again he caught himself. A totem? Peculiar choice of word. Wasn't that something to do with voodoo? Malcolm's talk of an occult war had clearly had an effect.

Winter rummaged among the clutter of Ordnance Survey maps on the back seat. He found his grey felt trilby, dusted it down and placed it over Hatherly's eyes, hiding the bullethole but not the frozen scream of the mouth.

He peered into the alley once more. There was a sweep of headlights in the distance, the nearby growl of an engine. A lorry, perhaps, reversing. He clicked on the dashboard radio and tuned aimlessly between the channels. A gust of static resolved into the clipped tones of the Home Service and then the sound of The Shadows playing 'Wonderful Land' on Radio Luxembourg. He listened to the feeble, fading signal as it clutched the airwaves, then he switched the tune off. It felt inappropriate in the company of a dead man.

He started the car and drove out of Knightsbridge, doing his best to ignore the body beside him. He had to get rid of it, clearly. There was no other choice. It would deny a decent man a funeral but his other options would lead to complications. Hatherly would have understood. Field agents knew how ugly practicalities could be.

Best not to report this to Faulkner, he reasoned. Malcolm had put the worm of doubt in him. He needed time to evaluate just whom he could trust.

He drove to the docks at Wapping, taking the side streets where he could. He let the car purr through the wharves, past the filthy Victorian warehouses with their shattered windows and grime-blackened names of sugar traders. Great cranes rose over rusting hulks of boats, their towering steel frames like a fossil army against the horizon.

A fog prowled the quays, grey and spectral. These docks were meant to be a place of activity. By night they felt like a place of abandonment. A place where things could be abandoned.

Winter tucked the car into a cobbled alley. He rooted around by the gear stick and found a tin of Simpkins travel sweets. He twisted the lid, reached inside and broke apart a congealed cluster of fruit drops. He popped one in his mouth and looked out at the docks. He imagined Telstar gazing down on them in disdain. This was an old world, an old Britain. Its time would soon be gone.

It was then that Hatherly spoke.

'Hurts…'

It was a single word, a single syllable, but it sounded

as though it was being torn from his throat. The dead man said it again and this time it was even more wracked. 'Hurts...'

Startled, Winter lifted the brow of the hat. Hatherly's eyes were open now. Something glimmered in the pupils; something alive, but not quite life. The mouth forced itself wider and there was the sound of bone grinding in the jaw.

'Hurts!'

The breath was rank, like the buried air of a grave. Winter almost gagged. He watched, incredulous, as the man's right hand began to move. The death-locked fingers juddered, creaked apart, unfurled.

And then, with uncanny speed, they reached for Winter's throat. The hand encircled his windpipe, clammy and determined. Winter countered Hatherly's arm with his own and tried to force it away but there was an extraordinary amount of power in the dead man's chokehold. His vision began to blacken at the edges.

Fighting to focus, channelling all of his strength into his forearm, Winter smashed the fist of the corpse into the dashboard. The undead fingers flexed and curled.

Winter's free hand snatched the pistol from his shoulder holster. He jammed the barrel of the Webley against Hatherly's head and pulled the trigger. A bullet tore through the man's skull and pierced the glass of the passenger door, striking the wall of a warehouse with a bright, fleeting spark.

A soup of blood and brain matter lay splattered on the

windscreen. If there had been life in Hatherly's body it was now expelled.

Winter lay back in the driver's seat, his heart hammering. And then, very much aware he had just fired a bullet without a silencer – the docks were bound to be patrolled – he exited the car. He hurried to the passenger door and dragged out Hatherly's remains.

There was the steady slosh of water against the wharves. From a nearby quay a ship's horn sounded through the fog. Winter opened the boot and gathered up a sheet of tarpaulin, unused since a camping trip to St Ives. He wrapped Hatherly's body inside it, coiling the ends and fixing them tight with twine.

He rolled the bundled body to the edge of the cobbles and looked down. The Thames waited. With a makeshift prayer he kicked the corpse away. It landed with a splash in the river, bobbed among the weeds and the empty ale bottles then sank into the dark water. As it vanished, Winter wondered if he had seen the tiniest stir of movement inside the tarpaulin.

He walked back to the car, took a handkerchief to the windscreen and drove away.

It had gone eleven o'clock when he returned home to Jubilee Close. He parked the Ford Zephyr in the drive, having smashed its passenger window. An attempted robbery was so much easier to explain than a bullethole. A damp rag had dealt with the remaining blood and brains.

He took a moment to look around the cul-de-sac, hearing the rumble of the overground line in the distance. This corner of Croydon always felt impregnable, a whole other life away. He could be another man here, sometimes.

He put the key in the lock, pushed at the frosted pane and called Joyce's name. The house was warm. A little too warm. The radiators were on full blast again. There was the queasy-sweet smell of washing drying in the heat.

He followed the sound of orchestral music to the living room. Joyce was in the spare chair, dozing as a Mantovani disc swirled on the Dansette. He watched her for a moment. As if sensing his presence in the room her eyelids opened. She gave him a sleepy but delighted smile. It was the smile of the girl he had met in Bentley's Shoes, all those Saturdays ago.

'Hello, Chris.'

He walked over and gave her a desperate hug. She put her arms around him in response, crossing her wrists and pulling him tight and close for a kiss. He buried his face in her black lacquered hair and inhaled her. A long moment passed. He heard the loyal sweep of the carriage clock.

Joyce knew what he did, to a point. There were lies, inescapably, but he had always taken care to emphasise the duller side of the service, the dossiers and the boxes. It made the conversations simpler.

She pulled away and looked at him, searchingly. 'What's the matter?'

He gave her the usual word. 'Work.'

'Talk about it?'

'Not now.'

'Later maybe? Your casserole's in the oven. I couldn't wait any longer.'

'It's fine. Thank you, sweetheart. I appreciate it.'

He left the room and walked to the kitchen, still in his overcoat. It was even warmer in here and there was a rich, comforting fug of cooking. He turned on the hot water tap and let it run. He reached for the plastic bottle of Quix washing-up liquid and squeezed a dollop onto the palm of his left hand. He ran it under the tap and let it foam. And then he scrubbed. He scrubbed until the water steamed, until his flesh hurt, until every trace of that dead man's touch had been erased.

He returned to the hallway. As he eased his shoulders out of his coat he saw a note by the phone, scribbled on a flyer for a local production of Gilbert and Sullivan. There was a single word on it, in Joyce's handwriting. *Malcolm.*

'Joyce,' he said. 'Did someone ring for me?'

'He said his name was Malcolm,' she called from the living room, shouting above a sudden surge of Mantovani. 'Said he works with you. Said it was urgent. Wouldn't say what it was.' She laughed. 'He sounded in a state!'

Winter slipped his shoulders back into his overcoat. He put his head around the door. 'I need to go out again.'

Joyce looked genuinely dismayed. 'You're joking... It's almost midnight!'

'I'm sorry. It's really important.'

'What's so bloody important?' she demanded, a rare but familiar flash of anger in her voice.

He reached for the word again and felt a swine as he said it. 'Work.'

4

The fog had found Belgravia.

Winter watched as it curled through the moneyed square, past the white stucco-fronted terraces. It came from the city's chimneys, its firesides and its factories, a throng of soot and sulphur that joined with the dank mists of the Thames Valley. It turned the streetlamps into hazy blooms and it condensed as oily smears on the windscreen of the Ford Zephyr.

The wipers turned. *So much for the Clean Air Act*, he thought.

It was cold in the car. The night air came through the broken glass in the passenger window. Winter had watched Malcolm's home for twenty minutes now, unsure what to do. There was an etiquette to these things, after all, a professional discretion. You simply didn't make direct contact outside of the Broadway office. If you had to meet it was in secret, and mutually agreed, as with the Fairbridge.

And yet Malcolm had called him at home, and spoken to Joyce. That was a breach of procedure in

itself. Something was wrong tonight.

There was a muted light in one of Malcolm's windows. A reading lamp, perhaps, or the television – if he even had a television, and knowing Malcolm he would prefer the wireless, or a volume of biography. Winter had spotted no signs of movement behind the glass and no one had left or entered the building by the front door.

He stepped out of the car. He could feel the fog on his skin, damp and close. The square was hushed. Mindful of the rap of his steps on the cobbles he crossed to Malcolm's townhouse.

The door was open, just an inch. Suspicious, Winter pushed it further. The heavy mahogany swung into a darkened hallway. Some fog floated in ahead of him.

Best to keep the lights off.

Winter entered the hallway, his eyes decoding the gloom. There was thick carpet beneath his shoes. A pigeonhole stood to his left, still filled with items of unclaimed post. He reached out a gloved hand and found a sturdy banister. He took the stairs slowly, as quietly as he could. These old Regency buildings could betray you. He reached the first floor. He climbed to the second.

A shape came barrelling out of the dark, a cannon of a man. He rammed into Winter, sending him stumbling back down the stairs.

Winter struck the wall of the landing. Winded, he struggled to his feet.

A headbutt. A fireflash of pain in the skull. The man had him by the coat collars, his fists bulging like meat.

Winter glimpsed a crested tie and military hair.

The man swung a punch. Winter ducked and the great blunt fist connected with the banister, splintering wood. Another fist came. This time Winter blocked it, then kneed his assailant hard in the crotch.

The man reeled. He took a third strike at Winter's head. Again Winter evaded it. The man's fist hammered into the Gainsborough print on the wall, the impact shattering the frame. There was a drizzle of glass.

Winter scrabbled on the carpet, seizing a shard. He slashed upwards in a brisk, vicious arc, slicing the glass into the man's face. In retaliation his opponent snatched a statuette from an alcove window, wielding the white marble like a club.

Winter dropped, twisted, dodging the Grecian nymph as it swung close to his head. He kicked at the man's arm and sent the improvised weapon flying into the wall. The nymph cracked in two. The man grunted, blinking, his face a mess of blood.

Then both men froze. There was the sound of a lock unlatching. A landing door opened. An elderly man peered out, wrapped in a candy-striped dressing gown, his sparse white hair awry. He had a stiff, regimental air. With ill-concealed disgust he appraised the broken statuette, the scattered glass, the ruined banister.

'Gentlemen,' he declared. 'Words fail me.'

Winter's opponent slugged the old man and knocked him out cold.

And then he was gone, bolting down the stairwell,

impossibly swift for his bulk. Winter pulled his gun and levelled it into the dark but the man was too fast. He was already out of the doorway. Winter realised he had no stomach for pursuit. Let the bastard run.

He took a moment to recapture his breath. The old boy at his feet wouldn't be waking any time soon. Winter stepped over the prone body and climbed the stairs to the third floor. He felt sure he could smell burning.

The door to Malcolm's apartment was ajar. Winter studied its edges, noting the shreds of burgundy paint, the buckled brass of the catch, the indentation in the woodwork. It had clearly been forced.

He nudged the door wider with the tip of his shoe. The bitter, burnt tang was more pronounced now. There was a sound, too. A rasping, a scratching. It was insistent.

He entered the apartment. There was a 78 revolving mindlessly on the turntable, the needle scouring its run-out groove in an endless loop. Each futile cycle was amplified by the small black speakers mounted above the door. The needle sawed through the dead vinyl.

The room was dim and warm, sleepily lit by lamps. A large leather sofa dominated the space, blocking his view of the floor. There was a tumbler perched upon it, a tiny swill of whisky in the glass. Winter noted the empty bottles of Glen Moray stacked against the side of the sofa.

The air was acrid. Something had recently been on fire in here. There was another scent too, oily and pungent. Kerosene, perhaps?

Winter stepped around the sofa, past the discarded

bottles and the strewn broadsheets. He saw the shoes first.

Christ. Malcolm.

The body lay on the floor, the arms and legs splayed, as if ritualistically. The clothes were singed – Winter saw the familiar paisley bow-tie – but the face, the flesh blackened and peeled by heat, was barely recognisable as Malcolm.

There were no eyes.

There were no eyes, and in the charred sockets someone had jammed a brace of snakes. A third, fat serpent filled the mouth. They coiled obscenely.

Winter's stomach spasmed in repulsion. This was ungodly. He snatched the rug from the back of the sofa and flung it over the body. It was the only decent thing he could do for Malcolm now. But he'd also done it, he knew, to try and bury the sight. It was too late, of course. He would always see it. The horror of it had branded his memory.

He looked around the room. If there had been time – and a chance – then Malcolm would surely have found a way to leave a clue. Some desperate final communication, secreted in plain sight. Winter's eyes picked over the ivory carvings on the mantelpiece, the hand-painted military figurines on the glass table, the Elizabethan globe in the corner, its undiscovered reaches patrolled by sea monsters. There were no family photos.

His gaze moved to the bookshelves. Milton. Marlowe. Bunyan. And there it was; a thin volume of Blake, bound in dark cherry leather. There was a flash of blue chalk on

its spine, the same discreet indicator they used to mark dead drops in the field.

Winter pulled the book from the shelf. It opened at the frontispiece. William Blake, it announced, 1757–1827, and it showed one of Blake's pictures, *Angel of the Revelation*. A towering, golden-curled figure stood halfway between the sea and the land. One hand clasped what looked like a page of verse, the other was raised to the sky, palm upturned, touching the edge of the picture as if testing the frame that held it. There was a light behind the angel, celestially bright, streaked with amber fire.

He knew what this meant. Good old Malcolm. Winter pocketed the book and left the room. As he did so he glanced, inevitably, at the body on the floor. There was a squirm of movement beneath the rug, coiling and serpentine.

Winter shinned over the padlocked gates of Matilda Park. Taking care to avoid the spear-tipped railings he dropped to the ground, landing in an autumnal mulch of leaves.

The fog was thicker now. It filled the park, great grey banks of the stuff, massing between the bony October branches of the trees. London's streetlamps looked like ghost lights in the distance, or ships at sea. Winter began walking, rain-slick leaves clinging to his shoes.

He soon found the statue. It was another of Blake's

angels. This one had granite wings, sweeping forward in the moonlight. They guarded another figure, a girl. She wore the crown of a queen. There was an inscription chiselled on the base of the statue and rainwater ran between the words. 'And I wept both night and day, And he wiped my tears away; And I wept both day and night, And hid from him my heart's delight.'

Winter plunged his fist into the earth. His fingers rooted in the wet soil. They found a metal spike and pulled it free.

It looked like a long nail. The centre band was knurled, the rest of it smooth steel. Winter wiped the dirt from the object and, with an effort, unscrewed the cap. Then he removed the lean winder that nestled inside the spike, pulling it carefully past the O-ring seal that was still tacky with glue.

There was a message wrapped around the winder. Malcolm's writing. The hollow spike also contained a sheaf of money – big notes – and a tiny sliver of microdot film, along with a business card. Winter pocketed them all and lobbed the dead-drop spike into a nearby bush.

It was then that he saw her.

'Joyce?'

Surely it was Joyce. She stood ten yards away from him, dressed in a coat he was sure he had once bought her – an anniversary present, maybe, or something for Christmas. She had Joyce's stance, the familiar chocolate-dot mole beneath the lower lip and a fringe of black hair that skirted her eyes, just as Joyce's did.

She was looking directly at him, her expression inscrutable. The fog wreathed her.

It had to be Joyce. But why was she here? It was impossible. He began to walk towards her, his eyes blinking through the condensation in the air. 'Darling?'

The woman's head tilted as he approached, as if only just aware of him. The shadows left her face. And they left nothing behind. There were no features. Nothing but blankness, a void of skin where the face of his wife had been.

And then the head tilted again, retrieving the shadows. A new face.

It was almost Joyce.

The woman regarded him. Still silent, still only half conceding his presence, she casually turned her back. Placing her hands into the pockets of her coat – a coat he had never seen before – she began to walk into the fog as if dismissing this whole wordless encounter.

Winter's memory flashed to the night before. He recalled the man he had mistaken for Hatherly.

He strode after the woman. He wanted an answer. He caught up with her. He grasped her arm.

It was as if he had seized live voltage. A blast of white light filled his vision.

Winter opened his eyes. He was alone in Matilda Park. There was a numbness in his hand, like an echo of some greater pain. Was it the arm he had been stabbed in? He blinked, uncertain. It felt as though a fragment of memory had just been snatched from him.

Had there been another person standing there just now? Someone he knew?

The fog had cleared, surprisingly quickly. He looked through the trees, past the wrought-iron Victorian railings to the city beyond. Dawn was on its way.

It was already Tuesday. Winter slunk the car into the cul-de-sac, as quietly as he could, aware of Jubilee Close dozing around him. There were no milk bottles on the doorsteps yet. The early morning light was clear and tinged with crimson.

He parked the Ford in the drive and walked the gravel path to his front door. There were no lights on in the house. The bedroom windows were shut. He paused, key in hand, scrutinising the lock. Had that grease-smudge of a fingerprint been there yesterday? Was that a fresh scuff in the paintwork? He glanced down. There was a single silver screw at the foot of the door, squeezed between the frame and the brickwork.

Good. Undisturbed. Just where he had left it.

Reassured, he turned the key in the lock and stepped inside his home. The empty hall had a stillness, the kind you only ever found in waking houses. He placed his keys in the dish by the door, shrugged off his overcoat and made his way up the stairs, his hand trailing on the smooth pine banister.

The door to the bedroom was closed. He turned the doorknob, gently. There was the cinnamon scent of

Joyce's perfume, the one she'd worn since that birthday in '59. And there was Joyce, asleep, one arm slung over the white sheets. She looked serene in the rose-coloured light that found the gap in the curtains.

He walked over to the bed, brushed the black fringe from her eyes and kissed her, softly, needing her to stay dreaming. *You beautiful girl*, he thought.

She shifted beneath the kiss but didn't wake.

Winter left the room, crossed the landing and entered the bathroom. He eased himself out of his jacket and placed it on the wicker washing basket. And then he unbuckled his shoulder holster and placed that and his gun on top of it.

He tugged a cord and turned on the wall-mounted heater. He could smell the dust as it began to burn on the bars. And then he switched on the electric light and studied himself in the mirror. It was an unforgiving reflection. He noted the pinprick fretwork of blood where that bruiser had headbutted him. He looked closer. His eyes were rimmed red and distant. Of late he swore he could see another man meeting his gaze in mirrors.

He inspected his bandaged arm. The bloodstain had grown, weeping through the gauze.

He needed to do something about that wound. TCP, perhaps. A fresh dressing. He turned to the bathroom cabinet and opened one of its doors. Joyce's bag of toiletries was stuffed behind it. It tumbled to the floor. Unzipped, it spilled some of its contents on the tiles.

He reached down to collect the scattered items.

Earbuds. A lipstick. And a rectangle of foil studded with tiny blue pills.

He examined them. Valium. Benzodiazepine. Mother's Little Helpers. He knew them from the service. Sometimes they helped to anaesthetise the darkness. Now they were prescribed to housewives. Was this what Joyce needed? A way to chemically numb her days? He felt a strange amalgam of guilt and betrayal. Could she not talk to him about this?

He returned the pills to the small leather bag, debating how and when they could ever discuss them. And then he spotted something else, tucked deeper inside the pouch. A fat hypodermic. It held a viscous amber liquid.

He removed the syringe, held it to the light. The liquid shone and the needle gleamed, threateningly long. He had seen one exactly like it, only hours before. It had been held by that silent man in the briefing room. It had been thrust into his arm.

Instinct made him turn.

Joyce was standing behind him. She had taken the gun from his holster and now levelled it directly at him, both hands clutching the grip. One of her fingers encircled the trigger. He saw that the gun did not shake as she held it. She matched his gaze.

Time held itself like a photograph.

'Joyce,' he said, uselessly.

In that moment he wanted her to be anyone but Joyce. But she was. She was his wife. She was the woman he loved, and she had his gun, and she looked prepared

53

to shoot him, here in this bathroom, in their bathroom, in their home.

Winter rushed her. He slammed her backwards. As her body hit the wall he seized her arm and fought for the gun. She resisted, invoking a strength he never dreamt she possessed. The gun twisted between them, pivoting in their hands.

There was a shot and the bonfire scent of cordite.

Winter felt a quick, slick wetness on the front of his shirt, tacky and thick. He looked down. Joyce was sliding against the bathroom wall, her white nightie riding against the tiles. There was a bloom of blood on the nylon.

'Joyce!'

Her body sank to the floor. She was still breathing. She was still breathing.

He stared at the hole the bullet had torn in her chest. It was the ugliest thing he had ever seen. He dropped to his knees and leant over her, assessing the wound, calculating her chances. She continued to stare at him. He watched as her nostrils tightened and flared, every breath a struggle.

Winter placed his hands either side of her face, brushing the familiar wayward fringe from her eyes. He knew this woman. He knew her.

'Jesus, Joyce,' he said, breaking inside.

He willed her to reply but she said nothing. Her eyes stayed on him and never left him.

He held her, then, as life left her body. He saw her

pupils shrink, then freeze, sightless. He was the last thing she would see in this world.

The bathroom was very still. Overhead the bulb continued to glow, hot and bright. It flickered almost imperceptibly. The remaining dust burned on the bars of the electric heater. And Christopher Winter cradled his wife, whoever she was, whoever she had been, as her blood dried on his skin.

5

They had come to the beach in the early hours, the girl tripping down the steps of the Promenade des Anglais, tossing her heels to the sky to go barefoot on the shore. Behind them the lights of the great hotels still burned, the grand dome of the Negresco stubbornly bright, reluctant to surrender its gamblers and drunks to the coming day. The moon was equally defiant, full and lemon-hued despite the first hint of a Mediterranean morning. The sea already held a firefly glitter of fishing boats.

'It's all bloody pebbles!' cried the girl, wincing as she crossed the clutter of stones that marked the shoreline. She was trying to dance, a giddy solo waltz fuelled by one too many brandy Alexanders. 'Can't they afford sand, for God's sake? It's disgraceful!'

She slipped and laughed. The man called Hart followed her on to the beach, watching as she became a silhouette against the water. What was her name? She must have said, surely. His mind was elsewhere. That telegram from London that waited in his room. British

Intelligence. It was a tempting offer they had made.

'Maybe they import them,' she continued, talking as much to herself as her companion. 'Individually selected by connoisseurs. Luxury pebbles, all the way from Whitstable...'

Antonia. That was it. A minor duchess or a countess or some slightly less impressive title. A blue blood. The English aristocracy at its flightiest and prettiest. They had met at the tables at the Palais de la Méditerranée only an hour before. She was already halfway to an irritation.

'Give it time,' he said. 'Pebbles turn into sand eventually.'

'Well, I think they've got a rotten sense of urgency.'

Antonia strode to the edge of the tide and let the froth lap at her toes. She took a red chiffon scarf from her throat and held it above her head with both hands, allowing the dawn breeze to fill it like a sail. The thin silk of her dress shivered around her, a second skin.

'This place. It's sublime.'

Hart placed an empty gin bottle on a rock. He took his eyes from her body and looked at the curve of the headland, the long, elegant sweep of coastal road fringed with palms and oleander. In the distance lay the slumbering peninsula of Cap Ferrat, jutting like an interloper between Nice and Monaco, its promontory just discernible by daybreak.

'La Baie des Anges,' he said. 'The Bay of Angels. They say it's where Adam and Eve came when they were booted out of Eden. The angels brought them here.'

Antonia looked out across the water, beyond the dark outlines of the yachts and their tight huddle of masts, out to where the horizon had begun to lighten. Her expression was suddenly sombre.

'Do you think there'll be another war? It's always special before a war, isn't it? Sweeter, somehow. Like you know it's precious without really knowing why. Or is that just the way we remember it?'

Hart shrugged as he stepped across the shingle. 'There's always a war. You don't necessarily have to see it to know it's happening.'

She turned to him, lowering her scarf to her chest. 'You're odd,' she decided. 'You're really rather odd.'

Hart considered this. 'And you're just a little tedious. I think we're even.'

For a moment she seemed affronted. 'Well,' she said, returning the billow of chiffon to her throat, 'you're not just odd. You're rude. Rude and ghastly. On balance I think I'm winning.'

She brightened again, her mood made mercurial by the brandy.

'Show me another one of your tricks.'

'Why?' His voice was flat, disengaged. The thought of that telegram in his room at the Beau Rivage still nagged at him. There were possibilities in that line of work. He could see that.

'Because I like your tricks. And I don't know how you do them. And I like that, too.'

Hart slipped out of his satin-trimmed jacket. He

placed it around her body, noting the arc of each shoulder blade, geometrically sharp beneath the bare skin. He wanted to trace his fingers along them, feel the truth of her bones.

'Here. Wear this.'

The moment of chivalry surprised her. 'Perhaps you're not so ghastly after all. That was positively gentlemanly.'

'Oh, I'm certainly not a gentleman, Antonia.'

Hart strode to the water's edge. The tide came for his shoes, washing over the leather. He unclipped his pearl cufflinks and rolled his sleeves along his slender forearms until they bunched at the elbows. It was a magician's gesture, unashamedly theatrical. He stood there, on the cusp of the sea, the wind loosening his black curls. There was a rim of sunlight on the horizon now. A snatch of gulls rose from the east.

He turned to Antonia as she came to join him. 'So what would you like to see?'

'Surprise me. Something even better than the flying spoons!'

Hart smirked, an arrogant crease to his mouth. He looked back at the ink-blue bay. And then he closed his eyes and inhaled, a deep, protracted breath. A nerve pulsed on his forehead, beating against the skin.

The sea began to stir. It was almost imperceptible at first, a tiny variation in the rhythm of the current. As Antonia watched, the gap between the waves narrowed, the tide folding back upon itself. The swell gathered, the waves piling and colliding in a clash of

spray. The gulls fled the commotion.

'Dear God,' she whispered.

A pillar of water emerged from the churn, climbing out of the waves. It seemed to sculpt itself as it grew, forging a rudimentary body from the sea. It was assuming the shape of a man.

No, not a man, realised Antonia. An angel, with a halo of spume and wings that dripped seaweed and saltwater as they unfurled. It rose above the shoreline, translucent as rain. Antonia could see the coastal stars through its face, almost where its eyes should have been.

She stared at it, incredulous. And then she stole a glance at Hart. The vein on his brow was drumming.

'How am I seeing this?'

'Because I want you to.'

She gazed again at the angel. It made her shiver beneath the borrowed jacket. 'What are you?' she asked Hart, just a little afraid of him. 'An illusionist?'

'Would you prefer an illusion?'

She shook her head, transfixed. The angel cascaded, its great wings pouring down. It was beautiful and it was impossible and it made her feel very small.

Hart opened his eyes. The shape collapsed, tumbling back into the tide. The torrent smashed into the sea and flung a barrage of water at the figures on the shoreline.

Antonia burst out laughing as the wave hit her. 'Am I dreaming?' she demanded, turning to Hart in her drenched silk.

He held her by the wrists and brought her close.

Her skin was slick and cool with seawater. The salt scent overpowered her perfume, the one he had noticed at the Palais, the one that had reminded him of an orchard. He sensed a pulse at each wrist, racing now.

'You shouldn't have to dream, Antonia. Only the blind need to dream.'

He explored her hands, feeling the peaks of her knuckles. She had exquisite bones. Ideal for the ritual he had in mind.

'My room?' he suggested, brightly.

6

Vienna was a whispering city.

Winter had come to it by the wine road that clung to the north shore of the Danube. Now, as he swung his hired Daimler along the Ringstrasse boulevard, past the baroque buildings and their alabaster saints, he imagined he could hear the phantom chatter in the air: the wire-taps, the eavesdrops, the stolen snatches of radio conversations; great ghost-drifts of intelligence that murmured through the city's colonnades and alleyways.

The October sun glimmered on the body of the car, reflecting statues stained sea-green by a century of Austrian rain. Winter saw rearing copper stallions, commanded by men in military plumage whose swords sliced at the gulls that perched on them. Somewhere along the way Vienna's imperial dream had curdled. Nostalgia had turned to decay. It was a remembrance of a place now, surrendered to history and haunted by the glories of the fallen House of Habsburg.

The Allies had carved it all up in '45, slicing the city like cake. British, American, French – and a portion for

the Russians. It had been an uneasy division of power. For a decade the defeated capital was ruled by everyone and no one, its four zones bleeding together in the shadows. Spies had naturally flocked to it like insects drawn to light. Eight years ago Vienna had regained its independence and now declared itself neutral. Of course, like all defiantly neutral places, it was nothing of the kind. The city was riddled with treacheries and betrayals. These were the faultlines of espionage.

Even the geography of Vienna made it the perfect playground for the intelligence community. The central district, its ancient heart, retained a medieval configuration of winding streets and pinched, cobbled lanes. It was a labyrinth at the best of times – and didn't the Schönbrunn Palace boast a genuine labyrinth in its summer gardens? Winter grimaced. The Viennese soul loved a maze.

The Daimler slowed. The Ringstrasse was congested today. Winter looked at the dull crawl of Volkswagens and Opels ahead of him. The only vehicles with any forward momentum were the motor scooters that tore brattishly between the cars. What were they called again? *Schlurfraketen*. Spiv-rockets. The perfect name. Envious, he watched them outrun the slog of afternoon traffic.

Winter moved his gaze to the rear-view mirror. The bullet-grey BMW was still there, tucked two cars behind. He had first spotted it on the autobahn outside Linz and it had appeared to be tailing him ever since. Always subtly, never quite declaring intent. Winter recognised its accelerations and fallbacks as feints,

standard operating procedure for a discreet pursuit.

He wondered who they were. East German intelligence? Or StB, the Czechoslovakian boys? They fished in Austria, he knew. For a moment he wondered if they might even be British Field Security, performing their usual gruntwork for the SIS. Again he tried to catch the face at the wheel but sunlight obscured the BMW's windscreen. No worry. He would allow them their fun and shrug them off near Stephansplatz.

To his surprise the BMW pulled to the right a minute or so later, escaping the crush of the Ringstrasse. Winter watched its tail-lights disappear into Innere Stadt. Perhaps it had been nothing after all. A holidaymaker or a returning businessman. You always tried to uncouple paranoia from professional intuition but there were times when the two inevitably tangled. He drummed his fingers on the Daimler's wheel and waited for his own chance to escape the jam.

It was almost dusk when he arrived at his hotel. It was an unassuming three-storey building near the Danube canal — or as unassuming as any building in Vienna could ever be, he reflected, noting the ornate pediment over its doorway. He removed his case from the boot. It thumped to the ground. There was a scent of roasted chestnuts on the air, blending with the ozone tang of the trams whose overhead wires criss-crossed the street in a glistening cat's cradle.

Finding his room, he lay on the bed in his shirtsleeves, his tie loosened at last. He reached for the cigarettes he

had bought at that kiosk in Calais. Capstans. A daft little tribute to Malcolm. He lit one and watched as the smoke sailed to the ceiling.

He wondered how many people knew he was here, on this bed, in this room, in this city. Someone had to know, for all that he had told no one and taken care to keep his movements sly and nimble. He was good, but he knew other people, on all sides, who were just as good. It was never easy to vanish. This world knew how to hunt its own.

He had left England two days ago: slipped away from Folkestone on that awful Tuesday. Faulkner had ordered him to take a leave of duty, of course, so his absence from the Broadway office would be less obvious than it might have been. But he suspected he was under watch. Whoever had killed Malcolm, whoever Joyce had been working for − and he was already entertaining some troubling possibilities in that regard − had to be keeping tabs on him.

For the moment he was severing all trust. He would operate alone. He couldn't trust the chain of command now. Something was compromised back home.

The radio was on, playing a buoyant waltz that didn't match his mood. He clicked it into silence and reached for his jacket, removing the calfskin wallet from the inner pocket. Inside, nestled among banknotes and tobacco coupons, was a small black-and-white photo of him and Joyce. He had been looking at it a lot. They were together on the front at St Ives, smiling in a rare British summer that hadn't broken its promise. August '57? '58?

He should know. Damn it all. He should know.

He traced the familiar lines of his wife's face, touched her smile, tried to exorcise the image of that bloodied body on the bathroom floor.

Why was he doing this? To persuade himself that their time together hadn't entirely been a lie?

He imagined her death might have made his memories sharper, more acute. It seemed to have had the opposite effect. All those shared days felt gauzy now, like fiction. He fought to remember the way they met, the kiss stolen in the arcade by Bentley's Shoes, their first, earnest lovemaking in that quiet bungalow on the Kent coast. None of it felt real now. It was as if he'd read it all in someone else's diary or seen it blown up on the big screen at the Gaumont. But if they were all lies, every moment, he had nothing. Was that worse?

He came close to crumpling the picture in his fist but he returned it to the wallet, sliding it neatly into the leather fold. Turning off the lamp, he prised himself from the bed and walked over to the room's lone window. It was evening now, and autumn dark.

Winter opened the curtain half an inch. Positioning himself in the shadow of the wardrobe he scrutinised the street. A couple passed by below, chattering brightly, a Pinscher on a lead. He watched an old lady cross the road, as regal as a Habsburg palace. And he saw a man – middling build, fair hair, early forties – standing by a tram shelter with the practised blankness of someone who really didn't want to be seen.

Winter focused tightly on the man, and wondered. If he approached him, if he walked into the street and confronted him, would that face blur and shift and rearrange? It wouldn't surprise him at all.

He took his gun from the holster, feeling its weight in his hand. Releasing the safety catch he levelled it at the window, aligning it with the gap in the curtains. His left eye tightened, expertly. He locked the other eye on the man below.

Not so invisible now, are you? thought Winter.

He saw the tremor in his fingers. It was minimal, almost imperceptible, but it was there. A quivering in the bones that nudged the gun a fraction of an inch from its target. He knew why, too. This was the gun that had killed Joyce.

He lowered the Webley, grudgingly reset the safety catch and flung the weapon to the bed. At that moment, as if by some extra sense, the man on the street looked up, his eyeline fixed on the darkened hotel window. Seconds passed. The man's gaze held. It seemed to probe the glass and the shadows that lay behind it. If he glimpsed Winter he didn't show it. His features stayed bland, expressionless.

And then, quite calmly, the man began to walk away. A car slid by, and then another, slow and obscuring, and soon there was no trace of the figure on the street.

Winter stood by the window for some time, watching the electric flash of the tramlines, their voltage sparking in the October darkness.

He rose early the next day, shaking away an ugly dream in which he had repeatedly put the gun to his mouth and shot off his own face. Each time he did so his features re-formed, unchanged, but his eyes filled with fragments of shrapnel until they were blind with the accumulated metal. Winter rarely dreamed. Sometimes he felt profoundly grateful for that.

Leaving the hotel at nine he found a coffee house in the Stephansdom Quarter. It was shabby and tobacco-stained but pricelessly quiet. He took a table close to the door, ordered a Konsul – ink-black with a whirl of cream – and looked out at the morning with its fitful drizzle. A grease-smeared bay window gave him a good view of the Stephansplatz, the main square dominated by the Gothic hulk of the cathedral. A keen crowd of tourists had already formed and were arming their cameras with flashbulbs against the morning murk.

The coffee arrived. It had a bitter kick. He felt a brief, homesick pang for Lyons Green Label Tea. He sipped it again and took his wallet from his jacket. No, he wouldn't look at the picture of Joyce, not today.

Outside the window a flashbulb flared, bright in the grey morning.

Winter opened the wallet and slid out a thin rectangular object. It was a business card, thin and pale blue, stamped with the words EMIL HARZNER, HARZNER PLASTICS. The address it declared in tiny embossed letters

was on a street nearby. He rubbed the card between his thumb and forefinger, stroking the words like Braille. It had a wealthy, superior feel to it. Harzner had money, and cared that you knew it.

Another flashbulb popped. This time there was laughter outside.

Malcolm had left this card for him. It had been waiting in the spiked cylinder at the dead drop in Matilda Park. As leads went, it was pretty unambiguous, but Winter still had no idea who Harzner was, or his connection to the events of the last few days. Clearly he was the man in Vienna, the one Costigan had been trading with. But how did he fit into the bigger picture? Winter stared at the card. If he hadn't left England so quickly he could have done some digging at the Boneyard, the dusty but scrupulously indexed kingdom of files in the bowels under Broadway. The place where manila came to die.

Again, a flashbulb. This time Winter glanced out of the window, taking care to tilt his gaze but not his body. The flash had been close. He suspected someone was photographing him, no doubt some bored security grunt assigned to document his presence in Vienna. It was all about keeping tabs, knowing movements. A camera was as crucial as a gun in this game.

Outside, through the smudged glass, an old man held a Box Brownie. He was gesturing at two laughing children, urging them to stand closer to the carved wooden figure in lederhosen that smiled cartoonishly outside the café next door. Winter looked beyond them.

He had glimpsed a familiar figure in the square.

The man he had seen on the street last night was standing in the doorway of a bookshop. He was perfectly motionless but his eyes were on the coffee house. Winter took the opportunity to properly appraise him. Yes, definitely early forties. Sandy, receding hair. He wore a camel coat and a ribbed pea-green fisherman's jumper, the roll-neck collar bulging at the throat. There were no obvious signs of concealed weapons distorting the cut of his clothes.

Winter chose to be bold. Fumbling for schillings he paid for his coffee and left the café. He stepped into the square, folding his coat collar against the drizzle that was rapidly turning to rain. He walked purposefully, though he had no real destination in mind. Stephansplatz smelt of ripe horse dung and there was the clang of morning bells, ringing out from the cathedral tower, loud and true.

He walked past a tavern and a post office. And then he stopped, pretending to be absorbed in a spinner-rack of postcards. There were tourist-bait pictures of the Schönbrunn and the Hofburg and a portrait of St Ruprecht, patron saint of salt merchants, keeping watch over the Danube canal. The cards were tatty and bleached by the sun. Winter peered between them, gazing through the rusted wire of the rack to the square beyond.

The man had moved. He was clearly keeping pace and now stood parallel to Winter across the street. He was as still as a bill poster, his head turned to the contents of a watchmaker's window.

There was a stiff rain now and people were opening umbrellas. Winter crossed the square, scattering pigeons from the flagstones. They took to the air in a rattled flap. St Stephen's Cathedral loomed over him, its single spire puncturing the sullen sky.

There was restoration work under way on the building's exterior. A grid of scaffolding lay against the ribbed vaulting, hugging the bays of the north wall, an ugly steel skeleton obscuring the beauty of the church. Winter saw tarpaulin mounted on a framework of wooden poles. One sheet rippled in the morning breeze, acting as a makeshift door. There was no sign of any workers.

He pushed through the tarp, entering a dim, enclosed space filled with loose bricks and chalky rubble. Turning, he saw a stone archway behind him, a limestone sculpture of a saint mounted in the alcove above it.

Winter examined the high, curving arch. A moment later he dug a foot into an indentation in the stonework. He gripped the groove with a gloved hand and began to haul himself up. Soon he was standing on the ridge of the apex, level with the face of the saint. He stood there, stationary, letting the minutes pass, watching the wind tug at the tarpaulin. He could hear the rain slowing as it pattered the plastic. Finally it dwindled to nothing.

The man entered, brushing his way through the thick sheeting. His steps were tentative, cautious. Winter observed him from his vantage point, watching as the back of the man's head tilted like a bird.

The man assessed the empty construction site, peering into the corners.

Winter sprang, leaping on the stranger. The sudden impact sent his pursuer sprawling to the ground, smashing his body against stone slabs.

Fighting for breath, the man twisted around, only to find Winter's hands closing for his throat. He blocked the grip with his fists and struck up into Winter's jaw. Winter retaliated with a thump across the man's teeth. There was a spray of blood.

The two men struggled, rolling over rubble, their tussle kicking up clouds of chalk and brick dust. They fought for dominance, trading fast punches, half on their feet, half on the floor. The man slammed a balled fist into Winter's stomach. Winter staggered back, buckling.

There was a brick on the ground. Winter seized it, eagerly, and swung it at his opponent. The man dodged the full weight of the blow but the edge of the brick connected with his left temple, scuffing the flesh. He clasped his head in sudden, blackening pain and sunk to his knees.

'Public-school prick!' he spat.

It was an East End voice, dry as sandpaper.

'What did you say?' demanded Winter, the brick held tight and ready in his hand.

The man looked up, his hand pressed to his forehead, blood trickling between the knuckles. He shot Winter a distinctly venomous look.

'I said you're a public-school prick, you great galloping cock!'

The man winced, as if the words themselves had exacerbated the wound. 'I'm Joe Griggs,' he said, more quietly. 'SIS. Malcolm's man, you bloody tool.'

Winter's expression was sceptical. 'You work for Malcolm?'

'Yes, mate. Do keep up.'

'Why should I trust you?'

'Because it'll save a right bunch of ball-ache, won't it?'

Winter considered this, too. And then he reached inside his overcoat and smoothly removed his Webley. He trained the gun at the man. This time his hand did not shake.

'What brand of cigarettes does Malcolm smoke?'

Griggs snorted, blinking in bewilderment. 'What?'

'Malcolm. What cigarettes does he smoke?' Winter kept the gun level. 'Tell me now.'

The man's mouth twisted, partway between a smile and a snarl. 'Do bugger off. How am I supposed...'

Winter's finger embraced the trigger. His voice was stone. 'I won't ask again.'

'Capstans! Capstans! Bleedin' Capstans! Christ, do you want his inside leg as well?'

Winter lowered the pistol.

'I'm Christopher Winter.'

'I know,' sighed Griggs. 'I wasn't labouring under the misapprehension you're Audrey cockin' Hepburn.'

The two men shook hands.

'Is there somewhere we could talk?' asked Winter, eyeing the tarp for signs of approaching workmen.

'Got just the place, mate.'

Griggs hauled himself to his feet, brushing at the chalk dust that covered his camel coat. He gave a crinkled, blood-smeared grin.

'So, Malcolm, then,' he said, brightly. 'How is the old fruit?'

Winter holstered his Webley and met the man's eyes. 'We really need to talk.'

7

Griggs led the way, up the ramshackle staircase to the room he was renting on the fourth floor. The building stood on Blutgasse, the narrow street that ran between the Domgasse and Singerstrasse, where some of the oldest houses in Vienna crowded together, hunching above the cobbles.

The two men reached the door at the top of the stairs. The landing was dingy, the light sparse. Griggs fished in his pocket and brought out a heavy, rusted key. He turned it in the lock. The door opened with a yowl of hinges.

'Excuse the glamour.'

It was a crate of a room, compact and cramped. Decades of cigarettes had yellowed the walls and left black whorls of ash residue on the low ceiling. The window at the far end was masked by wooden slats, allowing only a weak spill of light on the exposed floorboards. It was a practical place, a place for work. *You couldn't live here*, thought Winter, just before he spotted the rumpled sleeping bag and portable gas stove in the corner. There was an abandoned copy of *Parade*,

too, with a sulky, beehived model on the cover.

The room was crammed with the tools of surveillance. There were tangles of multicoloured wire, large wheels of reel-to-reel recording tape. A fat pair of headphones lay on top of a chest of drawers and a squat rotary telephone sat beside them. A film camera was positioned by the window, mounted on a tripod, aimed at the street. Numerous metal canisters were propped against the wall.

'I've got loads more out back,' said Griggs, nodding to the film cans. 'Got some terrific honeytrap stuff. There's this knockout little dancer from Hamburg having it away with the Soviet agricultural minister. Soon put a smile in your trousers, know what I mean?'

Winter ignored him. He picked up a chunky camera that had been left on a folding desk. It had a futuristic look to it.

'Polaroid?' he asked.

'Colour Polaroid,' clarified Griggs, smugly.

'Whatever next,' said Winter, turning the object in his hand. It was a weighty little thing.

'Haven't you heard, mate? It's the age of miracles. They've given us cheese-and-onion crisps and all sorts.'

Winter put the camera down and walked to the window. He peered between the wooden slats. There were tiny, dust-like gnats imprisoned behind the glass. For a moment he watched them flit uselessly, trapped between the panes. Then he focused on the street.

Another old Viennese building faced them across the cobblestones. This one was considerably less decrepit, its

pale grey façade in a superior state of repair. Its windows were shadowed and impenetrable.

'So that's Harzner's place?'

'Harzner's main office. His factory's just outside Graz. And he's got a mansion in the Vienna Woods. He's a man of property, you might say.'

'Who is he?' asked Winter, keeping his gaze on the building, though no movement could be seen behind its dark, boxy windows. 'All I know is that he's into plastics. Self-made man, I take it?'

Griggs joined him by the blinds. 'Yeah, pretty much. He emerged after the war. Lots of whispers that he'd been something rotten in Nazi high command but nothing that could be pinned to the bastard. We just don't have the intelligence on him, frankly. KGB might do but they don't share no more. Whoever he was, he remade himself. Came back as an industrialist in the fifties. Fancied himself as one of the big dicks of the new Germany.'

'Criminal connections?'

'Yeah, you could say. He's like a randy squid. Tentacles everywhere. We've linked him to European cartels in Berlin and Paris. But that's just mob stuff.'

The more Winter stared at the building the more convinced he became there was something odd about its windows. They refused to reflect light. It was almost as if they repelled it.

'So why are you watching him? Why did Malcolm assign you?'

Griggs gave a low whistle. 'Now you're asking the

big questions, Eton boy. All right, then. Our man Emil Harzner is what you might call an auctioneer. What does he auction? Secrets. Whose secrets? Ours, sometimes. Which is, to say the least, a liberty.'

'Who buys these secrets?' asked Winter.

'Whoever's got the readies,' shrugged Griggs. 'Russians. Chinese. Yanks. Even us lot if we raid the piggybank and the finance boys don't ask too many questions. But it's not always money that people offer. Sometimes it's other secrets. And he'll trade, if he reckons he can flog them on for a decent price.'

Winter reached inside his jacket, removing a marbled fountain pen. He snapped and twisted the barrel. Inside was a tiny sliver of microdot film, wrapped ever so carefully around the ink cartridge. It had been buried in the dead drop in Matilda Park, along with Emil Harzner's business card.

'What have you got there, mate?'

'You tell me, Billingsgate boy.'

Griggs took the fountain pen and moved to the desk. He settled into the canvas chair. Clearing some room, he tossed the headphones to the floor and reached for his microdot reader, a black cylindrical item that resembled an upright microscope. Selecting a pair of tweezers from a tray he plucked the miniscule fragment of film and slid it beneath the eye of the high-powered magnifying device.

Griggs scrutinised its contents with the air of an expert jeweller.

'Shaft me sideways.'

'What's on it?'

'It's a nasty little nerve gas formula. From the labs at Porton Down. Secret as Her Majesty's chuff. Malcolm gave this to you? Seriously?'

'Malcolm's dead,' said Winter, bluntly.

Griggs lifted his left eye from the microdot reader. 'What?'

'Malcolm's dead. He was murdered. In London. I don't know who by. Not yet.'

'You're joking.'

'Not really my sense of humour. Bit bleak.'

Griggs stood up, pushing the chair away. He was clearly winded by the news. Finally, he exhaled. 'The poor old sod. No wonder he's gone dark since Monday.'

He gestured at the microdot reader. 'So why did he give you this? What's the deal, mate? This is proper defence of the realm stuff.'

'I'm not sure,' admitted Winter. 'He didn't have a chance to brief me. I'm piecing all this together as I go. I imagine it's some kind of bargaining chip. And if Harzner's holding one of his intelligence auctions in Vienna then this might just be our bid. Do you have a photograph of him?'

'Harzner?' said Griggs, distractedly. 'I've got better than a photograph.'

He tugged on a cord that hung from the ceiling. A canvas screen unfurled in the corner, blank and square. With the blinds drawn tight to remove any remaining trace of light, Griggs positioned himself behind the

projector. There was a chuckling rattle of parts as the machine was switched on. The wheel of film began to spin. Dust specks swirled in the beam.

'Take a look. I shot this yesterday.'

The film hit the canvas. It was black and white and the silent footage had a stuttering quality, as if random frames were missing. Winter instantly recognised the street outside, the sturdy building opposite. This was Blutgasse, filmed from this very room. As he watched, the main door to the building opened and a young woman emerged. She had blonde hair and her strong, angular Slavic features had a hunting bird aspect to them.

'Who's the woman?'

'Harzner's private secretary. They're inseparable, those two. Lucky sod that he is.'

A man followed her out of the building. For a moment his face was obscured by an awning, allowing Winter to focus on his clothes. The shoes gleamed in the monochrome film. He wore a faultlessly tailored suit in dark check and there was an unorthodox number of rings coiled around his fingers. The hands were large, like hams bursting from the cuffs of his shirt. He carried a cane.

'Emil Harzner?'

'That's the feller. And he's ready for his close-up.'

The lens tightened on the man's face, the speckled image coming into focus. Winter estimated that Harzner had to be in his late fifties. He was heavily built, with a slab of a head. A grey, spade-shaped beard

framed his face. He had the look of a prosperous pilgrim or a Victorian botanist.

'He's got star quality,' said Griggs. 'I'll give the bugger that.'

As the footage flickered Harzner and the woman were met by a uniformed chauffeur who fussed them into a waiting Opel Kapitän saloon. Moments later the car pulled away and exited the frame. The camera kept focus on the empty street and then the image dissolved. An almost subliminal scrawl of numbers chased across the screen.

'So what do we do?' asked Griggs. 'Malcolm won't be giving the orders now. Do I keep this little surveillance operation going or what?'

A new strip of film began to thread through the projector. It was grainier and less distinct than the previous footage – clearly it had been snatched at night – but Winter knew this street, too. It was the one he was staying on. There was his hired Daimler, parked close to the hotel. It was obviously yesterday evening. Griggs must have been positioned close by, quite invisible. As a voyeur, he had talent.

'I mean,' said Griggs, 'who do we report to? Who's calling the shots now? Faulkner?'

Winter watched, distracted, as he saw himself on screen, opening the driver's door and easing out of the Daimler. It was unnerving to see himself so oblivious, so vulnerable. How had he not realised he was being watched? His professional instincts had failed him.

'I take it Malcolm did keep Faulkner in the loop on this?' asked Griggs. 'I know he was always a law unto himself...'

Winter saw himself turn to face the concealed lens. And his blood chilled.

The man on the screen, the man who wore his clothes, the man who had driven his car... That man had no face. He was eyeless, featureless, blank.

'I just want to know the chain of command,' continued Griggs. 'That's all. Keep it straight.'

Winter stepped closer to the screen. He extended his right hand and touched the image, the film playing on his flesh.

'Why do I have no face?' he asked.

'What do you mean?'

'The film. I don't have a face. Rewind it.' And then he said it again, more urgently, 'Rewind the film!'

Griggs did as he was asked, freezing the frame of Winter emerging from the car. And then he, too, approached the screen, his brow creasing as he peered at the image. He gave a considered snort.

'You're right. You don't have a face. Well, don't take it personally, mate. Probably just phosphor burn.'

Winter pressed the tips of his fingers to the canvas, tracing the void where his face should have been. 'I've seen this,' he murmured, almost to himself. 'I've seen this before.'

'All right,' said Griggs, bemused. 'You've seen it before. Now, I'm dying for a slash. Try not to get any weirder when I'm gone, all right?'

Winter barely registered the man's absence from the room. His gaze stayed fixed on the frozen image.

And then he turned away. He walked to the desk and picked up the Polaroid camera. This time he held it directly in front of his face. He stared down into the wide circular lens, seeing his head reflected dimly in the glass, the size of a toy soldier. He pressed the button that summoned an instant photograph. There was a high electric whine. The camera ejected a rectangular print, wet and empty.

Winter gripped the edge of the print between thumb and forefinger, willing the image to develop. It did so, killingly slowly, its vague, blurred shapes finally forming into a picture.

The nicotine-stained ceiling was captured perfectly. So were his clothes: the houndstooth coat and the thin knitted tie. But where his features should have been there was only a milky smear of emulsion. It was as if the chemicals themselves had refused to give him a face.

Sensing Griggs's return Winter crushed the print and stuffed it into his coat pocket.

'How's the existential crisis?' asked Griggs, irritatingly upbeat as he entered the room, the smell of carbolic soap on his hands.

'I'm coping with it,' said Winter.

'So what do we do now?'

'Now I'm going to knock on Emil Harzner's door.'

Griggs beamed, imagining he was sharing the joke. And then the grin died on his face as he realised Winter was serious.

'It'll compromise this entire operation!'

'Let's see how he copes with provocation. You stay here. Wait for my orders.'

Winter walked out of the room. As he did so he heard Griggs mutter beneath his breath. He caught the words. 'Public-school prick…'

Winter closed the door. He plucked the crumpled Polaroid from his pocket and tossed it to the floor.

8

Winter strode across the cobbles of Blutgasse, his pace brisk and purposeful. The throng of old houses reared over him, their shadows clustering on the pavement. He imagined that Griggs would be watching, still concealed in that vigilant little room with its slatted window. He wondered who else was observing him today on this hushed Viennese street.

Surveillance had its place, of course. But sometimes you had to punch the surface of the rock pool, just to watch the ripples. You never knew which of its hidden occupants might scurry into view.

It was the kind of move Winter favoured. A risk, of course, but he was prepared to ride the consequences.

He approached the door of Harzner's building. A polished plaque declared the man's name and occupation in neat black letters. EMIL HARZNER. PLASTICS. There was a curious decoration below it – a weather-worn knocker sculpted in the shape of a spider. The creature's legs cradled the brass ring that stabbed its bloated abdomen. *A queasy thing to have on a door*, thought Winter.

He was about to rap the knocker when he spotted the intercom on the wall. He jabbed the buzzer and heard it sound behind the door, shrill and insistent. A moment later a voice crackled through the grille. '*Ja?*'

Winter leaned close to the intercom. 'I'd like to see Herr Harzner, please.'

'You have an appointment?'

It was a woman's voice. He couldn't quite place the accent. Eastern European, he felt sure.

'I'm afraid not.'

'Then this will not be possible. I am sorry.'

Possibly Baltic.

'I promise I won't take up too much of his time.'

'This will not be possible. If you wish to make an appointment you must call the office.'

'I imagine you are the office.'

When the voice came again it contained a needle of irritation. 'Herr Harzner is not available this morning. You must make an appointment. Thank you and good day.'

Winter's gaze fell on the brass spider. Repellent thing.

'My name is Malcolm Hands.'

This time the grille remained silent. Winter tilted an ear, hunting for sounds. He felt sure he could hear the bassier tone of a man's voice, engaged in conversation with the woman. He imagined he was the subject for discussion. Moments later the intercom crackled again, the woman's voice returning with its familiar metallic edge.

'Please wait by the door.'

Winter smiled. God bless Malcolm. A name that

could open doors, even in death. He heard the sound of someone descending the stairs. Brisk heels tapped across the entrance hall, striking the wooden floor. A latch was unchained, a bolt drawn.

Presently the door opened.

'Herr Hands.'

It was the woman he had seen in the footage. Harzner's personal secretary. In person she was unexpectedly striking, her sleek features matched by fierce blue eyes that regarded him with a chill of suspicion. There was a long, fine scar on her left cheek, trailing below the eye. For a moment he wondered if it was a duelling scar.

She was tall, too, and her lean frame seemed coiled, as if the skin itself was restraining some inner strength. Winter recognised this quality. She could fight. Maybe she was more than an assistant. A bodyguard, perhaps? It was not unknown.

She gave a curt, obligatory smile. 'If you will follow me, please.'

She led him up the stairs, her movements compact and contained. She carried herself like a blade.

'What's your name?' he asked.

There was a fractional hesitation before she replied. 'Sabīne.'

'Nice to meet you, Sabīne. Where are you from?'

Again the information felt extracted, not offered. 'Latvia.'

'Splendid place.'

The building was smarter than the one Griggs was

holed up in but it felt smaller and narrower too. The walls seemed to pinch the staircase. Conversation abandoned, Winter and the woman passed through a clattering succession of glass-fronted doors and finally arrived at a sombre, windowless office, lit by an electric lamp. There was a fug of coffee and cigars – sweetened with the sickly aroma of lilacs – that made Winter very much aware of the lack of air in the room.

Harzner was at his desk, his eyes down as he studied some papers. He was a dapper whale of a man, not entirely accommodated by the width of his leather chair. Winter noted something else about him, too. For all his imposing physical presence he had a disquieting air of stillness.

He glanced up. Something flashed in his eyes. Was it recognition?

'Herr Hands,' said Harzner, a rising inflection hinting at surprise. 'You are a younger man than I always imagined. Perhaps war promotes us all beyond our years.'

'Herr Harzner. It's good to meet you.'

'Likewise. Please, do sit down.'

Winter did so, sensing the woman positioning herself against the wall behind him. He was aware that he had his back to the door.

'Do excuse the Viennese weather. It is capricious in autumn.'

There was an elegant apple pastry in front of the German, generously christened with icing sugar. Harzner was picking raisins out of it, his huge fingers surprisingly nimble.

'Would you care for some apfelstrudel? It's fresh. And especially fine.'

Winter waved the offer away. 'Thank you. I'm not hungry.'

'It is your loss.' Harzner plucked another raisin from the pastry. 'I imagine you find this a little... oh, what word do you have? Fussy? Fastidious? Is that it? I lose count of your marvellous words.'

He pinched the raisin between his thumb and his forefinger, regarding it with amused distaste. It left a tiny dark stain on the whorls of his skin.

'I was raised in poverty, I confess. And once a child has seen dead flies in his daily bread then the raisin is perhaps not so appealing.'

He added the unwanted raisin to a pile on an antique china dish. 'And now, do tell me, how may I help my dear friends in British Intelligence?'

Winter knew that this was a poker game. He had no idea how much Malcolm had known of Harzner's activities. Equally he had no idea how informed Harzner was about Malcolm. Had the two already communicated? All that he had was the microfilm. A nerve gas formula. It had to be a bargaining chip. But if it wasn't? What if Malcolm had wanted him to take possession of it for some other reason? It was a bastard of a thing to gamble.

'I have our bid,' said Winter, softly.

Harzner's eyes glimmered across the desk. 'Excellent. I trust it is of considerable value?'

'It is. Defence of the realm. We're reluctant to trade but we must.'

'Of course. The item for which you are bidding has, as you know, significant rarity value. There is much demand for it. From your nation's enemies. And your imagined allies.'

Winter took care to keep his expression neutral. 'It's absolutely genuine?'

Harzner visibly bristled, his great stillness momentarily broken. Winter caught the cloying perfume of lilacs again. This time he realised Harzner was doused with the scent.

'I have no wish to be insulted by Her Majesty's drudges.'

'I apologise, Herr Harzner. As you can imagine, we need to be sure.'

'And as you can imagine my reputation is above reproach. Perhaps I shall remove the British from the bidding.'

Winter gave a conciliatory smile. 'Again, apologies. Your reputation is beyond question. If I offended you, I'm sorry.'

Harzner's mouth curled beneath the thatch of beard, his lips parting to reveal gleaming veneers. 'Forgive me. I never tire of making British Intelligence crawl. Now, let me show you something. Sabīne, fetch the box.'

The silent woman detached herself from the wall and walked to a waist-high shelf behind Harzner. She took hold of a small rectangular casket and placed it on the

desk. It was a thing of exquisite craftsmanship, its silver frame inlaid with intricate dragonfly swirls of blue, green and red enamel.

Harzner opened a drawer and removed a tiny silver key. He placed it next to the casket, aligning it just so.

'I fear I am misunderstood by the intelligence community. I have no desire to know your secrets. I simply provide a service. I am a facilitator. To me mystery itself has a beauty. This casket is beautiful, yes?'

Winter nodded. The woman was standing behind him again.

'Sixteenth-century,' continued Harzner. 'You know, I convince myself that plastic is the future but I can only jealously admire the past. This casket originally belonged to a clockmaker. I acquired it from an acquaintance of mine. It was locked when I obtained it and it has remained locked ever since. I have never even placed the key in the lock. I have no idea what hides inside. It could be something as magnificent as a Romanov egg. Or as terrible as the stolen heart of a child.'

He pushed the casket across the desk. He nudged the key too.

'Each day I fight the urge to open it. And each day its secret becomes keener and sweeter. This is why you can trust me with your secrets. Are you that strong, Herr Hands?'

Winter picked up the key. It glinted tantalisingly in the light, as finely wrought as the box. And then he took the casket in his hand, feeling its solid, silvered weight on

his palm. Was that something rattling inside?

He threaded the key into the lock.

Harzner observed him. The man's breathing had subtly changed. His sweat carried the scent of lilacs again, filling the office.

Winter turned the key. He heard a faint spindling inside the lock. There was a palpable escape of pressure beneath the lid. The casket was unlocked.

Winter pushed it back across the desk to Harzner. 'There you go. You're even closer to knowing now.'

For a moment Harzner stared at the casket. And then he gave a bark of a laugh. 'How mischievous you British are. You have made it all the more delicious. Thank you.'

He rose to his feet. It was like a continent shifting in the room.

'The auction is tomorrow night. Come to my residence, perhaps at seven? It is das Krabbehaus in the Vienna Woods, just west of Lainzer Tiergarten. It shall be a pleasure to welcome you.'

He extended an immense hand. Winter clasped it, and they shook. The woman was there at his side again, still silent, still watchful.

'Your hand is so cold,' noted the German. 'You're like a dead man.'

'I've had terrible circulation for as long as I can remember,' smiled Winter, concentrating on concealing his dislike of Harzner. He wanted to leave this fuggy, oppressive room, breathe some morning air. 'The English weather doesn't help.'

'A kingdom of rain, I'm told.'

Winter nodded, mutely.

Harzner released Winter's hand. 'Tomorrow, then. I wish you luck in my auction. As you say, the best of British.'

The woman saw Winter out. This time there was no stilted pretence at conversation.

He stepped gratefully into sunlight.

9

Dusk had settled on the Vienna Woods.

Already dense with shadows, they reached beyond the western bounds of the old city, a sprawl of forest and rolling vineyards that crept to the foothills of the Alps. There was snow on the distant peaks.

Winter and Griggs had claimed a hill that gave them an optimal view of Harzner's mansion. They had been there for the best part of an hour now, crouched among the fallen leaves. Winter wore his tweed suit while Griggs was all in black, a knitted commando hat tugged low on his head. The soil had left cold, sodden patches on their knees and elbows.

Griggs had the field binoculars. He was keeping watch on Krabbehaus.

'What can you see?' asked Winter, instinctively whispering though they were quite alone on the knoll.

'More cars,' grunted Griggs. 'Some smashing birds.'

'Focus,' snapped Winter.

'Don't encourage me.'

Winter snatched the binoculars and put them to

his own eyes. Adjusting the focus wheel he brought Krabbehaus into view. It was perfectly named. Whether by accident or architectural whim Harzner's mansion resembled a squat crab, its brace of turrets rising like vicious pincers. There was something oddly nocturnal about it, even in the fading daylight.

He let the binoculars range across the view. A tall gate of curved steel guarded the entrance to the drive. It was open now, allowing a coal-dark BMW saloon to access the path. Winter watched it glide in, its tinted windows inscrutable. There were other cars in the expansive parking area, graceful limousines and more discreet vehicles, side by side on the gravel. An off-duty chauffeur slouched by a Volkswagen, the red twinkle of his cigarette picked out by the powerful lenses. Next to him stood a pair of women in evening gowns, as elegant as the car they reclined on. Other figures mingled in the gloom.

Winter shifted his attention to the mansion itself. There were already lights on in the windows of the great house. He let the binoculars roam across the walls, taking note of potential exits and entrances, assessing the geography as best he could. And then he looked beyond the building, to the grounds that encompassed Krabbehaus.

'Perimeter fence,' he stated. 'Ten feet. Maybe twelve. I can't tell if it's electrified.'

'Shouldn't be a problem,' said Griggs, patting the canvas knapsack slung around his torso. 'Crocodile clip, circuit breaker and a change of pants.'

'There are dogs, too. Pinschers.'

'I'll bullet the buggers if need be.'

Winter passed the binoculars back to Griggs. He stole a glance at his watch, squinting at the clock face in the fast-dimming light. It was almost time.

'Wait here until eight. Then find a way in round the back. Have a rummage. See what you can find. Photograph as many faces as you can. Basic intelligence sweep. We'll rendezvous at my hotel.'

'Yes, darling,' said Griggs. 'Shall I bring you some tea in the morning?'

'Just do your bloody job.'

Winter picked himself up, brushing soil from his suit. He peeled off his gloves and jammed them into his pockets. Griggs regarded him wryly.

'Some real flash gits at this bash. Who's your tailor? Marks? Or Spencer?'

Winter rubbed at the wet patches on his knees. 'I'll take the car to the front. You take the bike to the fence, northern approach. No lights.'

'Got it.'

Winter left Griggs on the hill. He had walked only a few steps before he turned to regard his colleague. His face was half shadowed, his eyes bright in the dusk. 'Good luck,' he said.

Griggs gave his customary crinkled grin.

'You too, you bastard.'

✦

Winter slid the Daimler along the curling gravel path to the main gate. The car was met by a member of Harzner's private security, a sour, brick-like man dressed in a dark olive uniform. His peaked cap and boots summoned echoes of another Germany. Winter showed him his ID, which was in the name of Malcolm Hands – an impeccable counterfeit fashioned overnight by a master forger Griggs had found in the Jewish quarter.

The guard opened the gate and waved Winter on. The moon was out now, brilliant and full, and it made the clawing turrets of Krabbehaus even more pronounced against the October sky. Winter eased the Daimler alongside a vintage tourer. Exiting the car with a perfunctory nod to a bored chauffeur, he strolled to the entrance of the mansion, his shoes crunching shingle.

There were concrete statues either side of the door, sculpted in a modernist style. They subliminally hinted at the shapes of insects but their skewed contours seemed to twist and shift each time he looked at them. Winter disliked them on principle. Give him Blake's angel in Matilda Park any day.

Winter rang the bell and heard it chime behind the hefty oak door. He was soon ushered inside and offered a glass of Saint-Émilion from a silver tray. The serving girl gave a joyless smile and continued to wheel through the murmuring crowd.

Winter swiftly felt very British and very ordinary. Hadn't Joyce chosen this suit for him? He crushed the

memory as soon as he thought it. Placing himself in a quiet corner he observed the room.

Who were these people? A few faces he knew from the files. The deputy commander of Italian security. His French counterpart. There was the director of Chinese Intelligence, his arm linked with an impassively beautiful girl who was neither his wife nor one of two European mistresses of record. Winter noted a KGB operative he had crossed on a particularly messy kill in Dortmund in the spring of '61. It would be prudent to avoid him.

He had no idea who the rest of the crowd were. They thronged beneath the high dazzle of chandeliers, thin, shimmering glasses in their hands, the men in black tie and the women in chic dresses. They wore power, too. Winter recognised it in their absolute poise, the clear lack of jealous glances at their fellow guests. Nothing in their eyes betrayed them. They were equals, whoever they were, and supremely confident. Winter sensed that these were the people behind the doors of the world.

'Mein Herr?'

A man was at his side. He was a unique specimen, flukily tall, a ragbag of bones in a tuxedo. His clothes seemed pinched and altogether too short, the ruby-studded shirt-cuffs revealing a waxy length of wrist. The face was equally long and bloodless, the skin taut over the hollows. A strangely surgical scent clung to him. Winter had the unshakable impression he was being addressed by someone whose body should, by rights, have been gifted to medical science.

'Forgive me,' the man said, his voice curiously high and tremulous. 'I am Albrecht, Herr Harzner's factotum. And you are?'

'Malcolm Hands,' said Winter, swiftly. 'I am here on behalf of Her Majesty's government.'

'Of course, of course.' The man gave a smile that belonged on a post-mortem slab. 'I should have recognised your fine British style.'

Winter ignored the slight. 'What time is the auction?'

'Nine o'clock. May I have your bid?'

Winter reached into his jacket and removed a plain sealed envelope. As he handed it over he asked, 'And how does this work, exactly?'

Albrecht adjusted the square gold-framed spectacles squatting above his gaunt nose. His eyes were surprisingly boyish. 'Herr Harzner will judge the bids. The one he finds the most attractive wins. It is not a complex system, Herr Hands. I wish you luck.'

'Thank you.'

Albrecht smiled again, just as repellently. 'And please, there is much entertainment on offer before and after our little auction. We have many rooms. And many delicacies. Whatever your pleasures, I am sure you will find satisfaction.'

Winter held the man's gaze. 'I'm happy with my wine, thanks.'

'You British. You are never quite able to relax, are you? No matter. Enjoy your wine. It is an exceptional vintage.'

Winter watched as Albrecht bowed and returned to

the throng. He felt as though his entire body had just been coated in a slug trail, cold and gluey. He placed his untouched wine on a table and continued to patrol the perimeter of the room. He took care to keep himself out of the KGB man's line of sight. In fact he meticulously avoided eye contact with anyone. After all, any of these people might have been acquainted with the real Malcolm Hands.

Watch over me, Malcolm, he thought.

He saw the woman, then, standing equally alone. Her face was concealed by a butterfly mask but he knew that profile and he saw the edge of the scar beneath the wing. It was Sabīne, Harzner's secretary. The Latvian, the one with the fighter's body. She appeared to be lost in contemplation, staring at a fresco that dominated the wall. It was a vision of biblical apocalypse, the world shattering beneath a sky of demons.

'Cheery sight,' he said.

She turned to him, the light of the chandeliers playing on the iridescent wings of her mask. They glittered, violet and green.

'You are talking about me?' she asked.

'I'm talking about the picture. I know I'd prefer something a little more soothing than the end of the world on my wall. But then that's not really Herr Harzner's style, is it?'

She returned her attention to the painting, falling back into silence. Winter found his eyes drawn to her left arm. Bared by the dress, it was decorated with an

elaborate tattoo, a snaking vine whose dark leaves encircled her flesh like creepers. He had never seen a tattoo on a woman before.

'That's remarkable,' he said. 'And this time I am talking about you.'

The compliment prised a smile out of her. It felt hard won. 'Thank you. I rarely have the chance to show it. Most people frown upon such embellishment.'

'I think it's astonishing. And really quite beautiful. Why did you have it done?'

Silence.

'Tell me. I'm intrigued.'

There was frost in her voice again. 'It is a private matter. I do not discuss it.'

'Is it something to do with Harzner? Is that it?'

She turned to him. Her eyes were an urgent blue behind the mask. She spoke quickly and quietly. 'He knows who you are, who you really are. And he knows that you have not come alone. You are in danger here. You should leave this house.'

Winter made sure that his face betrayed nothing. 'Why would you tell me this?'

'Your death is unnecessary.'

He reached for her arm, his hand closing around the tattooed leaves. He could feel the muscles coil and contract beneath the ink.

'What hold does Harzner have over you, Sabīne?'

'You are the one who appears to be holding me. If you continue to hold me I promise I will shatter your arm.'

He let go of her. 'Is that a threat?'

'Yes, it's very much a threat,' she replied, levelly. 'Well observed.'

She took a final sip from her champagne flute, draining the glass, then placed it next to a marble bust of a minor Roman deity. 'Now leave. There's still time for you. Your death doesn't have to happen tonight. It may be too late for your colleague.'

And with that she walked away. Winter watched as she melted into the swarm of partygoers, his mind picking at her words. What danger was Griggs in?

'A pity. Such a waste of your imperialist charm.'

There was a new voice at his shoulder. Winter turned, hating that he had been so easily surprised. It was the Russian, the one he had encountered that night in Dortmund, the one he had left beneath the bridge, cradling another KGB man's splintered skull.

Winter appraised him, calculating probabilities: height, weight, muscle power, the strong likelihood that the crease in his tuxedo was made by a holstered gun. Small calibre, he guessed. A pocket pistol. Very discreet. But no matter. Winter was armed too.

'Why would they send you?' the man asked.

Winter sensed a belligerent edge to the question. He examined the Russian's face, noting the sweat in the pockmarked pores, the bloodshot webs in the eyes, the telltale constriction of the pupils. The man wasn't drunk, not yet, but the wine was impacting. His reaction time would be compromised, his combat skills

impaired. The Russian had more heft but Winter would have an advantage, if it came to it.

'You are a killer,' the man continued. 'An assassin dog. You have no place here, unless you are here to kill.'

Tactical possibilities: side of the fist to the windpipe. Alternatively a fast, balled punch to the gut, assuming the abdominal wall would be unprepared. If he needed a weapon there was always the woman's abandoned champagne flute. Crack it on the marble, slash the jugular or blind the eyes.

'Are you here to kill?'

Exit possibilities: the crowd was behind them, lit by chandeliers and patrolled by Harzner's staff. This corner of the room had a degree more shadow but was just as exposed. There was a choice of doors. One led back to the main hall and the central arteries of the house. The other was frequented by waiters, replenishing trays and glasses. It had to connect to the kitchen. Too many people in either direction.

'You British were so proud of your code of honour in the war. And yet in Dortmund you shot our man in the back of the head. It was a coward's kill. Are you proud of that? Are your masters?'

The rate of the man's breathing had increased. There was a pink sheen to his skin, betraying a rush of blood to the veins. If he chose violence it would come now, and it would be swift.

'Would you care for a cigarette?' asked Winter.

The Russian stared at him, momentarily nonplussed. 'What?'

'A cigarette. Would you like one?'

Winter fished out a crumpled packet of Capstans, its lid still trailing cellophane. There were two cigarettes left. *Thank you, Malcolm.*

The Russian took one. Winter offered his silver lighter, the gesture equally conciliatory. The Russian's cigarette took flame. And then Winter lit his own. There was a mutual expelling of smoke through nostrils.

'About Dortmund,' Winter began. 'Your man had put a bullet in my colleague that afternoon. That was just as unnecessary. He was on his knees at the time. But he didn't plead. We do have a code, of sorts.'

The Russian took another drag, his eyes narrowing to red-rimmed slits as he inhaled. 'Two men dead, both loyal to their countries. And all because you came to kill another man who no longer believed in his. We are all rooks, every one of us. But this man Harzner has no loyalty, no country. He is his own nation. There is no compass for him, no east, no west. This makes him dangerous.'

'I know,' said Winter. 'But we want what he's got. And so do you.'

'So we waltz with devils,' said the Russian. 'I hope Her Majesty's government knows how to dance.'

He gave a flushed smile. And then he took his leave. 'Thank you for the cigarette. Capstans? Mr Hands' favourite.'

Winter dropped his own cigarette into the woman's glass. It was time to leave this room.

1∅

Winter found the architecture of Krabbehaus increasingly curious.

He stood in the main hall, before the grand staircase, mulling the dimensions of Harzner's mansion. There was something about its geometry that refused to make sense, something that almost defied the eye. The very angles of the house seemed evasive, deceptive, as if the walls and the high vaulted ceiling shouldn't meet in the places they did.

He sensed it, instinctively. It was an unease that pooled at the base of his skull. The house felt wrong.

Only Albrecht had seen him leaving the party. He had smiled across the crowd, almost conspiratorially, no doubt imagining the Englishman was off to sample the so-called delicacies in the upstairs rooms. Winter suspected the cream of Austria's whores were here tonight. He had already spotted them in the ballroom, women with a glassy beauty and something blank and untouchable in their eyes.

Let Albrecht think that. It was a good excuse for his

departure. And he would need a persuasive alibi if he was caught exploring the mansion's rooms before the auction began. If Sabīne was right, and Griggs was in danger, he had a duty to investigate – a personal duty, as far as the mission would allow. Hatherly's fate still troubled him.

Winter's hand smoothed his jacket. The pen was there in the inside pocket, still concealing its precious cache of microdots. He hated this blind auction business but that was the game they were playing. He just had to hope Harzner favoured the British bid. But if he didn't? God knew there was no decent contingency plan.

He began to climb the stairs, holding the pearl-coloured balustrade that clung to their extravagant sweep. It felt cool in his grasp but the surface was uneven, rutted and pitted as if fused from materials that didn't quite match. His hand moved over a succession of gnarled grooves.

He glanced at the balustrade as he climbed. A single word occurred to him. *Vertebrae.*

He couldn't shake the thought. That's what this was – a vast, coiling spine, built of bone.

Winter looked up. The ceiling seemed to be decorated with more bone, fashioned into a giant ribcage. And the white chandelier that lit the immense hall of Krabbehaus – was that also crafted from human bones? He peered into its dazzle, convinced he could see femurs and clavicles, fragments of skull, hollow sockets and jaws, all elegantly arranged around the lights.

Winter had heard of ossuaries, or bone churches,

as they were also known. Medieval shrines, garlanded with the skeletal remains of the dead. It was almost unimaginable that such a grisly concept could be replicated in a house in the Vienna Woods, in the second half of the twentieth century. He wondered if Harzner had inherited the macabre ornamentation – Griggs had told him that the mansion had once been a summer retreat for the Habsburgs – or if he had installed it himself. If so, how exactly had he sourced the bones? Some of them were terribly small...

Winter felt he was moving ever closer to a strain of human darkness he had never encountered before, something dreadful in the shadows of this world. It chilled him but he knew he had to keep focus. He had a gun and he had a mission. These would be his certainties.

The stairs took him to a wide, broad landing. There were taxidermied animals on display – a fox, a white leopard and a wolfhound. Their teeth were bared in mummified snarls, their eyes stolen by glass.

The walls behind the dead animals held framed cases. Winter walked up to one and saw that it contained a collection of mounted insects, individually labelled in neat copperplate script: cuckoo wasps, shield bugs, mayflies. Their thoraxes were skewered by tiny silver pins. There was a date, too: *1894.* And a word: *Gothenburg.* The paper they were mounted against was yellowed, like parchment.

He moved on. The landing branched into three passageways, spaced equally apart. They looked gloomier

than the rest of the house, lit by the dim glow of wall-mounted gas lamps. After a moment's deliberation he chose the middle passage.

Some of the doors were open, spilling light into the corridor. Winter walked past a succession of rooms, glimpsing half-lit couplings and other carnal acts. From one room came the sound of laughter, low and furtive. From another came what might have been a scream. It was hard to tell if it was agony or pleasure or something in between. He ignored it all.

A door flew open and a woman strode out. She wore only a velvet domino mask and a ribbon of black lace at her throat. Winter felt momentarily unnerved by her nakedness, by the sheer force of her self-possession. For the second time that night he felt deeply British. Joyce had always undressed in the dark. He heard a man call after her, his voice muffled, possibly gagged.

The walls of the passage narrowed, converging on a single door. It was different to the other doors; wider, taller, more elegantly crafted. There was a silver handle on it, carved in the shape of a rose, each petal intricately sculpted. Winter reached out to turn it.

He snatched his hand back.

The rose had pricked him, drawn blood. He sucked at his smarting thumb, and squatting on his haunches, examined the handle. There was a spiked metal thorn, located just below the bloom. A malicious little touch.

This time he twisted the handle more cautiously, lifting his fingers away from the hidden barb. He felt the

bolt shift, the hinges loosen. The door opened.

Another corridor confronted him. This one was darker, more tapering, its doors firmly shut. Winter couldn't quite see what lay at the end of it.

He tried to recall the shape of the building. He had studied it through the binoculars but the structure he had seen from the hill refused to map onto the mansion's interior. A corridor of this length didn't belong here. The dimensions simply didn't fit.

There was an unusual taste in his mouth. He took a moment to identify it. It was almost like diesel, just at the back of his throat. Odd.

Winter began to explore the passageway. He tested a couple of the doors and found that they were locked. He pressed an ear against one of them. He couldn't hear anything. Not even the sounds of the party below. The dark length of the corridor was completely hushed. This was clearly a private wing of Harzner's residence, off limits to the pleasure-seekers.

He continued walking, his vision struggling in the gloom. Something stung his right eye, causing him to blink. It was a drop of his own sweat, beading from his forehead. Another followed it, hitting his cheek. His shirt-cuffs, too, felt clammy.

The taste in his mouth was stronger now. A rising sense of nausea accompanied it. He thought of that metal thorn, the prick of pain in his thumb. Could it have been laced with a toxin? Christ, he was an amateur.

Yet another door waited at the end of the corridor.

Winter warily rotated the handle. This door, too, swung open.

He was back where he had begun.

Winter stood on the landing, at the top of the great stairs, by the stuffed remains of the fox, the white leopard and the wolfhound. And there were the mounted insects on the walls, their glass cases bright as mirrors as the light from the bone chandelier hit them.

He could hear the party now.

His internal compass spun. This made no sense. It was impossible. For a moment reality lurched.

Winter focused his thoughts. This was an illusion, he told himself. Momentarily inexplicable but just an illusion. It was something an opponent had designed to confuse and disorientate. Standard psychological combat procedure. Clever, but you could conquer it. You just needed to crack how it was done.

So how was Harzner doing this? Winter had a sudden vision of Krabbehaus as an immense Chinese puzzle box, its walls sliding and realigning in ever-shifting combinations. Hidden engines, concealed mechanics.

He balled his fists and scrubbed the sweat from his eyes. And then he entered the corridor he had originally chosen, the one that led to the door with the carved rose, the one with that damn silver thorn.

It seemed to be exactly the same passageway as before. Did it seem darker this time? A little narrower? Possibly. But then his vision was beginning to telescope, fuzzing at the edges. Winter wasn't sure if he could trust his eyes.

He stepped cautiously along the corridor, past the open doors and the shadowed couples, his senses alert for any trace of architectural subterfuge. He heard nothing, saw nothing. There was no hint of secret clockwork turning in the walls.

Again there was a strange taste in his mouth. The diesel flavour was gone. In its place was something brittle and metallic on his tongue. He found himself wondering if this was how mercury poisoning tasted.

A door flew open. The same door as before. And the same woman strode out, as defiantly naked as the first time Winter had seen her. But now there was something very different about her. Something terribly wrong.

There was the skull of a beast where her head should have been.

Winter stared, incredulous, as she approached him. The ribbon of lace at the woman's throat separated her body from the obscene thing perched above it. For a moment he assumed it had to be a mask, but no, her head would never have fitted. It was the elongated skull of an animal – a dog? A stag? A horse? – its eyes like craters, its jawbone riddled with teeth.

She strode past him, her flesh rippling, as soft as the skull was hard bone. The gas lamp played on the pitted cranium, illuminating the cracks and fissures that scarred its surface.

Winter felt sick. A sudden gag reflex flooded his mouth with bile. He was spooked now.

He took a moment to calm himself, to reclaim his

breath, to try and exorcise the horror of what he had just seen. It was an illusion. It had to be. It was either a theatrical trick or some kind of hallucinatory phenomenon. Yes, that was it: the toxin that had doubtlessly coated the thorn was a psychotropic agent. It was inducing visions, scrambling his mind.

And yet he remembered the priest in the church, the one whose body had erupted with insects. And then there was Hatherly. He could still see those dead eyes flashing open, lit by some unholy approximation of life. No psychotropic drug had summoned those visions. He had seen so much in the last few days, so much that was impossible, unaccountable.

Winter steadied himself. He was aware of a creeping heat in the corridor, accelerating the sweat seeping from his pores. He wrenched his tie and tugged at his shirt collar, prising it open. He had to breathe, even though every breath felt raw, tasting of metal.

Focus. He had to focus.

He took a step forward. As he did so the corridor kaleidoscoped. It seemed to tilt on its very foundations. The walls themselves began to pivot and wheel. One wall rose to meet the ceiling even as the ceiling itself shifted, chasing the opposite wall. The passage spiralled like a funhouse tunnel.

Winter lost his footing, convinced the floor was sliding beneath him. He rammed his hands against the wall, as if trying to hold onto a remnant of gravity. He shut his eyes, tightly. Was this only inside his mind? If so, then the corridor was his mind, reeling and treacherous.

Winter kept his eyelids closed, blocking the vertigo as

best he could. He concentrated on the sound of his torn breathing. As he did so he felt the whirl of the passageway begin to slow. His inner compass slowly settled, though his heart stayed tense, thumping erratically against his ribs.

Tentatively he opened his eyes, blinking through a sting of sweat. His senses were ready to be betrayed again.

The corridor had steadied itself. Or else his mind had shaken the deception. He gathered his wits and continued to walk. Each step felt loaded, a potential landmine, primed to shatter his hold on reality.

The door with the silver rose was deep in shadow. As Winter drew nearer he saw that there was something on it.

It was a spider the size of a fist. It crouched there, its legs splayed across the oak, its engorged abdomen pulsing beneath the gas lamps. The creature had a legion of eyes.

It wasn't there, Winter told himself. It had simply been plucked from his unconscious. Some psychotropic poison had stolen into his veins, rooted around in his memory and snatched the sight of that brass spider on the door in Blutgasse. It was a fever-dream image conjured by a clever combination of chemicals. That was all.

Winter reached for the rose handle. One of the spider's legs quivered. It curled and tapped against the wood, as if anticipating a moment to strike. The creature seemed fat with threat.

Winter hesitated. And then he placed his hand around the carved rose. This time he took care to avoid the thorn. He rotated the handle, sensing its inner mechanism click and shift.

There was a sudden, excruciating flare of pain, in the soft flesh between his thumb and his forefinger. The spider had punctured his skin. Now its legs were locked around his wrist. Winter shook at the thing, violently. It finally flew free of him. Hurled to the floor, it scrambled away, a scurrying blur.

Winter held his wounded hand. The bite throbbed, in time with his pulse.

He opened the door. And stepped into darkness. Absolute darkness, as thick as ink. It drowned him. His other senses raced to compensate.

He wasn't enclosed. He felt certain of that. He was standing in a room, not a passageway. A sizable, spacious room. And there was a sound, too. A low, seething drone. The sound of swarming. And it was growing closer in the cloying dark.

There was a skittering sensation across his face. A flurry of tiny wings, flicking against his skin. Something danced on his eyelids. Something else crawled at the edges of his nostrils, as if seeking entry. Blindly he batted them away. The frantic cluster of insects surged around his hands.

The drone was piercing now, a shrill, furious buzzing that bombed his ears. He felt something flutter on his lips. He spat it away and something else found his tongue. Winter collapsed to his knees, scratching at his face, desperately trying to tear the unseen swarm away.

At last the creatures abandoned him, their agitated drone fading to the far corner of the room.

Winter dared his eyes to open.

The enveloping blackness had marginally receded. Now there was the faintest suggestion of light. He glanced up and saw pinpricks of brightness. The more he looked the more there were, multiplying as his eyes adjusted. They were stars, he realised. He was looking at stars.

The stars were behind glass, framed by circular windows set in a high ceiling. Was this a private observatory of some kind? He hadn't spotted any such room from the hill.

There was something odd about these stars. This was Western Europe and yet he could see no sign of the Great Bear. In fact he couldn't recognise any constellations at all. It was a sky that seemed to belong to a different corner of the world altogether.

Winter heard music then. A melody that he took a moment to place. It was the tune that Malcolm had played on that broken piano in the Fairbridge. 'A Nightingale Sang In Berkeley Square'. It sounded spindly and spectral now, as if it was being played by an antique music box.

The melody was summoning him.

Winter picked himself up. He was a mess of sweat and nausea but he had to go on. He slipped his gun from his holster. Its cold weight was comforting in his hand.

He followed the sound of the music, his unsteady footsteps echoing in the empty room. He became aware that there was a shape ahead of him. Something white and luminous, moon-bright in the corner. At first he imagined it was a pile of discarded ivory silk. It resolved into a hunched figure. Its back was turned, its face concealed by lace and shadow.

Winter levelled his gun. 'Turn around slowly,' he said. He could hear his words reverberate along the walls.

The music box continued its clockwork serenade. There was a smell like stagnant water, a scent of weeds and dead ponds. Winter drew closer to the still, silent figure. It was wearing a wedding dress, he saw. There was something very familiar about that dress.

'I said turn around!' he demanded. The gun shivered in his hand.

For a moment the shape remained motionless. And then, almost lazily, it began to turn. It was his wife's wedding dress. He realised that now.

'Joyce,' he said, uselessly.

She raised her hands. Her flesh had the texture of rotted bark. The veil lifted. She had hollows for eyes, black as wells.

Winter tore his gaze away, repelled. He had to find Griggs. They had to escape this place.

He turned to retrace his steps. As he did so the room exploded into sudden, blinding light, so bright it almost had a sound. It made him stagger.

There was a panoply of mirrors, each as tall as a wall. They surrounded him, every last shining surface reflecting his own bewildered face. An infinity of faces, an infinity of Christopher Winters.

Except for one mirror. The man who stood directly in front of him had no face at all.

Winter flung his hands against the silvered glass. He confronted his reflection, determined to defy its mocking

blankness. For a moment he was sure he could glimpse traces of his features, blurred and obscured as though they had been wrapped in gauze.

It was then that the reflection spoke.

'We are the Half-Claimed Man,' it said, in a voice that was, and was not, his own. Winter realised his own lips had moved exactly in synch with the words.

Acting utterly on reflex now, he fired point-blank at the mirror. The bullet smashed the glass into shards. For a moment the reflection remained.

The pistol tumbled from his hand, clattering across the floor. Winter sagged, his knees buckling. He fell, the last of his resolve gone. His mouth was a flood of metal.

He lay there, broken, hearing the tinkling melody fade. He saw the mirrored walls rising from the ground, summoned to the ceiling by great, grinding pulleys. A puzzle box, he repeated to himself. A puzzle box. The house was a puzzle box.

As the walls slid away they revealed a blaze of chandeliers. There was a ring of partygoers watching him. They held drinks and they murmured and they laughed.

The elegant bulk of Emil Harzner walked towards him, his shoes as bright as black diamonds. He held a silver-topped cane that rapped the floor, triggering vibrations that knifed Winter's skull.

Harzner smiled. 'I trust tonight's entertainment has been to your taste, *mein Freund*?'

Winter saw what they had done to Griggs.

11

It took Winter a moment to register that the blood pooling in his left eye was not his own.

Another drop spattered his eyelid. He wiped away the thin, warm liquid and stared at the smear on his finger. It clung to the contours of his skin. It was another man's blood.

It was Griggs's blood.

Winter looked up, blinking to clear his vision. Joe Griggs was suspended some twelve feet above him, lashed to an enormous wooden wheel that swung in the air, manoeuvred by an intricate cradle of chains and gears. He had been stripped to the waist and his torso was criss-crossed with knife wounds, the gashes sunk deep in the flesh.

They were not frenzied or animalistic, these lacerations. There was a sense of ritual to them, a clear sense of purpose. As the wheel pivoted Winter saw that the struts supporting it were etched with symbols. They were pentagrammic in design, echoing the markings that had been inflicted on the man's body.

Griggs was alive, for the moment. He was chalk-pale

and had clearly lost a perilous amount of blood. From the twisted angles of his limbs Winter suspected that some bones had also been broken. The SIS man was breathing hard, his slashed chest heaving, exposing a knuckling of ribs that couldn't help but remind Winter of the macabre architecture of Krabbehaus.

He met Griggs's gaze. It was blank, full of a dread so overwhelming that it had nearly left him catatonic. Winter tried to flash some reassurance to his colleague but his gaze faltered. Ashamed, he broke eye contact, returning to the sickening maze of wounds on the man's body.

With a rusty jangle of chains the wheel moved across the room, orbiting the crowd that had gathered behind Harzner. As the disc spun more blood fell from the mutilated flesh. It dripped upon the partygoers. To his revulsion Winter saw a woman smile and slide her tongue across her lips, savouring it.

Two of Harzner's men broke from the crowd. They seized Winter by the shoulders and wrested him to his feet. He was half dragged, half shoved across the floor, the heels of his shoes scuffing marble, his fallen gun receding behind him. His senses were still a mess but the room was beginning to stabilise, shedding some of its dreamlike strangeness. There were familiar stars above him now. When he glanced at his hand the spider bite was gone. He fought to retain this clarity of focus. He needed it.

The partygoers were assembled in front of a large arched window, the floodlit spires of Krabbehaus visible behind the glass. He heard the crowd murmur

delightedly as he was brought before them.

Harzner was flanked by two figures. There was the woman – Sabīne. Her eyes were shadowed by the butterfly mask, her expression impenetrable. For all that she had warned him earlier that evening her posture now radiated total, unassailable loyalty to Emil Harzner. She stood by his side, silent, vigilant, a weapon.

To the right of Harzner was Albrecht. Winter only recognised him by his freakishly bony frame. His face was concealed by a layer of dark, moist clay, shaped into a grotesque approximation of human features. There was an oily sheen to it, like a sculpture in progress, pinched and twisted and reconfigured. It was like a primitive, shamanic mask. The wet clay soaked into the crisp collars of his dress shirt.

Winter was pushed before Harzner. The men released his shoulders but stayed close. Winter could sense their eyes on him as he shrugged his jacket back into shape. Part of his mind was already calculating their potential response times. The other part told him it was pointless. This was a bad situation. He had no gun. He was considerably outnumbered.

Harzner regarded him with an almost surgical disdain. Once again Winter was struck by the German's uncanny stillness. He was a big man and yet even sweat didn't dare to sabotage his composure.

'British Intelligence,' Harzner declared. There was an acid relish to the way he said it. 'I confess the irony of those words had not occurred to me until this evening.'

Winter said nothing.

'How did you imagine you could accomplish such a deception?' demanded Harzner. 'It is an arrogant thing that you do, you British. An arrogant thing.'

'My name is Malcolm Hands. I am here on behalf of Her—'

Harzner dismissed the lie, impatient. 'Please. You are not Malcolm Hands.'

'My name is Malcolm Hands. I am here on behalf of Her Majesty's—'

Harzner hit Winter in the teeth. The fist connected with a loud crack. Winter tasted a sudden rush of blood on his tongue. He glared back.

At Harzner's side, Albrecht put a long, emaciated finger to his crude mask, etching a ragged frown in the clay. The woman, meanwhile, simply looked on, detached.

The sudden violence had broken Harzner's unnatural air of calm. Now he recovered it, gathering his breath and holding the moment before speaking again. He was oblivious to a thick gob of saliva in his beard.

'You,' he said, thrusting a silver-ringed finger at Winter, 'are not Malcolm Hands. I know exactly who you are. I know. I know! How could you presume otherwise? It is an insult to my face, here tonight, in front of these people. Why would the British wish to insult me?'

'Herr Harzner, we have no wish to insult you, believe me.'

'So why assume my stupidity? Why try to deceive me, when I know you? When we have met, many times?'

126

Winter shook his head, perplexed. 'Herr Harzner, we have never met.'

'We are acquaintances.'

'I'm sorry. You're mistaken.'

Something wormed at the back of Winter's mind. Perhaps it was just the emphatic certainty of the German's words, their absolute conviction. It was almost enough to persuade him that they had, indeed, met.

But it was impossible. Harzner had been a stranger until Winter's arrival in Vienna. They had never crossed paths, he knew that. Winter had only just learned his name, after all. Until now the man hadn't even existed as a coffee-stained intelligence file.

And yet he seemed so sure that they knew one another.

Harzner regarded him, standing so close that Winter could hear him exhale. He smelt of tobacco and lilacs, just like their first encounter in the office on Blutgasse. Winter suddenly remembered the moment that Harzner had appeared to recognise him. Clearly he had been wrong to dismiss it as some paranoid flicker of imagination.

The German reached into the inner pocket of his tuxedo and produced a photograph. It was a glossy monochrome print, folded so tightly that the folds had scored sharp white creases. Harzner opened the photograph, almost delicately.

'So we have never met, you and I?'

Winter stared at the print. The first thing he saw was himself. A crease had sliced his face in two but it was unmistakably him.

It was impossible.

But there he was, a younger man, his hair darker, a little wilder, for all that it was slicked down with pomade. He was dressed in a suit he couldn't recall – a wartime suit, by the cut of it, double-breasted with wide slashes of collar, as had been the style in those years.

Harzner was next to him in the photograph. Significantly slimmer, equally younger, his beard trimmed tight to his face. They were laughing together, full of youth and mischief. Winter stared at his younger self's smile. It was not a smile he knew.

'Where did you get this?' he asked, his voice sounding small in the grand room.

'My archive is considerable,' smiled Harzner. 'You do remember that night in Aschaffenburg?'

'I have never been to Aschaffenburg in my life.' Winter knew that this was the truth.

Harzner hit him in the mouth again.

'Of course not. Perhaps you choose not to remember.'

'I don't know you,' said Winter, his lip wet and burning. The impact of Harzner's rings had split the skin. 'I have never met you. I have never been to Aschaffenburg.'

He girded himself for another assault. It didn't come. Pocketing the photograph, Harzner reached towards Winter and, improbably gently, corrected his tie. He then fussed over Winter's lapels, brushing lint from the tweed with his thick fingers.

'Good little soldier. Her Majesty is proud. Stay true to your lies.'

Harzner stepped back. His eyes moved to Griggs, hoisted above them. 'Your colleague was equally unwilling to make conversation. They do train you men damnably well.'

'I don't know that man,' said Winter, firmly.

This was a different kind of denial – prescribed operational procedure in the field. If the situation was hopeless you cut away a captured colleague like a gangrenous limb. If Griggs could hear him he would know that. And still Winter felt guilty as he spoke the words. No training could ever remove that.

'Of course not,' said Harzner. 'So the sight of his death will leave you quite unmoved. That is convenient for us all.'

He motioned to Albrecht, who now held a small ceremonial blade. It was sheathed in a scabbard of elaborately patterned gold, scored with symbols that mirrored the ones carved on Griggs's chest. Albrecht put a finger to the wet clay that concealed his face. This time he gouged a smile.

'Why do you have to kill this man?' Winter demanded.

'He is fortunate,' said Harzner. 'His blood has purpose. It won't be an empty spectacle, I assure you.'

The wheel lowered with a squeal of gears.

'My partners require forfeiture,' stated Harzner. 'They have certain expectations. It is a very old, very amenable arrangement.'

Winter glanced around the room. 'Your partners? You mean these people?'

The disc halted its descent with a shudder of wood. Albrecht unsheathed the knife. It shone, reflecting the gleaming chandeliers.

'These people? Of course not. Surely you remember?'

Winter sensed something stir in the room then. Something more than the blood hunger of a crowd. A presence. A thing that clung, that stole the air, dense and oppressive, like bad weather about to break.

'There is no need to kill him,' said Winter, as calmly as he could.

Albrecht walked towards Griggs. There was a sense of ceremony now.

'My lords of the hollow spaces,' said Harzner, his voice assuming the low, liturgical rhythm of a chant. 'My kings of bone and dust, my queens of the buried. Feast upon this life. It is gifted to you with devotion.'

Winter made to move forward but Harzner's men seized his arms. Pinioned, he could only watch as Griggs faced the knife. He saw the man's eyes widening, his mouth contorting, too full of fear to speak.

Winter fought the men's hold. 'No, you bloody bastards!'

There was a rush of breath in the room. A susurration, urgent and aroused, anticipating the kill. It was not a human sound.

Albrecht employed the knife. It sliced cleanly across Griggs's throat. And then it arced again, completing a ritualistic X. Blood spouted from the wound, the jugular pumping aggressively even in death.

The room fleetingly darkened, the light sucked from the chandeliers. A sonorous groan rumbled through the sudden blackness. It was a sound of gratification. And it had not come from the crowd, Winter was certain.

The lights returned, flaring for an instant. Winter stared around him, his arms still locked by Harzner's men. He saw delight on the faces of the guests. How could the people in this room witness a man's murder like that? Some were representatives of the world's intelligence services. Were they all complicit in this sickness?

Malcolm. Hatherly. Joyce. Now Joe Griggs. There were too many bodies behind him.

Harzner climbed the steps to a raised dais that gave command over the room, empty save for a tall, throne-like chair. Albrecht and Sabīne joined him as the crowd fanned in a deferential circle. Griggs was forgotten, a corpse now, his head slumped on his chest. The blood was beginning to dry on the carved symbols.

'*Meine Freunde*,' Harzner began, his voice velvet-warm. 'I thank you all for your patience and trust you have found diversion in my home. Our pleasures must wait now. It is time for the true purpose of our gathering. Tonight's auction is upon us.'

Albrecht handed him a white envelope. It was sealed with a stamp of burgundy wax.

'I have been impressed by your bids. So many secrets your nations are willing to surrender. Unbreakable ciphers. Atomic technology. A nerve gas formula. And all for a chance to possess the contents of this envelope.

It is clearly a powerful thing you covet. A profoundly powerful thing. I wonder if any of you truly deserve it.'

Winter sensed an irritation in the crowd. Harzner was just on the edge of baiting these people. It was theatre; a display of power.

'I know many of you have sought this item for many years. Your predecessors also pursued it. It is, shall we say, universally desired. But there can be only one nation that takes possession of it tonight, and that is by my choice alone. So I have given your bids much careful consideration. And I have chosen a winner.'

Harzner spread his palms in a gesture of mock reproach.

'Please. Do not go to war over this. It is so nearly Christmas, after all.'

He smiled, relishing the moment.

'The winner is China.'

There was a wave of surprise in the room, followed by a listless ripple of applause. Most took care not to react at all. The director of Chinese Intelligence acknowledged the win with a neat, appreciative bow. The woman on his arm beamed like a circus act.

'Please, General Shao. Come join me.'

Harzner extended a hand in invitation. As he did so his body spasmed. His smile froze and slowly collapsed, the teeth turning red with a swill of blood. He tried to form words but his throat could only summon a dry rattle. His fingers snatched uselessly at the air, the rings winking in the light.

Emil Harzner toppled, quite dead.

12

The woman in the butterfly mask withdrew the porcelain-handled knife. It was thin as a reed and glimmered with Harzner's blood.

She took the envelope. And then she seized the heavy, throne-like chair behind her and launched it at the window that dominated the room. The glass shattered like ice. Bracing her body she leapt through the splintered remnants, shielding her head with her arms.

In seconds she was gone.

There was chaos in the room. Harzner's men abandoned Winter and raced to their slain master. Winter took advantage of this and scavenged his gun from the floor. He swung it in a wide arc and put a bullet into Albrecht's head. It tore through the man's skull with a jet of blood and clay.

For Joe Griggs, he told himself.

Winter ran to the dais, pushing past the men as they knelt over Harzner. One of them saw him and moved to pursue. Winter spun the gun again and blasted the man in the collarbone, the punch of the bullet smashing him backwards.

There was a jagged maw where the window had been. Winter felt the night air gusting through it, chillingly sharp. It was momentarily intoxicating, a promise of escape from the horror of Krabbehaus.

He spotted Sabīne. She was scrambling across the floodlit roof, skimming the tiles, clearly targeting an optimum place to drop. She moved with a strange grace, all the more remarkable for the fact that she was in an evening dress. She had flung her shoes behind her.

Winter made to follow her, scraped by the glass as he, too, leapt through the ruined window. He landed with a judder on the roof, his feet sliding, betrayed by the sheen of rain on the tiles. He felt his balance give way. He fought to steady himself but he was already falling.

He grasped a chimney turret, his knuckles all but bursting as his fingers clung to the brickwork. His hand momentarily bore the weight of his body. This halted his descent but sent a hot lash of pain the length of his forearm. He clamped his teeth and endured it.

There was a commotion at the window. Harzner's men pushed their heads through the remnants of glass. There was a cry. And then the emphatic crack of gunshots, booming in the night. Bullets sparked against the tiles.

Regaining his footing, Winter set off across the roof. It felt treacherous, like sprinting on a frozen lake, but he kept his focus on the woman, watching as she vaulted a parapet and fell to a lower cupola. Soon she had dropped from the roof itself, using an outbuilding on the side of the mansion to stagger her descent.

He echoed her moves as best he could but misjudged the final leap. He landed with a slam of bone on the gravel drive, his knees taking the brunt of the impact. The off-duty chauffeurs regarded his arrival with amusement. And then, as one, they scattered as a whip of bullets ripped through the shingle.

Twisting his body into a marginally smaller target, Winter bolted across the drive, using the parked cars for cover. As he ran, bullets tore into the chassis of a BMW, studded the side of a Volkswagen. He had his gun in his hand but it would be pointless to fire in retaliation. They had the vantage point and the illumination; he'd be as good as shooting blind into the night.

The woman had cleared the drive and was now running for the lawns that enclosed Krabbehaus. Past the reach of the floodlight she slipped into the dark, a silhouette absorbed into shadows. Soon she was lost to his sight. She had to be making for the trees. And then, no doubt, the fence beyond, the ring of wire that ensnared the grounds. He could still catch her, he told himself.

Winter raced across the grass, the wet earth grasping at his shoes. He was straining his muscles to the limit now. He could feel ligaments burn, his heart protesting as his arms pistoned. There was fire in his side.

He passed the woman's discarded butterfly mask, tossed to the ground. He was close enough to hear her breathing, torn and urgent. He knew she was trying to keep her body focused, pushing her physical limits just as he was. Her dress glittered in the dark. He was closing on her.

It was then that he heard the dogs.

The barking was frenzied, rageful. Harzner's men must have loosed the Pinschers. Or else the dogs had been on duty and caught their scent on the wind. Their baying grew louder, ever nearer. They were closing.

He stopped. Sabīne had halted. She faced him now. They exchanged a wordless moment, both aware of their predicament. He glanced back and saw the dogs carving through the night, jaws bared to reveal dagger-ranks of teeth. Their eyes looked maddened, ready to burst.

Winter pushed the woman back. He levelled his gun at the first of the dogs. He closed an eye and pulled the trigger.

No bullet. The gun was empty. The Doberman sprang at him, its belt of a tongue spilling drool.

Now the woman pushed him away. He saw a flurry of silver. It was the blade, the same thin knife that had killed Harzner. She was wielding it against the dogs, her slashes vicious but expert. There was a pair of agonised howls and then the beasts were silent.

The woman recaptured her breath, the bodies of the dogs at her feet.

She wiped the blade clean on her dress. And then she replaced it in a fold, concealing its cold length against her thigh.

'Come on,' she hissed. 'We must go.'

There were lights in the field now. Torches, or maybe headlights, cutting through the dark. There was

a stir of voices in the distance. The lights began to slide across the lawn.

'Thank you,' said Winter. 'Who are you?'

The woman ignored him with a look that suggested the question was imbecilic. She turned and continued running, making for a copse of trees at the fringe of the grounds. Winter followed her, holstering his useless gun.

The oaks formed a dense thicket. The stout trunks reared into the night, lashed to the earth by ancient roots. Their branches were empty, snagging their sisters to create a vast, ragged cage. Winter looked behind him, past the collusion of trees. Across the field, the lights that were hunting them had shifted closer.

He was level with Sabīne now. She had stopped running. It was as if the trees themselves demanded a slower, more reverent pace. Winter and the woman stepped deeper into the shadowy coppice, decaying leaves crunching underfoot. A throng of moths parted as they passed.

He heard her gasp. There was a face nailed to the tree in front of them.

'It's just a mask,' said Winter, pragmatically. 'Some kind of totem.'

He peered at the object. Was it a mask? Its surface was as thin as paper. The texture was puckered, closer to parchment than human skin. The nose was flattened, the mouth a tight, shrivelled slit, the eyelids shuttered. If this face had once belonged to a man then it had been removed with clinical precision. Tiny nails pinned it to

the bark like a grotesque crucifixion.

The eyes flashed open, bright as fire.

'*Kuwaamba! Wageni ni kupatikana!*'

The words were unintelligible but their meaning was obvious. This was clearly some kind of occult sentry, stationed at the furthest edge of Krabbehaus, keeping watch for intruders. Winter wondered if the thing was futilely attempting to communicate with its dead master. He caught himself. How instantly all this insanity made sense to him now. He had stopped questioning any of it.

'*Wageni ni kupatikana! Konchaka!*'

The pair of them ran, pushing through the clutch of trees. Winter reached for Sabīne's hand but she flung his back at him. Her other hand held tightly to the white envelope.

Soon they had cleared the copse and arrived at the chain-link fence at the perimeter of the grounds. Winter hurried along its length, searching for the hole that Griggs would have cut a matter of hours ago. 'This way,' he said. 'There'll be a bike on the other side. We can use that.'

He found the makeshift opening, neatly snipped into the wire. There was a darkened road beyond it, and beyond the road the promise of the Vienna Woods.

On the other side of the fence a pair of headlights flashed. And then they flashed again in sequence.

Winter frowned, nonplussed. There was a black fat-tyred truck parked on the road, its windows in shadow. As he stared, a troop of men swarmed from the rear of the

vehicle. They held machine guns in their hands. Garanin 2B-P-10s. Standard Soviet military issue. One of the men gave a low shout and waved the others forward with an officer's practised slash of the hand. They weren't in uniform but Winter knew soldiers when he saw them.

He became aware of a small but insistent pressure at his ribs. He glanced down. The bitch had the blade on him.

'Move,' she said.

He had no choice. The two of them squeezed through the snarl of wire and emerged on the other side. The men met them on the road, their weapons levelled at Winter. Making a show of his compliance he raised his hands in the air.

'I'm not armed. My gun is empty.'

'It's true,' said the woman.

One of the troops came forward and flicked Winter's jacket open. He snatched the Webley from its holster and chucked it to the side of the road. It landed with a clang of metal on rock.

The men circled him. The tallest of their number – the one who had given the order – broke rank and walked towards Winter. He appeared to be in his late forties, his greying hair buzzed short and retreating at the temples. There was something sour and reptilian in his features. He seized Winter by the lapels and pushed him down, forcing his head to the wet road. He was strong. His fists pressed like weights on Winter's chest.

As he struggled for breath Winter found himself staring at the man's left eye. He couldn't look away from

it. It was surrounded by crossfires of scar tissue, trajectories of wounds where the flesh had refused to heal. In the iris itself was a pale, cloudlike formation. As Winter watched this cloud began to swirl, spiralling around the pupil.

The eye pierced him. The Russian said nothing but Winter could hear words, closer and louder than a voice. They seemed to collide and echo inside him, ricocheting in his skull. *Who are you? Why are you here? What is your mission?* The words were inside him and they felt like punches.

The Russian hauled Winter up by the jacket. Again the milky iris spun. *What is your mission? Why are you here? Tell me your name!*

The words faded. Frustrated, the man slung Winter to the road.

'Enough. I cannot read him.' There was a note of genuine exasperation in his voice.

He unzipped his jacket and removed a Tokarev semi-automatic. He casually levelled the weapon at the Englishman.

Winter faced the gun unflinchingly. It wasn't a show of resolve, he knew. Nothing heroic. He was simply exhausted, resigned to the moment. He had always suspected death would take him in just such an offhand way. An indifferent bullet on an unmapped back road in Vienna, the act of a man whose name he would never know. He had killed other men in exactly the same way. There was an inevitable balance to it.

'Malykh, no!' The woman had spoken. 'He's British

Intelligence! That makes him currency.'

'A liability.'

'We can trade him. The British will want him back.'

The Soviet officer considered this. Persuaded, he lowered his gun. And then he put a swift boot into Winter's face.

'Perhaps.' He gestured to a couple of the men. 'Put him in the back. Secure him.'

Half conscious, exhausted, Winter felt himself dragged to the rear of the truck. He glimpsed canvas and leather fastenings. And then he was pitched into darkness, landing in a sprawl of limbs on the floor. As he lay there his senses began to ebb, almost hungry for the dark. The last thing he noticed was a scent of gun oil and boot polish, the universal smell of the military. And then the world was black and still and untroubling.

The truck's engine turned. With a grind of wheels the unmarked vehicle rolled into the night.

13

The Thames looked sickly tonight.

Hart regarded the river as he crossed the wrought-iron span of Blackfriars Bridge. The water that moved between the great arches was sluggish, weighed down by silt and thickets of weed. It swilled to the mudbanks that flanked the river's edges, piled with clay and shingle. A few small boats swayed on the tide, tethered to the Embankment by fat cords of rope. To the east the dome of St Paul's shone like a crown.

The city's bells struck eight. As if in response a horn sounded from a distant Thameside wharf. The wind carried the scent of chestnuts and bitter tea.

London itself seemed ill this evening, thought Hart. It was the kind of illness that lingered in damp, cheerless rooms, bred by the rain. Something nagging and bronchial. The soot alone was inescapable in this city. It stained the buildings like the grime that lodged beneath your nails or the tobacco smoke that filled the cramped, rattling carriages of the Underground.

He looked up and saw gulls break the thick fog.

On a night like this walking through London felt like navigating a filthy lung.

Giorgio's Café was just ahead, on the corner of an alley in need of a streetlamp. The steam on its windows gave the light within a smudgy, homely glow. The word EATS burned in pink neon, next to the sticker declaring LUNCHEON VOUCHERS ACCEPTED. There was a photograph sellotaped to the pane. It showed a smiling Italian family, their faces bleached yellow by years of exposure to daylight.

Hart felt a mild shudder of distaste as he reached for the door. Such a common choice for a rendezvous. He'd expected a touch more class from these people.

The café welcomed him with a sudden, greasy heat. Hart made his way past the tight throng of tables with their citrus-bright Formica tops, hearing the sizzle of fry-ups and the hiss of tea-boilers as he edged around the other diners. The man he had come to meet was waiting in a booth at the far end. Hart slid into a green leatherette chair and joined him.

'Dreadful business, isn't it?'

The man glanced up with a frown, clearly confused by this introduction. 'I'm sorry?'

'The girl,' said Hart. 'The one in the news.'

There was a ketchup-spattered copy of the *Evening Standard* on the table. The headline read MISSING BARONESS — RIVIERA MYSTERY DEEPENS. Hart lifted a salt shaker from the front of the paper, revealing a grainy photograph of a smiling, elegant woman, a chiffon scarf at her throat.

'She's pretty, too. Such exquisite bone structure.'

He brushed a small spill of salt from the picture, his fingers tracing the contours of the woman's face.

'Antonia. Yes, that was her name. She looks like an Antonia, doesn't she?'

'I suppose so,' said the man in the booth, nonplussed.

Hart gave what seemed like a private smile. And then he ordered a cup of tea from the glum pinafored waitress at his shoulder. He picked at a palmful of coins, as if unused to such tiny transactions. The waitress took the payment and walked away.

'Anyway,' said Hart. 'Here we are.'

He studied his companion, noting the blunt cut and dull fabric of his suit. The man sat across from him had an earnest, distracted, academic air. Oxbridge, perhaps? Yes, there was a distinct reek of debating society and suppressed sexuality about him. Hart spotted a nervous sheen on his upper lip. This pleased him.

'I must say I was intrigued by your invitation. Less intrigued by your choice of venue, but then I suppose you chaps inevitably prefer a low profile. Still, there's a fine line between keeping a low profile and simply slumming it.'

'I'm glad you came,' said the man, doing his best to cover his evident unease. 'I'm Charles, by the way. Charles Bridelford.'

He extended a hand across the table. Hart ignored it.

'Hello, Charles. One of the Norfolk Bridelfords, are we?'

The man lowered his hand, unsure how to withdraw

145

it with any dignity. 'I'm not sure. I don't think so. Not much into genealogy, to be honest. More concerned with the future.'

'Oh, quite right. But then the future's an ongoing negotiation. At least you know where you are with your ancestors. Can I help you to the sugar?'

Hart indicated the bowl next to the copy of the *Standard*. Bridelford shook his head and took a quick sip of tea before settling the mug on the Formica.

'I'll get to the point, Mr Hart. We've been observing you for some time now—'

Hart cut across him. 'Did you think I hadn't noticed? You boys are charmingly clumsy.'

Bridelford acknowledged the interruption with a wan smile and continued. 'Naturally, the people I represent are very impressed. You have quite remarkable talents.'

'Talents? You make me sound like a child violinist.'

'Gifts, then.'

Hart reclined against the leatherette. There was amusement in his bright green eyes. 'Personally I'm rather partial to the word "powers".'

A nerve pulsed on his forehead, blue and urgent against the skin.

Bridelford began to cough. He put his hand to his mouth to cover it. Spluttering into the fist he tugged a handkerchief from his trouser pocket and pressed it to his lips. The coughing eased. He glanced down at the crumpled cotton square. It was dark with soot.

'Such an unhealthy city,' said Hart. 'I dread to think

what our pipes must look like. We're probably black as factory chimneys inside, aren't we?'

The waitress returned, placing Hart's mug of tea on the table. He took a sip of the milky swill and pinched his mouth in disdain. He put the mug down and did his best to ignore its existence.

'I should tell you, Charles, that this isn't the only offer I've received.'

Bridelford was still dabbing at his mouth. He scrutinised Hart with pink, watery eyes.

'The service?'

'Of course.'

'And they're appealing to your patriotism, I suppose?'

Hart twinkled. 'I do feel a faint stirring, I must admit. Must have been all that "God save the King" business at school.'

Bridelford leaned across the Formica. 'This isn't about patriotism. This is about ideology. It's about finding a better way. A way to make things fairer for everyone.'

Hart waved at the smoky cluster of tables that filled the café. 'Omelette and chips for all? Greasy tea doled out among the great proletariat? Or do we all get champagne and oysters?'

There was a sudden flash of conviction in Bridelford's gaze. In that moment he wasn't afraid of Hart. 'Communism will define this century.'

Hart snorted. 'Is that right? I don't believe in political ideologies, Charles. Compared to the oldest truths of this world they have the lifespan of flies. You'll have to find

another way to persuade me, I'm afraid. You might want to try self-interest. That usually works.'

Bridelford bristled. 'That's not our way, Mr Hart. I really hoped you might share our ideals.'

'So sorry to disappoint. Perhaps if I felt any kinship whatsoever with my fellow man I might give a damn. But dear God, they do tend to be tedious creatures.'

Hart rose from his seat as a kettle sang at the café's counter. He gave a tight, sardonic smile. 'No offence, comrade.'

Squeezing out of the booth he indicated the copy of the *Standard*, tapping the photograph of the missing baroness. 'She's still alive, by the way. I only required her hand for the ritual. I suppose I could have used the bones of a single finger but no sense in cutting corners.'

Hart strolled to the door, savouring the look he had seen on Bridelford's face. The bell tinkled as he stepped out into the Thameside chill, reaching for the packet of Woodbines in his overcoat pocket.

'Will you at least consider our proposal? Properly consider it?'

Hart sighed. The dull little man had followed him out. He turned into the lightless alley at the side of the café, hearing Bridelford keeping pace behind him.

'If you want money we have money. That's no problem.'

Hart kept walking as the wind from the river stirred the gutter. There was no moon above London tonight and the fog hid the stars. The only light to be seen came

from the surrounding streets and the glitter of the city beyond Blackfriars Bridge.

'Seriously, Mr Hart. We can accommodate you.'

Hart stopped, a lit cigarette between his lips, the flaring red dot the brightest thing in the alley.

'Like I said, Charles, I've had another offer.'

Bridelford coughed. For a moment he looked surprised. He tried to form a reply. And then he coughed again and kept coughing, a violent, uncontrollable sputtering that compelled him to clutch his chest. The sound was unbearably raw, as if the flesh of his throat was being torn away with each hacking spasm.

The man collapsed to the ground. He rocked on his knees for a moment. And then his mouth yawned apart and he vomited lungfuls of soot. It poured out of him, a thick, choking fountain of dust. More soot gushed from his nostrils and streamed from the ducts of his eyes, leaving his face streaked with grime. Soon his eyes were black and sightless, the corneas completely obscured by grit and filth.

Hart stood over him, a nerve drumming relentlessly on his forehead. He watched as Bridelford keeled onto the cobbles.

'One less Oxbridge Lenin to worry about.'

The voice belonged to another man, waiting at the darkened end of the alleyway. He broke from the shadows to inspect the body in the gutter.

'Charles Bridelford. One of our own. Damnably high security clearance, too. Wonder how much he's told

Moscow. Well, you've saved us a mole hunt, at least.'

'My pleasure.' Hart threw away his Woodbine, already bored by it.

The newcomer turned to regard him, his eyes cool and curious beneath the brim of his trilby. 'So you've made your decision? You'll work with us?'

Hart smiled, exhaling the last of the smoke between his teeth.

'God save the King, old boy.'

14

Winter was locked in what he took to be a disused farm building. As the days passed he came to know every chip and crevice in the stone of the room that held him. He counted the imperfections and saw how the walls darkened on mornings when the rain came, the water finding the cracks and staining the slabs like shadows.

The Russians hadn't chained or cuffed him but they hadn't provided a bed, either. The floor was hard granite. It had a token covering of straw, barely enough to compensate for the chill that arrived once the sun had gone. The straw was stiff and it crawled with cockroaches; Winter suspected there might be mice in the room, too, or possibly some shy rats, scraping in the corners at night. Sometimes he dreamt of their teeth, tiny and insistent.

The wind found him wherever he lay. There was a single, glassless window. In truth it was more of a break in the stonework than a window – much too small to crawl through but at least it gave him a view. If he stood

on his toes he could see a rusting tractor. Everything on the farm had the same ochre patina, brittle and decaying. An abandoned pitchfork lay against a gate and looked as though it might turn to copper dust if you touched it.

He could see tumbledown wooden buildings, their roofs submerged beneath great thatches of moss, vibrant green against the smoke-white sky. In the distance were the Alps, remote as clouds. At dawn Winter would observe the amount of snow on their peaks, committing to memory each melt or fresh fall. The next morning he would compare the snow level. By the second week of captivity it had become a compulsion.

He wondered if it was better to go mad gently or quickly.

More practically, the sight of the mountains gave him a crucial sense of location. He estimated that they were in Hungary, close to the border, perhaps by a matter of miles. It was an ugly, characterless tract of land, wherever it was.

The Russians had taken his suit, his shirt, his tie and his shoes. And then they had dressed him in coarse khaki trousers, laceless work boots and a baggy jumper riddled with holes. The wool had a pungent vegetable smell, as if it had been pulled from the soil, but then he was pretty pungent himself. The washing facilities were primitive, after all – a rag, a pail of lukewarm water and an ever-diminishing slice of soap. These amenities didn't appear every day, either. No one had brought him a razor and so there was a wiry scratch of beard on his jawline.

Surprisingly, the food wasn't too shabby. Some days he even found himself craving the chopped sausage with its pinch of paprika. Winter imagined he was being served the same plain yet palatable rations as the Soviet soldiers. After all, it took extra effort to prepare the kind of prisoner's gruel you expected to receive in these situations. It made sense to let him share the menu with the grunts.

He also suspected the Russians had a pressing need to keep him healthy. He was currency, ultimately. That's what the woman had called him. And every day he could feel himself healing, his body belatedly attending to its recent wounds. Yes, the cold that crept in at night still found every last ache and strained muscle but he sensed he was slowly repairing. Each morning, just after waking, he would absently prod the place where Harzner's ring had split his lip. The gash in the flesh had begun to close.

Some days he was allowed outside for brief spells of exercise. He would pace a small yard, letting his limbs flex and swing, savouring the autumn sky, the cool touch of air on his skin. The guards were watchful – and armed – but not entirely unfriendly. Winter's grasp of Russian was a little too basic for banter but he managed to cadge the occasional cigarette. They were a state-manufactured brand and tasted sour enough to cement his distaste for communism.

Most of his hours were spent in that cold stone room. It allowed him time to think. Altogether too much time. The monotony of his incarceration turned thoughts into scabs, things to be picked at. He found

himself mulling the same questions, again and again, his mind cycling through the events of the past few weeks.

Who had killed Malcolm? Another faction of British Intelligence? Some splinter of the SIS with its own agenda? If so, were they gunning for him too? Could he trust anyone now? Even Joyce had been part of it; part of a great lie that had coiled around his life without him even noticing.

He thought about the nature of the secret he had chased to Vienna. It had power, clearly. Power greater than the atom bomb, Malcolm had warned. Enough to make it desired by every intelligence service in the world. And yet it could slip neatly into an envelope. Was it a code? A formula? A blueprint of some kind?

Runes, Malcolm had said. Occult power. Knowledge made into a weapon in a war that had been fought for centuries, a war played out in shadows beyond even the ones Winter operated in. He had glimpsed a wider, more frightening world, that much was certain. He feared it might crack his mind if he wasn't careful.

The Russians possessed this secret now. He would have to take it from them, for his country and for Malcolm. And yet he was a prisoner: no gun, no plan, no expectation of release. But it was a mission, of a kind, and there was something reassuring about that.

Winter also considered the photograph that Harzner had shown him, the one of the two of them together. How could it even exist? He had scoured his memory in that cell and knew that he had never met the man. And yet there was the proof, irrefutable in black and white. Perhaps it had

been skilfully doctored. It was possible, he told himself. The British propaganda unit had disseminated doctored images during the war – Nazi bigwigs in compromising circumstances. But why would Harzner choose to do it? Had it been a psychological feint, meant to unnerve him? Perhaps. But it was a peculiar game if it was.

And then there was the thing he tried not to think about. The reflection he had seen in the mirror at Krabbehaus, the face that had gazed back at him with that awful blankness. That was one thought he tried to bury. But it found him in his dreams, and sometimes in the silence when he sat alone in the stone room and came close to despair. *We are the Half-Claimed Man.* The words knew him in his bones.

One day, in his third week of imprisonment, Winter was woken by the voice of a woman.

'Good morning, Christopher.'

He snapped awake, annoyed that his senses had been so negligent. It was the woman who'd called herself Sabīne. She had entered the room without him noticing and now she stood against the far wall, her arms folded. Her blonde hair was scraped back from her brow, underscoring her sharp features. She wore a tunic and trousers, cut to a military silhouette but lacking any distinguishing insignia. The guards had worn the same kind of covert uniform.

It was the first time he had seen her since the escape from Krabbehaus.

'Could I possibly trouble you for a bed?' he asked.

He was aiming for nonchalance but the words felt raw and lumpen in his throat. He remembered he had barely spoken in days.

She hinted at a smile. 'There would be very little point. You're out of here today.'

'Where am I going?'

'You're being traded. At the border.'

'I take it my people want me back?'

'Of course they do. You're quite an asset, apparently.'

Winter mulled this. It should have been good news but another possibility hovered – the Russians might be returning him to the men who had murdered Malcolm. If they were, his own life expectancy had just been significantly shortened.

'Who am I being traded for?'

'Someone the British have held for years. Someone our government wants returned to them. Personally I have no wish for this creature to be back on our soil. I cannot imagine your freedom is worth such a price.' She shrugged. 'Politics.'

'It's always politics. I take it you're here to interrogate me before I go?'

'Not as such.'

'Pity. A little professional torture might have helped break up the tedium.'

The intimation of a smile remained, no wider, no smaller than before.

Winter knuckled the sleep from his eyes. And then he focused on the woman.

'I need to say thank you for saving my life.'

'I saved your life twice.'

He tried to examine her face. It was obscured by the morning light, the pale glare of the window hiding the finer details of her expression. Her words had been matter-of-fact but had he seen something more playful in her eyes?

'So you did. Then I must thank you again, mustn't I? Although bearing in mind you put a knife to me and gave me to these sods I may demand a recount.'

He sat up, placing his spine against the cold hardness of the wall. He stretched his arms, expelling cramp from the muscles.

'Sabīne. I imagine that's not your real name.'

'Is Christopher Winter yours?'

He gave a wan smile. 'I hope it is. How do you even know my name?'

'Easily enough.'

Winter shook his head, amused. 'People like us never have the easiest of conversations, do we?'

The woman stepped away from the wall, out of the pallid light. There was a directness to her manner now.

'My name is Karina Ivanovna Lazarova. I am an officer of the First Chief Directorate of the Committee for State Security.'

Winter grunted. 'KGB. I imagined as much. How long were you undercover with Harzner?'

'Some years.'

'Two? Three? Five? You killed him easily enough.'

'As I say, some years.'

157

'It's impressive. Committed. I can't imagine what it must be like to go deep like that. A cover's one thing, but you really lived it. You must have known him very well. He must have trusted you. Did you feel anything when you killed him?'

'Why do you ask me this?' she countered. 'Professional curiosity? Or do you want reassurance that no, it's never easy? You know it marks you, every time. You've killed many men.'

'Targets,' said Winter, briskly. 'Faces in files. Backs of heads, sometimes. Men I will never know. And God knows that makes it simpler. Not easier, but simpler.'

There was a bruised silence in the room. And then Winter smiled as a new thought occurred to him.

'You know, it's a wonder you people are part of this. I thought you Reds had no time for the occult. Superstition's a tool to control the masses, right? Isn't that part of your motherland's glorious ideology?'

She regarded him coolly. 'I understand that you're an intelligent man, Christopher. I'm clinging to that thought right now.'

Winter prickled at the putdown. He didn't enjoy the sensation of feeling quite so foolish.

'And your colleague? The man who was about to kill me? Also KGB?'

'Malykh is my superior officer.'

'It felt like he was... breaking into my head.'

'Malykh has a gift,' stated Karina. 'A very rare and very precious gift.'

Winter had heard the rumours, of course. Concrete intelligence had proved elusive but the SIS had long suspected that the Eastern bloc had a programme of psychic research under way. Extrasensory warfare, the service had labelled it. Telepathy, telekinesis. The CIA were said to be at it too, naturally. His own government had a research lab in North Woolwich but as far as he knew these experiments had led to nothing but a drizzle of wasted time and deeply British embarrassment.

'You bother him,' Karina said. 'You may be the only man he's ever failed to read.'

'I'm sure there's a compliment in there somewhere.'

She smiled, properly now. It was like sunlight on frost. 'Perhaps. Or perhaps there's simply nothing in there worth reading.'

She stepped closer, bringing a faint scent of tamarind. The smile had gone, replaced by a purposeful expression. 'So no, I'm not here to torture you, Christopher. But I do have something to ask. British Intelligence has activated Operation Magus. What do these words mean to you?'

Winter scoffed at the question. 'Absolutely nothing. And if they did, would you really expect me to tell you? Come on. That's matches on the eyeballs time. You know that.'

'Of course I know that. I just thought I'd offer you the chance to tell me. Before Colonel Malykh arrives.'

Winter was irritated by the transparent threat. 'I'm not lying. I have no idea what those words mean. Where did you hear them?'

'We intercepted them. One of our listening stations. Your lines of communication are not quite as secure as you may hope.'

'Neither are yours, darling. It all balances out in the end.'

Karina nodded. 'Of course it does.'

'That envelope you took from Harzner. I imagine its contents are on their way to Moscow by now.'

There was the briefest pause.

'It's quite safe. I shall leave you now. Malykh will be here shortly. Keep your English resolve. It's very charming.'

'Thank you. I'll be sure to keep my home fires burning.'

As the woman moved to the door Winter called after her, his voice studiedly casual. 'Tell me, Karina. This secret that you killed a man for. Are you even allowed to know what it is? I nearly died for it and I haven't the faintest bloody idea…'

She paused. 'You'll soon have your suit back. And they're bringing a razor.'

She was gone. Winter felt himself relax at her departure: there was a conspicuous tension in his body that was only now dissipating. He didn't care to admit that the woman unsettled him. He told himself it was a purely physical response. He had seen what she was capable of, after all. It was like keeping company with a grenade.

He shifted against the wall and drew his knees towards him. Magus? The name of the operation hinted

at everything Malcolm had warned him about. Just who had ordered it? Faulkner? It was possible, but it was more likely to be a man he had never met, cloistered in some sunless corner of 54 Broadway, hidden in that labyrinth of dusty, furtive rooms.

Winter's entire career in the service had honoured one simple principle: did he need to know? He was beginning to sense he had never asked enough questions.

An hour later Malykh strode into the makeshift cell, kicking Winter in the thigh to rouse him. He had the same featureless uniform as the others but wore a long leather trenchcoat over the tunic. The leather was battered, webbed with deep cracks that echoed the scars on the man's face. The coat looked to be Soviet army issue. Winter imagined it had seen duty on the Eastern Front: Kharkov or Stalingrad.

He also noted the Tokarev semi-automatic, sat in its snug holster. And what appeared to be a sheathed blade slung low from Malykh's belt.

There were two men with the colonel. They held Garanin machine guns and positioned themselves either side of the door. Their presence felt like overkill to Winter, almost flatteringly so.

'What is Operation Magus?'

The Russian's voice was as cold as a lake.

'I have no idea,' said Winter. 'But I imagine you won't believe that.'

Malykh was upon him then, clamping Winter's head in his hands. Winter felt the fingers tighten. The man's nails

dug into the flesh at his temples, almost breaking the skin.

What is Operation Magus?

The voice was inside him, as close as his own. It was a worming, invasive thing. The man was searching out faultlines in his skull, hunting for points of entry. As Winter met Malykh's gaze he saw that clouded iris swirl like a miniature dust-storm.

What is Operation Magus?

It was like a live current touching his mind. Winter recoiled from it. He could see sweat beading on the Russian's brow, summoned by the sheer exertion of his will. A blue knot of veins grew angry and engorged on his forehead. The iris spiralled, almost mesmeric now.

What is Operation Magus?

Winter had no answer for him.

With a snarl, Malykh pushed him away. Winter hit the wall. He found himself snatching lungfuls of air.

Malykh's breathing was also ragged. He turned his back, determined to regain his officer's composure. Winter saw him swipe the sweat from his forehead.

'You defy me,' Malykh spat. 'How do you defy me? Have they trained you for this?'

He turned to face Winter again. This time there was a knife in his hand. He placed it under Winter's jaw, tilting the Englishman's chin. The blade was black, slender and glimmering. It was like a shard of ink.

'Tempered obsidian,' said Malykh. 'Sharper than steel or diamond. In Kaliningrad I cut out the heart of a witch with this knife.'

Winter felt the tip of the weapon flutter at his throat. He spoke softly, aware that even the tremor of his Adam's apple might provoke the blade.

'I'm not sure my government would appreciate damaged goods.'

Malykh let the knife loiter at Winter's throat. And then he sheathed it, the black glass sliding into leather.

'You are correct, of course. But I think you are already damaged goods, Christopher Winter.'

Winter laughed, sourly. 'What the hell's that supposed to mean?'

Malykh's lips thinned with distaste. 'There is nothing inside you. Where other men have souls you have emptiness. You are hollow.'

The words pricked at Winter. He remembered a stolen face in a Polaroid picture. Another blank face, confronted in a mirror. *We are the Half-Claimed Man.*

He fought his unease. 'You know,' he said, 'your comrade told me I was the only man you couldn't read.'

Something shifted in Malykh's eyes. 'My comrade?'

'The woman. Karina.'

'Lazarova? She has had no scheduled contact with you.'

'Well, she strikes me as something of a free spirit.'

'When was this?'

'About an hour ago. She was asking about this Operation Magus. I told her what I told you. I've never heard of it.'

Malykh evaluated this information. 'She had no authorisation to talk to you. I shall see that she is reprimanded.'

'I'm sure she was only being a good communist.'

'Oh, we are all good communists here, Christopher. Now, you must ready yourself. Your comrades are waiting.' A smile spread like a wound on Malykh's face. 'I understand they have missed you very much.'

15

The truck rolled through the dark, its headlights hunting the ground.

Two motorbikes flanked the vehicle, edging just ahead of it. Their riders wore goggles and helmets and kept precise military formation. Engines growling in synch, they led the way along the twisting forest road.

Inside, under the flapping, oil-spattered canvas, Winter felt every rattle and judder of the journey, every jolt of the tyres. He was in his suit. There were still flecks of blood in the tweed but it felt good to be in his own clothes again. Even the presence of his tie – a present from Joyce, he remembered – gave him a renewed sense of identity. He had shaved, too. A clumsy, hasty shave, one that had nicked and stung, but he was grateful for it.

He was cuffed now. His wrists rested on his lap, bound with cold metal. His gun was gone, of course. He felt oddly incomplete without it, as if some vital bone had been plucked from his body. His empty holster lay strapped against his chest. It only made the gun's absence more acute.

He shared the truck with a group of men, some of whom he recognised from the farm. The youngest was the guard who had given him cigarettes. Winter had made halting conversation about football with another. There was nothing amiable about any of these men now. Their faces were stern, their expressions focused. One soldier toyed with an American Zippo lighter, conjuring and crushing the flame. Winter found himself watching it with a vacant fascination.

Karina was next to him. He imagined she was acting as his personal guard, though nothing had been said. In fact she had remained silent throughout the journey. It wasn't a companionable silence and yet it wasn't a cold one, either. She struck him as someone who chose to conserve conversation like oxygen.

She had buckled a raincoat over her fatigues and her hair was covered by the smoke-grey fur of a Cossack hat. Winter regarded her sleek profile, the Slavic planes, noting how her mouth held a determination even in repose. She intrigued him.

He tried to make conversation again.

'Malykh told me he killed a witch. Is this true?'

The truck swayed over a pothole.

'He didn't kill her. He cut out her heart.'

'I might have assumed that was one and the same thing.'

'Then I might have assumed you were ignorant.'

Winter caught a ghost of a smirk on the face of the youngest soldier.

'A witch?' said Winter. 'A real one?'

'Yes. The Bone Mother.'

The trooper with the Zippo stopped teasing the flame. A moment later his thumb resumed its compulsive ratcheting.

'The Bone Mother?'

'The Bone Mother,' said Karina, evenly, as if explaining it to a child. 'The Forest Hag. The Snow Crone. Baba Yaga.'

Once again the man with the Zippo paused. This time he chose not to summon the flame.

Winter snorted. 'Baba Yaga? Even I've read that. In a kids' book. It's a folk tale.'

Karina looked at him, her eyes cold-bright in the gloom of the truck's interior.

'That's what folk tales are,' she said, simply. 'Warnings against everything that waits for us in the dark.'

'Come on. They're stories for kids.'

'Stories arm children against the dark. But only children are allowed to believe in them. As they grow old they lose their faith in stories. And everything that hides beyond the light becomes strong again.'

Winter shook his head. 'Sounds like the Church to me. And I know what you people think of the Church.'

Karina spoke calmly but intensely. 'This world doesn't belong to us, Christopher. We carve out our safe places. We light our candles. We say our prayers. But the world isn't ours. We are too small for it, too fleeting. You know this.'

'I know I've seen stuff I can't explain,' said Winter. 'That doesn't mean I'm prepared to believe in fairy stories.'

He waved his cuffed hands at the silent entourage of soldiers. 'And these men? They all believe in this stuff? Every one of them?'

'Of course. If they didn't they'd be dead.'

'Who are you people?' asked Winter. 'You're not like any KGB I've ever met. You seem to have imagination.'

Karina ignored the slight. 'We are a covert division of the agency, accountable only to a select part of the Council of Ministers. We fight the greater war, beyond the ideological squabble between our nations.'

'The true Cold War,' said Winter, remembering Malcolm's words in the ballroom of the Fairbridge. 'So you cut out the hearts of witches and steal runes from devil-worshipping plastics moguls. I had no idea you lot even existed.'

'Perhaps you should know,' said Karina. 'Perhaps you need us. Or do you imagine that the things that live beyond the light care about our politics?'

Winter smiled to himself. 'Oh, I'm quite prepared to believe Satan's a communist. I'm sure he only burns the bourgeoisie.'

He fell back into silence, feeling the wheels on the road, the rhythmic jounce of tyre rubber. A thought came to him.

'Tell me something. My colleague was tortured before he was killed. I saw the knife wounds on his body.

It looked pretty savage. Were you party to that?'

'I wasn't responsible.'

'I didn't ask you if you were responsible. I asked if you were party to it.'

'Albrecht inflicted the wounds. I could not have prevented it.'

'Yes, you had a cover to maintain. I get that. But I'm not sure I could have stood there and watched a man suffer like that. I'm amazed you could.'

'You denied that you knew him,' said Karina, with a sting of reproach in her voice. 'You clearly had your own cover to maintain. It's what we're taught.'

'Did you find it easy?'

Karina said nothing. Her face said nothing.

'So why do they do it?' pressed Winter. 'Carve those marks? I assume those symbols have some significance beyond simple sadism?'

She paused, as if debating whether to answer him.

'Harzner practised ritual demonology,' she stated. 'Think of it as a transmission. The symbols are the message. The spell, if you will. The flesh is simply the means of communication. You cut the symbols into the skin to send the message. It's flesh magic. Think of the body as a wireless set or a Morse transmitter. The pain clarifies the signal.'

Winter didn't hide his disgust. 'It's barbaric.'

'It's ritual.'

Winter scrutinised the woman at his side. 'You're pretty deep into all this horseshit, aren't you?'

'And you're a rational man, I take it?'

'I have to be. I kill men because somebody tells me to. When that's your job you need to trust that the world makes sense.'

The truck had been climbing for a while, its wheels moving from pitted tarmac to a smoother surface that had to be grass. Now the vehicle lurched to a halt with a final, rattling shudder. Winter heard the thrum of the engine die, felt its vibration leave his bones. They had arrived.

He was seized by the shoulders and pushed through the gap in the canvas. The air hit him, sharp and galvanising after the fug of sweat and diesel in the back of the truck. One of the soldiers shoved him like baggage. Karina put her hand to the man's arm, quietly dissuading him from doing it again. The Russian obeyed, reluctantly, allowing Winter to walk forward with a modicum of dignity.

Malykh opened the passenger door and jumped out, the soles of his boots thumping the ground. He buttoned his heavy leather coat against the night chill and gave Winter a quick, contemptuous look. And then he gave an order in Russian, summoning the rest of the squad behind him. The incognito troopers fell in. The motorbike outriders roared ahead, leaving ribbons of tyre track in the mud.

The group climbed a grassy incline, rising to a spot that gave them a view of the great, empty plain of the Hungarian puszta. It was a profoundly desolate sprawl of marshland, treeless and bleak. Even in daylight, Winter

imagined, it would be leached of colour, a landscape of dirt and scrub, broken only by pockets of rainwater.

This was the border. If Vienna was a place where loyalties shifted like mist then this was where the division between East and West lay scored into the earth.

An immense fence rose in the distance. It was forged from barbed wire, knitted into vicious twists, its vast, razored length dominating and defining the horizon. Winter estimated that it had to be as high as a house. As he assessed its span he saw bodies caught on snarls of wire, snagged like rag dolls. Political fugitives, no doubt, seeking escape but claimed by soldiers' bullets on the very cusp of freedom. Or perhaps the fence was electrified and their lives had simply been lost to a lethal surge of voltage. Whatever the case, they had been left there. Warnings, he imagined. Twentieth-century voodoo totems.

The fence was punctuated by wooden watchtowers. They squatted like crates on stilts, high above the ground. Some of them contained men with rifles. Others held a dazzle of searchlights. The guards tilted the drum-like discs into the night and Winter watched as the beams prowled the sky, cast against the stars and smudges of cloud.

One of the lights found them. Winter raised a hand to his eyes, squinting into the brutal white glare. He saw Karina beside him, bleached chalk-pale by the beam. Her arm moved to the small canvas bag that hung on her shoulder, her hand fluttering over it, almost protectively. It seemed to be an instinctive

action. Winter had noticed the bag in the truck and now he remembered how her hand had moved to it during the journey, just as automatically. He found himself wondering what the bag contained.

Winter and the Russians followed the path that had been carved in the mud by the motorbikes. The light stayed on them, bullyingly bright. It seemed to want to pin them to the ground but they kept walking. Finally the spotlight swung away, sweeping left, illuminating another dismal stretch of marshland.

Winter saw a cluster of vehicles parked at the border. One of them was a British car – a Jaguar Mk II sedan, its elegant curves incongruous against the functional struts of the fence. It signalled the presence of a bigwig. Faulkner himself, perhaps. Next to the Jaguar was a van, a drab Commer, as calculatedly anonymous as the Russian truck. Winter had no doubt which of the two vehicles would be returning him to Britain.

A group of men in suits and overcoats were gathered by the Jag. To their right was a knot of border guards, kitted out in caps and greatcoats, their dogs leashed but alert. Even at a distance Winter could sense the tension between the two factions. If Vienna allowed rival ideologies to breathe the same air, swill the same coffee, then the border burned away all such ambiguities. Here East and West came together to stand and stare, daring the other to flinch.

Yes, there was Faulkner. His silver thatch was unmistakable. He acknowledged Winter with a brisk,

businesslike nod. Winter felt almost proud to have prised the old bastard out of London. If Faulkner was overseeing this handover personally then it was clearly a big deal. Winter wondered again just who he was being exchanged for. He was curious to learn his market value.

There was an unspoken etiquette to all this. The Russian bikes had stopped some thirty feet from the British vehicles. It was a discreet, courteous distance, marking out a strip of neutral territory between the two groups. The exchange would occur in the middle of this space, the prisoners traded with precise timing.

Winter stood behind the bikes, flanked by Malykh and Karina. He could hear the engines hum, low and restless, as if the pair of M-72s were poised to tear away at any moment. One of the riders flashed a headlight into the dark. A moment later there came an answering flash from the Commer van.

Contact had been established.

One of the British men broke from the others. He stepped away from the Jaguar and walked towards the waiting Russians, his pace determined but cautious. He was a slight, stooped figure, wrapped in a sheepskin coat that seemed at least one size too big for him. The wind toyed with the unruly white hair that crowned his high, scholastic forehead. There was a thick woollen scarf at his throat.

Winter found himself shunted a few paces forward. Malykh had his arm, the Russian's fingers as tight as a clamp. Karina stayed close.

The advancing figure drew nearer, his breath trailing like smoke in the cold air. Now Winter could see that the man was in his sixties, possibly older. He wore a pair of horn-rimmed glasses, their owlish sweep accentuating his donnish appearance. And there was a book in his hand, plump with gilt-edged pages and bound in leather. It was the King James Bible.

The man met them at the midpoint. He announced himself with a wet, bronchial cough and tugged at his scarf, loosening the wool to reveal the white band of a dog collar at his throat.

'Father Neville Katsworth,' he declared. 'Her Majesty's exorcist.'

16

The priest regarded Winter with clear disdain.

'So you're the silly bastard we're freeing this monster for.' He coughed again, the edges of his glasses glinting as they caught the sweep of a searchlight. The beam momentarily haloed the clergyman's head, revealing a mottled terrain of skin, liver spots scattered like map markings.

Winter nodded. 'Yes. I am. Not that I have the blindest idea who I'm being exchanged for.'

The priest gave a bitter little chuckle. 'Been rather kept in the dark, have we?'

Winter smiled, bleakly. 'Seems to be standard operational procedure in my life these days.'

'Well, I hope you're worth it. Somebody must think so, anyway. Bloody deluded though they must be.'

'We have an agreement,' interjected Malykh, clearly impatient.

Katsworth turned to study the Russian officer. His expression held even more contempt than the look he had given Winter.

175

'Do we indeed? My government may have agreed, Colonel. I certainly didn't. But I'm here as a loyal servant. Their will be done. And to hell with the consequences. Quite literally, I imagine.'

Winter saw that the priest was toying with the Bible, absently skimming its pages with his thumb. It seemed like an anxious tic. The nail of the thumb was chipped, too, the flesh around it torn and raw. This was clearly a nervous man.

'So tell me,' he said. 'Who am I being exchanged for?'

'A hero of the motherland,' said Malykh, supplying an answer before Katsworth had a chance to speak.

The priest snorted, triggering another phlegmy combustion in his throat. He fingered his dog collar, as if keen to loosen it.

'A hero indeed. Is such a creature really a hero to you lot? A beast that tears the skulls from brave young boys? What a bloody perverted idea of heroism you people have.'

'We were at war,' said Malykh. 'I imagine you have no stomach for such a thing.'

Katsworth gave him a fastidiously cold look. 'I was with the Spanish Maquis in the battle for Paris. I cast out infinitely nastier bastards than you. And may I remind you – I'm the fellow who put this vile thing away.'

'I know,' said Malykh, levelly. 'And I'm sure that it remembers, Father.'

Katsworth met his eyes. 'I imagine it does.'

Winter looked beyond Katsworth, back to the huddle of people gathered around the Jaguar. He counted three figures – Faulkner and two men he took to be fellow agents. They had the burly, anonymous look of a private security detail. There was no sign of a waiting prisoner.

'So where is he, then?' Winter asked, genuinely curious. 'This man I'm being traded for? Have you got him in the van?'

Katsworth gave a teacherly shake of the head, his white hair rioting in the wind. 'Dear God,' he said. 'They really don't tell you anything, do they?'

He took the Bible in both hands and held it in front of him. There was a gilt cross embossed on the cracked leather cover. For a moment it shone with the borrowed dazzle of the searchlight.

'I advise you to stand away,' said the cleric. There was a sense of exhaustion to his words. It was the voice of an old man now, tired of the fight.

Winter fell back with the others, though he had no idea why he was giving ground to the priest. He saw the man's hands clamp the Bible, tighten around it, the leather binding buckling beneath his ragged fingers. Katsworth closed his eyes. He began to mutter, a low, incantatory drone of Latin, the words half heard, half lost on the wind.

Winter caught some of the phrases. *Libertas.* *Interminatus. Christus.* He knew enough of the language to guess their meaning. This was some kind of invocation to Christ, a plea for mercy and freedom.

As he watched, the clergyman's eyelids quivered. Soon they were fluttering at speed, rippling over the whites of his eyes. The priest's voice grew in volume.

Libertas. Interminatus. Christus. Monstrum.

Something shifted in the air. It was the faintest, subtlest change to the atmosphere, like the first trace of rain on your skin before the clouds broke. Winter was barely aware of it to begin with but then he felt it in the pores of his face. A sudden veil of moisture, hot and prickling, as if the air itself was beginning to boil.

He glanced around him. The Russians were concentrating on Katsworth, their eyes fixed to the priest as he brandished the Bible like a Hyde Park preacher. High in the watchtowers the guards were equally captivated, leaning over the walls of the turrets. Some of the patrol dogs began to whine. It was a confused, distressed sound.

Winter could hear something else, too, something barely perceptible beneath the ever-louder chant of Latin and the rising murmur of the wind. It was a noise like tiny, tinkling bells, a jangle of metal against metal. He looked for its source and saw a flash of silver in the darkness. There, tied to the wire fence, a collection of crucifixes spun and clashed, stirred by the breeze. Who had placed them there? Political protestors? No, it had to be the guards. *So much for their godless ideology*, thought Winter. Communism clearly only made sense in daylight. The dark demanded an older faith.

Katsworth continued to chant. Now his voice was almost confrontational, the words hurled against the

wind. He kept his left hand locked around the Bible, the book bending in his grasp. With his right hand he made what looked to be holy gestures. Winter recognised the sign of the trinity but the rest was a blur, the old man's fingers moving like nimble spiders. *Libertas. Interminatus. Christus. Monstrum.* The priest's eyes were white slits behind his spectacles.

There was another wave of wet heat. The moisture in the air clung to their faces.

Winter turned to Karina. 'What the hell's happening here?'

The patrol dogs howled, their anxiety escalating. It was a pitiful noise, torn from deep in the animals' throats.

Karina stared ahead, undaunted. 'You are getting your freedom.'

A sudden gust of wind swept the plain, a squall that raced across the marshland and made a rattling assault on the fence. The little knot of crucifixes rang as they smashed against the wire, clanging like keys.

And then there was a moment of impossible stillness. The wind was gone, the stars frozen. It was as if, for a second, the world had simply stopped.

Then came a sound like the sky tearing in two.

It roared over the puszta, as loud as a brawl of storms. Winter had read about sonic booms – modern jet fighters made them as they stabbed through the sound barrier – but this noise was beyond anything he had ever imagined. It had to be what an A-bomb sounded like in the very second of detonation.

A cobalt-blue light filled the sky, electrically bright.

Along the length of the watchtower every last searchlight shattered, the orbs of glass bursting as if ruptured by some intolerable internal pressure. The shards rained to earth. One struck Malykh as he raised a fist to shield himself. He gave a guttural Russian oath.

Winter also covered his eyes, as much against the glare of the light as the volley of glass. Squinting, he saw that the unearthly gleam had a point of origin. The light formed a tunnel, radiating from a bright blue hole that had been punched out of the darkness.

Something walked from the heart of the light.

For a moment it wasn't quite human. Winter glimpsed a flurry of shapes, blurring like photographic transparencies laid over one another. There was something subliminally insectile about them. Were those wings he could see, just for an instant? A multitude of legs? Winter had a sudden, shuddering memory of the creature he had encountered in that dark little church in Notting Hill, the one who had worn the body of a priest before all those bugs had tumbled out of him.

The figure solidified. For a moment its movements were twitchy, fitful, as if its limbs were remembering how to respond. And then it seemed to gather itself.

It emerged from the light as a woman.

She wore a black dress, formal in cut, and there was a neat black hat on her head, resting on a tight black bundle of hair. Her face was obscured by a veil, the lace freckled with black dots, thick as flies. A sharp, bony

jaw lay beneath it. There was nothing hesitant about her movements now. In fact she walked with an incongruous grace, her heels knifing through the sludge of mud and rainwater. She was as thinly elegant as a spider.

'Who is this?' Winter hissed, unable to take his eyes from her. The bright blue light shrank and dimmed as the woman approached. Soon it had disappeared completely, leaving only her silhouette.

'The Widow of Kursk,' said Karina, simply.

'Am I supposed to know who the hell that is? What's her real name?'

Karina spoke quickly, obviously irritated by the question. 'Her other names aren't meant to be spoken. They're meant to be carved in flesh.'

'She's some sort of demon, is she? I've already met one, in London. I had no idea these things even existed.'

Karina smiled, a little smugly. 'That's how most people get through this life.'

'I should have been told.'

'British Intelligence captured this one in 1949. They've held her ever since.'

Winter remembered Malcolm's mention of a captured demon. And yes, he had said Kursk, hadn't he? 'Held her where?' he asked. 'Some kind of prison?'

'Of a kind. It's called the Hollow. It's outside of our world. Outside our senses. Just like Heaven or Hell. Think of it as Purgatory, only no one's waiting for judgement in there. In fact no one's waiting for anything at all.'

Once again Winter felt his head lurch. Karina said

these things in such an infuriatingly matter-of-fact manner, as if she was explaining sunsets or gravity to a child. So now he had to accept that Heaven and Hell were real, did he? The remains of his rational mind – the part that had let him kill men in the name of his country – flinched at the thought. The rest of him surrendered to it. He had seen so much already. The sane world was smashed anyway. There was plenty of room for God and the Devil in its ruins.

'Why did we lock her away?'

Malykh pressed his black knife against Winter's ribs. 'Stop talking.'

Father Katsworth had his eyes open now. His skin was slick with sweat. It pooled in his pores, giving him the look of a pale dead fish in a dog collar. He was snatching icy lungfuls of air, desperate for breath. The Bible had almost been crushed in his hands. The leather binding was split, ripping through the gold-leaf cross on the cover. The priest gripped it as he watched the woman approach, and there was something uncomfortably close to fear in his eyes.

'Christ the Redeemer preserve us,' he muttered, forcing the words through his teeth even as he struggled to breathe.

The woman joined them. She had a distinctive scent, powerfully sweet, like marzipan or decay. Her skin was waxy, the colour of milk, seeming all the more bloodless against her black clothes. Winter peered through the veil that obscured her features, searching for her eyes. There

was no flash of white behind the lace, only a suggestion of something impenetrably dark.

She smiled, and her teeth were tiny and sharp, like a kitten's. 'Hello, Tobias,' she said.

It took Winter a moment to realise that the demon was speaking to him.

17

Winter frowned at the woman. 'Tobias?' he repeated, blankly. 'That's not my name.'

The Widow of Kursk extended a hand wrapped in a kidskin glove, studded with a pearl at the wrist. She swirled a lean finger on Winter's lapel, stroking the weave of the tweed. It was a strangely playful gesture. Familiar, even.

'Are you pretending not to know me, Tobias? How hurtful.'

Her eyes were like black marbles behind the lace. They reminded Winter of the dead gaze of porcelain dolls in Victorian nurseries. Even up close he found it impossible to estimate how old the woman was. Twenty? Forty? Sixty? She could have been any age. There was something unnervingly timeless about her.

'I don't know you,' he insisted. 'We've never met. And my name is not Tobias.'

The name felt curious on his lips, though. Tobias. As he said it aloud for the second time it seemed to prick a memory. It was the faintest shimmer of recognition but it was there,

and it disturbed him. It felt like a half-remembered snatch of melody, something he'd once known.

He could hear Malcolm's fingers on the broken piano in that bombed-out ballroom in Knightsbridge. *A nightingale sang…* That handful of discordant notes played in his mind.

The woman smiled at Winter. 'Tobias! Always such mischief with you! Such games!'

She took her hand from Winter's jacket. And then she lifted her veil, just a fraction, exposing wire-thin lips that were almost as pale as her skin. She extended her tongue and let it curl, tasting the night air.

'So much grief in this little world,' she declared, letting the lace fall again. 'Grief and loss and hurting. Everywhere! Such a tang. I'd almost forgotten.'

Winter glanced at Karina, wanting to share a look. But Karina had her gaze fixed on the Widow. It was like she was keeping watch on a cornered scorpion.

Malykh stepped forward. He gave a terse, military bow. 'I am Colonel Pavel Timurovich Malykh of the First Chief Directorate of the Committee for State Security. The motherland welcomes you home.'

Winter thought he caught a trace of discomfort in Malykh's voice. He certainly seemed to be wary of the demon's presence.

The Widow regarded the Soviet officer, unimpressed. 'Oh, are you tedious Stalinists still ruling Russia? Pity. I had so much more fun under the tsars. Tell me, Colonel, are we at war again? Will there be mourning? I am thirsty for mourning.'

'We are not openly at war,' said Malykh. 'But we have ideological enemies. We're trading with the British tonight.'

The demon regarded Winter again, a slit of a smile playing behind her veil. 'So, you have earned me my freedom, Tobias. Your country must want you very much indeed. I'd be flattered, if I were you. My deliverance is a considerable price for any nation to pay.'

Winter frowned at her, nonplussed. 'Why do you keep calling me Tobias?'

'Why do you keep denying it's your name?'

'This is Christopher Winter,' interjected Malykh, with a flash of irritation. 'He is a British intelligence operative. A crude gunman. A man of no true consequence.'

The Widow hissed through her teeth. 'Be careful you do not insult me, Colonel. I would not be traded for a man of no consequence.'

'Of course not,' stated Malykh, flatly.

The demon returned her attention to Winter. 'Oh, Tobias,' she smiled, her black eyes gleaming behind the lace. 'You always did confound them, didn't you? Never one to be documented and filed away. It's why I always found you so very appealing. The brightest butterflies can never be pinned.'

Winter shook his head in exasperation. 'I have no idea what you're talking about, whoever the hell you are. Let's just get this over with, shall we?'

'We should conclude the exchange,' said Malykh, briskly. 'We have an agreement.'

Winter felt the Russian withdraw the knife at his ribs.

And then the officer took a small key from his trenchcoat pocket and unlocked the cuffs. Winter kneaded his wrists, keen to stimulate the blood flow. His hands felt colder than ever in the raw Hungarian air.

'One moment,' said the Widow, imperiously. She turned her veiled gaze to Father Katsworth, still standing there with the crumpled Bible in his hand. 'I remember you, dear priest.'

The elderly clergyman shifted as she approached him, rising on his heels. He did his best to set his face into a fearless expression. A sheen of sweat still clung to him, his pores reflecting the moonlight.

The demon's voice had a coquettish lilt to it now. 'But then how could I ever forget my jailer?'

She carried the aroma of rotting flowers, rich and sickly. The priest's face wrinkled, betraying his revulsion.

'I'm surprised you remember,' said Katsworth, as calmly as he could. 'It's been nearly fifteen years.'

There was a black flash behind the veil. 'Time is not as you know it in the Hollow, Father. I have only known thirst. A thirst that did not require the passage of years to grow more profound. It was a thirst I imagined I would never sate. Even if I was free, would there ever be enough grief in this little world to sate it?'

'You're a bloody monster,' said Katsworth, spitting his words. 'You belong in Hell.'

'But surely God will forgive me? Doesn't he forgive everyone? Isn't that the way it works? I'm sure that's what the carpenter said...'

'I want to believe there are no limits to God's love,' replied the priest, fighting to keep his tone measured. 'But creatures like you make me doubt the reach of his mercy.'

'You make me feel very special,' said the Widow. She gave a smile like ashes in a grate. 'Now tell me. Who is there to mourn you?'

Katsworth fell silent. He kept his eyes on the woman but his jaw tremored, faintly.

'Surely there's someone in the world? Someone who would cry for you? It can't be only God who loves you, surely?'

'The Lord is my shepherd,' said Katsworth. 'I'll not want. He makes me down to lie.' The words sounded like a protective incantation.

The Widow gave a bloodless pout. 'Oh, don't bore me, priest.' She glanced at Malykh. 'Colonel, I sense your gift. Can you assist me?'

'We don't have time for this. We need to exchange.'

'Please, Colonel. Indulge me. It won't take a moment. I can't imagine he'll put up much of a fight. And we won't harm the dear man.'

Malykh walked forward with an air of reluctance. Sighing, he took the priest's head in his hands, sliding his fingers through the snowy hair to clasp the old man's skull. For a moment Katsworth continued his recitation. 'In pastures green, he leadeth me, the quiet waters by...'

And then he stumbled on the words of the prayer. They became broken, guttural, a random collection of sounds in the clergyman's throat. The milky whorl of

Malykh's iris started to swirl. The priest stared back, his eyes widening as the Russian's grip tightened. Malykh sunk his nails into the mottled scalp.

'For Thou art with me,' intoned Malykh, 'and Thy rod and staff my comfort still...'

Katsworth's mouth hung wide, saliva running from his tongue. His pupils matched the movements of Malykh's own, darting in parallel.

Winter looked on, remembering Malykh's assault on his own mind. He moved to intervene but a soldier pressed a gun muzzle against the small of his back.

'Toasted bread,' said Malykh, as if peeling the words from the man's skin. 'Toasted bread and a kind of sweetness... you call it jam. A fruit... damson. From the tree in the garden. It is your favourite. The clock in the kitchen is old, and slow, but these evenings it barely matters, for she is with you, and you don't notice the hours when she is with you. She's always made you forget them.'

'A wife?' asked the Widow, eagerly. 'Let me know her name.'

The tips of Malykh's fingers dug even harder into the priest's temples. Katsworth stared back at him, emptily.

'Harriet,' said the two men, in unison, one voice firm, the other broken.

Malykh finally released the clergyman's head. It lolled backwards, the eyes fighting to regain focus.

'Harriet,' said the demon. 'Not the prettiest name. But she will stand by your grave and grieve like a good Christian wife. Her sorrow will fill me.'

Katsworth glared at her. Breathless, his bloodshot eyes fierce behind his glasses, he found words. 'Goodness and mercy all my life shall surely follow me. And in God's house...'

With a quick, curiously eel-like motion the Widow of Kursk rammed a hand into the man's mouth. Her knuckles shattered his teeth on impact. She twisted her wrist, the pearl stud of the glove twinkling as she tore the tongue from his throat. She held it like a prize, the severed lingual artery spouting a futile gush of blood. Katsworth collapsed to his knees in front of her, catatonic with shock.

'I did ask him not to bore me,' the creature declared, casually.

Winter felt an overwhelming rush of disgust. He pushed towards the woman before the troopers could restrain him.

'What the hell did you do that for?' he yelled. 'There was no need!'

The demon raised her other hand, demanding silence. The moment was held. A second later the clergyman's head burst apart in a volley of blood and bone.

The Widow gave a jagged little smile behind her lace. 'Sweet Tobias. Do you really have no stomach for this anymore?' She tossed the tongue to the ground.

Malykh placed himself between Winter and the demon. 'Enough!' he said, addressing the Widow. 'This is not why we are here! We have an agreement with the British! You have violated it!'

'I have no agreement, Colonel,' the Widow spat. 'I never agreed to be held in that empty, hungry place. And why, I wonder, did it take you so long to deliver me from my exile? One might almost imagine that such an arrangement suited Mother Russia.'

She cast a black glance at the sentry tower. A young guard flung himself over the edge of the turret and smashed into the wet earth below. He lay there, face down, limbs splayed, a final exhalation of breath bubbling in the mud. The Widow ran her tongue over her taut lips. It was a repellently sensual motion.

'Perhaps my country cannot forgive me for the acts I committed in her name? Perhaps she now considers them cruelties? Time changes perspective for you animals, I'm told. Mine's quite the same, I assure you.'

She turned her gaze to a military jeep parked at the edge of the great fence. The demon tilted her jaw and the vehicle rose into the air, wheels spinning and a door flapping open. There were two soldiers inside. They had no chance to escape before it was hurled into the thick wire mesh, triggering a fusillade of sparks that lit up the dark with a bright violence of electricity. The ozone spice of voltage filled the air.

'I helped you to level Berlin,' declared the woman, proudly. 'I drank that city's grief and it was sweet.'

'Stop this!' insisted Malykh. His fingers were tight around the hilt of his obsidian knife.

'No, Colonel,' said the creature. 'I demand my sustenance.'

A bullet ripped through the earth at Winter's feet. He stumbled backwards as a second bullet followed it, slicing through the soil. Glancing up he saw that one of the tower guards had levelled a rifle. Another had drawn a revolver. Further shots came, studding the mud, clearly aimed with anger rather than precision. The sentries were shooting blindly, wildly.

Winter knew how vulnerable he was on the empty plain. The only available cover lay in the shadows under the watchtower's turrets – and chancing that direction would take him even closer to the guns.

He looked towards the British contingent. Faulkner was running, his coat gusting behind him as he was hustled to the Jaguar by the protective bulk of a secret service man. The car's headlights flared, its engine snarling impatiently in anticipation of escape. The other agent held his position, his gun anchored in a precise two-handed grip. The man took a pre-emptive shot at the watchtower, winging a guard in the shoulder. He was met with a rapid return of gunfire that forced him to fall back to the car.

Only then, as the agent was illuminated by the headlights, did Winter recognise the man. He had fought with him on the stairs in Belgravia, the night that he had found Malcolm's body.

It had to be him: the weight, the height, the surly confidence in the face, they all matched. Winter had never encountered the man in all his years in SIS. And yet here he was tonight, working security detail for the head of the service. Who was he? Did he really answer to Faulkner?

Or did he have another agenda, another master?

Two more British agents leapt from the idling van. They squatted by the doors, angling them into makeshift shields as the Jag roared a retreat behind them. Their handguns thumped. The man positioned by the left-side door took out one of Malykh's men with a brisk, efficient shot. The trooper fell close to Winter, pitching into the sludge. Malykh sheathed his knife, snatched his semi-automatic from his holster and blasted back. He abandoned Winter and ran to the shelter of the tower, evading a chain of shots.

It was a chaos of bullets now, all sides trading fire as the Widow of Kursk stood untouched and delighted in the centre of it all. Winter had planned to scramble through the crossfire towards his countrymen. Now he froze. Perhaps he'd be safer taking his chances with the Russians.

He needed a gun. He half slid towards the fallen trooper and – cursing the lack of holster on the man's belt – tore the tunic open. The soldier was still alive, staring up at him with young eyes. It was the boy who had given him cigarettes. He wore a white cotton singlet beneath the khaki. It was clammy and dark. Chest wound. Winter located a gun strapped to his shoulder. A small, snub-nosed revolver, a weaker gun than he wanted. It would have to do. He plucked it out, his fingers wet with the boy's blood. The soldier's eyes continued to track him even as his breathing cracked and faded.

The gun was booted from his hand. A fist followed, smashing into Winter's cheekbone and sending him sprawling to the ground. It was another of Malykh's troops, a thickset man with oversized hands. Winter struggled to rise, the mud sucking at his elbows. He saw his opponent unbutton his jacket and take out his own gun. The trooper trained the weapon on Winter and coiled a broad finger around the trigger.

A reed–thin blade skewered the man's windpipe.

The soldier crumpled, rasping, his hands clawing at his punctured throat. Behind him stood Karina. She withdrew the blade with a swift, surgical motion.

'I make that the third time,' she said. 'Don't you?'

Winter glowered at her. 'Christ, who's counting?'

He pulled himself to his feet and retrieved the gun that had been kicked from his grip.

'You know you just killed one of your own?'

Karina shrugged. 'He's not exactly one of my own.'

'What do you mean he's not one of your own? He's in your bloody army, isn't he?'

'We need to go, Christopher. We need to go now.' There was an unexpected urgency in her voice.

'We? We need to go? Since when is this we?'

Karina glanced behind her. 'Since the moment I killed that man.'

Winter knew there was no time to debate this. He turned and began to walk at speed, heading for the motorcycles waiting behind them, their engines idling. 'Come on, then,' he hissed to her.

He spun the gun in his hand and used its slab of a handle to cold-cock one of the riders. The man tumbled from the bike's seat, eyes rolling into unconsciousness behind his goggles. Winter caught the bike before it fell and hauled himself onto it, wrapping his thighs around its wide, brawny chassis. He felt the engine quiver like a constrained animal, its vibrations filling his bones.

The other rider simply stared at him, lifting his hands from his handlebars in a clear gesture of compliance. Winter knew without looking that Karina had her blade pointed in his general direction.

'Get on!' he told her.

She straddled the bike to ride pillion. As her arms encircled his chest Winter pulled the clutch in and slammed his left foot down, knocking the bike into first gear. The engine responded with an eager growl.

'Karina!'

It was Malykh's voice, startled and furious. He had seen them climb on the bike. Now he bolted from the shelter of the watchtower, his long leather coat trailing on the wind as he ran. He was reloading his pistol with a fresh clip of ammunition.

Winter opened the bike's throttle and released the clutch. The vehicle juddered and sprang forward with a stomach-stealing lurch. It gained speed, almost hungrily, its wheels carving through the soil, scattering thick sprays of mud in its wake.

Malykh fired after them. 'Karina!'

Winter was riding by muscle memory. It had been

years since he had last sat on a bike – and God knew he had never attempted to master a military beast like this one – but his body seemed to know what to do, even if the M-72 felt dangerously wilful beneath him. He let the speedometer's needle climb, conscious that he was serving the bike rather than taming it.

'Keep it straight, you idiot!' yelled Karina, above the rattling roar of the machine.

Winter corrected the bike as it tilted, its wheels skimming a treacherous stretch of rain-drenched earth. He took his eye from the twitching needle on the instrument panel, determined to keep his focus ahead of him. The empty plain swept by in a blast of air. Soon they were racing past the truck that had brought them there, their sheer speed rippling the canvas that clung to the vehicle's sides.

The motorcycle jumped from the wet grass to the coarse tarmac of the road, landing with a jounce of tyres. Winter felt the wind on his skin, cold and numbing. There was a rush of exhilaration in his blood, a heady surge of adrenalin and gratitude. This was freedom. This road, this simple country road, was suddenly sweet and infinite. Above him the October sky seemed equally endless. He had an urge to race away from everything, all the madness and the darkness of the last few weeks. He could do it. So easily. Just let the needle climb. Don't look down and don't look back.

Karina's arms were locked around him, her muscles hardening as the bike gathered speed. They were bound

together now, in a way that he sensed rather than entirely understood.

No, there was really only one road, he knew. They had to go deeper into this world, straight into its heart, however insane, however terrifying.

Winter gunned the throttle. Beneath a sprawl of stars the bike tore north.

18

Berlin felt haunted by rubble.

It was piled in great colourless hills between buildings still pockmarked by wartime bombing. Some of the debris had been shovelled into tidy mounds, awaiting turfing and the planting of trees, but for the most part the war remained unburied, for all that a skyline filled with cranes and construction work promised the future. A fine dust of shattered brick and stone lay upon the city, and when the wind rose over these open graves of masonry the dust found the eyes, infiltrated the throat.

Rubble. It was everywhere. Berlin had an asphalt pallor.

This was a wounded place, thought Winter. He wondered if it could ever heal. Hitler had dreamt of it as the capital of a Thousand-Year Reich, something shining and eternal, only to see it razed by the strength of Soviet firepower. The great *Strafe* had levelled half the city, the bombs falling day and night, relentless as an Old Testament judgement. The centre had been flattened in the final battle of 1945, a sustained artillery assault

reducing the great streets to a charred wasteland as the Red Army routed the Nazis.

Winter thought of the Widow of Kursk. He imagined her walking among the gutted buildings, the ruined streets, over the corpses of soldiers and civilians strewn on the cobbles. God, she must have feasted on this city.

And now Berlin had a fresh wound. The Wall had come overnight and cut the city in half, severing its arteries. The major transport links of the S-Bahn and U-Bahn lines had been broken. Squares and canals had been divided. Even houses had been sliced in two with ruthless communist pragmatism, doors tied and windows choked with bales of barbed wire. It was as if someone had turned a knife in the city's still-raw scar tissue.

Winter gazed out across West Berlin, over the bomb-wrecked buildings and emerging tower blocks. He saw the Europa-Center in the Breitscheidplatz, a cradle of scaffolding supporting its modernist bulk of steel and glass. It was already a giant of a building. It should, by rights, have dominated the horizon. But it didn't. It was the Wall and the Wall alone that ruled this city. Even when it was hidden from view it was all that you could see.

Maybe that was how this whole strange business of magic worked, he mused, sipping the remains of a thick, grainy coffee. Huge ideas, unseen but unimaginably powerful. Invisible to the everyday eye but always there, regardless, shaping the world.

And walls were there to keep things out, of course.

They had reached Berlin that morning, after a night

of travelling. The bike had taken them as far as the town of Lauchhammer, only to be unceremoniously abandoned in a backstreet. A Russian military motorcycle would be just a little too conspicuous by daylight, and nowhere more so than in West Berlin. And so, in the early hours, they had stolen a Volkswagen coupe sat in a hushed residential street, hotwiring its engine as its owner – a dentist with a taste for opera and hunting, to judge from the paraphernalia that littered the top of the dashboard – slept unaware.

Winter had taken the wheel, Karina closing her eyes in the passenger seat, her hands protectively clasping her bag. Once again he wondered what was inside. She must have slept for some of the journey but whenever he took his eyes from the road to glance at her she was staring back, her gaze mirroring his, lit by the glow of the dashboard.

Dawn had found them on the autobahn. Its emptiness at that hour made its endless lines feel even more hypnotic than usual. The concrete lanes flashed by without ever really seeming to change. Winter felt as though he was in stasis, only the reverberation of the car reassuring him that they were actually moving. Already tired, he had to concentrate to ignore the infinite blankness of the German motorway system. It made him ridiculously heartsick for England. All he asked for was a damp green verge, a Little Chef.

Reaching the fringes of West Berlin they had driven to an old SIS safehouse placed in the Neukölln borough.

Karina had been against the idea and Winter, to be honest, had his own qualms – he still wasn't sure how far he could trust the service, or, indeed, how far the service trusted him. But he knew that Britain's European safehouse network traditionally used operatives recruited years before, people whose contact with London was remote at most. These were satellite operations, divorced from the main intelligence hub, and that made them just a little easier to trust, he reasoned.

The contact at the safehouse was a petite, vinegary German woman in her late sixties. Frau Weissbach wore her hair wrenched in a tight grey bun and carried a fug of Muratti cigarettes that extended to every stale little corner of her home, from the vase of ailing flowers in the entrance hall to the nicotine-yellowed cupboards of the kitchen. She had quibbled over Winter's credentials at first – his pass code was out of date, part of a set of protocols that had been upgraded some months ago – but he had managed to win her over with a mention of Malcolm. She had responded to the Englishman's name with a sudden, fond smile. Karina, at that point, had quietly sheathed her blade.

Winter had stolen a couple of hours' sleep in a drab room decorated with thick-framed watercolours of agricultural fairs. He had drawn the curtains against the sun. The bed had been hard but it was, at least, a bed, his first for weeks. Even the stiff, chemical-scented sheets were a luxury compared to the floor of that farm building.

It had been a brief but useful sleep. No dreams to speak of. Only images, as fleeting as sparks: the Widow of Kursk with her unfathomably black eyes; Father Katsworth, clasping the Bible, about to die; a white light, more piercing than the lights on the watchtower, a light as vivid as fire, bright enough to blind, bright enough to wake him…

Rising, Winter had washed and shaved, pressing the towel against his face and holding it there for a moment, inhaling its strangely comforting laundry scent. Then he had exchanged his rumpled, grimy tweed suit for a pinstriped one he had found in the wardrobe. Just as every drawer of the safehouse held forged papers and documentation, each wardrobe offered a choice of clothes, from discreet business suits to counterfeit police uniforms. The cut was a little old-fashioned – as if he cared – but it just about fitted and, teamed with a new cotton shirt, made him feel considerably fresher, even if his shoes were still encrusted with the mud of the Hungarian border.

'You look like a Frankfurt banker,' Karina had said, meeting him in the kitchen for a breakfast of schlackwurst, herbed cheese and poppy seed rolls.

'Pity,' Winter had replied. 'I wanted to look like a fugitive British Intelligence agent.'

Now the two of them were sat outside at a terrace café in the Charlottenburg district, close to the flea market. An aroma of fresh eels, coffee and cabbage drifted from the stalls. There was rain in the air, along with the ever-present

dust. An uncommitted drizzle hit the morning edition of the *Berliner Morgenpost* that Karina was reading, spattering grey stains on the newsprint.

Winter glanced at the headline. Back home that starchy aristocrat Alec Douglas-Home had just succeeded Macmillan as prime minister. It was the first piece of news he had seen in weeks. As the paper asked if this was good news for Germany Winter realised how utterly untethered he felt from Britain. No, not just Britain – the world. Sat here in Berlin, his future uncertain, he felt outside of everything. Absolutely everything. The world he had known now felt like a small, ignorant thing, burying its head beneath the blankets to keep the dark at bay.

He moved his gaze to Karina, watching as the drizzle fixed a stray lock of blonde hair to her forehead. He had a sudden sense of her as one of those hollow Russian nesting dolls, the ones stacked inside one another. Faces behind faces, identities within identities.

'Who are you?' he asked, genuinely curious.

She turned a page of the newspaper. 'Do we need this conversation, Christopher? I'm whoever I need to be.'

Dear God, she was exasperating. 'I'd prefer a straight answer.'

'Then you might be in the wrong profession.'

Winter was determined to press the subject. 'Well, you're clearly not Soviet Intelligence. Not unless that was a pretty unequivocal act of resignation back there at the border. So that's twice now you haven't been who you claim to be.'

'Christ, who's counting?' she replied, casually mimicking Winter's voice. She clearly had a talent for accents.

'Is your name really Karina Lazarova?'

She continued to study the newspaper. 'Is Christopher Winter yours?'

She had asked the same question in the farmhouse. This time Winter heard the Widow's voice. *Hello, Tobias...*

He regained focus. 'If we're going to be a team I think I should know your name, don't you?'

'Whatever makes you imagine we're a team?'

'The fact you haven't stabbed me yet?'

She allowed herself an ambiguous smile. 'There's a whole day ahead of us.'

'But we're here together, aren't we?' Winter insisted, nodding to the busy tables around them. 'There must be a reason for that. You don't strike me as someone who seeks out alliances. So you need me, don't you? If you didn't we wouldn't be sat here. I think we're partners.'

For a moment she continued to scrutinise the newspaper. And then she folded it and placed it next to her glass of black tea.

'We are not partners, Christopher. We are not a team. I don't need you. You don't need me. I don't trust you. You don't trust me. Is that understood? If it is, we can proceed.'

'Naturally,' said Winter. 'But I took all that for granted. First rules of engagement in this line of work. You know that.'

'What line of work do you imagine I'm in?'

Winter took a moment to drain his coffee. The accumulated grain at the bottom of the cup gave it a final kick.

'Well, offhand I'd say you specialise in death and bullshit. And you're very good at both. But you obviously have an agenda. I can only presume we're after the same thing. That piece of intelligence that Harzner auctioned off. The code or the rune or whatever the hell it is.'

Karina regarded him closely, watching as Winter returned his cup to the saucer. 'Harzner told me you know exactly what it is.'

'Did he?' said Winter, wiping a smear of froth from his lips. 'He was mistaken, then. My briefing was pretty vague. Circumstances.' He dabbed at his mouth with a napkin. 'So that's why you're keeping me around, is it? You think I can help you make sense of this thing?'

'I understand it perfectly well.'

Her reply was almost defensive, thought Winter, intrigued by this sudden flash of emotion, cracking her customary composure.

She spoke again, her words a little more measured this time. 'Believe me, I've always understood its power.'

'Always? How long have you been chasing it?'

'A lifetime.'

Winter saw something in her eyes then, something older than her face. A weariness matched by a kind of fire, a resilience and a determination. In that moment he felt he was finally glimpsing the truth of who she was.

'You don't seem old enough to have lived a lifetime,' he told her, half teasing.

Karina didn't return a smile. 'It's been my life.'

She said it so matter-of-factly and yet Winter sensed these words were raw. He'd never considered himself an empathic person – empathy wasn't high on the list of requirements for a government-sanctioned assassin – but now, facing this puzzle of a woman across a café table in the rain, he felt a fraction closer to understanding her.

He knew the life she meant, knew it well. It whittled your heart out in the dark hours, left you empty. You formed a shell around yourself and then, one day, the shell was all you were. What was it Malykh had called him? Hollow inside. The Russian had been right. Even his marriage, his life with Joyce, had clearly been some kind of sham. Hollow inside, all those years.

'Karina,' he said, softly, 'are we still being watched?'

She moved her gaze. The men were still there. There were three of them, wrapped in slate-grey overcoats, standing altogether too still amid the swirl of the market. They had been there for ten minutes now, conspicuous as statues.

'They haven't moved,' she said, letting her eyes stray past the men to settle on the bright colours of a fruit stall. 'Who do you think they are? British Intelligence?'

'Stasi, I'd imagine,' said Winter. 'We can't come this close to the East and not expect to attract attention. They know we're here. They just don't know what we want. It's routine surveillance. I wouldn't worry. I'm more

concerned about your friend Malykh knowing where we are.' He paused. 'Tell me,' he said, 'this gift of his, the eye. It's called telepathy, right? I know the Russians have been conducting tests since the end of the war...'

'It has nothing to do with science,' said Karina. There was an intensity to her voice, just enough to unease Winter. 'And it's not a gift. He stole it. In a village north of the Caspian Sea he took the eye of a devil. Cut it out and used it for his own. He will find me soon enough. Perhaps you should not remain in my company longer than you can help it.'

'If the Russians have that code then I'm not going anywhere.'

'Oh, the Russians don't have the code,' said Karina, unexpectedly brightly. 'I do. Naturally I gave Malykh a false envelope. The code it contains is quite inessential.'

She raised a hand, summoning the waiter as Winter stared blankly at her. 'Time to go, Christopher. The richest man in Berlin is waiting for us.'

19

The taxi slowed to the kerbside on the grand avenue of Kurfürstendamm, finally released from a squabble of midday traffic.

Winter saw their destination through the drag of the cab's wipers. Hotel Fabelhaft was a regal, imposing building whose five portly storeys had seemingly defied the war. It bore none of the artillery scars or wounded stonework that so characterised the city. It looked invincible, in fact, a world away from the bomb-blasted remains of the Fairbridge in London. A cluster of international flags hung from its brick brows, their colours muted in the Berlin rain.

It was a downpour now, rapping on the roof of the Mercedes and striking its bonnet with quick, vicious pecks. As the wipers crawled a doorman in a swallow-tailed coat broke from the hotel's entrance and walked to the car, a large umbrella in his hand. He sheltered Winter and Karina as they left the taxi, accepting a tip with a nod.

They entered the Fabelhaft through a revolving door. The carousel of glass turned at a stately pace, its tall,

bronze-edged panes reflecting the bleak skies outside.

The lobby was an expanse of cream and coral and crystal, lushly carpeted and decorated with altogether too many gold-framed clocks. A succession of bells marked the quarter-hour, chiming in synch. They were the only sound in the luxurious hush.

Like all great hotels, the Fabelhaft made you feel as welcome as it did unworthy. Winter began to feel remarkably self-conscious about his mud-crusted shoes, which were already trailing filthy footprints on the deep-pile carpet.

He looked around the foyer as Karina went to the reception desk, noting the cheerless parade of businessmen, the coiffed old women in stoles, the staff who seemed to glide past, powered by pure discretion. This place bled wealth. Above him he saw a web of pneumatic tubing, an antiquated communication network propelling messages in cylinders through the arteries of the building. And this was the age of satellites, he thought.

Karina returned, removing her Cossack hat and squashing it under her arm. 'The restaurant's on the third floor. Herr Unterbrink is waiting.'

They crossed the lobby to the lifts. A gleaming bronze rectangle of a door slid open, revealing a caged interior. A man in a tailcoat the colour of liquorice drew back the metal lattice and welcomed them in. He was polite enough not to smile. The lift ascended with a whisper and a soft lurch of motion. The floors scrolled past, their numbers illuminating coin-sized slots set into the walnut

panel to the side of the door. No one spoke.

They exited on the third floor. A curve of corridor led them to the restaurant entrance. The maître d' welcomed them with an expert blend of attentiveness and disdain.

'You are Herr Unterbrink's guests? Please, follow me.'

He led them inside, through a towering set of doors decorated with embossed horses. The restaurant was vast, easily as big as the lobby, an ocean of white cloth and silver cutlery beneath a sprawling fresco of summer skies. Marble columns rose from floor to ceiling. It was surprisingly dim in the room, despite the chandeliers that hung like ornate anchors. The wattage of the lamps was low and thick velvet curtains obscured many of the windows, restricting the light from outside.

A quartet was playing. Winter couldn't place the piece – something by Handel? – but the strings sounded half-hearted, as if the players weren't entirely enjoying themselves.

The maître d' walked them through the tables. There were only a handful of diners, either businessmen and their mistresses or old, awkward couples, resenting one another over silent spoonfuls of soup. Winter noticed that they had all taken the tables on the outermost orbit of the dining area.

A smell hit his nostrils. At first he thought it must be food, some pungent mix of aromas drifting from the kitchen. But it was far from appetising. And it became more pronounced the deeper they walked into the dining area.

A man sat at a far table, alone in the shadows. The ring

of empty tables that surrounded him made him seem even more solitary, framing his isolation. As Winter approached his table he realised that this man was the source of the smell. It slunk from him like the stench of drains.

He was an improbable presence in the gilded surroundings, dressed in a suit that wasn't just shabby but dirty, stained with patches of grime and food spills of indeterminate age and origin. The jacket was ragged, its buttons chipped or missing entirely. The fabric trailed snags of wool and the fraying pockets hung from their seams. His shirt-cuffs were the colour of rust.

He was wearing gloves despite the fact that he was indoors. They were a grubby pair of knitted mittens and his fingers protruded through them like worms poking out of soil. The man's nails were dark with dirt and dried blood, a contrast to the immaculate cutlery he held in his hands.

So this was Unterbrink. The richest man in Berlin, Karina had claimed. More like the richest vagrant, thought Winter. And to think that he had been fretting about the state of his shoes.

The man must have been in his late fifties, possibly older. His hair was a tangle of greasy black fronds while his skin was the shade and very nearly the texture of curdled milk. It clearly wasn't a face that had known daylight terribly well. It spoke of a lifetime of windowless rooms.

The maître d' bowed, sharply. 'Herr Unterbrink. Your guests.'

For a moment it seemed that Unterbrink hadn't heard the words, or had chosen to ignore them. He continued to eat, taking another slice of goose liver from the terrine in front of him. And then he looked up, his eyes contracting, almost mole-like, as if wary of anybody that might bring in the outside world and disturb his carefully calibrated gloom.

He nodded an acknowledgement with a minimal tilt of the head, determined to savour his food.

Karina took a chair, dismissing the maître d's attempt to seat her. She held on to her bag, placing it upon her lap. 'Guten Tag,' she said. Winter took the seat next to her, waving away the maître d's offer of a menu. He had to force himself not to flinch at Unterbrink's odour.

'Fräulein Fabre,' grunted the German, with no warmth to the greeting. 'It has been some years.'

Fabre? Another identity, no doubt. Just how many did this woman have?

'I very much appreciate you meeting us like this,' said Karina. There was a French inflection to her voice now, all trace of Eastern European accent erased, the very rhythm of her words subtly altered. She was good, thought Winter, grudgingly.

'As you know I rarely engage in these matters directly,' said Unterbrink. A portion of goose liver tumbled from his fork and made a fresh smear of grease on his suit. He casually snatched it from his lapel and lobbed it into his mouth. 'Your proposal, however, was compelling.'

'It's really not one I made lightly,' said Karina.

'I should trust not. It's a remarkable offer.'

Unterbrink finished eating and tossed his cutlery onto the plate. It landed in a haphazard clutter, defying restaurant etiquette with the assurance of the very rich. He pushed the plate away from him, drained a glass of brandy and then reached inside his threadbare suit. He pulled out a slim rectangular box of gleaming brown and gold. It was a tortoiseshell cigarette case, a bird of prey chiselled upon its surface. He held it in a way that told them he wanted the object to be admired, not touched.

'1862. The work of Ernest Keep. The shell is hawksbill sea turtle and the eyes are mother of pearl. Commissioned to commemorate Von Bismarck's appointment as Minister President of Prussia. Five cases were made. Two survive. Naturally I also have the other. Would you care for a smoke?'

He flipped the case open, revealing a neat parade of cigarettes, each one decorated with a tiny ribbon of red silk.

Winter smiled, dryly. 'I take it your cigarettes aren't a century old too?'

Unterbrink blinked and turned to Karina. 'Who exactly is this man?'

'As I told Herr Beltz, he's my associate. You can trust him.'

'I would prefer not to be placed in that position.'

Karina leaned forward in her stiff-backed chair. She spoke softly. 'He's with me. Or our deal is off.'

Unterbrink snapped the case shut and returned it to

his pocket. Disdain crawled on his face.

'Please, Fräulein. Our desires are well matched. You want what I possess and I want what you possess. We are in no position to bargain or threaten one another. But you can understand that I'm curious. I have always known you to work alone. Is he also with the Order of Leaves? I thought you were the last of them.'

Karina kept her face expressionless. 'He's with me, Herr Unterbrink.'

'We're partners,' said Winter, with a pointed look at Karina. 'A team.'

Karina buried a murderous glint. 'We are associates.'

'Associates. Very well. You have the item with you?' There was a tremor of anticipation in Unterbrink's voice, something very nearly lustful.

'I do.'

Karina unbuckled her bag. These past few days Winter had begun to imagine it was welded to her body. He watched her reach inside it and remove something wrapped in smoke-grey tissue. Slowly, carefully, she lifted the object out of the bag's grasp. It had the unmistakable shape of a bottle. The tissue fell away to the table.

'My god,' said Unterbrink, with a sharp, astonished breath. '*Unglaublich!*'

It was indeed a bottle. A bottle of wine, and clearly one that was exceptionally old. There were no markings upon it, no trace of manufacturer's labels. The bottle's curves were imperfect, slightly uneven, obviously crafted by hand. There was a weathered, crumbling cork

jammed into the top of it. The glass itself was olive-dark but it shone in the gloom of the restaurant, as if it had the power to find and magnify any available light.

At first Winter assumed the bottle was empty. But then, as it turned in Karina's hands, he saw a tiny ripple of liquid run the length of the glass, like a raindrop on a window.

'May I hold it?' said Unterbrink. There was reverence in his voice.

Karina handed it across the table. He held it almost hesitantly, as if afraid it might shatter in his grasp at any second. 'The provenance is assured?' he asked, unable to take his gaze from the object.

'Of course,' said Karina. 'Taken from the Church of Saint John, the Hermit of Pskov, when the Bolsheviks seized the land. It's been in safekeeping since 1917.'

'I had heard the speculation, of course. Every collector has. I never dreamed it could be so real. So utterly precious.'

Unterbrink let the bead of liquid tip its way back to the bottom of the bottle. And then he spoke, very quietly.

'And the third day there was a marriage in Cana of Galilee, and the mother of Jesus was there,' he intoned, almost to himself. 'And when they wanted wine, the mother of Jesus saith unto him, they have no wine.'

The bottle turned and shimmered.

'The ruler of the feast had tasted the water that was made wine and knew not whence it was. But the servants which drew the water knew.'

Winter glanced at Karina, incredulous. She met his gaze

with a look that told him to simply accept this moment and say nothing. He looked back at Unterbrink.

The German had brought the bottle close to his face. His tiny, crumpled eyes were watering as he peered into its depths, through the shadows in the glass.

'By God,' he whispered, as the bottle glinted and gleamed. 'The most desired vintage in history.'

'I imagined you would be pleased,' said Karina. 'I know how long the Reliquarists have been seeking this piece.'

'All my life,' said Unterbrink. 'I only wish there was more of my life left in which I might savour it.'

'You're one of the only men alive who will savour it, Herr Unterbrink. Why do you need to count the days?'

Unterbrink nodded. 'Such a thought is always a comfort to me, Fräulein Fabre.'

'So we have a deal, then?'

'We do.'

Unterbrink seemed reluctant to hand the bottle back to Karina. For a moment he clung to it, almost protectively. And then, because he had to, he passed it back across the table. His eyes stayed upon it, watching as it was wrapped in tissue once more and returned to the bag on Karina's lap.

'I'm curious,' he said, as Karina buckled the bag. 'The object I'm trading is an item of immense rarity, of course, and one that many others have sought over the years. I'm well aware of its market value and I'm willing to make an exchange. But you and I both know that it's

not… well, it is hardly the contents of that bottle, is it? Why would you even make such a trade?'

Karina answered him levelly. 'Because you have it. And I want it. It's really that simple.'

Unterbrink considered this. And then he gave a brittle little laugh. 'Very good. Your philosophy echoes my own, Fräulein Fabre. I believe we can do business.'

He took a battered leather wallet from his jacket pocket. He prised a card from its folds and handed it to Karina. It bore the words '*Die Wendeltreppe*' and a small but elegantly executed illustration of a spiral staircase, black ink on gold. There was an address, too: 49 Falke Spur, off Potsdamer Platz. That was the furthest edge of West Berlin, Winter knew. Close to the Wall.

'Be there this evening. Say six? Herr Beltz will be in attendance. We shall trade, you and I.'

'It will be a pleasure,' said Karina. She rose and Winter stood up too. The other diners in the room immediately focused on their meals.

Unterbrink reached for the crisp white napkin placed on the table. It was rolled in a silver ring decorated with a bulbous fish. He used it to dab at his mouth, staining the cloth. 'One last thing,' he said, between dabs. 'This city has eyes. Perhaps the keenest eyes in Europe. I am aware that your arrival in Berlin has not been unobserved. You would do well to ensure absolute discretion in these matters. I have no wish for the Stasi to involve themselves with my business.'

Karina nodded. 'You have my assurance, Herr

Unterbrink. Absolute discretion. And should I need to kill them, I will be absolutely discreet, I promise.'

Unterbrink stared at her, unsure if she was serious. And then, taking it as some kind of dark joke, he laughed again. '*Drollig*,' he said. '*Sehr drollig*.'

Winter and Karina walked through the half-lit dining room, aware of conversations stopping at tables as they passed, cutlery hovering in people's hands. The maître d' met them at the door. There was a small bottle of cologne in his hand. He fussed at them with a jasmine-scented mist.

'My apologies,' he said. 'Herr Unterbrink is a valued patron but like so many wealthy men he has his eccentricities. I trust you shall not judge the Fabelhaft unfavourably.'

'It's fine,' said Winter, bristling at the liberal application of cologne. 'In England we call them the stinking rich.'

The maître d' regarded him blankly.

This time they took the stairs to the lobby. Karina walked ahead of Winter, her hand on the ivory banister.

Winter kept his voice low, for all that they were alone in the stairwell. 'So am I really supposed to accept that was the wine of Christ?'

Karina shrugged. He didn't have to see her expression; he could sense the dismissive chill.

'Accept what you wish,' she said. The Eastern European accent was back.

'And the Reliquarists,' he continued, turning on the stairs to follow her. 'Who are they?'

'You'll meet them soon enough.'

Winter found himself irritated all over again by her aversion to straight answers. 'Unterbrink mentioned something else,' he continued, as they came to the last stack of stairs. 'The Order of Leaves. He said you were one of them. The last of them. What did he mean by that?'

Karina fell into silence. She strode into the broad expanse of the lobby, Winter behind her, matching her pace.

'Tell me,' he insisted. 'I need to know.'

She stopped and turned. 'No,' she told him. 'You do not need to know. You want to know. You must realise there's a difference.'

Winter examined the defiant tilt of her face. When he spoke his voice was calm.

'Karina,' he said, 'whatever it is you're after, whatever you're chasing, there will come a point when I'm going to do my job and take it from you. You realise that, right?'

Her gaze was equally cool. 'I will take your life before that, Christopher.'

She pushed through the revolving doors and out into the wet street, raising a hand to hail a taxi from the rainy blur of traffic. With a choice curse Winter followed her.

20

The night gave ghosts to Potsdamer Platz.

Once, Winter knew, this had been Europe's busiest, liveliest plaza, a bright throng of shops and theatres, raucous beer palaces and stately dance halls. The Nazis had rallied here in torchlit swarms, hoisting swastikas, spellbound by Hitler. The Führer's speeches had echoed among its streets, loud and mad and violent. Napoleon, too, had marched through the majestic boulevard of Unter den Linden, less than half a mile to the north, parading beneath the chariot of the goddess of victory, claiming it for his own.

It was a place of weeds and wire now, barren in the moonlight.

This was a no-man's-land, a desolate expanse, blasted to the ground by war. The great churches of the Französischer Dom and Deutscher Dom still stood in the Gendarmenmarkt but they were shells, bombed-out husks. The Reichstag, once the seat of the German parliament, a baroque symbol of permanence and power, had been gutted by fire. The shattered building was

ringed by wild grass and sickly trees, abandoned now, like a thing left to die.

The Wall separated the ruins of the Reichstag from the Brandenburg Gate, halting the grand sweep of the road. The great slab of whitewashed concrete rose against the sky, crowned by guard towers and gun emplacements. It wasn't quite as tall as Winter had always imagined – fifteen foot at most – but its unrelenting monotony was every bit as oppressive.

The Wall wasn't the only barrier to freedom, just the most obvious one. A quarrel of barbed wire marked the approach to the Todesstreifen – the death strip, they called it – while angular tusks of steel had been hammered into the ground, acting as tank traps. They looked like a graveyard of toppled crosses. Landmines waited beyond.

This was the city's greatest scar and it was still raw. It scored through the very heart of Berlin, marked by the red and white stripes of the checkpoints, the black and white stripes of the crossings. Winter could just about read the propaganda posters on the other side. He couldn't translate every word but they were clearly exhortations to the glory and the purity of communist rule. *Die Einheit macht stark. Die Macht des Volkes.*

The eastern side of the divide was conspicuously emptier than the western half. Many of the buildings ravaged by war had recently been razed, allowing the sentries in the watchtowers a cleaner line of fire – handy when you were shooting potential escapees. The buildings that remained were husks, their windows

vacant frames. They shared the Soviet half of the city with newly erected blocks of housing, drably functional in design. There were washing lines strung between the towers, the cords glinting as they caught the searchlights.

The western side of Berlin had suffered just as much damage but it had chosen to preserve its survivors. A defiant corner of the Hotel Esplanade still stood on the wasteland. There were a handful of shops, too, incongruous among the rubble. But Winter knew there was no illusion of normal life in this place. It was a tripwire landscape, nervy and tense. This was the blade edge of the Cold War.

A church tower bell tolled across the city, deep and heavy.

'It's time,' said Karina. 'Let's go.'

They had positioned themselves in the shadows beneath the rail line but the area was too exposed for them to imagine they hadn't been seen. Winter had watched the border guards as they moved in the towers. He had seen them raise their binoculars, scrutinising the dusk as it turned into darkness. Simple routine? Or genuine suspicion? He couldn't be sure but it was all too easy to imagine his face in the sights of their rifles. True, they were in the western sector and free to go where they wished but Winter remembered the Stasi agents in the market. The KGB had to know that he and Karina were here in Berlin. It would be stupid to take chances. And besides, he had a professional affinity for the shadows.

They left the cover of the underpass as an S–Bahn

train rolled above them, its sluggish rumble sounding in the girders, shuddering through the metal. They took care to keep close to the viaduct, passing under hoardings for Opel cars and Old Red Fox whisky, posters engaged in their own small war against the communist slogans on the other side of the city. The rain had stopped some hours ago but it pooled between the cobbles and dripped from the gantries. The tarmac glimmered like oil.

The streets behind Potsdamer Platz were just as deserted as the main square but they were concealed from the sight of the guard towers, a fact that lent them a furtive, conspiratorial quality. They held the occasional shop, closed now for the night, and rows of residential houses, their windows intermittently lit. There was a scrapyard on the corner of Stresemannstrasse, its clutter of iron pipes and engine parts left to rust in the forecourt. The remains of a family car looked almost spectral in the moonlight.

There was mist in the air now, idling in the dark.

A solitary figure stood on the street, dressed in a belted, ankle-length coat and a narrow-brimmed trilby, tilted to obscure the face. The presence was so perfectly motionless it seemed to be a fixed point in the shadows, a shape rather than a person. And then, almost imperceptibly, the figure moved, shifting its head to catch the streetlight. Winter glimpsed a silvery beard and familiar, reproving eyes.

'My God, it's Faulkner...'

It made no sense. Why would the head of SIS be

waiting there, on an empty street in Berlin, entirely alone? There were no other agents to be seen, no sign of any security detail around him. It was, at the very least, a profound breach of field protocol.

'Sir?'

Winter's tone was courteous but wary. He sensed Karina tauten beside him, bracing for combat. He touched her arm, cautioning her to hold back. Across the street a gas lamp sputtered and hissed, its light faltering.

The man strode towards them. His pace was fast, determined, his steps heavy on the road. As he passed an empty phone kiosk the light inside the box flared, as if experiencing a sudden surge of voltage.

'Sir Crispin,' began Winter.

The man seized him by the throat. The assault was so abrupt, so unexpected, that Winter had no chance to block the move. The hand encircled his windpipe and tightened. Faulkner's grip was surprisingly strong.

Winter grasped his assailant's wrists. He fought to break the chokehold but the crucial leverage escaped him. The hand continued to close, seemingly determined to crush the bones of his neck.

Winter battled to breathe. The street around him began to fade. So did the face of Faulkner, with its strangely dull, filmy eyes.

Winter's vision didn't darken as his senses retreated. It turned white. A fierce, pure, brilliant white that engulfed his eyes.

It was absolute and it was everything.

White fire. It consumed him.

And then Faulkner's grip slackened. Karina was on his back, her right arm locked around his throat. She gave a twist of muscle, wrenching the man's head, almost cracking the upper vertebrae. Faulkner reeled, struggling to shake her, break her purchase on his body. Karina grimaced, clung on, maintaining the pressure until Faulkner finally surrendered his hold on his agent.

Flung to the ground, Winter hit kerbside concrete. He lay there, dragging air into his lungs as gutter water seeped into his suit. In seconds the brilliant white light was gone from his eyes. As his vision stabilised he saw Faulkner totter backwards and smash Karina repeatedly against a stone wall, using his bulk in a bid to dislodge her. She hung on to him, her face contorting as she tightened her forearm around his throat.

And then, with a final heave, she was hurled away. There was a thud of flesh against stone. She landed with a grunt, her bag slapping the wall. Faulkner had shrugged her off, discarded her as an irritant. Now he returned his attention to Winter, moving with clear purpose.

Karina scissored her legs around Faulkner's, snagging him. He kicked her feet away and continued walking.

Winter's chest heaved. Pain carved through his lungs. He reached for his Russian gun, his fingers trembling as they found the holster. Precious seconds wasted.

Karina had her blade in her hand. She had spun into the space between Faulkner and Winter, plucking the knife from her skirt. She crouched now, tossing the

blade's porcelain handle from palm to palm. And then she sprang, slicing forward with the reed-thin weapon.

Faulkner blocked the blade. Its razored edge swept through his hand. There was no wound, no laceration, not a drop of blood. Only a ghost of an indentation where the knife had passed. A second later it was gone. The man had felt nothing.

Winter snatched his gun from the holster. He focused and fired at Faulkner's left shoulder. The bullet tore straight through the body, leaving a smouldering hole in the coat. It struck the wall with a metallic howl. The man barely flinched.

This wasn't Faulkner. This was something else.

Winter shot the creature in the face. The flesh rippled, like water, as if the bullet had punched into a clear pond. For a moment Winter glimpsed a multitude of faces, shifting and blurring.

A car passed, at speed. There was a sudden dazzle of headlights.

Faulkner's face was gone. He had another one now, similar but a stranger's. The silver-streaked beard remained but everything else had changed, fractionally, like a face pieced together from a partial memory. It was almost Faulkner. Almost.

The man stood there, blankly. There was no trace of the determination that had animated his features only seconds before. He regarded Winter impassively. And then he turned, his hands digging into the pockets of his overcoat. He began to walk away, his shoes sounding on

the flagstones of the quiet street. Soon he was lost to the Berlin mist.

Winter looked at Karina as she hurried towards him. 'You're impressive,' he said, collecting his breath. 'You know, I rather think you could kill me, if it came to it.'

She didn't smile. 'I want to know what that was,' she said.

She offered her hand and Winter took it, hauling himself up from the kerbside. Back on his feet, he loosened his tie and tore his shirt collar open. His throat felt raw, the skin smarting from the attack.

'I have no idea,' he said. 'But those things are following me.'

'You've seen something like that before?'

He nodded, briskly. 'I saw one in London. I thought it was somebody else. Somebody I knew. Their faces change. God knows what they are. I hoped maybe you could tell me.'

Karina peered into the drift of mist. There was no sign of their assailant. The city had erased him.

'It just walked away... What do you mean their faces change?'

'Didn't you see it happen? It was Faulkner!'

She turned to him, confused. 'Faulkner? Sir Crispin Faulkner? The man at the border?'

'Yes! It had his face! And then it... changed. Became somebody else. That's what they do. Are you seriously telling me you didn't see that?'

Karina evaluated Winter's words. 'I saw that man

take a bullet in the face and walk away. But he wasn't Sir Crispin Faulkner. I have no idea what you saw.'

Winter dragged a hand through his cropped curls, tearing at the roots. 'I am not going mad,' he insisted. 'That's the one thing I tell myself in all of this. I am not going mad. Because you seem insane. And yet you tell me this is how the world is. So when people like you say you have no idea what I'm talking about then, well, Christ, I really feel alone.'

Karina reached for his hand. Her fingers were calloused but warm on his cold skin.

'I didn't see it,' she said, calmly. 'That doesn't mean it didn't happen.'

Her touch was unexpected. Winter nodded, not ungrateful. And then he shrugged her hand away. He didn't want to need it.

'You'd better check that bloody bottle of yours. Priorities.'

Karina quickly unbuckled her bag. She lifted out the bottle and delicately unwrapped the tissue. Exposed, the glass gleamed, its imperfect curves catching the streetlight.

'Thank God,' she said. 'It's intact.'

There was a sound like thunder rolling over the city. It came suddenly, a rumbling that seemed to bruise the very air. They looked up and saw a pair of fighter jets slash through the evening clouds, trailing scars of vapour. Republic F-84s, noted Winter. American planes, scrambled from the air base. They were moving at speed but it was impossible to tell if this was a genuine threat

response or just a piece of intimidatory theatre, routine on this frontier of the Cold War.

'We need to move,' said Karina, stuffing the bottle back into the bag. 'We're late as it is.'

Die Wendeltreppe stood at the far end of Falke Spur, its name declared in a Bauhaus font on a tarnished metal plate. It was the only surviving shop in the street, though the state of its health was questionable. Its windows were grilled, their bars colonised by rust, and the paint of its frontage, once a pale shade of blue, peeled in flaking clusters, revealing crumbling brickwork beneath. The shop's exterior had a sickly, almost diseased aura, as if its decay could be contagious, transmitted by touch.

Karina twisted the iron handle. The door opened with a pained, reluctant crack and a tinkling of bells.

'*Guten Abend*,' she said, addressing the dusty hush within.

The shop was lit by candles. There were too few to provide any decent illumination but as Winter's eyes grew accustomed to the gloom he saw the chaos of junk around him. There were objects everywhere, arranged with no obvious logic: a dead carriage clock shared a shelf with a porcelain harlequin, antique apothecary bottles sat next to a brass incense burner, the single scuffed shoe of a ballerina rested against a child's violin. There were books, too, placed in haphazard islands on the floor, their bindings faded, unreadable.

'*Guten Abend*, Fräulein Fabre.'

A man emerged from the recesses of the shop. He made his way towards them, expertly navigating the teetering books. He could only have been in his thirties but there was already a stunted look to him, something wormy and hunched, burrowed inside his suit. Just like Unterbrink his skin had an ashen cast that suggested a life untroubled by the sun.

'Herr Beltz?' The French inflection had returned to her voice.

The man extended a hand. 'Yes, indeed. I am at your service.'

'I'm sorry we're late,' said Karina. 'We were detained.'

'Please, think nothing of it. Time seems of less consequence inside these walls. It's one of the joys of our business.'

'And what is your business, exactly?' asked Winter, shaking the man's hand in turn. 'Junk, I take it?'

'Items of antiquarian interest,' said Beltz, coolly. '*Historische Objekte. Sammlerstücke.* And you are?'

'Just an interested party.'

Beltz's eyes seemed to flinch from the light, even in the shop's candle shadows.

'He's with me,' said Karina, quickly. 'Unterbrink knows.'

'I wasn't informed about this man but if Herr Unterbrink is aware of him then his presence is not a problem. You have the item, of course?'

'Of course,' said Karina.

'Then please, if you will both follow me.'

Beltz led them deeper into the shop. It was surprisingly large, a half-lit warren of nooks and corners, connected by sets of wooden steps. Elaborately framed paintings lay stacked on the floor, denied a place on the walls by the sheer crush and clutter of shelves. They passed a sculpture of a seahorse, carved from coral the colour of old teeth.

'So you call yourselves the Reliquarists?' asked Winter, casually.

Beltz walked ahead of him. 'We try not to use that name on the outside.'

'The outside? The outside of what?'

'The outside of our world,' stated Beltz, as if this was the only answer imaginable.

There was a staircase in the heart of the shop. It coiled in concentric circles, a whorl of wrought iron, spiralling down and down, through one floor, then another, then another, the stairs extending to a distant basement, deeper than the shop's exterior suggested. It was a dizzying, almost hypnotic helix, lit by a corkscrew parade of candles.

'Remarkable,' said Winter, genuinely impressed.

'We think so.'

Beltz led them down the staircase. Their shoes rang on the succession of metal grilles. Winter found himself fighting a surge of nausea as they twisted into the depths of the building, the three of them moving in tight rotation. Their candle-cast shadows filled the walls, stretching like putty.

At last they reached the basement, a drab, brick-

walled storage area where even more junk lay heaped in the corners. The room had a smell of oil and electricity. Old generators murmured against the walls, their dials obscured by grime.

At the foot of the staircase was a wide, circular trapdoor, rather like a manhole cover. Beltz knelt down and picked up an iron bar. He dug it into the recessed edge of the trapdoor. With a grunt he prised the hatch open.

Stale air rose from the open hole. There was darkness beneath, tar-black.

'Herr Unterbrink is waiting,' declared Beltz.

This city held another secret.

21

It was like clambering into an inkwell.

Winter descended the ladder that led into the thick dark under the trapdoor. It was built of rigid steel, bolted to the wall below. Its rungs ran with condensation, cold as ice water. They chilled his hands as he held them, one slick metal bar after another. Beltz was below him, Karina above.

He moved cautiously, knowing he was entering a space it would be tricky to escape from. The tactical part of his mind disliked that fact immensely. Only curiosity – and a grudging trust in Karina – persuaded him that this was an acceptable risk.

He let go of the last bar and dropped to the ground, falling to a surface that felt hard and uneven, as if a great expanse of rock had been crudely flattened. Karina landed beside him. Puddles sloshed around their shoes, reflecting electric light. Beltz had a torch in his hand and was sweeping the walls, exposing a barrel-vaulted tunnel ahead.

It was a dank, subterranean place. Water seeped from

the walls and dripped from the joists that supported the makeshift ceiling. A small portable heater stood in the shadows, glowing orange as dust smouldered upon its grille. Another heater was placed a little further along the tunnel and yet another glimmered in the distance. They did little to dispel the pervasive, bone-deep cold. It was like striking matches in the Arctic, thought Winter.

'This way,' said Beltz. His voice was low now.

They began to walk. Winter saw bundles of cables entwined on the ground. Other cables were clipped against the walls, coiling into the dark. A web of blue and green wiring hung from the ceiling, stitched through the cracks in the stone. Pipes and tubes ran the length of the passage, disappearing into fissures, their purpose uncertain.

Winter knew about this network of tunnels beneath the city. He had seen the files on Operation Stopwatch, known one of the men who had worked on it with the CIA, a brusque, brandy-loving service legend named Wickersham. A decade ago British Intelligence had run an intercept operation in a secret tunnel half a mile long, across the border from West to East Berlin. The tunnel had been located three hundred yards from the American sector, right under the very snouts of the Russians.

A battalion of tape recorders had plugged into the trunk telephone lines that connected East Berlin and Leipzig, tapping the covert traffic between Zossen and the army headquarters at Adlerhorst.

Back in London, in poky old Chester Terrace, on the edge of Regent's Park, a team of analysts had pored over

the high-grade Soviet ciphers, trying to make sense of the stolen chatter. Winter always remembered Wickersham telling him that the operation had lasted precisely eleven months and eleven days, a fact he never failed to describe as 'positively Biblical'.

The KGB then bragged that they had known of the tunnel's existence all along, and had fed the British and the Americans a stew of lies, misdirections and strategically sacrificed truths, all the better to coat the bullshit. Winter only knew that Wickersham had taken a bullet one night after cards at the Silversea Club in Mayfair. Some said it had been a London gangland hit, payback for his part in an unsavoury gambling scandal. Others knew a pointed message from Moscow when they saw one. Winter wondered if this was the same tunnel. The British had abandoned it in '56, after all. Perhaps these people, whoever they were, had found another, equally furtive use for it.

A rumble echoed through the dark stone of the passage. It took half a minute to pass, reverberating with a heavy, slow-fading roar. They had to be close to the U-Bahn line down here.

There was a light ahead. Two pools of light, in fact, both a sickly lemon colour, glowing against the tunnel walls. Winter soon perceived the source of the illumination. From a distance it looked like the severed head of a horse but it was a wartime gas mask, nailed to a joist. There was an oil lamp inside it. The light flickered through the wide, empty eyes of the mask.

To the left was a hefty wooden door, its frame carved out of the rock. Beyond it the tunnel continued, receding into solid dark.

The door was open, revealing a sunken anteroom. Inside this chamber a pair of gas lanterns hung from the ceiling, perched on hooks. There were lumpen sandbags piled against the walls, soaking up the water that swilled in the far corners. More incongruously, a set of elegant, glass-fronted display cabinets stood in the gaslit shadows, their shelves filled with objects that hid like secrets but glittered like treasure.

Winter took it all in. There was something church-like, almost sacred about this space, buried here beneath the city.

'Fräulein Fabre. Herr Winter. You are welcome here.'

The smell was unmistakable. Unterbrink sat at a rough-hewn wooden table whose legs rested at crooked angles. There was an open ledger and a fat bottle of Rémy Martin in front of him. He rose, still dressed in the decrepit suit he had worn for lunch. He scrunched his eyes against the beam of Beltz's torch. 'Please, Herr Beltz. We have no need for unnecessary light.'

Beltz switched off his torch. Two other men emerged from the half-light. Their clothes were equally as shabby as Unterbrink's and they shared his maggoty pallor. And just like him their eyes were pinched and shied from direct contact.

A sudden burst of water fell from the ceiling, spattering the stone floor.

'Your place of business, gentlemen, I take it?' There was an irresistible edge of sarcasm to Winter's voice. He sensed Karina flinch, clearly wary of him antagonising these people before the deal was done.

'No, not as such,' said Unterbrink, choosing not to acknowledge the taunt. 'More a place of contentment. Reflection. A chance to savour everything we have accumulated over the years.'

Winter gazed around the chamber, his eyes drawn to the curious contents of the cabinets. He saw a jagged shard of iron – a spear tip, perhaps – paired in a display case with a simple wooden plate. In another cabinet lay a solitary nail, rusted to the colour of blood, and in yet another was what looked like the remains of a winged sandal. There was a sword, too, its length inscribed with Latin script.

'Strange place to keep all this stuff, surely?'

Beltz interjected. 'We believe that beautiful things become truly beautiful in shadow. Why would we wish to share all this with the world above, with their poisonous museums and foul galleries? The gaze of others diminishes that which is precious, makes it commonplace, unremarkable. Other people are bacteria upon beauty.'

'That's just a little elitist.'

'We are an elite, *mein Herr*.'

'Imagine if the world had never seen a Goya,' said Unterbrink, blinking in the gloom. 'Never beheld a Bruegel. Imagine if yours were the only eyes that had ever glimpsed their perfection. How much more beautiful

they would be, no? So it is with our collection. We bury these objects to make them shine.'

'Interesting philosophy, Herr Unterbrink.'

'More than philosophy, *mein Freund*. It is our duty and our purpose. The precious things of the world must remain precious. And now, of course, we are about to make a significant addition to our collection. Fräulein Fabre, if you please?'

Karina nodded and stepped forward. She unbuckled her bag and removed the bottle, passing it to Unterbrink. This time he held it with the obvious delight of a man who would never have to hand it back.

'*Danke*,' he whispered.

The other men gathered around him, staring at the object. The glass had a jade shimmer, even in the dim light of the chamber.

'We are quite certain of the provenance?' asked Beltz.

'I trust in the Order of Leaves,' said Unterbrink, turning the bottle in his hand, half lost in wonder. 'They have always had our respect. We have been rivals for centuries, after all.'

He nodded to one of his colleagues. The silent man walked across to a cabinet and unlocked a thin drawer beneath the glass front. He came back holding two objects, one in each hand. He passed the first of them to Karina.

She took the item with obvious reverence. It was a sliver of parchment, perhaps five inches high by three inches wide. It seemed closer to cloth than paper, fraying at its edges and darkened by age to a tobacco-stain shade

of yellow. The scrap was completely blank.

'Give me your lighter,' she said to Winter.

He handed it over. Karina conjured a flame and held it beneath the piece of parchment. For a moment Winter wondered if she actually intended to set fire to the thing. And then, as heat rose from the quiver of fire, the yellowed scrap began to curl, and to change.

A series of shapes emerged from the fibres, ghostly at first and then gradually more distinct. Winter saw triangles bolted onto circles, circles fused with squares. Within these strange markings letters of the alphabet mated with geometrical symbols.

They were sigils, he realised, as if accessing a submerged memory. Runes. The cipher codes of magic.

'Dee called it the Language of Fire,' said Unterbrink, taking his eyes from the bottle to watch the symbols materialise. 'A sacred lexicon, with the power to summon a force beyond dreams. How fitting that the fire of our century finally reveals it.'

Karina absently returned the lighter to Winter, her gaze fixed upon the parchment. 'The Ingolstadt fragment,' she murmured, marvelling. 'How long has it been in your possession?'

'Since 1953,' said Beltz. 'The Prussian dealer had no idea of its worth. Poor man. It felt like theft.'

'One item closer to your goal,' said Unterbrink. 'I understand your happiness, believe me.'

'You have no idea,' said Karina, almost to herself. 'This is the final fragment.'

'My God,' breathed Unterbrink. 'You have assembled the entire grimoire?'

'Every page,' replied Karina, smiling in the gaslight.

'I see now why you would trade this for the wine of Christ.'

Karina said nothing. She remained transfixed by the symbols, taking in every scratch and curve of ink.

'Your life's work is over, Fräulein Fabre,' said Beltz, dryly. 'However will you occupy yourself now?'

'Give me the second item,' said Karina. 'We need to complete this deal.'

Unterbrink nodded his blessing once more. The silent man passed the remaining object to Karina.

It was a sturdy iron key, corroded but intact. It looked functional rather than elegant, with chunky, serrated teeth and a plain metal loop. Winter watched as Karina turned its rusted bulk in her hand. It seemed weighted with history.

Unterbrink gestured to the bottle of Rémy Martin on his desk. There were dusty brandy glasses arranged next to it. 'Please, will you not share a cognac? Alas only a miracle could allow us to share the wine...'

Winter heard a sound then. He had just caught it beneath Unterbrink's rattle of a laugh. A faint, quick sound. It had come from the tunnel, from the passage beyond the chamber. He tilted his head, cocking an ear, focusing his gaze past the door. Had there been movement back there in the dark? Perhaps it had been water spilling through the rock, or the reverberation of the U-Bahn.

'Are we all done here?' he asked.

'Please, *mein Herr*,' said Beltz. 'Let Fräulein Fabre relish this moment. She has accomplished something very special.'

Winter turned to Karina, directing his words at her alone. 'If the deal's done then we should leave. No sense staying down here longer than we need to.'

She was silent for a moment, continuing to stare at the symbols. And then she nodded, briskly. 'Let's go,' she said, placing the key and the parchment into her bag and buckling it. 'Herr Unterbrink, Herr Beltz, it has been a very rewarding transaction for all of us.'

'Such knowledge you hold now,' said Beltz, quietly. 'I must say I'm envious.'

Another noise from the tunnel. This was closer. Unmistakably the sound of movement.

'Of course,' Beltz continued, 'we might ask whether such knowledge should even be in your hands.'

Winter glimpsed a sudden shadow at the mouth of the chamber, cast from the passage beyond. A man's shadow, holding a gun. Another armed shadow approached behind it.

They had been betrayed.

Winter seized the bottle of Rémy Martin from the table. He hurled it into the tunnel. It smashed as it hit the rock, exploding in a hail of glass and dousing the passage with pure cognac. A second later he wrenched one of the gas lanterns from its hook. He flung that, too. As the lantern shattered its flame ignited the trail of alcohol. Fire

reared in the passageway, quick and vicious.

It bought them only a moment. Startled, the men in the tunnel recoiled, allowing Winter and Karina a chance to retreat into the chamber, chasing cover.

Stamping on the flames, the men took position at the entrance to the anteroom. They were the same men from the market. Stasi agents. Framed by the blaze they fired warning shots into the lair of the Reliquarists.

'No guns!' cried Beltz. 'Not in here! You promised me!'

A stray bullet struck the sacred wine bottle. The green glass burst apart. Unterbrink gave a hoarse, disbelieving scream.

Karina snatched her blade from her dress, ready to engage. As she did so Winter wrested one of the cabinets from the wall. It tipped forward, its treasures clattering; he steadied it and crouched behind, pulled out his stolen Russian revolver, took a breath and fired back. He heard the bullet whine as it ricocheted across rock, seeking a place to embed itself. This was not a smart place for a gunfight.

Karina squatted beside him, sharing cover. 'Contingency plan, Christopher?'

'Not sure. Can't you just kill everyone in the room?'

'I can't promise that I can.'

'Damn. I was banking on that.'

A bullet flew above the cabinet, clipping its corner, studding into the wall beyond. These were no longer warning shots.

Karina nodded towards the entrance. The wooden door frame was ablaze. 'That's the only exit we've got. Thank you for setting fire to it.'

Another bullet glanced against the wall, sparking on the rock. There was a fug of cordite in the air now.

'We know the tunnel extends past this chamber,' Karina continued, her words cool and unhurried. 'It has to run deep beneath the city.'

'It might be a dead end,' said Winter.

'We're in a dead end. I'd rather have a possibility, wouldn't you?'

Winter bobbed above the cabinet and blasted his gun. The Stasi agents blasted back.

'You're right. Let's move.'

They abandoned their makeshift cover. They were clear targets now.

Unterbrink and his two silent colleagues were flat against the far wall, as if attempting to merge with the rock itself. Beltz, however, was frozen in the crossfire, cringing as the bullets arced past him. Winter seized him by the collar and shoved him forward, using his twisting, protesting body as a shield. He propelled the man the length of the chamber, firing around his head as they scrambled to the exit.

Beltz jerked as a Stasi bullet thumped into his shoulder, flooding his shirt with blood. As he howled Winter threw him at the men, knocking them backwards.

Winter and Karina dodged the flames that licked the doorway. They ran headlong into the darkness, kicking

through pools of cold tunnel water, expecting to slam face-first into rock at any second. There was barely any light in this part of the underground labyrinth, not even the sickly glow of a gas lantern.

Winter reloaded, spun and fired, the shot briefly illuminating the span of the tunnel. The bullet took down one of their pursuers. Winter scowled. The shot felt lucky, not earned.

Karina tore right. 'This way!'

Another length of passageway, as dark as the last. They pelted down it, Karina's blade flashing silver.

Something else glinted in the shadows, just ahead of them. A huge steel plate, set into the black rock. The words 'BERLINER VERKEHRSBETRIEBE' and 'ACHTUNG!' were stencilled upon it. There was a handle attached to the plate. It was a hatch, some kind of utility door. And it was rattling in its hinges. Karina lifted the bar that unlocked it. It creaked with disuse. The door swung back. They tottered on the edge of a drop. There was a violent, almost blinding rush of air. A U-Bahn train roared past in a blur of heat and metal, carriage after carriage after carriage. The rails of the underground screamed beneath its thundering bulk.

The other Stasi man was almost upon them. He raised and steadied his gun. Karina pivoted, her blade severing the main artery of his wrist. The gun spun from the man's hand. He pitched onto his knees, cradling his slashed flesh. Blood pumped from his wrist.

Karina took a step towards him, her knife poised for a finishing strike.

'Leave him,' said Winter, sharply.

'Why?'

'Because you don't need to kill him, do you?'

Karina turned, her eyes contemptuous. 'Are you reproaching me, Christopher? You kill men for your job!'

'I said leave him. He's not one of Harzner's dogs to be diced up.'

'I thought you wanted me to kill everyone in the room?'

There was a sound of movement behind them, deep in the tunnel. It was the pounding of feet. There were more men in pursuit. The two Stasi agents had clearly only been an advance guard.

Winter cast a glance across the U-Bahn line. There was a ridge of rock on the other side, running above the tracks. A maintenance path, perhaps. It looked just about big enough to walk on.

'Come on,' he said. 'We'll follow the line. Find a way out through the U-Bahn.'

'You seriously expect us to cross electrified rails?'

Winter waved a hand at the tracks. There were two running rails and a third, parallel rail, higher than the others and set apart from the wooden sleepers.

'It's the third rail that closes the circuit. That's the one with the contact points. Don't step on that and you'll live.'

'There'll be another train coming any moment...'

'So we should get on with it, shouldn't we?'

Winter jumped down onto the tracks, small stones scattering beneath his shoes. There was no vibration in

the rails, no indication of an oncoming train. Good. They had time. He began to cross the line, keeping to the gravel where possible. He stepped over the bullhead rails and the welded iron anchors and the greasy corpse of a rat.

The third rail waited. It seemed to murmur with power. Winter could almost feel the slumbering voltage. He moved across it with a wide, wary step.

Karina leapt down after Winter and followed him across the tracks. Reaching the other side of the rails the pair hauled themselves onto the ridge. It was more of a ledge than a walkway, extending only a foot or so from the rock wall. Placing themselves side-on against the granite – the only way their feet could stay on the lip – they edged deeper into the tunnel, almost scratching their way by their fingertips.

Soon the gloom gave way to solid shadow. The only illumination came from the red glimmer of signal lights in the distance. It was unbearably warm.

They heard a rumbling. It rapidly gathered in pace and volume. The rails quaked and rattled, as if sending a warning through the steel.

There was a train coming, hurtling through the dark like a punch of light.

Winter and Karina became motionless. Without even breathing they stood flat against the tunnel wall, their eyes locked shut. They stayed frozen as the train passed in a hot roar, scorching metal, spraying oil, its carriages buckling and rocking, impossibly loud, impossibly close.

22

The man stirred as the canvas mouth of the tent was pushed open. The Algerian sun flooded in, the desert light illuminating the khaki womb that enclosed him. The tent's interior was bare and functional. No tables, no clocks, no boards, no charts. No ornamentation of any kind. Only the lone wooden chair, military plain and stiff as bricks against his spine.

The flap closed, returning the tent to a state of sweltering gloom. There was a scratch of shoes on a hessian mat. Someone was walking towards him.

Jürgen Scholz let his tongue play against his lips. He could still taste the whisky, burning in the cracks. He remembered how the Englishmen had doused his broken skin, purifying the very wounds they had inflicted. It had been a curious act of kindness. The stinging alcohol had run with his blood in a pale red stream, spilling onto his chest. It had made him think of communion wine and his childhood church in Tremmen. With that last thought he had slid into unconsciousness.

His hands were still bound. Scholz glanced at the

hanks of rope strapping his wrists to the arms of the chair. There was a numbness in his fingers. He flexed the muscles of his left hand and sensed a disconnect in the nerves. The finger that held his wedding ring was swollen and black and lay at an ugly angle. It didn't respond at all.

'I understand you're quite a resilient fellow,' said the man who had entered the tent.

Another Englishman. Scholz felt sure he hadn't seen this one before, though the faces of his captors were blurring now. He looked younger than the other men, his black curls worn a little looser, a wilder, more mischievous energy in his green eyes. A cream linen suit hung on his slender frame and there was a battered leather holdall slung across his shoulder, stickered with bright, colourful travel labels. Trinidad. Bali. Macau.

Scholz sensed something else about him. A coiled and tangible darkness, as if he had altogether too much shadow for one man. This one was a practitioner, that much was certain. He held magic inside him, and a lightless magic at that.

The newcomer smiled. 'Do we even have your real name yet?'

Scholz grunted, conjuring only a swill of phlegm in reply. He realised he had teeth missing.

'My name's Hart, by the way. I know we'll only be briefly acquainted but I think there's always a place for manners, whatever the arena.'

The Englishman dumped the bag on the floor and unzipped it. Scholz glimpsed a flash of something cold

and silver, piled upon neat white cotton.

'I can only apologise for the methodology of my colleagues,' Hart continued, airily. 'I'm forever embarrassed by their lack of subtlety. There's really no reason why the exchange of information should be quite so messy. Such unpleasantries are always avoidable, don't you think?'

Scholz replied through cracked teeth. 'Go to hell.'

Hart considered these words. 'All in good time, old boy.'

The Englishman approached the chair. Scholz felt a hand seize his jaw, tilting his head towards the best available light. Hart was scrutinising his wounds with the detached air of a surgeon. A finger lifted the half-shuttered lid of his left eye, breaking a crusted seal of blood.

'Yes, this is a pretty vulgar job,' Hart declared. 'But then I imagine they did try asking you nicely.'

Scholz stared into the man's clear eyes. His charm was clearly part of the interrogation process, a calculated bid to unsettle and confuse. A clever, theatrical Englishness. No doubt he would soon be offering him tea and sandwiches. At least a fist in the face had an honesty to it.

Hart gave another, tighter smile. 'I'll ask nicely too, then, just in case it saves us some bother. Where is the Tall God's Cave?'

Scholz heard those words again, the ones that his interrogators had pounded into his skull over the past two days. Once more he kept his face composed.

'I have no idea what you mean,' he muttered, tiredly.

He let his head sink against his shoulder, making a show of willing himself back into sleep.

Hart lifted his jaw again and leaned closer, only a breath away from his face. The Englishman's skin carried the scent of lavender water. There was sand in his hair, Scholz saw, and a vein like a fine blue line of ink on his brow.

'We are adepts, you and I,' said Hart.

His voice was hushed now, as though these were private words, exchanged between equals, not interrogator and victim. 'We have a certain bond. A higher loyalty. One that places us beyond nations. Beyond this conflict. We should, I think, answer only to knowledge. And so I'll ask you again, in the dear spirit of knowledge, and in the ancient and darling name of magic... where is the Tall God's Cave?'

Scholz met the man's eyes, unimpressed.

'You're chasing devils, Herr Hart. Why do you bother? You're clearly halfway to being such a damned creature yourself.'

Hart's pupils flitted from side to side. For a second Scholz imagined he saw vulnerability there, a fleeting trace of what could have been guilt or fear. He had caught that look in the eyes of other occultists, the ones who knew the price of the path they had chosen but whose commitment remained absolute, their craving for the blood-rush of magic too deep, too embedded.

The Englishman turned away. Dropping to his knees he rummaged inside the holdall.

'Here. Take a gander at this.'

He had a rolled parchment in his hand. Dispensing with a knot of ribbon he flung it at the floor of the tent. The parchment uncurled with a sigh of air. It was brittle and faded, stained with age. Scholz saw that it was a map of the world, the names of the nations inscribed in antique calligraphy.

Hart pressed a brogue to the edge of the map, keeping it from scrolling back upon itself.

'It's a little old, I know, but it's beautifully done, don't you think? So much character.'

He dipped into the bag once more. This time he retrieved a small rectangular casket, roughly the size of a book. It was an ornate object, showily so, its silver panels inlaid with intricate dragonfly swirls of blue, green and red enamel.

As Scholz looked on the English warlock fished in the left-hand pocket of his jacket. His fingers plucked a tiny silver key from the rumpled linen. It looked as though it belonged to a music box. He placed the key in the casket and turned it. The lid slid open to reveal a glimpse of scarlet lining.

Hart turned the glittering box upside down. And then he shook it, impatiently, as if trying to dislodge its contents.

'Come along, Antonia.'

Something dropped from the casket. At first Scholz thought it was an animal. A bird, perhaps, or a sizable insect. And then he saw that it was the bones of a human hand.

Hart smiled. 'Oh, don't be bashful, dear girl.'

The skeletal fist crouched upon the parchment. The bones were young and white and intact, still stitched together by ligaments and gristly with sinew. The hand had a shudder of life to it, Scholz saw. It quivered, almost shyly, on the painted coast of Asia.

'Are you familiar with bone magic, by any chance?'

Scholz made no reply. Perspiring, he kept his gaze on the bones, watching as the knuckles hunched above the contours of the old map.

'I've made quite a study of it,' Hart continued. 'Some claim it's the oldest magic on earth. I think that's very possible. Bones are potent things, after all. The symbol of our own death, buried from birth within our flesh. Just imagine those ignorant Neanderthals, watching as the bodies of their elders crumbled and peeled away. What power there was in that process. The great, long, silent levelling. It would have awed them. I mean, gosh, what's the discovery of fire compared to the discovery of death?'

The bones squatted like a cornered spider.

'And then of course there's blood magic. I've always seen it as a close relation to the craft of the bone. A little more romantic, perhaps. More passionate, you might say. Certainly a great deal messier.'

Hart had extracted a small knife from his pocket. He closed in on Scholz and tugged at the rope that bound the German's wrists, exposing raw red weals where the knot had been. Scholz struggled but his strength was gone, his muscles fatigued by the beatings.

'The beauty of it is, of course, that as parallel branches of body magic they're completely compatible.'

Hart made a swift and precise strike with the blade. It sliced an arterial vein on Scholz's right wrist, an inch above the rope. In seconds blood began to jet from the wound.

'I want you to think of your little secret. The one you're trying so hard to keep from me. Let it flow in you. Let it run in your veins.'

Scholz's blood spattered the bones. The cadaverous fingers twitched and flexed, christened by the bright red spray.

A nerve began to drum on Hart's brow. 'Go on, Antonia. Be a sweetheart. Show me where the Tall God's Cave is.'

For a moment the hand spun like a maddened compass. And then it skittered across the parchment, trailing smears of blood. The bones navigated the map as if chasing a scent, scurrying across coastlines and continents, click-clacking over oceans. Finally they settled.

Hart clapped, the knife between his palms. 'Oh, she's very good, isn't she? Such a clever girl.'

Jürgen Scholz's vision darkened. The last thing he saw was the bone hand, sat on the map. The forefinger rose, trembled and tapped twice on the coast of Africa.

23

Schweigenbach felt entombed by forest.

The tiny village lay deep in the dense green heart of Bavaria, encircled by towering firs. The shadows of the trees made it curiously sunless and there was a hush you could almost weigh. Winter estimated that they were some twenty miles from Haselbach but this place seemed to defy maps and compasses and signposts. It felt half buried, hidden from the world like a stone under moss.

It seemed to be outside of time, too. Certainly it was hard to imagine that the war had come anywhere near here. Winter could almost sense the clocks turning more slowly around him, keeping to their own private rhythm. No, he corrected himself – Schweigenbach wasn't outside time. It was heavy with it. There was history here, a sense of a much older country surviving among the cobbles and shuttered windows of the cramped, curving lanes.

They had arrived late that morning, the engine of their hired Daimler the loudest sound in the village. There were more cats than people on the streets, observing them from doorways and walls, at first curious and then

indifferent. Finally the cats had ignored the two strangers entirely, content to lick their fur in the weak noon sun or return to their secret paths between the clutter of houses.

The people were altogether warier. Eye contact was brief, a smile even more rare. They were old people, Winter noted, every last one of them. Where were the young people of Schweigenbach? Little wonder the place was so quiet, he thought. The noise and energy of Berlin seemed a world away.

They soon found a tavern in the heart of the village. It was oak-gloomy inside, decorated with dull brass. It had a charred smell, as if haunted by a past fire. Winter and Karina sat in a corner and shared a dark and treacly local beer before asking the landlord for directions to Schattenturm.

'There's nothing there,' he told them, collecting their dimpled glasses and placing them on a copper tray.

'But I imagine it's still there,' Karina countered, glancing up. 'Schattenturm itself?'

'The tower? An ugly thing. Empty now. You are historians? Researchers?'

'Just tourists,' Winter smiled, wiping a froth of beer from his lips.

'We rarely get tourists. Even more rarely in this season.'

'We heard it was beautiful in autumn. Didn't we, darling?'

Karina shot him a sharp look. 'We did. Darling.'

The landlord took a charcoal pencil from his bib and sketched directions on a paper napkin, smudging the map

with the edge of his hand as he drew. 'There's nothing there,' he stressed again, handing the napkin to Winter. Karina gave the man a handful of Deutsche marks for his trouble and he pocketed them with a grudging but appreciative smile.

Winter excused himself from the table and went in search of the toilets. He found the gents at the rear of the tavern, at the end of a thin corridor lined with a series of commemorative plates. They were garish tourist kitsch, each plate depicting an eighteenth-century hunting scene in bright, sickly oils. There were slain boars and snarling dogs and red-cheeked men with muskets in their hands. Even the blood looked as cheery as an oompah band.

The toilet itself was poky. A crookedly aligned wooden door opened to a windowless space with a modern, chemical smell, at odds with the tavern's attempt at authentic Bavarian charm. Winter heard water gurgle in the brass pipes that crept from the cisterns to the ceiling. There was a small, boxy radio fixed upon the wall, and a dull, folky song half crooned, half crackled from its grille.

Winter used the urinal. As he did so the light in the room dimmed, faintly. He glanced up at the lone light bulb that hung from a frayed cord attached to the ceiling. There was an odd darkness in the glass, almost as if a shadow was growing inside it. The sound of the radio also faded, the song decaying into splutters and hisses. The signal was dying. Winter was convinced he could hear a competing signal, growing stronger. A man's

261

voice, guttural and rasping. It made sounds that might have been words. Moments later the song returned, still faint and interrupted by pops and clicks of interference.

Winter soaped his hands. He let the water pour from the old taps until it was nearly scalding. Curiously, he began to feel colder, even as the steam rose in the sink, clouding the edges of the mirror. He knew his circulation was terrible but this was something different. The temperature in the room had changed, dropped by degrees.

A chill fell like a breath on the nape of his neck. His flesh prickled, almost warningly. He had spent so much time in the field that sometimes he could sense somebody else's presence by bodily intuition. But no, he was alone in the room. The cubicle door was open. And yet his senses were cautioning him.

He took stock of himself in the mirror. It was a stark light and an unflattering angle and he winced at how drained he looked, how pummelled by the madness of the past few weeks. He felt sure there were new lines on his face.

The light went. The room turned black. The mirror gleamed in the sudden shock of darkness, the glass silver-bright. Winter stared into it and saw a skull where his face should have been. It was as if his flesh had been ripped away, exposing the bone beneath. He saw his eyes reflected as sockets, two hollows that gazed back, sightless as death.

The song was gone. The man's voice was back, louder and even more animalistic than before. The sounds that

tore from his throat broke into static as they roared through the radio's grille. For a second Winter sensed another figure in the mirror, a shape struggling to wrestle itself out of the glass. A bare-chested man, wounded and smeared in blood...

And then the light bulb flared into life again. The song returned to the radio, the signal clean and clear. Water swilled in the pipes. Winter found himself clutching the sink, his fingers tight around its porcelain edges. His breathing was urgent.

The door to the toilet opened. A man came in. Portly, fifties, dressed in a hacking jacket. Hint of ex-Luftwaffe. Winter had seen him at the bar with his wife. The two men nodded to each other. *Guten Tag.*

Winter dried his hands with a paper towel. He resolved to say nothing of this to Karina.

They left the tavern and followed the route that led to the forest, climbing up and out of the village on a narrow, twisting trail. The streets of Schweigenbach soon faded behind them. They didn't attempt conversation and the silence thickened as they walked. Even the sounds of nature seemed muted in this place. There were none of the usual scratches and cries of the countryside, no sense of life moving among the leaves and hedges.

Winter glanced up, his gaze caught by a sudden flap of wings. He saw ravens circling high in a pale, pebble-coloured sky. The birds, too, kept their distance here. He

watched as they spiralled above the brooding woodland and the stillness of the meadows beyond. In the distance he could see the snow-topped peak of the Great Arber, rising above the treeline.

A stone-strewn path took them to a bridge over a brook. As they approached the crossing Winter stopped, astonished by what he saw.

The bridge was wreathed in ladybirds. They dotted every available inch of wood, as bright as blood. Some of them crawled by themselves, others pulsed together in clumps, like a single organism. Karina saw them too but she continued walking. As she crossed the bridge the insects shifted in a haze of tiny wings, scattering around her.

Winter followed her across, batting away the mist of ladybirds. The old wood of the bridge creaked beneath his shoes. He looked over the side. The water below was almost motionless. Thickets of weed sprouted among mustard-coloured rocks.

Beyond the bridge lay a path that led deeper into the forest. The trees were like a shroud now, the vast branches of the evergreens obscuring the sky, greying the light. Their huge, serpentine roots erupted out of the soil. The air had the smell of autumn, of things withering, turning dry.

The path narrowed as it took them under the trees. They found themselves pushing through clusters of brambles that swarmed at either side. The ragged plants coiled like snares, studded with thorns. Tattered remains of cobwebs drifted from their branches.

Winter realised that the hush of the forest was now absolute. There had been clouds of flies before but their background drone only truly registered now that it was gone. He listened to his own breath. It was impossibly loud. The silence felt like another presence in the woodland, close as a person.

'God, it's here,' said Karina.

The tower was taller than the trees. It rose above them, old and soot-dark and nearly windowless. Great green vines encircled the base, wrapping themselves around the structure as if trying to wrest it back to earth. A lone turret speared the sky. It all belonged in a picture book, thought Winter. Some childhood tale of witches and giants.

'Schattenturm,' murmured Karina, almost to herself.

He stole a glance at her, watching as her eyes widened and darted. She was gazing at the tower with something close to awe. No, not awe. She was altogether too cool for that. It was a kind of satisfaction. This was clearly a moment she had anticipated for a long time. He was almost tempted to smile on her behalf.

They stepped into the tower's shadow, the October air becoming marginally colder around them. There was a formidable wooden door set into the stonework, medieval in its plain, functional design. A heavy brass lock was bolted onto it, flaking with rust. Karina dipped inside her bag and retrieved the equally rusted key, the one the Reliquarists had traded with her. It matched the look of the lock precisely. They belonged together.

She thrust the key into the keyhole, sliding its teeth

into the waiting aperture. There was a scrape and a rattle of metal. She was about to twist the key when she paused. She placed a hand against the brass plate. And then she pushed, gingerly at first and then more purposefully. The door opened with a grinding of old hinges. It was unlocked.

Winter frowned. 'What the hell did we need a key for?'

Karina peered into the shadowed doorway. 'Clearly it wasn't the key we needed, Christopher. Just the name on the key.'

'I thought this was meant to be a prison tower.'

'Not for some time, it seems.'

They entered, pushing the old door as wide as its age would allow. The light inside was sepulchral, barely illuminating the leaden dark of the tower's interior. Winter felt his senses sharpen in the cool gloom.

'Let's take this carefully,' he said.

'Of course.'

Nature had crept into this place. It had found the cracks and the gaps. Moss grew between the flagstones and pale, sun-starved weeds clung to the walls. There was a distinct smell of mushrooms too, rich and woody. Winter squinted into the dark and saw oily fists of fungi in the far corners.

They moved forward, pushing past a waist-high metal grille that had clearly been some kind of security gate. There was a wooden desk behind it, its surface stained with ink and pitted with holes. Beyond that was

the start of a staircase, narrow and spindling.

'Look at this,' said Karina, her voice a whisper for all that they were alone.

She pointed at the stairwell wall. A finger of light fell onto it from a high window, revealing markings gouged into the stonework. There was a whole series of them. The symbols were etched deep, the stone crumbling in their grooves. Somebody had clearly carved them out of the wall with remarkable persistence.

Winter recognised the shapes from the parchment the Reliquarists had given Karina. They were the same strange geometric assemblies of lines and numbers.

'These are runic,' he said, surprising himself with his own certainty.

'My God,' said Karina. 'You've actually been paying attention.'

Winter followed her up the stairs. 'I'm a fast learner. And I know code when I see it.'

At first the symbols kept a distance from each other. They were regularly spaced, ten or twelve inches apart, twenty at most. But as Winter and Karina climbed the steps the shapes began to multiply and cluster. By the fourth turn of the tower's stairs they had become more frenzied, etched with less care but greater insistence, scratched rather than chiselled into the stone. It was as if they were breeding, thought Winter.

There was a room at the top of the staircase. Once it must have been the highest cell in the building, as tall as the tower itself, but its hefty, brass-trimmed wooden

267

door had been left wide open. Now it was just a bare, echoing space, infested with runes. The symbols covered every inch of the room, the walls and the ceiling, salt-white against the dark stone.

A solitary window allowed a slice of light. The light struck a bundle in the corner of the room. The bundle was the body of a man.

Winter approached the figure, cautiously. It was wrapped in an odd muddle of clothes. The coat was a filthy velvet, cut in a formal, foppish style that reminded him of powder-faced men in old paintings. The shirt was equally grimy but its loose wing collar and tattered tie seemed closer to this century. The trousers looked like Elizabethan breeches, buckled below the knee and tucked into torn white stockings, while the feet were clad in a sturdy pair of soldier's trench boots, presumably from the Great War. It was like a jumble sale across the ages.

The body was that of an old man. A very old man, judging by the way the skin had shrivelled like a dying apple. The parched flesh clung to the contours of the bones, its surface mottled with moles. The hair was ash-coloured and bedraggled, spilling onto the man's chest until it was indistinguishable from his beard.

Something else caught Winter's eye. The body was surrounded by what looked like slivers of wax. The thin, translucent strips lay in little mounds on the floor of the cell. Winter found himself reminded of discarded snakeskin.

And then he noticed something else. The body was breathing. As Winter watched, the man's sunken chest

rose and fell beneath his shirt, the movement almost imperceptible in the gloom.

He glanced at Karina. The blade was already in her hand.

'He's alive,' said Winter.

'Are you pig-witted, boy?'

The voice stirred in the man's throat. It sounded dry and ragged. The vocal cords had clearly been neglected for some time.

'Am I what?' asked Winter, incredulous that the man had spoken.

'Pig-witted,' repeated the man, the words rumbling out of him as if he was shaking off sleep. 'Ignorant as a shit-nut.'

His eyes snapped open. They were a fierce blue, incongruously bright in the old face. The man fixed his pupils on Winter.

'Observant fellow, aren't you, boy? Quite the gannet eye. Of course I'm bloody well alive.'

He switched his attention to Karina, noting the glint of her blade. He smiled, summoning a natural charm for all that he was exposing a mouthful of ruined teeth.

'And you, girl? Do you mean to kill me? I wish you luck with that. I truly do. But I fear it'll be a waste of your day. Still, I won't stop you. The attempt may be diverting.'

He began to sing, softly to himself, his cracked old voice struggling to keep the melody.

'Death is my sweetheart, who never holds me true… My cruel little mistress, my cold wife too…'

The song ended in a private chuckle. The man fixed his eyes on Winter once again. There was an urgency to his words now.

'I'll tell you one thing, sir. Don't fear your death. Embrace it. We spend our years in dread of it but by Christ we should crave it. A life without an ending is no life for any of God's works.'

Karina stepped forward, sheathing her blade.

'Who are you?' she asked.

24

The question hung like the dust suspended in the half-light.

For a moment the man in the cell seemed affronted, as if Karina had insulted him by asking who he was. Something cold and proud flared in his eyes. Then his face puckered into a smile, one that deepened his creases, leaving his skin looking like pale, weather-worn leather.

'It appears my legend has receded. Very well.'

He began to gather himself, elderly bones shifting beneath his mismatched clothes. He raised his body with a struggle and rested it against the wall, framed by the frenzy of runes. And then he tossed a stray lock of hair from his face and let his jaw jut forward. It was a haughty, almost theatrical gesture. Winter momentarily glimpsed a much younger man, one who seemed utterly certain of himself and his place in the world.

'There is much that I am,' the man began, his voice now surprisingly resonant. 'Much that I have been. Thief. Cripple. Occultist. Swindler. A stealer of men's wives and a forger of coins.'

He put a hand to the side of his head, sweeping his hair back to expose a malformed ear. It looked like it had been clipped, sliced with a knife. An old wound, clearly, and it had healed badly. The edge of the ear was now a scarred curl of flesh, darker than the skin surrounding it.

'They lopped me in St Albans. A public shaming. The mark of a forger. In years gone by people knew what that mark meant. Now I seem to have outlasted its meaning. A tiny but sweet victory, don't you think, girl?'

Again there was a decrepit grin. Karina regarded him coolly.

'I was once made a baron of Bavaria,' the old man continued, 'for all that England had branded me a criminal. Some say I was a fallen priest, too, and I may have been but Christ, it's so long ago, and one forgets. I was considered a warlock but I called myself an alchemist. Some say I trafficked with devils. Others believed I consorted with angels. Sometimes even I didn't know the difference. Heaven and Hell… they speak the same language, you know.'

'She asked you who you were,' said Winter, tersely. 'Straight answer. No more bullshit.'

The man gave an imperious flash of his eyes. 'A blunt and tiresome fellow, aren't you, boy? But then I forget what it's like to know urgency. So I shall tell you my name – or one name, at least, for I have a choice of many, depending on my mischief. I am Sir Edward Kelly. You may know me as a scryer and a colleague of Dr John Dee. A friend, in fact, for all that I took his wife.'

Winter saw Karina react, almost imperceptibly, to the

272

sound of the name. He turned back to the old man. He had never heard of an Edward Kelly but he had certainly heard of Dr John Dee. Malcolm had mentioned him that day in Broadway Buildings as they had stood beneath the portrait of Sir Francis Walsingham, Queen Elizabeth's spymaster. Dee had been some kind of court astrologer and a founding figure of Britain's intelligence network. But that was centuries in the past.

'That's impossible,' said Winter. 'Dee lived four hundred years ago.'

The man gave a tiny, impatient sigh. 'Impossible is a word an alchemist quickly unlearns. It's a manacle. My God. Only four hundred years. I thought it was longer…'

Winter glanced at Karina. 'Are you going to tell me you believe him?'

Karina crouched down, keeping her gaze level with the old man's eyes. She spoke calmly. 'What are you doing here, Sir Edward?'

'I knew it,' said Winter to himself. 'Of course you believe this shit.'

'Why am I here?' the old man echoed, his eyes searching Karina's. 'Didn't you come looking for me, girl?'

Karina shook her head. 'I had no idea I'd find you. I only knew the tower was here. They locked you up? In Schattenturm?'

'Schattenturm…'

Kelly savoured the Germanic syllables as he repeated them. 'Of course. I'd forgotten its name. Yes, I was imprisoned after my trial in Prague. A rival accused me

273

of poisoning the emperor. As if an alchemist would ever use anything as commonplace as poison.'

His eyes flickered, as if he was unlocking deep memories, undisturbed for years. 'Or was it after my arrest in Olomouc? I seem to recall I was once accused of theft from the royal library. A book of scholarly demonology. Now Dee had a magnificent library. Magnificent. The accumulated lore of centuries. Oh, he had such books at Mortlake. Such beautiful books.'

'Why are you still here?' asked Karina. 'It's not a prison anymore. You're free to leave.'

'I did leave,' said Kelly, keeping his eyes on her until Winter sensed he was being pointedly ignored. 'I left years ago. Before the wars, whatever wars they were. But I came back. Because the world eventually grinds you down with its sunrises and its sunsets. After a while you realise there's so little point to them. Weary, perfunctory things. Sometimes I think they're just for show.'

'You're telling us you can't die?' said Winter.

'No. If you listen, boy, I'm telling you I cannot live. Not easily.'

'You're saying you're immortal?'

Kelly clapped his hands, slowly and sarcastically. The contemptuous sound filled the bare cell, echoing between the stone walls.

'Every alchemist's dream. An elixir to outfox the reaper. Not the sweetest dream, I discovered.'

Winter moved his eyes over the pathetic figure. 'So I see.'

'You're an Englishman,' said Kelly, with a hint of confrontation in his voice. 'What line of work?'

'I'm British Intelligence.'

The old man gave a hiss of appreciation through his broken teeth. 'Oh, are you indeed? Dee was an intelligencer too. One of the first, with Walsingham. You're one of his children, you know. Still playing in the shadows for the queen. Or is there a king on the throne of England now?'

'It's a queen,' said Winter. 'Queen Elizabeth.'

Kelly absorbed this latest piece of information. There was a wry glimmer in his eyes. '*Semper eadem.* Ever the same. She had that on her coat of arms. How right the old virgin was.'

Karina leaned closer. 'How did you meet John Dee?'

Kelly stared at her. He seemed transfixed by her fine scar. He reached for it with a bony finger and she allowed him to trace its pale arc. He moved across her skin, slowly, like a fascinated child. And then he put his finger to his cracked lips and kissed it. He began to speak.

'I first came to the great house in Mortlake in March of 1582. Dee told me he had watched the sky that day. He had seen it turn to the colour of blood. No doubt some would account for that with science but science was young and magic was old and we listened to magic. It was an age of signs, after all. There had been talk of a new star in the heavens.'

Kelly began to absently scratch the back of his hand. As he spoke, the scratching intensified.

'I knew Dee by reputation. The queen's conjuror, we called him. The finest mind in England. Walsingham made use of him, of course. He outfoxed the Catholics with his clever little codes. Dee could hide words within words, conceal symbols within symbols, meaning within meaning. It was a language of shadows. But he wanted more. He wanted a language of fire.'

Kelly dug a nail into his skin. There was a weak trickle of blood. He ignored it and continued talking.

'That was Dee's dream. He imagined he might conjure obedient spirits from the flames. And they would be at his call, these creatures, flying in fire across the world to carry his secret words. Over peaks, over lakes, behind the very backs of the Spanish dogs as they plotted to overthrow our queen and restore the Roman Catholic faith. It was to be a language of fire and sky, in the service of England.'

Kelly tore away a sliver of skin. Winter stared at the hand. Somehow he imagined that the flesh beneath, newly exposed, would be supple and young, renewed like a snake's epidermis. But it was every bit as old as the rest of the man. He watched as Kelly tossed the waxy fragment to the floor, adding to the pile of discarded skin. Winter wondered if this was what immortality meant. It wasn't eternal youth at all. Just endless old age. No wonder the poor bastard craved death.

'But Dee was no scryer,' Kelly continued, eyes bright and alert in his ancient face. 'He was blind to the visions in the black glass. That was my gift, you see. He required

my talents. And so he took me into his home at Mortlake and we were partners in this great work.'

'The black glass?' pressed Karina.

'The scrying glass!' spat Kelly, with sudden impatience. 'The stone in the frame! The obsidian window, girl!'

He put his hand to the stone floor and began to grind his palm against it, scouring away the centuries of accumulated dust and grime. He swept his hand in an urgent, circular motion, clearing a plate-shaped space in the dirt. And then he tapped his nails on the dark stone, insistent that they grasped the meaning of his words.

'I looked into Dee's black glass and I saw angels. They weren't spirits. They were angels. They came out of the white fire that grew in the glass, out of the flames that gathered like clouds. They came to greet me, girl, and I was frightened at first. They're terrifyingly beautiful. As beautiful as lightning in summer darkness. You imagine you might lose your eyes just to gaze upon them. And my eyes wept blood.'

'Angels...' whispered Karina. 'My God. I always believed.'

Kelly's voice grew quieter, more guarded. 'I saw them,' he declared. 'I saw the archangel Uriel, the one who had warned Noah of the flood. There was Michael, of course. And Raphael. And Madimi, the child, with the face of gold and the laughter that sounded like song. She was always my favourite, Madimi. I imagined she was God's favourite too. I would have killed for her.'

He fell silent, his eyes lost in memory.

277

'What did the angels show you?' asked Karina, softly.

Kelly's eyes fluttered, returning to the moment. 'A new language. The oldest language, as old as Heaven. Never spoken by human tongue, never placed on a page by man's hand. They taught me it, the angels, and I would speak what I had learned, even as my eyes ran with blood. And Dee would write it down, every detail, every letter, every word. He said it was a celestial alphabet. He called it Enochian. The *Claves Angelicae*. The angelic keys. He knew that they would unlock the universe for him. For England. We'd show the Spanish brutes. God was on our side.'

Winter gestured to the symbols carved on the cell walls. 'These are the same runes, right? The ones they showed you? The same alphabet? This Enochian stuff?'

Kelly shook his head. There was a crack of despair in his voice. 'No, boy. Not the same. I cannot remember what they taught me. I try to recall it, and some days I think I'm close, but the more I carve on the walls the more maddened I become. There is an enchantment upon me. An enchantment of silence. It lies upon this land but it's mine. Even my mind has been silenced.'

'Who did this to you?' asked Karina.

'Dee,' replied Kelly, calmly and resentfully. 'Dee did this to me.'

Karina nodded. And then she unbuckled her bag. 'There's something I need to show you.'

She delved inside, retrieving a small book. It was as slim as a hymn book but it had the anonymous look of

a private journal. There were no words on its bruised leather cover, which folded shut like a wallet, two flaps joined by a pair of scuffed metal studs. The edges of the pages inside were ragged and uneven.

'Give me your lighter,' she said to Winter.

He fished it from his pocket and passed it to her. She struck a pale yellow flame, marginally brightening the gloom.

Karina handed the book to Kelly. 'Take a look, Sir Edward.'

Kelly took it, almost warily. He balanced the book on his palm, let his fingers brush the binding. And then he popped the studs and carefully unfolded the cover flaps.

Winter watched as the pages turned, lit by the lighter's flame. They seemed to belong to a dozen different books – some were plain manuscript, yellowed with age, some were smooth slices of vellum, others were brittle pieces of parchment, almost like rice paper. They varied in size and shape, too. Some pages were little more than fragments, clearly orphaned remnants of other journals. Some were charred by fire, others warped by exposure to water. A couple were bandaged with tape. All of them were bound together now. The leaves of this book had clearly been assembled from many places, many sources, over many years.

A thought struck him. Of course. The order of leaves…

Each page held a symbol or a series of symbols. They looked like the runes on the walls: lines, letters and

numbers, arcane splices of language and mathematics, just like the one Winter had seen on that scrap of paper in the Berlin tunnel. They were drawn in ink, charcoal, pencil. One seemed to have been set down in blood, faded to a dull burgundy stain. Kelly flicked through the mismatched pages at increasing speed, the symbols blurring as he did so.

Finally he closed the book. He regarded its cover for a moment, as though studying the imperfections in the leather. And then he looked up, a mix of bewilderment and disgust in his eyes.

'Why in Christ's name have you done this?'

It clearly wasn't the reaction Karina was expecting. In fact she seemed taken aback. Her face was usually so cool, so impassive, that the slightest tremor in her composure betrayed her.

'I've gathered it all,' she told him. 'Every last page.'

Winter could hear a proud, wounded tone in her voice. It reminded him of a well-intentioned child confronting an inexplicably furious parent.

'I know what you've done, girl. I want to know why.'

She met his eyes. 'I am of the Order of Leaves. This has been my life.'

Kelly seethed. 'You've given your life to this? To this idiocy?'

Karina nodded. 'It's been my duty. All that I've known.'

Kelly seized her by the wrist. His hand encircled it with surprising speed and strength, closing tight around

the bone. Winter never imagined anyone could do that to her and still be breathing a second later.

'Listen to me, girl,' the old man hissed, his voice grave. 'In the end we knew them for what they were. Murifri, the greatest of angels, came to me and said, "Hell itself is weary of Earth. The Son of Darkness cometh now to challenge his right, and seeing all prepared and provided, desires to establish himself a kingdom." Those words will burn in me forever!'

The light from the window faded, lost to cloud. Kelly's face paled in the shadows of the cell. For a moment he looked almost like a ghost, haunting a different century.

'Soon the visions in the glass terrified us,' he continued. 'We knew them then, Dee and I. These angels we had summoned were fallen. They named themselves the Ascendance but they were devils. Their fire was unholy. They sought to claim our world, rule it with flame. All that was done was lies!'

He stared into Karina's eyes, his gaze accusing. 'What you have gathered is a work of darkness! Damn you, girl, Dee wanted it lost!'

She shook her head, calmly. Now there was no trace of her startled reaction to Kelly's disapproval. The muscles of her face had buried it completely.

'No. He didn't. He told you he'd destroyed the grimoire but he hadn't. He couldn't bring himself to do it. It was knowledge. Dee believed that all knowledge was sacred. You know that, Sir Edward.'

'Don't presume to speak to me of Dee, you insolent

child!' spat Kelly. 'There was nothing sacred in this matter! He burnt every volume! In Prague! I witnessed it!'

'No,' said Karina. 'You only saw the originals burning. Dee copied everything. Every word he'd transcribed. Every rune. He had followers. Acolytes. Other alchemists. He shared it among them, across Europe, across the world. He concealed it over five continents. Nobody knew who else possessed the pages but his knowledge survived. It was preserved.'

Kelly's eyelids quivered. He continued to clasp Karina's wrist. 'It was destroyed. Dee assured me it was done.'

'We are the Order of Leaves,' said Karina. 'It is our duty to defend the Language of Fire.'

Winter had the impression she was reciting a vow, as if these were words she had known since childhood.

Kelly released his grip on her wrist. He threw the book to the floor. It landed with a slap of leather on stone. Dust rose around it like smoke.

'Dee's final folly,' he breathed, exhausted by the conversation. 'No wonder he ended his days in poverty, telling fortunes to idiots.'

Karina retrieved the grimoire. She held it up to Kelly's face. It was a gesture that should have been provocative. She made it seem conciliatory.

'You should know I'm going to destroy this.'

Kelly looked between the book and Karina. 'That's not your *duty*,' he retorted, twisting the last word into a jibe.

'I know it's not my duty. But it's my decision.'

'Why?'

'Because I'm the last of the Order,' said Karina, emphatically. 'This would survive me. And the world has too many people who want it. It needs to be destroyed. I just had to know for sure what I've given my life to. Thank you, Sir Edward.'

Winter heard a sound then. It came from beyond the tower, a faint, distant droning, almost like a hum of wasps. The forest was so abnormally quiet that the noise had registered immediately. Winter crossed the cell to the solitary window and peered out over the treeline.

He could see nothing at first. The sky was empty, a colourless expanse of cloud. But the sound was growing closer, louder. Now it had a rhythmic, mechanical quality to it.

It was the sound of rotor blades.

25

A helicopter was approaching, cutting through the sky from the east, its blades a grey haze.

Winter immediately recognised the squat, snub-nosed design and elongated tail. There was no telltale red star stamped on its fuselage but it was unmistakably Soviet military. A Mil Mi-4 – known to NATO as the Hound. An ugly but nimble assault and transport craft. And this one was armed – Winter saw the brace of gun pods fixed beneath the nacelles – making its incursion into Western airspace all the more audacious.

'Stay down!' he yelled.

The guns flashed, the twin barrels releasing a stammer of bullets. The volley studded the tower's exterior, ripping into the stonework. Tiny chips of granite flew from the window's frame, spitting into the room like hail.

Karina shook away the shower of debris. She had instinctively fallen to shield Kelly. 'What the hell's going on?'

Winter was flat against the wall, gun in hand. He tore a quick, cautious glance outside. The helicopter hung

like a giant grey dragonfly, droning as it hovered. The whirl of its blades made a downdraught powerful enough to touch his face. Winter squinted into the warm rush of air. The craft's canopy window was obscured by reflected sky but he could just glimpse the helmeted figures inside.

'Russian army. Acquaintances of yours, I imagine.'

'Damn them. How did they find us?'

'Christ knows. But they're here.'

The chopper waited, its gun pods idle for the moment. And then it tilted, banking to the left, nudging even closer to Schattenturm. Its incessant blades were loud as hammers now. This was a targeting approach.

'Down!' cried Winter, hurling himself to the floor.

There was a fresh barrage of gunfire. This time the bullets violated the room, shrieking through the aperture and striking the far walls with a flare of sparks, some stabbing into the carved runes. Others fell into the corners with a tinkling of metal. The sound was strangely musical.

Winter lay there with his face in the dust, his gun still tight in his hand. The bullets had changed the room. This empty cell felt like a trap now, every inch of it potentially tripwired.

He concentrated on the rumble of the rotor blades, using its volume to judge the craft's proximity. The drone had diminished. In seconds the sound was significantly quieter, receding to the right. Moments later it was fainter still, the murmur of blades moving behind the opposite wall. The chopper was manoeuvring, circling the tower, no doubt preparing for another attack.

Winter eyed the gun in his hand. It looked redundant now, almost ludicrous. He knew he was utterly outmatched in firepower but his mind still dialled through the tactical possibilities, each more improbable than the last: a single, ridiculously lucky shot into the cockpit, straight into the pilot's skull; an equally blessed bullet into the fuel tank, igniting a fireball that would, in theory, put the chopper into a death-spin. Perhaps a crippling round into the rotors themselves?

No. He might as well throw the bloody gun. See what good a lump of metal did against a fully armed Soviet military assault helicopter. He glanced across at Karina, who was still shielding Kelly with her torso. She had her blade in her hand. The thin, sharp reed glimmered in the cell's half-light. They exchanged a look that told him they were sharing the same thought. Yes, they could race down the stairs and run into the forest. But they would be picked off in seconds.

Winter raised himself from the floor and, absently brushing dust from his suit, positioned himself directly in front of the window. He knew he had just become a target – and a clear one at that. Every instinct he had rebelled at the thought. The sensation was queasy, almost vertiginous, as if his body was firing warning signals through his entire nervous system. But he stood there, stock-still.

He embraced his gun with both hands, locking his fingers into a cradle, keeping the weapon steady. He aimed it ahead of him, into the sky, and waited for the chopper's return.

He wondered if this was a death wish.

The hum of blades intensified. The sound was building from the left, implying that the helicopter had almost completed its arc around the tower. And yes, there it was, suddenly shining gunmetal-grey against the anaemic sky of Schweigenbach.

Winter watched it approach, saw it tilt once more, the nose dipping, the guns levelling. It moved with a strange, impressive grace, an insectile predator, perfectly calibrated to kill. He could see that the craft packed other armaments beside its guns. There were four air-to-surface rockets strapped to the fuselage, bristling with lethal possibility. One of them would kill them instantly, he knew. All four would doubtless take down the tower, reducing it to so much forest rubble.

Winter matched his gun against the craft. He imagined the pilot was smiling. *Sod him*, he thought, and smiled himself.

The helicopter simply hovered there, marking time. Its blades clipped the air, suspending it above the trees, the branches quivering in the downdraught. It seemed in no rush to fire. As if sensing some unspoken stalemate, Winter hesitated around his own trigger.

'Throw your weapons to the floor.'

There was a new voice in the room, cold and resonant. Winter knew it at once.

'Do it now.'

Winter let his gun drop from his fingers. It hit the ground with a jolt of metal. Outside, the blades of the

helicopter continued to thrum.

Winter turned from the window, his hands raised in a reflex gesture of surrender. Malykh was framed in the cell's doorway, draped in the dark folds of his leather trenchcoat. There was a pistol in his hand, aimed squarely and unequivocally at Winter's head. Two troopers flanked him, dressed in the unmarked fatigues Winter had come to associate with this unit. They gripped Garanin machine guns, potentially targeting everyone in the room.

Winter understood. The helicopter had been a distraction, a ruse that had enabled Malykh and his troops to enter the tower unseen and unheard. Now they controlled Schattenturm's sole exit. It was textbook infiltration technique.

Damn. He should have been sharper.

Malykh stepped into the room, his boots ringing on the bare stone. He nodded to Karina, the gesture curt and perfunctory. The gun remained on Winter.

'You too, Lazarova. Drop the blade.'

Karina paused, visibly reluctant, considering a clearly limited set of options. Then she opened her hand and let the blade tumble from her palm. It struck the ground with a spindly clatter. Winter glanced across at her. There was something furious and newly vulnerable behind her eyes. He sensed that she had just torn off a part of herself.

The blade rolled across the rutted floor, stopping just short of Malykh's boots. The Soviet officer reached down to retrieve it, taking care to keep his gun locked on Winter. He turned the slender, porcelain-handled

weapon in his hand, watching as it glinted among the shadows, catching the fractional light in the room. Its hilt was decorated with carved leaves.

'This blade of yours always intrigued me,' he began, conversationally. 'It is unique. Clearly not standard military issue. I chose never to ask how you came to own it. I wanted you to confide in me. I waited for that.'

Malykh traced a gloved finger along the silvered edge, as if daring it to cut him.

'Such a profoundly elegant thing it is. So fine. So fierce. So much like you.'

His forefinger found the tip of the blade and rested there. The crowning spike pushed against the soft leather of his glove, indenting it, almost piercing it.

'Graceful. Remarkable.'

Malykh folded his fist around the blade. His mouth, too, tightened, forming a determined ridge. The leather began to pucker, creasing as his fingers exerted pressure. He grunted.

'And yet, in the end, only a weapon.'

He exhaled, sharply, his mouth twisting at the edges, determined to contain a reaction.

'And any weapon can be bested. Broken.'

Malykh opened his fist. The blade was balanced on his palm. The razored edge had slit the glove, splitting the leather across the span of his hand. There was blood on the knife, bright and oily. It dripped from the Russian's fingers.

'You simply need strength. And spirit. Ideology, you might say. Always the superior weapon.'

Once again he crushed his fist into a tight ball. This time Karina's blade buckled, contorting like a length of wire. Malykh gave a final, triumphant grunt and tossed the ruined weapon to the floor.

'We shared ideology once, you and I. Or so I imagined. Did you always intend to betray the motherland?'

'Something you should realise,' replied Karina, her words cool and measured. 'I've never known a motherland.'

Dee's book was in her left hand. Winter's silver lighter was in her right. She struck a flame and brought the two objects together.

Malykh observed her, implacably calm even as the soldiers either side of him raised their guns, ready to respond. 'You could never allow yourself to do that. We sought that book for so long, Karina. I've seen you kill for it. You could not let it burn.'

Karina shook the book by its covers, exposing the pages within. The lighter glowed a hot yellow against the tattered wad of paper. She moved it closer, close enough for the thin dance of fire to tease a corner of parchment.

'So kill me before I do it. Or could you never allow yourself to?'

Malykh swung his semi-automatic, training it upon her chest. He fixed it there for a moment. And then he shifted target again, returning his aim to Winter. There was a crisp click as the pistol cocked, its hammer now primed for a shot.

'I will kill your English friend.'

'So do it.'

Winter felt the gun upon him. There was a prickling dryness in his mouth. He heard the throb of the helicopter's blades merging with the beat of the pulse in his temples. He glimpsed a white light at the very periphery of his vision. The edges of his world were becoming milky, gauzy. It was like a creeping blankness, claiming his sight. He had experienced this sensation before. He had faced death then, too.

Winter fought the phenomenon with a rapid succession of blinks. The room snapped back into focus.

'You have no desire for him to live?' asked Malykh.

'Not my concern. Do what you wish.'

The parchment began to smoulder.

'Your focus is admirable,' stated Malykh. 'You are an exceptional soldier.'

Winter locked his gaze with Karina's, searching for a private connection. He found nothing in her fixed, defiant stare. In that moment he had no doubt that she would allow him to die. Perhaps that was how men like him should go, said the small, close voice he always heard at times like this. A dispassionate act of execution. An assassin's death. There was a neat symmetry to it, after all.

He nodded to her. *Do it. Burn the bloody thing. Cast it back to Hell.*

Her face was set. Only the fractional shift of her pupils told him she was making a decision.

'I'm sorry, Christopher.'

Winter girded himself, resolved to the bullet. *Let it be fast, at least.*

Karina flung the book to the floor. It landed at Malykh's feet with a soft smack of leather on stone. The Russian regarded it for a moment, a quiver of satisfaction around his mouth. And then he picked it up, pressing his bloodied glove to the smouldering edge. There was a final, desultory wisp of smoke. It rose into the air and was gone.

'So you do have loyalty. I only wonder if it's to the book... or the Englishman?'

The same question had just occurred to Winter.

Malykh thumbed through the pages, the runes passing before his eyes in a flicker of ink. Karina watched him and said nothing.

'Fascinating,' he declared, his voice detached. He closed the grimoire and placed it in the pocket of his trenchcoat. 'It was worth the years of pursuit, then. Though I imagine you never doubted that.'

Again she met him with silence.

Malykh closed the space between them. He took Karina's jaw with his right hand, tilting it towards him, his glove leaving a smudge of blood on her chin. His other hand slid into her hair. And then he pulled her head close and took a terse, possessive kiss. Winter saw him shut his eyes as he did so.

Malykh let their lips part. When he opened his eyes again Karina was looking back at him with undisguised contempt. He paused for a moment, observing her. 'Everything was a deceit, then.'

Karina nodded.

There was a brief but telling flutter of muscle, just beneath Malykh's clouded eye.

'At least I took my pleasure from your body,' he said. Winter felt an absurd flash of jealousy at the thought.

Karina gave a brittle smile. 'Yes. If only I could say the same.'

Once again a nerve pulsed beneath Malykh's eye.

'How did you know we were here?' Karina asked him.

'The Stasi. They shared their recently acquired intelligence on this tower's location. Your friends beneath Berlin were, I am told, exceptionally obliging. All it required was the application of a little light. Such sensitive eyes they possessed. Altogether too much time in darkness. It cannot be healthy.'

He looked down at Sir Edward Kelly. The old man had said nothing since the Russians had entered the cell. He was huddled against the stone wall, his angular bones bunched together, as if trying to wrap himself into the shadows, disappear entirely.

Kelly regarded Malykh in turn. And then he scrabbled in the pocket of his breeches. With a surprisingly deft flick of his fingers he sent a coin wheeling into the air. It spun with a wink of gold in the gloom.

'How do you do, sir. I find myself imprisoned for counterfeiting. Apparently it's a crime. I always approached it as art.'

Malykh snatched the coin from the air. He scrutinised it for a moment and then flung it aside.

Kelly's eyes brightened mischievously. 'I fear my talent may be underappreciated. They're masterpieces, you know. Aren't they, boy?'

Kelly sent a second coin spinning from his fingers. This one he pitched at Winter.

'An adulterator of the queen's purse, they called me. It sounded rather grand, I thought. And just a little saucy.'

Winter caught the coin. It was roughly the size of a half-crown but felt heavier on his palm. It had been forged from silver and was remarkably untarnished for all that it appeared to be centuries old. There was a depiction of a man stamped upon it. His hands were clasped against the crude lines of his face, hiding his eyes, as if deep in prayer or penance.

'May saints preserve us from the judgement of the ignorant. We know art is transcendent, don't we, my pig-witted boy?'

Kelly held a fistful of coins now. Another gold one spun in the direction of the trooper to Malykh's left. The young soldier stiffened his grip on his gun, uncertain how to react. The coin fell to the floor, landing on its side. It rolled an inch or two towards the cell door before toppling into dust.

'Enough theatre,' said Malykh. He struck a boot at Kelly's hand, kicking the remaining coins from the old man's fingers. 'I know exactly who you are.'

As the coins scattered into the shadows the Russian placed his boot on the alchemist's hand. He pressed down

hard, the boot leather creasing as he did so. There was an autumnally dry crack of bone. Kelly's wrist shattered beneath Malykh's heel.

'The Widow of Kursk told me everything about you.'

Saliva surged at the edges of Kelly's mouth.

'She... endures?'

'Of course she endures. A creature like that is beyond any notion of death. But you know this, Sir Edward. You bargained with such demons. You made our world welcome to them.'

Kelly stared at Malykh's clouded, scar-cradled eye. He snatched his words between agonised breaths.

'I see... I am... not... the only one... to... trade... with devils...'

Malykh took Kelly's head in his hands. He clamped the old man's temples, his knuckles pale and sharp, pushing against the skin.

'We do what is necessary in this war.'

The Russian's iris began to swirl.

'The Widow told me that you knew a place,' said Malykh, his words unhurried even as Kelly writhed in his grip. 'A place of water and stone and shadow, where the stars wait, perfectly aligned. A place where angels could enter our world.'

Kelly flailed, his bones buckling, as if electricity was riddling his body.

'You and Dee endeavoured to hide this place from history. But new history waits for us in this century. So tell me. Where is this place?'

Kelly fought against Malykh's grip, his body struggling in protest, but the Soviet officer held him firm. The iris spun, remorseless and insistent.

'The location, if you will.'

Winter looked on in revulsion. He remembered the fierce sensation of violation, the way Malykh's mind had scraped like a knife in his skull. This interrogation seemed even more violent, even more vicious, as if Malykh was determined to gut Kelly's soul itself in pursuit of the information.

'The location, Sir Edward.'

Kelly was foaming with spittle and bile now. His mouth was stretched wide, the jaw nearly at the point of dislocation. His eyes had rolled upwards, the pupils vanishing beneath the lids and exposing tiny webs of veins at the base of the eyeballs.

Malykh dug his fingers even deeper, breaking the old man's skin. Water began to seep from his clouded eye. He blinked it away, keeping focus.

There was a howl. For a moment Winter assumed it had come from Kelly's throat. But it was closer than that. He looked up. The runes that Kelly had carved into the ceiling were cracking, fracturing. As Winter watched the arcane symbols began to warp and elongate, widening, deepening. In seconds the entire ceiling had splintered. Fine grey powder drizzled from the newly formed fissures in the stone.

Winter glanced at Karina. They exchanged a mutual look of incomprehension.

And then Kelly did make a sound. It was a rattle, dry and hollow.

Malykh released the alchemist's head. It lolled against the stone floor, the tongue protruding between the broken teeth. Winter saw Kelly's chest tremor, ever so faintly, rising and falling beneath his ragged shirt. He was still alive, still breathing. But his body had the ungainly sprawl of an abandoned doll and his eyes were the colour of fog. It was obvious that his mind had been eviscerated.

Maybe this was the closest Kelly would ever come to death, thought Winter. It was a kind of consolation, at least.

Malykh turned in satisfaction. He wiped his wet cheek with his knuckles.

'So,' he smiled. 'The history of this century is Russia's to write.'

26

The truck slowed as it neared the gate, a furious spiral of snow in its headlights.

Such weather was rare for October but not entirely unknown. Snow could come like a brigand in this part of Bavaria, descending from the peaks and stealing briskly through the towns and villages tucked beneath the Alps. One of these cold white storms could last an hour. Another could last a day, choking the remote roads and crippling the ranks of telephone poles hammered into the valleys. This one had blown in that evening, the blizzard swelling as the light dwindled, gathering strength in the dark.

The truck's wheels crawled, grit sticking to the tyres as they rolled over black ice. The vehicle sounded its horn, a single, insistent blare. Behind the gate a lone, scarf-muffled figure nodded in response. There was a dissonant jangle of metal. The chain-link gate swung wide. The truck rumbled forward, juddering over a grille in the ground, the impact loosening snow from its roof and sides.

'*Shevelis! Shevelis!*'

Christopher Winter was pushed through the slit at the rear of the truck. Tarpaulin slapped his face, slick and damp against his skin. And then he felt the snow upon him. It was wet in his pores and briefly blinding. He screwed his eyes against the biting gust, a mouthful of flakes turning to water on his tongue.

The truck had brought them to some kind of industrial complex. A factory, perhaps, or a power plant. It rose out of the night, a bully of a building, all concrete and soot and steel, its featureless walls throttled by pipes. A thick chimney discharged clouds of smoke – or was it steam? – that drifted into the swirl of snow, indivisible from the flurry. Another, thinner tower stood next to it. This one had a furnace glow, bright as magma. Its interior burned a baleful red.

Winter looked beyond the ugly, forbidding structure. The horizon gave precious few clues to their location. He saw the rugged sprawl of the Alps, a shadowy belt of trees, the intermittent wink of a transmitter mast in the hills. The countryside was moonless and made even less distinct by the haze of snow, but they were clearly some distance from the nearest town. This was some kind of clandestine Soviet base, hidden in the heart of NATO territory. Cheeky bastards.

The journey from Schweigenbach had taken hours, the truck hugging the rural back roads. Winter sensed they had headed north but it had been hard to maintain his bearings while slumped in the back, staring at his

mud-spattered shoes, hearing only the engine and the grind of the wheels as a fug of military-issue tobacco filled his nostrils.

'*Shevelis!*'

There was a thud of boots on tarmac, crunching through the snowfall. Two troopers had jumped from the truck. They stayed a vigilant two steps behind him, their machine guns trained at his back. Winter glanced over his shoulder and saw Karina follow him out of the truck, her blonde hair whipping her eyes as she emerged into the blizzard. There were two guards on her, too. One of them shoved her. She turned and glared, her body tensing, every muscle clearly containing the impulse to strike back.

They crossed a wide, empty yard, the snow swirling around them. An assortment of vehicles sat in the parking bays: cars, vans, lorries, each as scrupulously nondescript as the truck that had brought them here. One particularly large vehicle was draped in camouflage netting, tethered to the ground by bolts and cables. It was the chopper, Winter realised, as they passed the crudely concealed shape. There was no mistaking the bulge of the sleeping blades, the long spear of the fuselage. It must have arrived directly from Schweigenbach, moving under radar.

Malykh strode ahead of them, his coat open to the blizzard. He led the way to a set of unmarked double doors in the side of the building. The doors were lit by a piercingly bright spotlight, high upon the wall. Their windows were small and rectangular, the glass reinforced with grids of wire mesh. There was an intercom next to

the left-hand door. Malykh jabbed the buzzer and spoke into the grille, his words a gruff, impatient collision of Russian syllables.

Moments later the doors were unbolted. Winter instantly felt the heat of the building's interior on his skin. At first he imagined it was simply the contrast with the cold of the night. And then he realised that the temperature inside the building was queasily warm. It felt like a heavy, industrialised kind of heat, as if they were stepping into a forge.

There was something else, too. An overwhelming smell. It was the scent of something overripe and sickly, like spoiled meat or burst fruit. Winter took a moment to place it.

It was the tang of an abattoir.

Malykh conferred with the man who had unlocked the doors, a greying, mournful figure in a drab brown workcoat. As the man listened he stared at Winter and Karina, his expression impassive. Then he nodded, his eyes remaining unreadable.

Orders given, Malykh turned and left the building. The doors were closed behind him with a scrape of bolts. Winter peered through the mesh in the glass, watching as he strode away into the yard. The tall figure of the Soviet officer was soon lost to the snow and the dark.

Malykh had ignored them entirely. There had been no farewell threat, no boast about their imprisonment. This in itself was a statement. In Winter's experience few captors could ever resist such grandstanding. It was

as if he and Karina warranted no further consideration, the pair of them simply dismissed now that Malykh had extracted whatever secret had reduced Kelly to a blind, mindless husk. That kind of indifference was another, subtler show of power.

'So what did he say? Are we being left here?'

Karina nodded, her eyes fixed on the man in the workcoat, watching as he returned a jumble of keys to his belt.

'For the moment. We are to meet the evaluator. Immanuil.'

'First-name terms. You know him?'

'We are acquainted.'

Winter pursed his mouth. 'In a good way?'

'It's Immanuil. I doubt a good way even exists.'

The guards marched them down a long corridor. The walls were panelled with steel plates, dulled with age. The presence of so much metal magnified the heat, brought it even closer to the skin. Winter felt his shirt-cuffs begin to dampen. He slackened his collar and glanced up. There was a tangle of pipes on the ceiling, chasing the length of the corridor. As he passed beneath these pipes he heard them rattle and shudder, vibrating like engine parts.

The sickly-sweet smell was growing stronger. This had to be a meat factory of some kind. Winter did his best to ignore the pervading aroma of carcasses.

They were deep inside the building now. Presently they reached an entirely unremarkable door. The man in the workcoat unlocked it and then stood back as the

guards pushed Winter and Karina through.

The room was wide and dark and bare. A simple wooden desk waited within, one plain plastic chair positioned behind it, two more in front. The desk held a green phone, a neat array of pencils and a silk-shaded electric lamp, the only illumination in the room. The chairs cast skinny shadows, stretching to the open door.

There was an overhead radio on, low but noticeable. It was playing the Beatles. Winter knew the song. 'She Loves You'. Joyce had liked it. He had always meant to buy it for her.

They were led to the chairs. The guards placed themselves against the wall, their guns cradled in their arms. Winter and Karina waited, perched on seats that had the functional, uncomfortable feel of school furniture.

Two minutes passed, the only sound the muted harmonies of the Beatles. Then came a jingle for Radio Luxembourg, incongruously jolly in the hot, dark room with its abattoir smell. The radio signal faded, broke into a crunch of static, returned. And then came the sound of footsteps from the corridor. They were surprisingly soft, almost delicate.

Somebody entered the room. The figure was bewilderingly small, four foot high at most, dressed in a miniature tweed suit buttoned tightly across a pigeon chest. He wore a tie, too, blue with a thin silver stripe, knotted high against the starched collars of a crisp white shirt. The clothes looked altogether too neat, too formal for the person wearing them, like a child dressed by a parent for a wedding.

The newcomer took his place behind the desk, laid a pair of manila folders on the wooden top and adjusted the lamp with pudgy, undersized fingers.

'I trust you are not too warm. I understand the heat is quite unpleasant for your kind.'

It was a boy's voice, its timbre unbroken. Winter peered past the glare of the lamp, studying the figure on the other side of the desk. The face was smooth and unlined, the features still unformed. He saw a button nose, a small moue of a mouth and a thick shock of ash-blond hair, scraped to the left in a harsh parting. It was a boy's face but the eyes, impenetrable in shadow, belonged to something older, something else.

'I take it this is an interrogation?' asked Winter.

The boy smiled. 'No. This is simply an introduction. My name is Immanuil. I will be your evaluator in the months ahead. Please consider me a partner, not an interrogator.'

'A partner?'

'Yes. Of course. A partner. In our mutual journey towards understanding. It is easier that way. Less ugly, less awkward. We may even become friends. We can play, like friends.'

He beamed and smoothed a hand across the folders, running his fingers over the security classification stamps. Winter saw dried blood on the skin and what looked like hairs trapped beneath the tips of the nails. He was reminded of a cat's claws after a fight.

'I know how you play, Immanuil,' said Karina. 'You're a monstrous little bastard.'

Immanuil giggled. 'Karina Ivanovna Lazarova. Just one name among many, it seems. You always seemed such a good soldier. I do look forward to knowing you a little better. You are a tantalising prospect to me. So many layers to peel and to taste.'

'I'm thrilled at the thought.'

'You're at a disadvantage, of course. You are familiar with my methods. Most people have the delight of discovery.'

'You don't look old enough to have methods,' said Winter, cutting in. 'Frankly you don't look old enough to piss in a straight line.'

Immanuil ignored the taunt. He moved his hand to Winter's file. It was considerably thinner than Karina's.

'And you, Christopher Winter. An equally intriguing subject. A British Intelligence officer... and yet perhaps something more.'

Winter frowned. 'What do you mean?'

Immanuil opened the file. Winter saw a photograph of himself, ragged and unshaven. He remembered it being taken that fortnight he was held in the farmhouse. There were other photographs clipped alongside it. He saw a shot of himself and Karina at the pavement café in Berlin. Another placed them near Potsdamer Platz, their faces blurred but recognisable, clearly captured by the long lens of the Stasi.

'Colonel Malykh has added his own intelligence to your file. He states he was unable to penetrate your mind. He's not entirely convinced you even have a soul,

as most would know it. Isn't that fascinating? A puzzle. A challenge. So succulent.'

Immanuil's eyes darkened, glittered. Winter remembered the black eyes of the Widow of Kursk.

'My name is Christopher Winter. And that's all you're getting, you stunted little sod.'

Winter knew these words were a bluff even as they left his mouth. This child, or this creature, or whatever it might be, had already begun to prise himself under his skin like a tapeworm. He was determined not to show his unease.

'You know the truth of what I say,' Immanuil goaded, softly. 'There's a voice inside you, isn't there? When the world is quiet? A voice that insists there's more to you than you know. You should listen to it some time, Mr Winter. It may be wiser than you imagine.'

We are the Half-Claimed Man…

'I'm an operative,' snapped Winter, forcing himself to ignore the awakening whisper in his head. 'I take orders. I get things done for my country. That's my job. I don't need to think about it too much. Can you understand that?'

Immanuil giggled again. 'So like your empire. Defiant in defeat. A brave British face as the flags fall and the lights go out. Burying your failure behind another rousing chorus of "Rule Britannia".'

'Well, I'll let you know when I'm prepared to take psychiatric advice from a commie demon.'

Immanuil sunk a tooth into his bottom lip. 'You know, I have never cared for that word.'

'Demon?'

'Commie. So pejorative.'

'You're no communist,' countered Karina. 'You have the ideology of a scorpion. And the heart of one, too.'

'And what would you know of the heart, Karina Lazarova?'

Immanuil opened her file and turned through the sheaves of paper inside, studying the tightly typed paragraphs and the occasional scrawl of ink in the margins.

'Sexually active and yet no history of lasting emotional commitment. Presumed inability to form close relationships with either gender. No fear of physical intimacy, clearly, and yet such intimacy has only ever been demonstrated in pursuit of a private agenda. I may as well be reading the psychological profile of a whore.'

Karina gave a cold smile, refusing the bait. 'You're more of a whore than I am, Immanuil. You're selling yourself to the Russian army. Tell me, what do they pay you? I can't imagine you have any need for roubles.'

Again the dark eyes glittered. 'All I ask is professional satisfaction.'

There was another burst of static from the overhead radio. This one was louder than the last, a sudden eruption of white noise that hissed and sputtered from the ceiling. It faded as quickly as it had come, returning to the murmur of Radio Luxembourg. Now they were playing Eddie Cochran. 'Three Steps to Heaven'.

'How many of you bastards are there?' asked Winter.

'Communists?'

'Demons. Though my side might argue they're pretty much the same thing.'

Immanuil closed Karina's file. He brushed a small, smooth hand across the manila cover. 'And you really believe that your side is above consorting with my species?'

'Oh, you're a species, are you? You make it sound like you belong in this world.'

'And where, pray, should we belong?'

'I imagine you belong in Hell.'

Immanuil grinned, revealing a parade of milk teeth. 'We make our own Hell, Mr Winter. Some of us are better architects than others.'

Karina brought herself closer to the desk, her manner persuasive. 'You have a nice situation here, Immanuil. You've found a way to coexist. And that's good, given we usually try to kill or banish filth like you.'

Immanuil gave a brief, boyish laugh. 'You do try.'

'But maybe the world's going to change soon. Maybe there's something on its way, something older and so much more powerful than you. Something that will shake up all our cosy little alliances. It's going to come like a storm and rip through everything we have built, every nation, every empire. And when that happens I wonder what place there will be for your kind. For any of us.'

Immanuil considered her words. 'The Ascendance, you mean?'

Karina nodded. 'The Ascendance.'

'I knew of Malykh's mission. Your mission. I never imagined it was so close to completion. Have you truly found

a way to summon them again, after all these centuries?'

'I think we have. And I think that's just what Malykh intends to do. God help us when he does.'

Immanuil matched her gaze. The smile was gone. 'I doubt God will hear you above the screams of his children.'

The demon dismissed them. He gave a brisk order in Russian and the guards stepped forward, toting their guns. Winter and Karina stood up, scraping their chairs across the floor. They were led from the room at gunpoint.

Winter glanced back as he reached the door. He saw Immanuil nudging the orderly line of pencils into an even neater row. He was singing, too, matching the melody on the radio with a high, surprisingly sweet voice.

'We're to be taken to the detention cells on level three,' said Karina as they were marched down the corridor.

Winter nodded. 'I imagine we're not going to see daylight for a while.'

He looked down at his shirt. The heat had left swampy patches in the cotton. The smell of animal meat was still in his nostrils, inescapable.

'God, this place. I think I'd prefer a Gulag.'

Karina leaned in to him. 'I know this building's schematics.'

'We can get out?'

'Not easily. And not soon. I hope you have a taste for cat food.'

She gave another of her ambiguous smiles.

The corridor continued. Winter heard the pipes rumble and groan above them, water sluicing through the factory's plumbing. There was a whisper of static, too, hissing from the radio grilles positioned at regular intervals along the ceiling. One of the speakers suddenly emitted a roar of white noise, as if someone had spun the volume dial while tuning into interference. The sound faded seconds later. There was an echo, almost subliminal.

It sounded like a human voice.

Winter realised something then. For all the heat of the building there was a distinct chill on his flesh. He could sense it on the nape of his neck, just between the collar and the hairline. It was like ice against the skin.

Another growl of static. This time it came from the walkie-talkies pinned to the troopers' tunics. The sound was harsh, brittle, metallic.

They carried on walking.

'The Ascendance,' said Winter. 'I take it these are the things that Harzner was dealing with?'

Karina shook her head. 'No. There are entire pantheons of demons, some more dependent on human worship than others. Whatever Dee and Kelly were summoning doubtlessly had their own agenda.'

'Which is?'

Karina quoted Kelly's words. 'They sought to claim our world, rule it with flame…'

'Christ. Just give them the bomb and be done with it.'

There was a thick set of fire doors ahead, the glass panels reinforced with wire mesh, just like the ones at the

entrance to the building. As the escort party approached the doors Winter caught sight of their pale, blurred reflections. He saw what he assumed was his own face, distorted by the fluorescent light thrown on the glass.

It was another face entirely.

A shape tore itself out of the glass. It was the figure of a man, bare-chested, his almost transparent torso daubed with blood. The guards panicked, loosing bullets at the sudden apparition. The carbine cases spat and ricocheted in the narrow corridor.

The shape moved at speed, plunging a hand into the face of the nearest soldier. Phantasmic fingers pierced the man's skin, sinking knuckle-deep inside him, reaching beyond his eyes, into his skull. The fist tightened and the soldier screamed.

Winter seized the opportunity. He snatched the gun from the guard and slammed the weapon's butt into the man's stomach. The trooper doubled up, crumpling to his knees. Karina kicked him across the jaw then spun her leg into the other Soviet soldier, her heel connecting with his crotch. As he tottered she aimed a hard, balled fist at his face, smacking him unconscious. The guards collided and fell to the floor in a heap of khaki, out cold.

Winter stared at the translucent figure in the corridor. Even after all that he had encountered, all that he had seen, the rational part of his mind still rejected the sight in front of him. It was impossible to process.

The spectral presence spoke.

'All right, you prick?'

Joe Griggs stood before them. His flesh shimmered, like seawater lit by luminescence.

Winter struggled to form words. 'How...? You're... dead.'

'I know: I'm a ghost, you daft twat. And no, I can't explain. You don't get a debrief. Not on this side.'

'How did you find us?'

'Been following you for a while. Turns out I can get around through radios and reflections. Tried to say hello in the gents, back in the village. You weren't having it.'

Winter continued to stare, mesmerised by the sight of his undead colleague. He saw the knife-slash at the man's throat, viciously deep above the series of ritual shapes carved into his chest. The lacerations still looked fresh, the blood wet in the wounds, as if refusing to coagulate. They glimmered beneath the glare of the overhead lights.

Winter extended a hand. He felt his fingertips turn cold.

'I'm sorry,' he said simply. 'Christ, Griggs, I'm sorry.'

'Yeah, well, you did stand by and let me die, you bastard. But that's protocol, isn't it? I'm not going to rattle my chains at you. Not that I've got chains or anything like that. God knows what I've got. I thought at least I wouldn't still have these flamin' wounds...'

Griggs glanced at Karina, put out by the fact she was regarding him with what appeared to be professional fascination. 'She on the level?'

Winter nodded. 'I trust her.'

'Don't trust no one, son. Amazing what a different

perspective you get on the other side.' He noticed Griggs's voice had a remote, hollow quality, as if it was reaching them from somewhere deep and distant.

Karina's eyes flashed to Winter. 'We need to go.'

She knelt down and unhooked the keys from the belt of one of the troopers, then eased the man's pistol from its holster and tossed it to Winter. She took the other guard's gun for herself, her face full of distaste for the chunky, oily weapon. Clearly she missed her elegant blade.

'She's right,' said Griggs. 'Get going, mate. They'll soon know something's up. This place will be choked with Reds.'

Winter hesitated, then began to follow Karina down the corridor. He turned to look back. Griggs's wraithlike form was beginning to fade beneath the harsh fluorescence.

'What's it like?' he asked, softly.

'What's what like?'

Winter gestured, uselessly. 'This. You.'

'One thing you've got to know,' said Griggs. 'You shouldn't be afraid of it. Worse things to be than dead, I reckon. Now get going, you prick. Move yourself!'

The figure dissolved. In seconds all that was left was a quiver of dust in the air.

Winter and Karina ran. They moved deftly through the building's shadows, keeping their footfalls as light as possible as they navigated a dim warren of doors, backstairs, empty service corridors and half-lit storage areas. Karina seemed to know the way. They almost encountered a pair of soldiers at one intersection but they

flattened themselves against the wall and the moment passed with a mutual held breath.

Finally they arrived at an outlying utility door. Karina spun the keys in her hand, jiggled a few in the heavy padlock, found the one that fit. The door opened into a whirl of snow that immediately turned to steam as it met the escaping heat of the building.

There was a familiar sound in the sky. A steady beat of rotor blades, cleaving through the air. They looked up to see the helicopter climb away from the factory, its tail-lights winking as it banked into the night.

'Malykh,' said Karina. 'Damn him!'

Winter shielded his eyes from the flurry. 'Where's he heading? That place Kelly told us about?'

'It has to be. He knows the place of summoning. He's already on his way.'

'And do you really not have a clue where it is? Come on, there must be something. What did Kelly call it? A place of water and stone and shadow, right?'

'Where the stars wait,' completed Karina. 'I don't know. It was said to be a sacred area. Somewhere holy, known to Dee.'

'A church? A shrine? Where?'

Karina rounded on him, all of her suppressed anger breaking now. 'I don't know, Christopher! I don't know! We've searched for centuries!'

Winter stared at her, startled by the emotion in her face. And then a thought occurred to him. A recent memory. He reached into his trouser pocket, dug into the

cotton folds and found the coin that Kelly had thrown to him in Schattenturm. He lay it on his upturned palm. Flakes of snow blew across its surface.

The face of a man, stamped into silver, his hands clasped together in penance or prayer.

'May saints preserve us.'

Karina peered at the coin. And then she smiled. And the smile broadened.

A security klaxon sounded. A searchlight spun on the factory roof.

They ran into the snow-swept dark.

27

The Trans Europ Express shone in the frost-bright morning.

The sun swept its red and cream livery, playing along the sleek length of metal and glass. The train was heading south, to the edge of Germany, to her southernmost border, bounded by the Alps. It clung to the rails beneath imperious limestone peaks and lush green slopes, passing cold, wide lakes that had once been unassailable glaciers. The sky above the mountains was crystalline, the gift of Bavaria's status as the bridge between Northern Europe and the warm Mediterranean countries.

The train sped on, riding the electrified line, scattering a cluster of birds.

Winter stirred in his seat, aware he had slipped into a slumber. The click of the wheels on the tracks was as regular as a heartbeat. It matched the rhythmic pounding of blood he heard in his temples, the familiar tattoo between sleep and waking. He opened his eyes and saw the craggy Alpine escarpments snap into focus, perfectly framed by the broad window of the

compartment. Venetian blinds sliced the view.

They had caught the dawn train at Augsburg, abandoning another stolen car in the early morning shadows of an alleyway. The rails, he knew, were the fastest way to reach their destination, an isolated region at the very brink of the map. Daltzenwalt. It was the only place they could go, Karina had reasoned, if the coin was truly the clue that Kelly had intended.

'It's the Basilica of Saint Cenric,' she had told him, hours earlier, scrutinising the face on the coin. 'It has to be. I know this representation of the saint. It's also on a fragment of stained glass kept at the sacramental museum in Munich. I removed one of Dee's texts from the same museum, years ago.'

Malykh was already under way, of course, assuming he was heading to the same place they were. There was little hope of beating him there, even if that helicopter he was using would demand one – possibly two – pit-stops. An interception was the best they could hope for, and even that possibility felt increasingly fragile as the train continued to clatter past the Alps. The mountains were so huge that they barely seemed to recede in the window.

Winter had succumbed to a shallow, unsettled sleep, turning over many thoughts. The death of Malcolm still nagged at him. The image of that ritually desecrated corpse in Belgravia was unshakable. Who was behind it? Who had sent that warning? He still suspected someone in British Intelligence rather than a foreign power or some outside interest. But who? And what was their agenda?

Operation Magus. What was it?

Usually he relished his status as part of the apparatus of government. It made him feel efficient. But God, he had so rarely asked questions of anyone. Not since his first kill. It had all been duty. And you didn't question duty. Questions made cracks, and cracks grew. Cracks could grow until nations fell. Everyone in his line of work knew that.

He moved his gaze from the window and studied Karina. She was sat across from him, leaning forward on the plush red seat, her body tight with concentration. There was a steak knife in her hand, liberated from the train's dining carriage. He watched as she repeatedly scraped a block of flint along its serrations, attempting to sharpen it. The motion was methodical, her expression fixed. Occasionally a tiny spark would flash between the steel and the flint.

'Why do you use a blade?' he asked.

She kept scraping. 'Why do you use a gun?'

'I was given a gun.'

'I was given a blade.'

Another spark spat from the knife.

'You know what I mean,' pressed Winter. 'You clearly favour a blade. I can tell you're lost without one. Why do you like them so much? I'm curious. Professionally. Indulge me.'

Karina raised the knife, aligning it with her eyeline. She closed her left eye, inspecting the serrated edge in the clear light from the window. And then she carried on

sharpening, striking the flint against the steel with even swifter strokes.

'Do you feel anything when you kill someone?' She asked the question lightly, almost casually.

Winter considered this. 'I try not to. But it's inevitable, isn't it? You take a life. You can't ignore the size of that. You just can't let it touch you.'

'But it's so easy with a gun. You pull the trigger. You fire the bullet. The bullet hits the body. The bullet takes the life. You disconnect. You've released yourself of the obligation.'

'What obligation?'

'The obligation to feel the truth of what you've just done.'

Winter found himself bristling. 'I know what I've done. Every time.'

'You know what you've done, Christopher. But do you feel it?'

'Of course I do. You feel it the moment you do it. The life that's taken. The energy. Whatever it is behind the eyes. You feel it all right. You feel that theft. And yes, that's a physical sensation, even with a gun, believe me. It's like a hit of nausea. You have to absorb it. Catch it in your muscles. Move on.'

Karina gave a half-smile. 'I think you're confusing it with recoil.'

Irritated now, Winter let his breath escape between his teeth. 'So what's so superior about the blade?'

Karina paused again to examine the knife. She spun

the elegant rosewood handle in the air then tossed the pilfered blade from palm to palm, assessing its weight and efficiency. She seemed unimpressed.

'It's all about connection, Christopher. Connection and consequence. When I use a blade there's no divide between me and my weapon. We're all one thing. Me, my hand, the knife, the person I'm hurting, the life I might be taking. Nothing separates us. Nothing insulates me. We're one.'

Winter was unconvinced. 'What is that?' he smirked. 'Buddhist bullshit?'

Karina tilted her head, shook a stray lock of hair from her eyes. The light from the window struck her skin, accentuating the pale scar tissue that ran between her brow and her cheek.

'Think whatever you want,' she said and carried on sharpening. For a moment the steady rasp of the knife was the only sound in the compartment.

'Who gave you that? The scar? If you don't mind me asking.'

She didn't look up. 'My family.'

Winter stared at her, unnerved by how easily she'd given the answer. The revelation seemed so nonchalant, so matter-of-fact. She might as well have told him the name of her first pet. 'How do you mean? Your family?'

'I had many cousins in the house in Valencia. No brothers, no sisters. Just cousins. All of us were there that summer. Rafael was being taught the truth of the blade. And so was I.'

'He did that to you?'

'He had to know how it felt. So did I.'

'How old were you?'

'I was six. He was five.'

'And there were adults there? Making you do this?'

'Of course. We were raised by the Order.'

Winter shook his head, repelled. 'Jesus. That's cruelty.'

Karina pondered this. 'It's education.'

Winter watched as she continued to file the steak knife. He tried to see a trace of that wounded child.

'You know what I think,' he began. 'I think you don't feel anything at all.'

She raised an eyebrow. 'Please. Do enlighten me further. I'm sure your insights are first rate.'

Winter took a small, thoughtful breath. And then he spoke. 'You don't feel anything because you were taught to feel too much, too soon. I think this world is like a live cable to you. It's coiled there in the corner, sparking. And it scares you. You know exactly what happens when you touch it. So you've made damn sure that you never touch it, not really. Not so that it hurts. You talk about being one with your knife but I think you keep everything – everyone – at arm's length. You've numbed yourself.'

'Fascinating.' The word was glacial.

'It's true, though, isn't it? You don't get close to people. That's obvious. I don't think anybody could ever get close to you. Whoever you're pretending to be at the time, of course.'

'And you get close to people?' asked Karina. 'Really?'

'Closer than you.'

There was a quiver of motion in the air. Winter sensed it against his face, as near as a breath. He turned to see the knife embedded in the seat next to him. It had pierced the soft red fabric, exposing a yellow seam of stuffing.

'Weighted just a little too much to the left,' observed Karina. 'I really must bear that in mind.'

She reached over and plucked the knife from the train's upholstery. As she leaned across him Winter caught the scent of tamarind on her neck, in her hair.

'The circus clearly missed out on a rare talent,' he said.

She gave a compact smile. 'Just like the psychiatric profession in your case, it seems.'

Karina returned the block of flint to her bag. And then she carefully wrapped the blade in that day's newspaper and placed that in the bag as well.

'I don't need you to make sense of me, Christopher. I know you're trained to evaluate people in the field. You see them as a collection of moving parts, don't you? Tics, idiosyncrasies, vulnerabilities: they're all opportunities. Spot a traitor. Exploit a homosexual. Persuade an idealist to your nation's cause. So when you say you get close to people... well, that's all that you really mean, isn't it? People are easier to take apart the closer you get to them.'

Winter mulled this.

'I think we're both screwed,' he concluded.

The sunlight had suddenly dulled. Winter glanced out of the window and saw a bruise of clouds above the Alps. Spots of rain had begun to speck the glass. 'Well,

the weather's certainly changed. I think there's a storm waiting for us.'

'We're on the windward side of the mountains,' said Karina. 'It'll blow over the peaks.'

'That's some wind.'

'A foehn, they call it. A rain-shadow wind. They're surprisingly warm. So warm that the people of the Alps know them as snow-eaters. They can melt the slopes. Sometimes they can flood entire valleys.'

Winter regarded the sky as it darkened. The clouds cast charcoal shadows on the summits. 'It's come out of nowhere. No wonder these mountains are treacherous.'

Ten minutes later the train slowed with a stench of brake fluid. It slid into a small Alpine station, all timber and flower baskets and chocolate machines. Winter saw the wind bother the hand-painted signs that hung from the corrugated arches above the platform, jostling their chains. A handful of passengers left the train. A handful stepped aboard. Soon the engine returned to life and the wheels began to grind again, building speed along the track.

'We're close to Daltzenwalt,' noted Karina. 'That last stop was Krugendam.'

The door to the compartment sliced apart and closed again. A woman had entered, keeping her back to them as she manoeuvred her luggage. Winter watched the newcomer wrestle a leather portmanteau and a silk hatbox onto the silver rack above the seats. He found himself appreciating the elegance of the stranger's legs, the trim, enticing curve of her skirt. He hadn't permitted himself

to feel arousal for quite some time. It came in a rush now.

The woman settled into the seat opposite him. She placed herself next to Karina, close to the wide, rain-flecked window. She absently adjusted her blouse, smoothing a fold in the cotton. And then she looked up and smiled at Winter.

It was Joyce's smile.

Winter stared. This was the face of his dead wife. He knew every detail of it. The chocolate dot of a mole beneath the lower lip, the one he had always made a point of kissing. The puckish tilt of the nose. And the eyes. He remembered those eyes looking back at him in bed, those first nights of marriage when they had held each other tightly into sleep to the sound of the BBC Home Service.

It was the woman he had killed. It was Joyce. She was alive and sitting just across from him. He knew it was a lie. And she had been a lie too, of course, whoever he had been married to all those years. But just for a second his heart surged.

The woman with Joyce's face turned to the window, observing the sky with oddly empty eyes. The rain was gathering on the glass now, the beads hitting one another and splitting into streams. The downpour shimmered on the woman's face, imprinted by the light from outside. As Winter watched her features seemed to run with the rain. In moments another face was there.

The woman met his gaze again. This time she had the smile of a stranger. A woman who was almost Joyce. Almost.

Winter felt his body go cold. He remembered Hatherly's double, standing wordlessly beneath the streetlight in Notting Hill. And that man with Faulkner's face they had fought in Berlin. What in God's name were these creatures? Why were they hunting him?

He glanced at Karina, trying to signal his unease. She shot back a puzzled look. Clearly she had seen nothing.

There was a judder of light above the Alps, a flash so bright that it lit the window with a blue electric glow. The glass flared like an X-ray. Lightning cracked the sky above the peaks, illuminating the dark brawl of cloud, the forks fine and spidery. Seconds later there was a rolling groan of thunder. They were nearing the heart of the storm, at speed.

Winter heard another noise then, only just discernible as the thunder faded. A scraping sound, the sound of nails, sharp enough to make glass squeal. He turned to the door of the compartment and glimpsed a bone-pale hand, slipping from view. It had scratched a long, ragged trail into the transparent surface. There was something feral about the marking, more animal than human.

Winter got to his feet, buttoning his jacket to hide his holster. The woman watched him stand. Her eyes were filmy, gauze-like.

He spoke to Karina. 'I just need to stretch my legs, darling. Touch of cramp.'

His eyes flicked to the woman. Then he looked at Karina again. 'Keep your cutlery handy. You never know, you might need it.'

326

Karina nodded her understanding. Winter reached for the door handle and slid it back. He stepped out of the compartment, shot Karina a final look and closed the door behind him. He traced a finger along the gouge in the glass. It had been etched unnervingly deep.

The corridor was gloomy despite the wealth of reflective surfaces that made the Trans Europ Express feel so modern in sunlight. Winter walked along its dim, narrow length, feeling the train tilt and shift beneath his feet, the throb of the engine vibrating through the spine of the locomotive. The wind had begun to hit the windows, agitating the metal frames. The body of the train rattled and creaked around him.

There was a pneumatic hiss from just ahead. Someone had activated the automatic door.

Winter kept walking, passing the boxy chain of compartments that held the other passengers. Their occupants were in shadow, their faces turned away from him, everyone lost to the spectacle of the storm above the mountains.

One man turned as Winter strode by. His face was blank, as featureless as stone.

Winter kept his pace brisk as he moved down the corridor. The dining carriage was just ahead of him. He stepped through a succession of automated doors. They slid and hissed in sequence, leading him on, closing behind him.

Winter entered the dining area. A rich mix of soup, meat and coffee instantly hit his nostrils. The gleaming

carriage was full of people but there was no noise, no hubbub, just a heavy, unnatural hush. Meals were untouched, drinks still high in their glasses. As one the figures at the tables turned their heads to regard him. None of them had eyes. He saw smooth, blind shells of flesh where faces should have been.

The Widow of Kursk sat among them, all in black, as ever. She smiled her kitten smile beneath her veil.

'Tobias! Such a pleasure. Do join us. It's time you were told the truth about yourself.'

28

Winter's first impulse was to reach for his gun. It felt futile even as his fingers found the handle of the weapon. Bullets against demons. A stolen Russian service pistol against things that were beyond human. Hopeless. Useless.

His hand fell to his side, empty. He stood there as the train swayed, staring at the sightless throng of figures. There was something predatory about them, for all their silence and blankness. He felt the presence of something primal. Something that sensed his life and desired it.

'What are these creatures?' he asked.

'Oh, don't be afraid of them,' said the Widow. Her voice was poisonously smooth. 'They're part of the great order of things. Isn't that how your kind refer to it?' She gave another bloodless smile. 'Yes. The great order of things. Words you use because you're terrified your tiny world is really a mess of pain and chaos and unjustness. Quite a comfort to you in times of need, I imagine. And that's every moment of your lives, really, isn't it? Such sweet, breakable things you are.'

The carriage rocked, buffeted by the force of the storm. As the train shook, the wall-lights flickered and dimmed. It was then that Winter saw the bodies of the waiters, discarded in the corners of the carriage. A pair of corpses, their heads reduced to stumps of flesh. Blood and cranial matter stained the walls behind them.

He fought back his revulsion. 'These things have followed me since London. I want to know what they are.'

The Widow's eyes glittered behind their lace shroud, black and deep. Winter sensed she was savouring this moment of revelation.

'Very well. They have no true name, of course – I'm not even sure they have language, let alone thoughts – but over the centuries they have come to be called the Almost. I think it suits them, don't you?'

Winter grimaced as he heard the name. 'The Almost? Almost what?'

'Oh, just the Almost. You've seen the faces they steal. They're almost the people you know, aren't they? It's how they get close to you. Once they have your scent.'

Winter could feel the eyeless things regarding him. 'What do they want?'

'Why, you, of course. Isn't that obvious, Tobias?'

He kept his words measured. 'I've told you. My name is Christopher Winter. Now tell me why they're here.'

The sky splintered. The lightning was close. So close Winter could almost taste the voltage through the windows. He saw the Widow's lace lit by blue light. For

a moment the veil became transparent. The face beneath it was as old as the world.

'There are borders,' the Widow began. 'Edges. Limits. Partitions. Life and death. The great and ancient opposition. It keeps things neat, don't you think?'

Winter felt an unease building inside him. It was bone-deep. He looked up at the skylight and saw the clouds spark and glimmer, riddled with electricity. 'Keep talking.'

The Widow continued. 'There are those who defy the natural order of things. Souls who fall through the cracks between life and death. Alive, when they should be dead. They are judged to be aberrations. Irregularities. Nature hates mistakes.'

'And the Almost? Why are they here?'

'They cleanse the world,' declared the Widow. 'They hunt the mistakes. And they fix them. Gatekeepers, if you wish. They stand between the dead and the living. And they keep the great division pure.'

She relished her words now. 'I'm told you see them in your final moments, just at the point of your crossing. They wear the faces of the people you know. Friends. Loved ones. Your family. It's a lie, of course. But I'm sure it helps.'

Winter's mouth was dry. 'What do they want with me?'

The carriage juddered. A couple of brandy glasses tumbled from a table and smashed. The wind struck with even more force than before. Now it had the strength to tilt the bulk of the train itself.

The Widow set her mouth in mock sympathy. 'Oh, Tobias. I thought you might have understood by now.'

There was a taste of bile in Winter's throat. He sensed his heartbeat quicken. 'Tell me.'

The Widow let the tip of her tongue play against her jagged teeth. She was definitely enjoying this.

'Well, I imagine you're meant to be dead, aren't you?'

The voice in his skull whispered again, closer than ever before. *We are the Half-Claimed Man.* He kept focus, forced himself to ignore it.

'Don't be stupid. How can I be dead?'

'I assume the question is more... how can you be alive?'

Winter felt a sudden shudder of rage. He wanted to rip his gun from its holster, take aim at this creature, at all these filthy, unholy creatures. Make them go away forever, out of his world.

'I'm not dead!' he shouted, defiantly.

The Widow was clearly amused by his anger. 'Well, Colonel Malykh certainly believes you're alive. I doubt he would have sent me to kill you otherwise. And yes, you breathe. You bleed. You do seem to be alive, Tobias. But the Almost are never wrong. You've cheated them, haven't you?'

Winter fought to make sense of the demon's words. 'You're telling me I should have died on duty?' he scoffed. 'I've missed a bullet somewhere down the line? Is that what you mean? I've cheated death?'

'Not quite. You've died already. And yet you're

alive. You're a contradiction, Tobias. They don't allow contradictions. Too impure.'

Winter's blood was frost now. He could feel the cold in his veins, in his arteries, running the length of his nerves.

'So why haven't they taken me already, then? They've had plenty of opportunity.'

'You must have seen through them. They're unstable, these creatures. As fragile as rain. They need you to believe in the face they've stolen. Yes, you think you recognise them at first, but they need to convince you. Truly convince you. Without that they are nothing. They'll simply walk away.'

'They've only just come for me.'

'They've hunted you for years. Walked this world in search of you. The longer you defy death the greater their determination to claim you. They must have picked up your scent of late. I wonder why? Perhaps the fact you're finally engaging with the true nature of reality...'

Winter glanced at the blank horde in the carriage. They sat stiffly in their seats, their heads motionless, fixed upon him. He thought of the lethal stillness of a cobra, primed to strike.

'Well, they're not pretending to be anyone now, are they? What's the matter with the bastards? Given up?'

'Not at all,' said the Widow, with another pale slit of a smile. 'I imagine they're simply waiting for me to kill you.'

'And just how do you intend to do that?'

'With flair, of course.'

The chant of the wheels had changed. They sounded lighter on the tracks now. Winter felt a subtle shift in reverberation through the plates of the carriage floor.

He looked out of the window, past the fat spots of rain on the glass. The express was approaching a vast, curving bridge, built upon a viaduct that spanned a deep river valley. Alpine cliffs rose against this edifice of steel and wood, their rocky escarpments towering above the green spears of firs in the forest below. The pillars that supported the bridge were sunk deep into the gorge, claiming the land. A body of grey water churned beneath them, lapping at the concrete struts, whisked by the storm.

The train was gathering speed, preparing to pound across the bridge, outrace the wind and the lightning. It blasted its air horn.

Winter remembered the last time he had encountered the Widow. He recalled the watchtower lights shattering, the furious gale that had swept the Hungarian puszta.

'This storm is your work, isn't it?'

The Widow gave a mock bow beneath her veil. 'I'll take no true satisfaction in killing you, Tobias. Usually death is a pleasure for me. I feast on grief. I find it succulent. Sweet mourning. I imagine your death will be a dry, bitter thing, for who will mourn you?'

She gave a smile that tore into her cheeks like fish hooks. 'I have never met a soul more alone in this world. You have no one, my darling.'

Winter didn't blink. 'I don't want your sympathy,' he told her.

'And yet,' she said, as if catching a scent, 'perhaps there is someone in this world who will mourn you. She's close by, isn't she? It won't quite be grief, I'm afraid, but a sadness, just the same. It will add a little flavour to your passing, at least. A piquancy. Better than nothing.'

The Widow's smile contracted. 'I wonder who will mourn her, Tobias?'

Winter lunged at the demon. He went for her throat, his fingers closing around the bone-white flesh. And then he tore his hands away. She had burned him. It had been like grasping raw ice.

Startled, he staggered back, stumbling into a table, scattering glasses. His vision failed him. All he could see was a thick red smear, obscuring everything.

The Widow came back into focus through the crimson haze. 'Why, Tobias,' she cooed, her manner almost motherly, 'I do believe you're crying.'

Winter reached for his eyes. His face was wet and there was a scent of copper in his nostrils. He dabbed at his cheeks. When he looked at his hands they were bright with blood. He was weeping blood.

It was like holy stigmata.

'My name,' he roared, his larynx cracking, 'is Christopher Winter!'

His voice filled the carriage, louder than he had ever heard it. He stood there, shaking, another gush of blood streaming from his eyes. He blinked it away, ignoring the sting. As his vision cleared he saw that the Widow

had flinched, edging back into her chair. For a moment she seemed to have almost been afraid of him.

For a moment he had been afraid of himself. It had felt surprisingly good.

'You're more than you know,' she hissed, hunching in her weeds. 'So much more. But I'm done with you now, boy.'

The storm broadsided the carriage. It hit with a brute thud against the windows, making ragged cracks in the glass.

Winter turned. He had to get back to Karina. He ran to the door of the dining carriage. It refused to open. He hit his hand repeatedly against the glass but the automatic mechanism had frozen.

The wind pummelled the train again. This time the carriage lurched. Glass and china tumbled from the tables, smashing to the floor.

The wheels facing the storm had been torn from the tracks. Now they fought to regain a grip on the rails. There was a screech of steel grinding against iron, its pitch almost unbearable. Sparks spat against the windows in a fiery drizzle.

There was another furious volley of wind, even more violent than before. This one ripped the train from the bridge.

The locomotive reeled and shuddered over the edge of the viaduct, slamming through brick and fencing.

Winter clung to the edge of a table as the carriage tilted around him. He felt his stomach plummet as the

room upended. There was a hail of plates and cutlery. Bottles and glasses hurtled past his head, smashing against the opposite wall. For a moment he was almost weightless, his legs kicking against air.

The body of the train howled. It was a wounded, protesting sound, the cry of metal wrenched out of shape, twisting and shredding, enduring the absolute limits of what it could withstand. The chain of carriages was on the brink of tearing apart, its couplings buckling, pushed to breaking point.

Gravity seized the express. Winter heard the screams of passengers as the flailing locomotive plunged past the cliffs below. There was a rush of rock outside the windows, passing at sickening speed.

He let go of the table and landed on the upturned ceiling. Falling to his knees he wrapped his head in his arms, bracing himself as best he could. The train hit the water. It felt like a fist in his gut. Winter's lower jaw slammed against the upper part with a crack of teeth.

For a moment the carriage bobbed, suspended. And then the windows began to darken as the water stole the light. The wall lamps had already expired in a shower of sparks. The carriages were sinking. Soon they would be buried in the murk, engulfed by the silence and gloom of the lake.

Winter knew he only had seconds. The windows would shatter at any moment, pulverised by the pressure of the water. They were already beginning to rupture, cracks spreading like veins in the glass. The carriage

was on the verge of flooding. The water would seize it, fill it, claim every last inch of air.

He looked around. The faceless creatures lay in a sprawl of limbs around him, their hands reaching for his legs. He kicked the quivering fingers away. The Widow had vanished.

The light from outside was almost gone. He had to squint to see his surroundings.

He was standing on the ceiling, among the tiles and light fittings. The rows of dining tables hung above him as if poised to fall. It felt wrong; nauseous. Winter's senses instinctively rebelled but he made himself focus. He saw the long, rectangular skylight, close to his feet. If he could just break the glass then when the windows shattered the inevitable rush of water would act in his favour. The pressure, he reasoned, would propel him out of the carriage.

He stamped a heel against the centre of the pane; stamped it again. And again. And again. The skylight refused to break. It was reinforced glass.

Winter grabbed his gun and took aim at the skylight. The bullet made a hole the size of a shilling. This time the glass cracked, chipping around the point of impact. He stamped once more but it remained maddeningly intact.

Winter's eyes chased around the darkening carriage. He saw an emergency fire axe on the wall, secured next to a bright red extinguisher. He seized it and hurled the axe-head against the skylight. The cracks deepened.

The windows burst in a shock of glass. Water roared into the carriage, sweeping the shards ahead of it in a jagged tide.

Winter heaved the axe again. This time the skylight shattered beneath his feet.

The torrent overwhelmed him, cold and fierce, pounding his body. The force of the water thrust him through the broken remains of the skylight and out into the grey depths of the lake. The Alpine water felt sharp as pins against his skin.

Winter swam. He kicked away from the train's wake, fighting to escape the grasping vortex. He had snatched a breath a second before the carriage had flooded but he could already see it leaking away in a silver chain of bubbles.

He had one thought. He had to get to Karina.

Winter turned in the water, his eyes tightening as they peered through the murk. The express had drowned, contorting as it sank. Every window in every carriage was shattered and dark, as empty as eye sockets. Winter saw the lifeless bodies of passengers floating in the flooded compartments. They drifted like weeds in the water, their faces oddly serene.

He had to find her.

Winter felt a sudden, wrenching spasm in his lungs. It felt like they were being wrung with razors. That last breath had just expired. He had run out of oxygen. His vision began to blacken as carbon dioxide swamped his blood. He felt himself floundering, drifting away from the wreck of the train.

Every instinct told him not to breathe but as he slipped to the brink of consciousness his brain triggered an involuntary inhalation. His mouth flooded with foul-tasting water. It filled his nostrils, surged into his throat. He felt his windpipe contract, trying to repel the rush by reflex.

Winter saw absolute darkness. Then he saw a familiar white fire in the darkness. It was distant but it was growing brighter and closer. He surrendered to it as the lake prepared to take his life.

Karina took him instead.

She took him by the collar of his jacket, hauling him up through the weight of the water. She kicked her long, muscular legs against the current, arcing towards the daylight that shimmered like a promise above them.

They broke the surface of the lake, smashing into light and wind and air. Winter spluttered, choking up water. And then he filled his raw lungs with huge, hungry breaths.

The lake was calm now. The storm had receded. The sky was bruised but it had begun to lighten to the east. A squabble of mountain birds circled above them, the only movement in the landscape.

Winter lay his head against Karina, watching the birds as they wheeled. She placed a hand beneath his chin, extended an arm and swam, sidestroke, for the bank.

29

The ocean met the desert on the Skeleton Coast.

It was an uneasy truce between land and sea. The urgent Benguela Current brought the chill of the green Atlantic to the fierce heat of the Namib dunes. This union created a sea mist that could shroud the barren coastline for days, rolling in from the icy breakers. It was the only source of moisture in the sun-punished landscape and the jackal packs that prowled the black lava ridges licked its salt dew from the rocks.

'*Cassimbo*,' said Bagamba, keeping the wheel of the jeep level. 'It's an Angolan word. The fog of the sands.'

Hart nodded and held the edge of the windscreen as they sped across the shoreline, scattering a dawn parade of ghost crabs. He watched as the terns wheeled above the surf, the mist beading on his face. Early mariners had feared this remote and hostile coast – the gates of Hell, the old Portuguese sailors had insisted – and it still had a reputation as a maritime graveyard. Seal skulls and bleached whale ribs littered the dunes like votive offerings placed before the remains that had truly earned this place its name.

And there they were, saw Hart, as the banks of oceanic fog thinned and retreated. The wrecks of ships that lay like spectral carcasses. Tugs, liners and tramp freighters. Scores of them, colossal, rusted statuary now, their crumbling hulls and blackened anchors claimed by the sand in an act of burial that would take an eternity. The *Eduard Bohlen*, the *Dunedin Star*, the *Otavi*. All of them run aground, victims of the rocks concealed in the waves. An arch of whale bones stood in the shadow of one vessel, clearly a makeshift grave.

The old military jeep tore past the wrecks, moving at speed, its wheels cutting deep tracks into the damp sand. Bagamba fell back into silence, his eyes on the fiery granite massifs that rose in the distance. The Angolan had barely spoken on the journey north from the Ugab River. Absorbed in his driving, he would offer Hart the occasional scrap of local knowledge or folklore, facts about geographical phenomena or bush magic, each aside delivered in a minimum of syllables. Hart had a natural curiosity about the magic but he met the rest with an ill-disguised colonial disdain. In truth he was grateful for his guide's reticence. It was already a wearying journey and small talk, he knew, would make it hellish.

They had met in a clammy, surly bar in Windhoek, two nights before. Hart had arrived in South West Africa looking for a guide, someone with transport who knew the Namib wasteland in forensic detail. Bagamba had been introduced to him by a friend from the high commission, an habitual drunk and weekend

occultist by the name of Albert Tattersall. Hart was sure he had seen something shift in the Angolan's guarded, bloodshot gaze the moment he had shared the name of their destination but the pair had shaken hands and blessed their deal with the first of many whiskies bankrolled by the British taxpayer.

'To the desert,' Bagamba had toasted, with a wide but wary smile, one that clearly respected the region's formidable reputation. 'May the land be kind to us.'

'Bottoms up, old pip,' Hart had rejoined.

With a rattling chassis the jeep took them inland, away from the shore and deep into the dunes, outrunning the darting lizards that scurried across the parched plains. Soon all trace of the coastal mist had gone and a dry heat made the salt flats shimmer. Hart unscrewed the cap of the canteen and took a swift swig, just enough to slake his thirst. The water was warm and tasted faintly of steel but he was grateful for it. The sun was climbing in a viciously bright African sky.

'This place,' shouted Bagamba, above the straining thrum of the engine, 'the bushmen call it the land the creator made in anger.'

Hart tore off a strip of spiced dried meat and contemplated the ochre canyons of volcanic rock that towered above the sands. The Namib was said to be the oldest desert in the world but somehow it felt outside of time, too absolute an emptiness to be constrained by clocks or calendars or any of the apparatus man had created to govern the years. This was a true wilderness, a place where

names fell away and lives seemed immaterial. It was brutal and desolate but it endured. Above all, it endured.

The jeep crested the spine of a dune. Engine gunning, it ploughed down the incline, tyres whipping up a storm of sand.

It was then that Hart heard it. A low howl, almost like thunder. It echoed around the vehicle and rolled across the plain, gathering in volume. Bagamba had told him to expect it. They had reached the fabled roaring dunes of the Namib and this phenomenon was simply the sound of air trapped between sand grains, agitated by the jeep's passing. It still unnerved the Englishman. There was something ancient and wounded about it.

'Christ, that's a mournful noise,' Hart remarked.

Sunlight flared on the driver's sunglasses. 'The desert does not mourn, my friend. It barely knows you have lived.'

An hour later the jeep slowed to a halt beneath a rocky outcrop. Hart looked up. Centuries of sun had scorched the side of the escarpment a dark shade of amber. Black cracks in the cliff-face hinted at the network of caves concealed within. He felt a rush of anticipation. This was the place he had sought for nine years. He was here.

Now that the engine had stopped the silence of the desert felt total. It seemed to weigh upon the land. Bagamba stepped from the vehicle, the slam of the driver's door as loud as a gunshot in the gorge. His khaki shirt was blotted with sweat and his head gleamed like polished onyx. He reached into the back of the jeep,

retrieved a stubby, industrial torch and casually slung a rifle over his shoulder. The pendant of porcupine quills at his throat glimmered in the sunlight.

'This way, Mr Hart.'

The sand was treacherously soft. Hart felt his boots sink as he walked around the jeep. He took the other torch and glanced behind him at the undulating ridges of the dunes. From a distance they had an intricate natural pattern, almost like animal stripes. The desert, he saw, had already erased the vehicle's tracks.

He set off after Bagamba, climbing past rocks and scrub and scrawny trees whose shrivelled branches belied their obvious hardiness. As he climbed he inspected his left wrist, alerted by a throb of pain. The skin was blistering either side of his silver-link watch strap. Tilting his straw panama against the sun he kept walking, breathing air as brittle as dust.

A boulder awaited them on the cliff path. It was taller than the surrounding rocks and had a sullen, solitary quality. It was daubed with a petrograph of a hand, the red ochre fingers spread wide in an obvious symbol of warning. Hart knew that this pigment would have come from human blood, mixed with the powdered remains of a rock rich in iron oxide. All tribal ancestor cults used this method to create paint – it wasn't so much art as a summoning of their forefathers' souls. This was a sentinel stone, part guardian, part deterrent.

He struck a match against its side and lit a cigarette. He needed one very badly.

Bagamba stared at him, mouth turned down, clearly unimpressed. And then the Angolan pocketed his sunglasses and led the two of them into a black crevice in the side of the mesa.

The crack in the rocks took the men into a tight, winding tunnel, part of a cave complex that threaded the interior of the cliff. The dank chill came as a relief after the heat of the land. The pair pressed on into the passage, their torches illuminating an agitated flicker of sandflies. The air, already stale, was soon soupy with the scent of sweat.

Antelope. Springbok. Jackal.

Torchlight trailed across the rock walls, revealing crude representations of desert animals, daubed in the same earth-red hue as the hand on the boulder outside. And there were other shapes painted on the pitted limestone. Slashes of ochre pigment made circles, squares and triangles, the symbols overlapping, conjoining, creating new shapes. They were spaced at precise intervals along the length of the tunnel.

Hart recognised them at once. They were runes. Primitive, but unmistakably runes. So his theory was quite correct. These markings were six thousand years old. Those Elizabethan alchemists hadn't been the first after all.

The passage widened into a cavern. Solid rock surrounded them now, removing the last splinter of daylight from the tunnel's entrance.

'Here,' said Hart, urgently, his torch picking out a final petrograph, one that filled an entire wall.

It was the outline of a man, painted in the colour of blood. The neck of the figure was curiously elongated while its fingers tapered like talons. The eyes were simply circles, empty and sightless. Hart imagined they had stared out of this rock, stared into darkness, for millennia. He brushed away the blind termites and tok-tokkie beetles that were crawling across the surface and let his hand follow the lines that rose like wings from the figure's shoulders.

Paintings like this were more than just decoration or illustration. They were shamanic, Hart knew, the result of trance visions by medicine men. This art was part of a ritual, an attempt to pierce reality, to summon spirits through the rock itself. It was a dialogue with the unknown, just like Dee and Kelly's angels, the ones they had glimpsed in a scrying glass. Something had been seeking entrance to this world for a very long time indeed.

Hart heard a pounding in his head. It was the pulse of his temples, throbbing at the lack of oxygen, but just for a moment it sounded like the insistent tattoo of ancient drums.

'The Tall God,' said Bagamba.

Hart slung his cigarette to the cave floor. 'That's a nineteenth-century mistranslation. This is the Rising God. The one who ascends. The Ascendance, if you will.'

He glanced at his guide, the edge of his mouth curling with scorn. 'You should know that, shouldn't you?'

There was silence in the stale, heavy dark of the cavern. And then Bagamba spoke again.

'And you, Mr Hart, should not know that.'

Hart felt a searing flare of pain.

He looked down, wordlessly, his mouth hung open in shock. Bagamba had a blade in his hand. It was thin as a reed and crowned with a porcelain handle, sculpted into a garland of leaves. The Angolan twisted the weapon, deep between Hart's ribs. And then, equally swiftly, he extracted its slender, bloodied length.

Hart tore at the man's sleeve, clutching at the khaki. As he scrabbled for a hold the stitching split, exposing an arm inked with a coiling pattern of leaves, darker than the skin.

Bagamba turned, leaving Hart to crash to his knees, one hand clasping the wet agony of his wound, the other reaching after his assailant. A vein on his forehead tremored as he fought to conjure a hex – a desperate blood bane or a shadow scythe, anything he could hurl – but pain flooded his body, killing his concentration.

Hart collapsed to the ground. He heard Bagamba walking away, his boots echoing through the ancient limestone gallery. The Englishman lay there, snatching at breath, his face close to the still-smouldering cigarette. And then, summoning what strength he could, he began to crawl along the slick belly of the cave, dragging his body through the grime and the beetles and the dark.

At last the magician hauled himself up, one hand seizing the gnarled grooves of the rock wall. He staggered forward, hunched double and a mess of blood. He could see the entrance to the cave. A crack in the blackness.

The light was close now, the desert bright as fire. He impelled himself towards it.

It was August 1947 and, in a land majestically indifferent to his fate, Tobias Hart was about to die.

3∅

The Basilica of Saint Cenric lay like a pyre of bones upon the lake.

The ruins had to be centuries old. Maybe even a thousand years, imagined Winter. From the shore the stark remains of the monastery appeared almost to float upon the water. In reality they crouched upon a mass of rock.

The jagged granite that bore the building rose out of a glacial hollow, carved into the land by ancient ice. Barren crags loomed behind the promontory, their peaks eclipsed by mist, marking the boundary of this secluded Alpine valley.

It was an astounding feat of engineering. Winter could barely conceive how the monks might have quarried and hauled the slabs of limestone, let alone build a shrine to God on such an inhospitable site. The power of faith, no doubt.

One of the twin bell-towers was bomb-blackened, a simple cross crowning the surviving spire. Its sister tower was shattered, the stairs inside exposed like vertebrae. The exterior walls were smashed and charred. Artillery

fire, guessed Winter. The war must have found this place. The basilica had clearly been caught in the Allied push into Bavaria. Now it had been abandoned to the elements. The edifice had already begun to fuse with the landscape, nature merging with masonry. Granite and limestone, ice and mortar, melding into one.

Winter looked down and saw the church mirrored in the lake. The remnants of the towers twisted upon the water, their reflections reaching across the still, flint-dark surface. The sight unsettled him. He had felt an unease in his gut for hours now, ever since they had followed the long curve of the lake into the valley of Daltzenwalt. It was an apprehension that seemed to find solid form in the ruined bulk of the basilica.

He returned to the business of preparing his gun. The weapon was dry now and he racked the slide to return the cartridge to the chamber. It was a familiar ritual and there was something reassuring in the weight of the parts as they slotted into place. The tremor in his hand? He told himself it was purely from the cold.

'Is this really a plan?' he asked, without glancing up.

Karina had been tossing her stolen knife from palm to palm, still preoccupied by the blade's dynamics. Now she paused.

'You have an alternative, Christopher? Tell me.'

Winter shrugged. 'No backup. No contingency. No idea of the ground plan. No sense of how many of them there might be. And, yes, no alternative. I think that covers it, don't you?'

She placed a hand on his arm. As ever her touch surprised him.

'You're frightened, aren't you?'

Winter was about to dismiss her with a flash of his eyes. And then, to his own surprise, he chose to be honest.

'Yes. I bloody am. And I have no idea why.'

'So tell me what you can.'

He took a breath, determined to make sense of his thoughts.

'Something happened, back on the train. Something I can't explain. There was blood coming out of my eyes.'

'Blood? You were wounded?'

He shook his head emphatically. 'No. It's like I was weeping blood. Just like Kelly said happened to him. It was streaming down my face. I couldn't stop it. And here's the thing. It didn't hurt. Not for one moment. I felt... powerful. Like it made me stronger, somehow. And I saw it scare her. It scared the demon. And if it scared a demon then just what the hell was happening to me?'

He met Karina's gaze, almost daring her to answer.

'The Widow says I have another name. She also tells me I should be dead. I've seen a photograph of a man who looked just like me, and it was like looking at a picture of a stranger. Your friend Malykh says I'm hollow, that there's nothing inside me, nothing at all. My entire life in London feels like a lie. God knows who my wife was. And I stand there and I weep blood and it feels good, because just for a moment I feel stronger than the man I am.'

He was shuddering now. Karina's hand tightened

around his arm. 'You came back for me,' she said, gently. 'That's the man you are, Christopher.'

Winter drew another, deeper breath. And then he nodded, briskly, impatient to end the conversation and focus on the mission at hand.

'Come on, then. Let's retrieve this bloody book of yours.'

Karina released her grip. She kept her eyes on him a moment longer.

They set off into the dusk, moving with purpose as they followed the pebble-strewn path that clung to the lip of the shoreline. The sun had just set, leaving only grey light on the lake. Fragments of ice glinted in the water. There was a profound stillness in the air this evening. No wind disturbed the trees.

The path led them directly to the basilica. They slid around the back of the building, stealing past the bulge of the apse, the part of the church that held the sacred altar. It was windowless, a solid expanse of limestone, pitted by bullet scars, scorched by shell-fire. Good cover.

Karina killed the single sentry.

There was a stone wall. A small door stood in the centre, the wood warped and rotten. Winter pushed it open, taking care to deaden the groan of the hinges. They had to stoop as they squeezed through the low, tight opening.

The cloister courtyard lay before them, its flagstones riddled with weeds. They crossed it quickly, hugging the twilight as they passed the shattered remains of a

fountain. There was snow on the ground. Just ahead was the cloister itself, the two-storeyed walkway that adjoined the south wall of the monastery. They slipped inside its deep, cold shadows.

To one side were the windows that overlooked the courtyard, each arch bisected by a tall stone mullion. On the other side was a row of gloomy wooden doors, leading to long-abandoned monastic cells. Karina was about to walk past them when Winter raised a hand. He tilted his head in the direction of the nearest door.

There was a crackle of static, faint but discernible. Electric light fell upon the flagstone, illuminating the crack beneath the door.

They exchanged a look. And then a nod.

Karina nudged the door with her fingertips. It swung inwards, disclosing the back of a Russian radio operator. He was hunched over the dials of a squat wireless set, a pair of thick felt headphones fixed to his ears. A tall aerial sprouted from the top of the box, its silver length quivering as the man spun the controls, shuffling through the wavelengths.

Karina brandished her knife in the half-light. Once again Winter paused her. He stepped into the cramped, spartan cell and curled his forearm around the radio operator's throat. The Russian was large and he struggled, reaching in vain for his sudden assailant. Winter gave a final, tidy twist and the man slumped forward. A lit cigarette fell from his mouth and rolled across the trestle table. Winter picked it up and took a guilty but grateful drag.

Karina had caught the tumbling headphones. Now she watched as Winter leaned over the Soviet soldier's prone body. He was studying the controls of the radio set.

'You're going to use that?' she asked.

Winter gave the main dial an exploratory twirl. The mutter of static increased. He turned it again and the sound faded. 'We have listening stations throughout this region. They'll be earwigging Soviet military chatter. Someone's bound to pick us up.'

'You told me you didn't entirely trust your people. Now you want to make contact with them?'

Winter kept his eyes on the dial. There was little choice now. 'I think we could do with some backup, don't you?'

'I've never believed in backup. I think I may have a philosophical problem with it.'

Winter didn't acknowledge her. He hooked the headphones over his ears. The dial turned in quarter-inches, prowling the kilohertz as Winter hunted for the emergency protocol frequency. Finally he located it. He brought the microphone to his mouth, keeping his voice as low as he could.

'Knightsbridge to Royal Oak. Knightsbridge to Royal Oak.'

He heard only the whisper of dead air.

'Knightsbridge to Royal Oak,' he stated again, the words as loud as he dared. 'Knightsbridge to Royal Oak. Mercury protocol. Repeat. Mercury protocol. Location: the Basilica of Saint Cenric, Daltzenwalt. Engaging the

opposition. Support urgently required. Acknowledge.'

A crunch of static filled the headphones.

'Engaging the opposition. Acknowledge. Please acknowledge.'

Again there was no reply, only the sputter and hiss of long wave.

'Knightsbridge to Royal Oak. Knightsbridge to Royal Oak. Mercury protocol. Acknowledge.'

No voice came.

Frustrated, Winter tore off the headphones. He had the feeling he had flung his words into the dark.

'Let's go,' he said, tossing the microphone on to the table.

They exited the cell, taking care to close the door and bolt it. And then they moved into the arcaded walkway, heading for the holy heart of the church. They could feel the weight of the building around them, its accumulated centuries of dust and worship. The hush of the ancient stones was total. It threatened to betray their footfalls at any moment.

Karina killed the next sentry.

The walkway led to the south side of the vaulted nave. They stole past the remains of the chapel, avoiding the rubble that lay underfoot. The altar was ahead of them. And there was Malykh, unmistakable in his distressed leather trenchcoat. He had his back turned, conversing with two armed troopers.

They paused in the shadows of the sepulchre. Winter assessed what he saw, strategising as best he could. Rows

of empty pews cluttered the nave, haphazardly arranged. They would afford limited cover and a tight, tricky exit.

He looked up. Tiers of galleries flanked the side aisles, their tall, austere arches buttressed by sturdy limestone columns. Superior cover, excellent sightlines. You could see the entire church from up there, he imagined. Exit potential? Problematic.

They had dealt with three Soviet soldiers. Now three more were grouped in front of them, the two troopers cradling Garanin machine guns, their commander armed with a semi-automatic and a knife, both holstered for the moment. Winter judged the combat possibilities, calculating angles and advantages, estimating likely response speeds.

They had passed the empty helicopter on their approach to the basilica. How many men could it hold? Six? Or Eight? Winter tightened his eyes in concentration, desperately trying to recall the schematics of the Mil Mi-4. There had been a technical briefing, a couple of years ago...

Karina had already flung her blade.

Winter barely saw the knife slice the air before it embedded itself in the gun arm of the nearest soldier. The man howled in shock. His hand spasmed, reflexively dropping the weapon, which fell with a clatter of steel on stone. The other trooper spun, instantly alert, aiming his own gun at the shadows.

Damn her impulsiveness, thought Winter, hotly.

Karina tore into the nave, her body a lethal arc of

358

limbs. The second trooper tried to squeeze his trigger but Karina's heel had already connected with his jaw, executing a perfect spin kick that smashed the teeth from his mouth. He staggered back, his gun stammering bullets at the ground.

Malykh reached for his pistol, the motion cool and assured. Winter levelled his own gun and ran into the nave.

A single bullet pierced a flagstone in front of him. A wisp of dust rose from the hole. The impact had been inches from his foot. An expert shot.

Winter looked up. Two snipers waited in the upper galleries that watched over the sacred hub of the church. They had been positioned on opposite aisles, hidden behind the broad marble colonnades. Now they had emerged, long-barrelled Dragunov rifles in hand, heads nestled next to their weapons as they peered through mounted sights. Winter could feel the stare of the guns upon him, almost pricking his skin.

So it had been eight men after all.

Karina was about to tear the knife from the trooper's arm. Winter nodded to her. And then, reluctantly, he let his pistol tumble from his hand. Karina hesitated for a moment, her eyes furious. And then, acknowledging him, she stepped away from the wounded man, raising her hands in a grudging show of surrender.

Malykh clapped his gloves together, the slap of the leather slow and derisory. The sound echoed among the arches. The snipers in the upper galleries remained fixed on target, one gun on Winter, one on Karina.

'Look at the pair of you. Two lambs hungry for the knife.'

He stepped closer, the scar tissue creasing around his eye as he smiled. 'I imagined you would find a way to join us. I was informed of your escape. As you see, we are quite prepared for guests. But I am curious. How did you learn of this monastery's location?'

Karina glowered at him. He had stepped provocatively close to her. She stayed silent, defiant, keeping her gaze on him as he circled her.

'Your dedication impresses me,' said Malykh. The words sounded genuine. 'But then you are nothing if not resourceful. Such obsession is a remarkable fuel, clearly.'

He turned, dispassionately plucking her weapon from the trooper's arm. The man grimaced and clutched the wound, blood rushing through the sleeve of his tunic, running over his knuckles.

Malykh revolved the blade in his hand, vaguely incredulous.

'This,' he declared, solemnly, 'is a steak knife.'

Karina said nothing.

'Oh, you brave little soldier,' he smiled. 'Scrabbling in your mother's kitchen drawer for weapons. Fighting a war of attrition. Such spirit you have.'

'I take it you're going to kill us,' said Winter, bluntly.

Malykh was still amused by the knife. 'After you have made such an exceptional effort to be here? You must think me unkind. No, I intend for you to witness the culmination of your quest. Why would I deny you that?'

Winter compelled Malykh to meet his eyes. 'You're going ahead with it, then? You intend to use the book?'

'Of course. Modern psychology tells us we must face our demons, must we not?'

He gestured to the snipers. They hoisted their rifles and began to make their way down from the upper tiers. In the nave the soldier with the bloodied jaw raised his machine gun. There was satisfaction on his face as he levelled it at Karina.

'We must do it at dawn,' stated Malykh. 'There is precise ritual to be observed. And so much to prepare.'

Winter exchanged a glance with Karina. This threatened to be a long night.

'I shall share a story with you as we wait for the sun.'

Winter stirred from a flimsy slumber. Malykh crouched in front of him, the edges of his coat brushing the flagstones. He was in semi-shadow, lit by the glow of a portable lamp that had been positioned close to the altar. The Russian's voice was hushed, almost conspiratorial, but loud enough to cut into Winter's thoughts.

'Oh, good,' replied Winter, his words powdery in his mouth. He realised he badly needed some water. 'I like a story.'

It had to be the empty hours between night and morning, he guessed. Perhaps two or three o'clock at most. Winter's watch had shattered on the train but he could see sharp Alpine stars through a gap in the basilica's

roof. The sky was deep black. There was no hint of dawn. For a moment he remembered glimpsing London's stars through the ruined ceiling of the Fairbridge Hotel. That seemed a century ago.

It was bitter in the church. A nocturnal cold had penetrated the building and seeped into the stones. Winter sat up, sliding his back against the wall of the nave. He placed a hand on a flagstone. It was icy to the touch.

He looked across at Karina. She was wide awake, unruffled by the muzzle of the machine gun that had been aimed at her head for the last few hours. Her confiscated knife lay on a military-issue canvas table. There was an armed man behind Winter, too, his gun held at point-blank range. No wonder the Russians hadn't bothered to cuff them.

'So what's the story, Colonel?'

Malykh balanced on his haunches. 'It is the story of a child,' he began, his voice low and resonant in the vast, vaulted space of the nave. 'A boy who lived in a village in the Great Steppe, north of the Caspian Sea. A credulous, dreaming boy who was told of a spirit that walked the grasslands and the rivers. A creature with a heart like black apples, dead upon the branch. It had many names, for it had many faces, for there were many children. Some said its skin was like old leaves, carried on the wind. Others claimed it was an animal, almost a bird. A great crow with the eyes of a cat. My grandfather said its wings were as wide as the night. But I knew he was only trying to scare me. Grandfathers enjoy that, don't they? Especially

with boys who shudder at the sight of their own shadow.'

Malykh spoke slowly, choosing his words with care. They were clearly weighted with memory.

'I knew it as the Eyes of the Harvest, though that translation is inadequate. Words so easily grow weak between our languages. It was the name my family had always called it. A bad spirit. A demon, of a kind. As old as the seasons. Its touch would take your memories, they told us. Every precious moment of your childhood, every mother's kiss, every Christmas morning. All of them stolen, lost forever. Your mind would be left like an empty well. Can you imagine anything more frightening to a child? Some nights I was so sure I could hear it breathing in my room, close to my bed, come to drink my memories.'

Malykh smiled, ruefully. 'And then I grew older. And I was no longer afraid of it. I knew it for what it was. A peasant's tale. Something to make children run home early from the fields, before the sun sank. What word do you have for it in the West? A bogeyman. *Strashilische.*'

The smile faded. 'But I knew nothing of the truth of this world. One warm autumn night it came to my family's farm. It feasted. And I ran. I ran from the screams of my parents, my sister.'

Malykh's expression hardened. A muscle moved beneath his skin.

'Many years later I came back to my village. I looked for this creature and I found it, deep in the woods, living in a hovel of stones. It seemed very much like a

363

man to me. I had my knife and I took its eye. I took it for my own. And I heard it scream as I cut the eye from its head. I knew then that these things could be small and afraid, just like us. I would not let them hide in the dark any longer.'

Winter found himself focusing on Malykh's left eye, the one surrounded by scar tissue. He saw the clouded pupil contract in the half-light, almost as if it was cowering. Now, more than ever, that eye seemed out of place, a stolen thing. It belonged to another face. A face as old as the seasons...

'This war,' said Malykh, spreading his hands, expansively, 'this war we fight at the edges, in darkness... for me it's a private war.'

He rose from his knees, keeping his gaze on the prisoners. Behind him the soldiers continued their preparations, standing around the altar.

'I want them to be afraid of us,' he declared. 'I want them to tell tales of us to their bastard children. How we fight them. How we drag them into the light. And how they scream. We live our lives afraid of the dark. Let the dark be afraid of us.'

Karina shook her head. 'You're about to tear this world open, Malykh. And when you do this war of yours won't be at the edges anymore. You won't be fighting them in the shadows.'

Malykh nodded. 'I will fight them wherever I must. It's my duty.'

'You are opening Hell!' Karina retorted, spitting the

words with a sudden anger. 'You have no idea what you'll bring into this world!'

'I don't,' said Malykh, calmly, his face set. 'But I know that I shall be standing there to meet it. I won't be afraid, Karina. And the dark will have no hold over me.'

The sky was raw with dawn.

Winter could see a vivid red daybreak through the high clerestory windows that rose above the nave. The clouds looked like bloodstained banks of snow. Soon a hazy, crimson-grey light filled the basilica's interior. Morning began to touch the old stones. Some of the building's shadows retreated but the chill of the last few hours persisted.

The Russians had readied the place for some kind of ritual. Symbols were chalked on the walls above the altar. Winter recognised them as the runes from Karina's book. He imagined they had been copied with meticulous precision. More chalk glyphs marked the broad columns extending the length of the nave arcade. As ever the symbols made no sense to him but their presence – their sheer quantity, the specific choice of runes to replicate – had an ominous sense of purpose.

A casket of incense hung above the altar. A thread of smoke drifted upwards, thickly scented.

A circle of bones had been laid upon the flagstones. The arms and legs marked the perimeter of the ring, femurs and fibulas forming a chain with the severed

bones of the hands and feet. Fragments of the spinal column completed the skeletal arc. Within the circle was the skull, perched like a prize on top of the ribcage.

These were no ordinary bones. They were grotesquely pretty, studded with gemstones and embroidered with gold. The ribs had been bound with pearls. Sapphires glared from the sockets of the skull. Bejewelled rings decorated every finger, some of them wedged together in pairs, while the mouldering teeth were capped with a gilt-edged grin. The effect was vulgar, macabre, almost fairground tacky.

These were clearly the bones of Saint Cenric himself, plundered by the Russians from a concealed vault. Worshippers must have ornamented his remains centuries before. Winter had seen pictures of bones like this in the Sunday supplements – martyrs' relics, they were called, displayed and venerated as a piece of medieval church theatre. No doubt the Russians had ransacked the old boy's crypt in the night. The bones were almost comically gaudy but there was a very real, very violent sense of desecration in the way they had been torn apart and commandeered for this ritual.

Winter exchanged a glance with Karina. There was nothing encouraging in her eyes. He saw the trooper standing behind her, felt the equally unwavering gun at his own back.

Malykh stepped into the circle of bones. He carried a small black bowl that contained a thin layer of water. He was taking care to keep it level. It had to be some kind of scrying device, thought Winter, surprised at how quickly

such terminology came to him now, as though he had always known it.

Malykh set the bowl upon the floor, some inches from the skull. And then he stood back, unsheathing his knife with an air of ceremony. He grasped the black blade with both hands and raised it in front of his face, the obsidian length glinting as it caught the early light. The knife carved the air in a succession of quick, complex movements. Malykh was mirroring the runes, Winter realised, echoing the shapes and strokes of Dee and Kelly's unearthly alphabet.

The Russian began to chant as the blade swiped the incense-scented air. The sounds he made were guttural, indecipherable, more like grunts than words. The soldiers joined in, hesitantly at first, their voices rising from a murmur to a fierce, urgent clamour that echoed between the walls of the monastery.

The water tremored on the surface of the bowl.

Malykh's chant built to a climax as sweat beaded on his forehead. And then, with vicious speed, he plunged the black blade into the remains of Saint Cenric. There was a sickening scrape of metal against bone until the knife rested in the jewelled ribcage. The sapphires embedded in the skull regarded this violation impassively.

Malykh steadied his breathing. It was all that could be heard in the sudden silence of the nave.

And then there was a sound. A flash of movement.

Something had struck the flagstones with a hollow clatter.

Winter glanced at the ground. He saw a chubby green cylinder roll across the floor of the basilica. It came to rest by his shoes, hissing vapour. In the second it took him to identify it as a standard British commando smoke grenade the thing had detonated. A choking fug billowed upwards, smelling like a bonfire.

He hurried to cover his face. He could hear the clang and hiss of more grenades as they tumbled into the nave. As smoke filled his vision he saw muzzle flashes from the transept, heard the unmistakable stutter of Bren guns. The Russian trooper behind him returned fire over his shoulder. And then the man's gun fell from his hands. Winter felt a spray of blood against the side of his head.

He reeled, half blinded by the stinging smoke. It had found his eyes. Tears streamed out of his ducts. His throat burned.

Winter groped his way through the smoke, making for Karina, the retort of automatic weapons splintering his eardrums. The world was a sudden chaos of darkness and fire, snatched between the slits of his eyes. Any relief that British forces had found the basilica was tempered by the thought that a bullet would probably rip through his body at any moment.

He stumbled into a corpse, still warm on the floor. He felt rough khaki fabric and a slick of blood. It was the trooper that had been guarding Karina. She was gone.

Winter kept moving, crouching low, forcing his eyes to open, to clear away the tears. The smoke was thinner on this side of the nave and he could just about see the black-

clad British commandos. He had no idea how many they were but they were hugging the cover of the columns, emerging to loose rounds at the Russians. Their guns sputtered, the barrels of the Brens crackling, flashing fire. Bullets studded into ancient masonry. Winter ducked down, evading the hot quarrel of the crossfire.

He saw Karina. She was facing Malykh, the knife back in her hand, seized from the table as the guards were distracted. He had the obsidian blade in his. They were baiting each other like circling animals, locked in the moment, matching hard, unblinking stares. The smoke around them glittered with muzzle flashes. Winter wanted to intervene but something in the way they were measuring up to one another told him this was a personal duel.

Karina was the one who broke the impasse. She lunged, striking for Malykh's chest. He parried the attack. There was a brief, bright flash of sparks. Malykh twisted his knife against hers, urging blade against blade. He flexed his forearm, forcing her wrist to contort at an agonising angle.

She wrenched her blade away. And then, just as swiftly, she stabbed at him again. This time she aimed for his face. Once more Malykh expertly blocked her. He tore his knife upwards, smiling grimly as it stripped skin from her knuckles.

Karina didn't flinch. She bit down on her lip, matching his stance exactly, the two of them hunting for vulnerabilities, for a sliver of opportunity. Anything they could exploit.

Another jab. Another deflection. The blades locked, scraped, sliced apart. The obsidian was sharper than the steel but Karina's moves were nimbler, less telegraphed.

Malykh punched her in the face.

The force of the blow knocked Karina to the ground. The knife fell out of her hand, hitting the flagstones. She scrabbled to retrieve it but Malykh's boot was on her arm. He stamped on her wrist, making her fingers curl and clutch air. And then he reached down and locked his fist around her throat, his grip tightening until her veins bulged, blue and rigid. The black blade hovered in his other hand.

'Brave little soldier girl,' he murmured, smiling.

Winter scrambled in the smoke for a gun.

Karina had landed in the ritual circle, jewelled finger-bones scattered around her hair. Fighting for breath she managed to twist her head to the left. The skull glared back at her with its blind sapphires. The scrying glass lay inches away. She grabbed it with her free hand and swung it upwards, smashing the bowl into Malykh's face. It was obsidian, just like his knife, and its serrated rim sliced into his temples with a whip of blood.

Winter ripped a revolver from the holster of a dead trooper. He levelled the weapon, squinting into the smoke.

Malykh staggered, loosening his hold on Karina's throat. In that instant she rolled, reclaimed her knife and thrust it into his side. It pierced leather, khaki and flesh, sliding through his ribs to skewer his left lung.

Grimacing, she urged the hilt of the blade deeper, as deep as it could go.

'Karina...'

Malykh swayed, looking down at her. There was accusation in his eyes but something else, too. Something like regret.

'Don't you want to see?' he asked her, his words broken by snatches of breath. 'Don't you want to know?'

Blood and saliva frothed in his mouth.

'Don't you want to show them... we're not afraid?'

There was a gunshot. A bullet thudded into Malykh. He tottered, fighting to stay on his feet, determined to deny its impact. And then another bullet came, puncturing his chest. He fell forward, his knees buckling, his legs collapsing, his life taken.

It wasn't Winter who had fired the shots. The gun he held was empty.

A silver-haired man in a neat pinstriped suit stood behind the fallen Russian, a Webley & Scott pistol in his hand. He had grey, watery eyes and wore a paisley bow-tie.

Winter looked at this newcomer in disbelief. It was impossible.

The man standing there before him was Malcolm Hands.

371

31

Winter knew all about disorientation.

He had experienced it in the field, long before the madness of the past few weeks. Sometimes it was deliberate, a calculated act of psychological warfare, intended to destabilise. The Red Chinese were particularly expert at it. He remembered that room in Peking in '61, the one with altogether too many walls.

Sometimes it felt like mental dislocation, sometimes purely physical. It was the same experience each time though, the moment flashing into absolute focus even as the gravity of reality fell away.

Winter saw Malcolm standing there, alive, and he knew that familiar trapdoor sensation in his gut. In a moment this would make sense, he told himself. For now, however, he was reeling.

The smoke had nearly dissipated. The door to the nave stood open, letting the dawn into the church. Only one Russian soldier was still alive, the youngest of the squad. A British commando nudged the barrel of a Bren

gun against his ribs. The boy was bleeding from the mouth and he had lost his front teeth.

Malcolm stepped through the broken circle of bones, kicking the skull of Saint Cenric out of his way with undisguised disdain. It rumbled across the flagstones, rolling to rest against the altar.

'Bloody amateurs,' he muttered.

The SIS man acknowledged Winter with a crisp, brittle smile.

'They claim that communism's the future, don't they? But by God they're medieval peasants at heart.' He glanced around him. 'Just look at this carry-on. It's a circus.'

Winter stared at his old friend and colleague. He stared at every tiny, familiar detail, everything he had almost forgotten in the last few weeks. The birthmark beneath the left eye, the scattering of pockmarks on the right cheek. Winter nearly told himself it was like seeing a ghost. But then he had seen a ghost and ghosts had no sweat in their pores, no razor burn on their throat, no signature scent of Bell's whisky. Malcolm Hands, it was clear, had never been remotely dead.

There was only one word he could possibly form. 'Malcolm?'

This time the smile was warmer. 'Hello, Christopher. How are you? You have done astonishingly well. I've always had faith in your talents but this has made me very proud. I never quite imagined you'd get this far.'

Winter cut through the compliment. 'Malcolm, what

the hell's going on? I saw your body in London. I thought you were dead.'

'Tradecraft. Deception. Illusion. It's our sordid little theatre, dear heart. You know that.'

'I saw your body.'

'You saw a body,' Malcolm corrected, airily. 'Some poor, half-barbecued bastard, recruited for the cause. A particularly bolshie political prisoner, as I recall. I'm told there was a resemblance. And to be fair, your judgement at that moment was hardly impeccable. You were very nearly concussed, were you not?'

Winter remembered the fight on the stairs in Belgravia, the blinding impact of the headbutt from that thug in the regimental tie, brutal enough to knock his senses for six.

'He worked for you? That man on the stairs?'

'Muscle, nothing more. Come now, don't be jealous. He has none of your remarkable initiative.'

'Why would you do this?' Winter demanded, a wounded edge to his voice now. 'Why wouldn't you tell me, Malcolm? We're friends! Didn't you trust me?'

At the edge of his vision Winter saw Karina crouched by Malykh's body as the men confronted each other. She slipped a hand inside the dead officer's trenchcoat and extracted the book.

'I trusted you enough to give you this mission,' said Malcolm, briskly. 'My methodology may be a tad unorthodox but then Faulkner would never have signed off on it. Just great, rolling cloudbanks of bureaucracy in

that man's mind. Precious little lightning. Far better for you to be outside the system. Much more useful.'

'Useful for whom, Malcolm?'

'For all of us, Christopher. But especially for you. You're always at your best when you're free of the apparatus. No sticky departmental politics, no checks and balances, no triplicate. None of that messy business of accountability. Pure forward momentum. The perfect, efficient instrument. And one given a certain fire in his heart by the fact of my death. We're nothing without motivation, Christopher. I had to make it compelling, naturally.'

Winter shook his head, still struggling to make sense of Malcolm's presence, let alone his words.

'You should have trusted me. I didn't need to be deceived, Malcolm. That was a shitty thing to do.'

Malcolm reproached him with a twinkle. 'Come now, Christopher. We map shadows. We walk in mirrors. We are the architects of mazes. This is our calling. It's what we do.'

He turned to regard the captive Russian trooper. 'And now, perhaps, we should start to take care of extraneous details. Keep it neat, keep it tidy.'

Malcolm blithely shot the prisoner in the chest. The boy flailed as the bullet hit him. And then he sagged to the ground, his tunic darkening with blood.

'He was unarmed,' said Winter, appalled.

'Well, naturally,' smiled Malcolm. 'If he'd been aiming a gun at my head I'd have already shot the little bastard.'

He pivoted on his heel, shifting the pistol towards Karina. The charm was gone. 'The book, if you please.'

'She's with me,' said Winter, quickly. 'She's not a Russian operative, Malcolm. She was undercover.'

'I don't give a damn. She has what I need. And I'll happily take it from her corpse if I must.'

He levelled the gun, pragmatically. 'The book. I shan't ask again.'

'Don't shoot her, Malcolm!'

'I trust she's bright enough to ensure I don't have to.'

Karina glared at the pistol trained upon her chest. The commandos had also turned to target her. The barrels of the Bren guns hovered, anticipating the chance to fire. Resigned, she passed the book to Malcolm, resentment in her eyes.

The SIS man snatched it from her hand. He turned the leather-bound pages, inspecting the glyphs. Curiosity mixed with satisfaction on his face.

'Oh, this is excellent. Excellent. It's all here, just as I hoped. What a remarkable achievement. Shall we consider it your legacy, dear girl, or does that sound premature?'

Karina's voice was composed. 'If you use that book then the legacy is all yours, believe me.'

She turned to Winter. 'Perhaps you need to choose your friends with greater care, Christopher. This one doesn't reflect well on you at all.'

Winter watched as Malcolm paced the flagstones, leafing through Dee's grimoire just as Malykh had done in Schattenturm. The parallel made him uneasy. A

dozen or more questions pushed at his lips.

'Look, Malcolm, what's going on? Straight answer. No bullshit.'

Malcolm closed the book with a snap of leather. 'Long is the way and hard, that out of Hell leads up to light.' There was a hint of something mischievous moving at the edges of his mouth. 'I take it you remember your Milton?'

'I said no bullshit, Malcolm.'

'You do remember studying Milton, don't you? Then again, perhaps you don't. Perhaps all that you truly recall is the name of your school. Shrewsbury, wasn't it? Or did we choose Dulwich?'

'Dulwich,' said Winter, instantly, automatically, unthinkingly.

'Very good, Christopher. The essential framework is all there, of course. I imagine the finer details feel a little less defined. Fog and static where memories should be. But then you never dwell, do you? You barely glimpse the holes in your mind. They're entirely natural, you tell yourself. That's how we taught you to regard them. You're all about forward momentum, after all. The perfect instrument. No place for nostalgia in an assassin's life. No need to look back.'

Winter felt a familiar shudder, rooted in his bones. He had experienced the same sensation confronting the Widow of Kursk on the train. A sense of certainties collapsing. *We are the Half-Claimed Man…*

'Did you really think that was your life?' pressed Malcolm, openly taunting him now. 'Buried away

in suburbia? That neat semi-detached in Croydon? Mantovani and a tipple of sherry to soothe away the blood of the men we sent you to kill? The fragrant wife by your side?'

Winter saw her body on the bathroom floor. 'Joyce?' he murmured, only half in the moment.

'Joyce,' smiled Malcolm. 'Dear, loyal, dead Joyce. Do you know, it's been so long I've quite forgotten that girl's real name. Louise, I think. Or was it Lucy? She was dedicated, I'll give you that. She kept that cover immaculately. And for such an astonishing length of time. I imagine the poor girl could have eventually died of boredom before you put a bullet in her stomach.'

Winter sent a fist across Malcolm's face. Two commandos immediately moved to restrain him, seizing his arms. Malcolm took a moment to wipe the blood from his mouth. He smirked at the sight of his bloodied knuckles.

'Oh, I am sorry. Were you expecting a card of condolence, dear heart? It was rather awkward. I did just so happen to be dead.'

Winter lunged again. Once again the commandos wrestled him back.

'You were human wreckage when we found you in Africa,' stated Malcolm. 'A ruin of the man you had been. No more than a husk. A marvellous blank, in a way. Pure potential. From that day on I sculpted you. I created the perfect instrument for our purpose.'

Winter thrashed as the commandos held him. 'What

379

are you talking about, Malcolm...?'

'There was always a chance your memories might surface, of course. Luckily we had a chemical solution. We applied it on a regular basis. And then post-hypnotic instruction kept you equally in check. The mind can be such a malleable thing. Especially if it's not entirely intact in the first place.'

Winter remembered the syringe of orange liquid he had seen in the debrief room, the phial of the same bright, viscous fluid he had found in his bathroom cabinet, hidden in Joyce's toiletry bag. He saw the hot white light of the interrogation lamp, felt his thoughts being burned away by its glare.

'Why did you do this to me?' His voice was small now. 'Tell me why you've done this, Malcolm...'

'I keep telling you. I needed an instrument: wilful, resourceful but ultimately obedient. Someone I could hone. Who trusted me implicitly. A friend. Someone who would one day lead me to this place, to this moment. To fulfil their destiny, I suppose you'd say.'

'I'm a bloody assassin!' protested Winter. 'I kill people! I don't have a destiny!'

Malcolm stepped closer. 'Each kill you made was for me. All part of the greater ritual. Every assassination I sanctioned was also a blood sacrifice. Every shabby little traitor, every wretched defector. Every death I ordered in Her Majesty's name. Their blood fed the cause and we became stronger.'

Winter stopped struggling. He felt a cold jolt of realisation. Blood? Sacrifice? Ritual? Now it began to

make sense. Malcolm Hands was no better than those demon-worshipping bastards who had murdered Griggs in Vienna.

'You're part of it,' he said, half smiling as the truth hit him. 'You've always been part of it, haven't you, Malcolm? This bloody war of magic…'

'Tradecraft,' corrected Malcolm. 'Indivisible from magecraft. The British intelligence service was built upon it. We are all of us magicians, in a way. Some of us simply stand a little closer to our founding principles. John Dee would understand.'

'You killed Hatherly. You killed my echo man.'

'And I brought him back to life, after a fashion. I'm only a dabbler, after all. I'm no magus.'

Winter battled to process it all. 'Why? Why would you do that, Malcolm?'

'The more you saw of the power of this world the more you believed. The more you believed the stronger you were. I knew what I was doing. Pity, I know. I rather liked Hatherly. He was reliable.'

'You've betrayed me,' said Winter. 'You've betrayed everyone.'

'I set the snare. I hooked you in, back in London. Portobello, to be precise. And then I placed you on the board, like a good little rook, and the game was on. You fought the Russians on my behalf. You found this godforsaken place for me. And you guided me here, as I knew you would, given a chance, because you're exceptional. I haven't betrayed you, Christopher. I've wielded you.'

Another commando had entered the nave as Malcolm was talking. He wore wire-framed lenses and had the preoccupied air of a technician. He wheeled a compact khaki-coloured machine, roughly the size of a small upright cabinet.

The soldier rested the apparatus against one of the central columns. And then he unfolded a hinged metal plate to expose a copper-fronted display, all illuminated glass and quivering needles. The clutter of dials implied it was some kind of field radio, distinctly more advanced than the Soviet model in the monk's quarters. The trooper flipped a switch and the machine emitted a high, urgent whine, its array of dials simmering with electricity. It looked utterly incongruous against the ancient stone.

Malcolm strode over and handed the book to the radio operator. The man began to leaf through it, nodding as Malcolm's lean, emphatic finger indicated certain of the runes. The soldier slipped on a pair of headphones and pushed a cable jack into the side of the device. He rested the book on top of the unit, its pages splayed.

Karina watched it all. She flashed a cautioning look to Winter.

'Do you know what Dee called this place?' asked Malcolm, amiably, returning to Winter. 'The basilica of the burning star! They did so love their strange portents in the heavens, those chaps. And now, of course, we have placed our own stars in the firmament.'

Malcolm tilted his jaw, his gaze rising to the vaulted ceiling and, it seemed, the sky beyond.

'Telstar 1. Telstar 2. And, as of this month, Telstar 3, though that one we've managed to keep a little more hush-hush. We can do discretion when it suits us. Not everything needs to be a flag-waving opportunity.'

'Telstar? Communications satellites?' said Winter, nonplussed.

'Exactly. We have forged new stars, Christopher, and cast them into orbit around this planet of ours. The white heat of twentieth-century technology, up there in the heavens, circling over us, higher than the towers of our cities. It's a rather grand feeling, the future, isn't it?' He smiled, ironically. 'God save the New Elizabethans!'

The technician unlocked a drawer at the front of the machine. It slid from the cabinet, revealing a keyboard almost like a typewriter's. There was no alphabet embossed on the brass keys, just an array of shapes – strokes, slashes, curves. Edges of squares, slivers of triangles, broken halves of circles. Mathematical fragments. The operator nudged his glasses to the bridge of his nose, squinting as he studied the runes in the grimoire. And then, meticulously, intently, he began to type.

Malcolm's gaze swept the remains of the bone circle, contemptuous.

'They say our empire's in decline, don't they? But we're not the ones playing ju-ju with the bones of saints in 1963. Jesus, they may have nuclear warheads but just look at their magecraft. They're barely more advanced than witch doctors.'

There was a chatter of type. A thin strip of copper spooled from the rear of the machine. It was stamped with symbols. Dee and Kelly's glyphs, enshrined on the ticker-tape. The technician had created a sequence of runes from careful application of the keys, assembling the shapes fragment by fragment.

The man glanced at Malcolm, clearly reluctant to take his eyes from the device for more than a second.

'Relay bounce commencing, sir,' he stated, a trace of awe in his voice for all his attempt at terse military professionalism. 'Kressbronn listening post transmitting to Goonhilly Earth Station in Cornwall, closed frequency. Telecommand sequence will be received by helical antennae in approximately two minutes. Signal override will occur in approximately four minutes.'

Malcolm nodded, satisfied. And then he turned to Winter again. 'The Elizabethans used obsidian scrying stones to commune with the great beyond. All they were really doing was transmitting and receiving signals. And that's just what we're doing, only with infinitely more power. Beaming Dee and Kelly's runes to the stars. There's an obsidian–plated transponder at the heart of each satellite. White fire, black glass. The principle's exactly the same. Only the technology's changed.'

He relished his next words. 'And this time we have the power to truly bring them into our world. Not just as visions, glimpsed by sorcerers. A sacred presence that will stand among us. Naturally we shall welcome them in the name of Her Majesty.'

'Signal encode complete, sir,' said the radio operator. 'Pulse modulation commencing.'

There was a new sound from the transmitter. A shrill, ascending oscillation. A fresh cluster of lights lit up.

'Telstar's a massive project, Malcolm,' said Winter. 'You're not doing this alone, are you?'

'Of course not. There are plenty of us in government and industry furious at what's been allowed to happen to our empire. You've seen it for yourself, Christopher. Our influence has absolutely corroded since the war. Too many politicians content to put the wishes of other countries first. Independence. Immigration. Every fashionable rallying cry chipping away at our nation's strength. Soon we'll be a tiny, frightened island, bullied by the big boys. Is that really how you want this century to play out? I don't. Today we have an opportunity to correct that course. A chance to ensure the British Empire endures into the next century and beyond.'

He indulged a seraphic smile. 'We shall build Jerusalem. A new world, burning and glorious.'

'Telecommand sequence received,' said the operator, raising his voice above the growing thrum and whistle of the machine. 'Orbital alignment complete. Two minutes to signal override.'

'And this is the way you build a new world?' countered Karina. 'By opening Hell?'

Malcolm dipped into his jacket pocket, reaching for his hip flask. He took a swig then wiped his mouth, wincing as the whisky stung his split lip.

'They came to me as angels,' he said, simply.

'The Ascendance are far from angels,' said Karina, exasperated. 'Why don't you try and understand what they really are? What you're about to do?'

Malcolm swallowed another swill of whisky before pocketing the flask. 'I said they came to me as angels. When I was a child. They were beautiful. Their power was beautiful. You know how you can sense power in ice? In a glacier? Something immensely still and clear and old but you know it can reshape a landscape, given time? That's just how they seemed to me.'

He smiled again, more fondly this time. 'They came to William Blake too, you know. They're quite the inspiration.'

Malcolm returned his attention to Winter. His voice was lower now, more confidential, as if he was sharing some private understanding between the pair of them. The whisky clung to his breath.

'You knew them too, Tobias.'

The technician spoke again. 'Final telemetry authenticated. Signal override confirmed. Telstar 1, Telstar 2, Telstar 3. Transponders locked.'

Winter fixed his gaze against Malcolm's. 'My name is Christopher Winter.'

'I know. I christened you. It seemed appropriate. Winter's the season that buries everything, after all. The one that makes the world blank and white. But your real name is Tobias Hart.'

Winter caught a sound then. At first he thought it was a whispering among the stones of the basilica. And then he

realised it was coming from beyond the building's walls, a sibilance loud enough to be heard above the whine and hum of the machine. He stared through the windows of the transept, searching for the source of the noise.

Outside, the lake itself was hissing. The water was churning, broiling, seething into steam.

'Your name is Tobias Hart,' repeated Malcolm. 'You were the single greatest warlock this century has known. Wilful, unpredictable and quite devastatingly powerful. Sometimes magic itself seemed to cower from you. You were a great asset to us in the war. I also counted you as a friend.'

There was a sudden, oppressive energy in the old church. Everyone assembled in the nave could feel it against their skin. A tangible force, potent as a waiting storm, pushing against the atoms of the air, as if willing them to shatter, to explode, to release it into the world. Something unseen but insistent. Something that demanded existence.

'Naturally we named this project Operation Magus. It was only fitting.'

As the lake roared and boiled around the basilica great gusts of heat swept the length of the nave. Beads of moisture clung to the stonework before streaming down the high walls. In seconds every surface of the monastery had a slick, weeping gleam, like fast-thawing ice.

Malcolm quickened his words. 'In 1947 we found you in Africa, half dead. Technically you were dead. Briefly. A near-death experience, they call it. The great tunnel,

the white light. You flatlined. Your soul had been severed from your body. The doctors in that squalid little field hospital managed to revive you. But not all of your soul came back.'

Winter wanted to run, to push this all away. But there was an inescapable weight of truth to what Malcolm was saying. He knew that now.

'Part of you was left behind. Part of you – perhaps the best part – has been missing ever since.'

Winter simply stared at Malcolm. The same bloody words rumbled inside his skull, triumphant. *We are the Half-Claimed Man...*

Beyond the window the lake erupted, throwing scalding funnels of water into the sky. The furious heat filled the church.

'Don't you see?' said Malcolm. 'This isn't life that you have now, Tobias. It's taxidermy.'

In the centre of the nave a whirl of white flame tore into existence, the light at its heart as bleak as ice, as brilliant as a sun. The circle of fire revolved, carving itself out of the air. Winter stared at it. It looked like a rupture in the skin of the world.

'I think it's high time you met the man you were,' said Malcolm. 'He's waiting for you.'

There was a scream that bled into an electric shriek of overwhelmed circuitry. The transmitter had exploded, its dials shattering. Winter turned and saw the operator's charred body, the man's limbs spasming as life burned out of them. His uniform was shredded,

his spectacles cracked and blackened. It was as if some immense surge of energy had filled him, channelled by the machine. It wasn't any kind of earthly voltage, Winter knew.

The book, too, was smouldering, wreathed in thick, dark smoke.

Malcolm didn't flinch. 'Ignore it!'

The halo of white fire widened, deepened, blazing even more fiercely now as it eclipsed the altar. It was an opening, Winter realised, staring into the bright, blank abyss. A portal. A gateway.

He had seen it before. It was the white light that lay beyond life.

Malcolm gave a crisp snap of his fingers. Winter was thrust closer to the ring of flame. The commandos forced him down by the shoulders until he was on his knees, his body buckling. He raised his eyes, the heat of the uncanny fire on his face. There were shapes emerging. Figures were forming, coalescing out of the rage of light, their bodies sculpted from the pure white flame. They were dazzling, incandescent. Winter had to tear his eyes away. It hurt even to glimpse them.

They shone like the first morning.

And then, his eyes smarting with sweat, he forced himself to look. His eyelids were slits, screwed tight against the brilliance, but he tried to focus on the central figure, the one who stood in front of the others. He felt sick with dread but he let his eyes open, the lids trembling as they widened.

He saw Tobias Hart. He saw himself.

'Oh dear lord,' said the man with his face, smirking broadly. 'We've rather let ourselves go, haven't we?'

32

Winter wanted to recoil but the blazing figure transfixed him.

'My God,' he whispered, incredulous.

It was like gazing into a mirror only to find a memory staring back. A dim, nebulous memory, but one that became sharper the more he looked at it. It was his own face but it was as strange as it was familiar.

He knew his face. He knew the creases in the skin, the telltale grooves, the contour lines of experience accrued across the decades. This shimmering, phantasmic reflection had none of that detail, nothing of the forty-six-year-old man he had become. The features were his own, yes, but younger, smoother, not quite so hard around the jawline. He saw a bright boyishness he couldn't imagine he'd ever possessed.

The smile, too, belonged to a different man. There was a curl at the edges of the mouth, a hint of something arrogant, potentially cruel, as if the muscles were animated by altogether darker impulses. Winter had seen that smile before, he realised. The faded black-and-white

photo that Harzner had shown him in Krabbehaus, the one he had no memory of ever being taken. The two of them together, smiling hugely.

He had sudden, absolute recall of the moment captured in that picture. Aschaffenburg, 1946. A grand party beneath a high summer moon. It was vivid enough to taste, to feel, to inhale: the sour trace of Goldwasser liqueur on Harzner's breath, the swampy clutch of his handshake, the final, agonised scream of that evening's entertainment...

Winter shook himself free of the memory, repulsed by what he remembered. Just what kind of man had he been?

'A man who was never afraid to trade morality for strength.'

Tobias Hart had spoken again. The voice was Winter's own, only lighter, more sardonic, almost playful. Winter heard it just as much inside his skull as echoing around the nave.

'I mean, do come on. A squeamish assassin? I've never heard of such a thing.'

Hart was floating above the flagstones, dressed in a six-buttoned double-breasted suit, its flamboyant cut belonging to the 1940s. The thread of the tweed glinted as though woven out of light. The other shining beings rose behind him, impossible even to glimpse now that they were fully manifested. Winter sensed rather than saw them, a shudder of something unearthly at the edge of his vision. He had no idea if they were angels or fallen angels or demons who had stolen the

names of angels but even their shadows were searingly, blindingly beautiful.

Winter kept his eyes on Hart, convinced they would turn to ash if he so much as glanced at the Ascendance. 'You're not me,' he said, less emphatically than he wanted. 'I have no idea what you are but you're not me. You're not who I am.'

Hart laughed, indulgently. 'Oh, you brave little husk of a man. So adorably spirited. I'm rather proud of what I left behind.'

'You are not who I am!' Winter protested again, louder, more adamantly. 'We're not the same man! My name is Christopher Winter!'

Hart regarded him. The mischief in his face was gone, replaced by something colder, more determined.

'No, my name is Tobias Hart. You, on the other hand, are a cage of meat and bone. I'm going to take your flesh. You will be my body in this world. I will walk in you.'

Winter fought to understand the words, to grasp their implication. 'And what happens to me?' he demanded. 'What happens to me when you take my body?'

Hart gave him a sharp, disdainful look, as if losing patience with a slow child. 'I'm simply reclaiming what's rightfully mine. I'm sure you can comprehend that if you try.'

Malcolm stepped an inch or two closer to the maw of light. Some of his usual assurance had gone. He seemed apprehensive as he approached the spectral figure of Hart. The scent of whisky leaked through his pores.

'I brought him to you, Tobias. Just as I promised I would. Just as I said.'

Hart turned to appraise Malcolm, as if perceiving the SIS man's presence for the first time. 'You brought him, did you? I rather imagine he found me himself.'

Winter could hear Hart's words a beat before they were spoken. Somehow they were already inside his head, echoing in anticipation, almost persuading him that they were his own. He wanted to shake them out of his skull.

Hart spread his hands. They trailed a pale shimmer of fire, leaving a burning after-image in the air. 'Malcolm. Dear friend. Here I am, so nearly in the flesh.'

There was no warmth to the words but Malcolm smiled anyway, a sheen of sweat above his lips. 'We're close now, Tobias. Everything we've always worked towards. Jerusalem!'

Hart's eyes were like shards of emerald, clear, hard and bright. There was a sense of immense power compacted in the pupils, like lightning crushed into specimen jars. They sparked and they glimmered.

'Jerusalem!' he echoed, derisively. 'O clouds unfold!'

Malcolm nodded vigorously, missing the scorn in Hart's voice. 'We always dreamed of it, Tobias! A new world to burn away the ruins and the filth of this one! A world where you would lead us! The greatest warlock of the century! This is just how we planned it!'

Hart paused, pursing his lips in mock deliberation. 'Oh. Was that the plan? I rather thought the plan involved me dying in considerable pain in some

miserable little corner of South West Africa. No?'

Malcolm made to reply but his throat clutched at his words. 'I… Tobias…'

'You wanted me dead, Malcolm. You wanted me dead for quite some time.'

Malcolm shook his head, emphatically. He forced himself to find his voice again. 'That's not true,' he insisted. 'We were always friends! Why would I want you dead?'

Hart's gaze was accusatory. 'I was simply an asset to you. And all good assets are potential liabilities. We both know that. I think I frightened you, Malcolm. And if I didn't frighten you I certainly frightened Whitehall.'

A preternatural energy seethed in Hart's eyes. 'Somebody clearly feared my ideological sympathies might drift one day. As if such choices concerned me. What's politics compared to magic, after all? Why would I choose between East and West when I could learn to tear a man apart with a single thought?'

'The service valued you. I valued you.'

'You sent me to Windhoek,' spat Hart, cutting across Malcolm's words with a sudden, clipped fury. 'It was your intelligence I was following!'

'It was solid intelligence!' protested Malcolm. Behind him the commandos nervously hitched their guns.

'Absolutely solid,' hissed Hart. 'You knew what I would find there, Malcolm. You knew exactly who would be waiting for me in Africa. It was an immaculate trap, I'll grant you that. Pity I spoilt your plan by not actually dying. Deeply selfish of me, I realise.'

'I swear to you, Tobias, I had no idea! I would never have sent you there if I'd known!'

Malcolm took another tentative step across the stone floor, as if to stress his loyalty. 'And besides,' he continued, betrayed by sweat, 'why would I go to all this trouble now if I wanted you dead?'

'Because you're an opportunist, Malcolm. It's your traditional career path. You saw the chance I had to return to this world, to rule it in the name of the Ascendance. And you wanted to be part of it. You wanted to walk in my shadow, as ever. Well, my shadow's a pretty dark place, *dear heart*.'

Malcolm backed away from the burning figure. 'You came to me in visions,' he said, a trace of hurt in his voice now. 'Just like an angel. You promised me our Jerusalem. All I had to do was reunite you with your body. I've done that! I've brought it here!'

Hart smiled again, more cruelly. There was a pale dance of flame at the edges of his mouth.

'Bring me my bow of burning gold! Bring me my arrows of desire! Always so obsessed with Blake, weren't you? All those quaint notions he had of Heaven and Hell. I should share my own notions with you, Malcolm. They're a little more informed. Personal experience, you know. Hard won.'

Malcolm hesitated. For all that he was afraid the thought clearly captivated him.

His eyelids flickered. 'Tell me,' he asked, softly. 'Tell me about Hell.'

'Of course, Malcolm. Of course I will. But first I think we need to establish a common frame of reference, don't you?'

Hart raised his left hand, clenching it into a fist. Vicious white flames swarmed around it.

'Let me broaden your concept of Hell.'

Winter felt his body quiver as he watched. There was an electric shudder in his muscles, as if he was sharing in the unearthly energy that Hart was summoning. It felt seductive. The faintest shiver of power, deep in his bones. He hated how it made him feel.

Malcolm staggered back, staring in horrified fascination at the fire swelling around Hart's hand. Hart tightened his fist and Malcolm's body was wracked by a fierce spasm, one that seized his spine and tugged it taut. Malcolm writhed, wrapping his arms around his chest as if trying to suppress something massing inside him.

His shirt flooded with blood. Tusks of bone pierced the cotton, carving their way through his flesh. The ribs were being plucked from his body, cracked apart inside him and pulled out of his torso like spears.

Malcolm screamed. And he continued to scream as his face tore like fabric, exposing the clutter of teeth and muscle and ganglia that pulsed beneath his skin. Soon all that was left of his mouth was the throat that had been ripped through his jaws.

Malcolm crumpled, hitting the ground in a slop of blood and body parts, spilling out of a Savile Row suit. His fingers poured over the flagstones, a wet mess of tissue

and nerve endings crowned by a gleaming set of knuckles.

Malcolm Hands had been torn inside out.

Winter stared at the remains. Part of him felt repelled. Part of him – a part he didn't even want to acknowledge – felt exultant. He could still taste the power that Hart had invoked. It was intoxicating.

He finally glanced away. Karina was looking at him across the church, her face grave. For a moment he couldn't meet her eyes.

'Well,' said Hart, matter-of-factly. 'I trust that was theologically illuminating for you, Malcolm.'

The commandos opened fire, their Bren guns flashing. The bullets simply melted in the air, dripping in a spatter of lead to the floor.

Hart seemed to regard this development as deeply tedious. He opened his fist and the circle of flame expanded behind him. The swirl of white fire quickened its revolution. The portal pulled the soldiers towards it, a strange gravity dragging their bodies across the flagstones. They kept firing even as their boots skidded closer to the burning maw. And then, their guns still flashing, the men disintegrated, atomised by flame. There wasn't even dust where their bodies had been.

Hart turned to Winter. He extended a hand. 'Come now,' he said. 'I think it's time.'

Winter hesitated. He saw Karina moving across the nave towards him. He turned his head away from her. As if compelled he raised his left hand to Hart. Their fingers were perfectly mirrored. He wanted to refuse the

hand but it was part of him. He knew that now. And it promised so much. Hart's voice was like honey in his skull. *Take our hand*, it told him. *It will complete us. Make us whole. Make us one. We will be alive. Finally alive.*

Winter reached out, almost without conscious thought. He touched the hand. There was a shock of contact.

The unholy fire permeated his body. It suffused him. He could feel the light surge in his blood, blaze in his veins. His heart throbbed like a sun. And he could taste it all – the thump of every last pulse inside him, the burning rush in his capillaries, the sway of the tiny hairs in his skin. Even the saliva on his tongue was impossibly sweet.

No! It was Hart who was experiencing this, Hart who had stolen his senses, Hart who was finally tasting life again. The two of them were fusing, fire and flesh. Now even their thoughts were merging, becoming one.

As Winter convulsed he fought to preserve himself – everything that defined him, everything he knew as Christopher Winter – but the power that raced through his bones was exhilarating. Part of him wanted to surrender to it, to know it absolutely.

He inhaled, a hungry drag of breath, deep into his lungs. He could smell the lingering cordite of the soldiers' guns, the burnt flesh of the radio operator, the sickly organic aroma of Malcolm's remains. And there was something else, too. The scent of tamarind. A perfume. Karina's perfume, he remembered. She was close to him.

He tried to look at her but his eyes were elsewhere.

He saw a man's body, some distance below him. The

vision was hazy at first but it soon solidified. He seemed to be floating above this man, higher than the ceiling fan whose slats made a rhythmic sweep through thick, sticky air. He felt detached, an observer.

The figure was sprawled on a canvas bed, one arm flung to the side, the other locked to his left thigh. He was bare-chested and there was a blood-blackened wound in his abdomen. The man was alive, but barely, the slow rise and shudder of his chest the only sign that he was still breathing.

It was Hart's body, he realised. And then he caught himself. No. It was his body, lying on a makeshift bed in a cramped, half-lit operating room. The sheet was spattered with blood. There was an insect drone in the air and a heavy, fetid heat. This was Africa. That desperate little desert hospital.

Now he remembered. He had died in this room.

He remembered it all. He had left the cave, stumbling into the sun, clutching the stab wound, haemorrhaging life with every step across the sand. A party of Dutch geologists had found him, quite by chance. They had laid him in their truck, put water to his lips and driven like devils across the dunes. The medical station had been part of a former German colony, all but abandoned. He was delirious when they reached its door, murmuring about angels, and vengeance.

He saw an oxygen mask clasped to his face, fogged with moisture. A ramshackle array of catheters and surgical drips surrounded his body. One tube punctured his side, draining fluid from the wound. The transparent

plastic was yellowed with age and smudged with grime. Another tube delivered plasma from a bag mounted on a metal pole. The bag clenched and unfurled as it pumped. Beyond the bed corroded medical equipment thrummed and wheezed and sporadically bleeped. The entire room felt stained with rust and disease.

Three surgeons hovered over him in green gowns, their faces obscured by surgical masks. The thin fabric clutched their teeth as they breathed. The lead surgeon held a scalpel and used it to bat away a mosquito before plunging into the wound again. Their voices were low, the language impenetrable but the urgency of their words unmistakable. In the background was the steady electronic pulse of the heart monitor.

The pulse abruptly changed tone. Now it was a harsh, insistent whine. It cut through the voices of the surgeons, the loudest sound in the room. The upward tick of light on the monitor display became a flat line, the white horizon that declared death. The surgeons huddled over the body, a flap of hands and medical tools. The whine of the monitor became louder, more piercing, a screech that built in pitch until it seemed to drill through the world...

He was elsewhere again.

At first he thought he was blind. And then he realised he was suspended in total, perfect darkness. It encompassed him like a black womb. It felt still and silent and serene. No sound, no motion. No breath. He didn't even have a heartbeat here.

It was death and it held him. He wanted it to hold him forever.

There was a sudden, soundless flare of white fire. It tore open the darkness, atomically bright. He had no idea if the light was above or below him – there was no sense of such things in this place – but he felt himself moving towards it, the black void forming a tunnel around him. The white light was waiting and he knew exactly what it was. It was the light beyond life. It was eternity.

He smiled and gave himself to its radiance.

And then something grabbed him.

A hand had locked itself around his leg. It had come cleaving out of the darkness, a hand that had altogether too many fingers. It clutched him like a current. A throng of hands followed it, equally set on snatching him away from the light. The numberless fingers of the countless hands coiled and tightened.

The white fire began to recede. It became a pinprick of brilliance in the distance. Now he knew exactly which direction he was moving in. The mob of hands was hauling him down. He felt a gathering heat. It was inside him, throughout him. It was as if his soul itself was blistering. He plummeted, burning as he fell.

Hell had claimed him.

Tamarind. He could smell tamarind.

Winter was back in the basilica. He saw Karina standing in front of him, her face close to his, alarmed but determined. She had seized his lapels and was trying to shake him free from whatever force had overwhelmed him.

He grasped her hands. He could feel Hart rising inside him, demanding existence. He had no idea how much time he had now but in this moment he was Christopher Winter. And he had a choice.

'We have to stop this.'

Another convulsion rocked his body. His head jerked back. Karina kept hold of him, steadied his arms.

'How do we do that?'

Winter had to force the next words through his teeth, defying every instinct in his body.

'Kill me.'

She shook her head, emphatically. 'No. I'm not doing that. I'm not doing that!'

His hands encircled her wrists. 'Get a gun. Get a knife. Use whatever you need. Just kill me. It's the only way we can stop this. Do it!'

Karina broke his grip. 'I'm not killing you, Christopher!' She stepped away from him. 'We can undo this.'

Winter indicated the burnt-out radio behind them. 'Look at it! It's destroyed!'

'We can find a way!'

'There's no time! Karina, you've got to do it! Kill me before he takes this body!'

There was a pale blaze in his pupils now. White fire. 'Please,' he implored her. 'Kill me. End it.'

She looked at him a moment longer, a decision building in her eyes. And then, with a cold certainty of purpose, she walked over to Malykh's body and picked up the obsidian knife that had fallen to the ground. She

weighed the weapon in her hand. And then she crossed back to him, her face emotionless.

Winter watched her raise the knife. He saw the reflected glare of the Ascendance dance on its edge, a dazzle of light. As she turned the black blade towards him he had a sudden, striking memory. He saw Joe Griggs, strapped to that sacrificial wheel in Krabbehaus, a knife at his chest...

'Wait!' he hissed.

The blade was perfectly still in her hand.

Winter tore his shirt open. His chest was heaving as he breathed. Karina saw the vicious thread of scar tissue on his abdomen.

'This is how they do it, right? How they channel the magic? You said they carved the symbols in people's bodies. You told me it was the most powerful magic in the world. Well, that knife's obsidian. That's what you need, isn't it? Carve the symbols in me! Send this bastard back to Hell!'

Karina shot him a protesting look. 'I have no idea what symbols to use!'

'There must have been something in the book! Something you saw!'

She shook her head, frustrated. 'They were summoning runes... They can't repel. Why would the Ascendance give Dee the means to banish them?'

'He would have found a way. Him and Kelly. They were smart. They would have had a safeguard. A defence. Maybe it's here...'

Their eyes tore around the basilica, the walls and the arches, the arcades and the aisles. They looked at it all, the wooden crosses and the marble finials and the carved motifs of martyrs' faces. There was too much church to find anything in.

'They would have given us a clue,' said Winter. 'Like that coin he gave me...'

Karina heard his words as she scoured the church. And then she paused. And she walked away from him, quickening her pace as she crossed the nave. Keeping Malykh's knife in her hand she reached down and retrieved the jewelled skull of Saint Cenric, scooping it up by the jawbone.

She strode back to Winter, proffering the relic.

'The face on the coin,' she said. 'The saint wasn't praying. He was hiding his eyes.'

She took the knife and worked its tip into the pits of the skull. The blade slid beneath the sapphires that had been wedged in the eye sockets. In moments she had prised the gems from the bone hollows. She tossed the skull to the ground and let the sapphires roll on her palm. There was a tiny glyph etched into the back of each stone. The language of fire.

'You were right,' she smiled. 'A safeguard.'

The glare of the Ascendance filled the basilica. Winter had an impression of vast white wings unfurling. Their brilliance burned at the edges of his eyes. There were no more shadows now. Only the light of the Ascendance, a light that would claim the world.

'Quickly,' he hissed. 'Do it!'

Karina thrust the knife towards him. And then she hesitated, clearly unwilling to put the blade to his body.

'You're going to feel it,' he told her, his voice as calm as he could make it. 'Just keep going. Whatever happens, don't be afraid of it.'

Karina nodded, numbly. She gathered her resolve, tightening her grip on the hilt.

The blade punctured Winter's skin. He grimaced as the obsidian tip sliced into him, cold and insistent. It moved across his chest, dragging the incision sideways. A bright ribbon of blood rose to the surface and trailed behind the blade. It had a rich scent, coppery and sweet.

The knife continued its arc. Karina glanced again at the sapphires, memorising each crucial stroke of the runes. And then she threw the gems to the ground and seized the hilt in both hands, pushing the blade's edge deeper into Winter's chest. His blood ran on her fingers, sticky and warm.

Winter screamed as his flesh tore. The obsidian was pitilessly sharp. It scored him like razor wire. He felt Karina lift the knife away but it was only a momentary relief. Seconds later it pierced him again, carving a new and equally bloody arc.

He reached for her wrists, wanting to stop her, to wrest the knife away. But it was Hart he could feel in his hands, Hart who was fighting to live. Winter forced his fingers away from her. They snatched at empty air, spasming in shock.

The blade moved quickly. Karina's face was determined. She overlaid the second symbol on the first, creating a conjoined glyph on Winter's body. Outlined in blood, a moon encircled two mirrored triangles, the disparate shapes united by three undulating lines, like waves. She kept the blade moving, her mouth locked tight, her hands rigid around the hilt.

Winter flailed, his body protesting. It wasn't just the pain of the black knife tearing through his skin. Each cut burned as if his soul was being seared.

Hart was inside him, one with his flesh.

Karina made a final wound, a long diagonal incision that completed the rune. And then she stood back, repulsed by what she had done, and flung the knife to the flagstones.

Winter crashed to his knees. His chest ran with blood. He threw his arms behind him, his ribs pushing against his bare skin as he took air into his lungs.

The rune began to glow, every carved, bloodied line gleaming with white fire.

A surge of energy struck his chest, punching through him. It lit every nerve, every blood cell. Winter howled as it pierced him, consumed him. He was a conduit now, a channel for this unearthly force.

He could hear Hart's voice in his head, louder than the pain. It was raging, crying for life.

Winter's body buckled, the glyph of blood blazing on his chest. It felt as though his soul was being severed in two. The agony was almost unendurable, a pain that was

beyond the body, beyond the physical limitations of the flesh, a pain that terrified him because he had no idea if it would ever end.

A final, anguished scream filled his skull. And then, still raging, still defiant, Tobias Hart was torn out of him and cast back to Hell, forever.

Winter trembled. The fire and the pain had left his body. The man that he had been was gone.

The circle of white flame roared and then vanished. There was a rush of wind where the burning maw had been. It seemed to snatch all the light from the church. All that remained of the Ascendance was an after-image, a pale, wraithlike echo of great white wings and shining eyes. The vision lingered, like the sun imprinted on a retina. And then that too was gone.

Winter collapsed to the ground. He lay there, his face on the floor of the nave, hearing his own breathing. He pressed his chest against the cold stone, relishing its chill against his raw skin. His eyes adjusted to the sudden gloom. The shadows slowly disclosed their shapes. He watched as the marble columns came into focus, emerging out of the grey.

And then he gathered himself and got to his feet. Karina moved to help him but he pushed past her, making for the tall wooden door at the basilica's entrance. He staggered towards it, knocking into the scattered pews, his legs betraying him.

He put a hand to the heavy old door and stumbled into morning. The daylight made his eyes run and the

shock of Alpine air scraped his throat. Winter kept walking, away from the ruined monastery, over the stone path and its weeds, his chest dripping blood on the snow.

He took it all in. The sky seemed limitless above the eternal peaks of the Alps. It was dizzying, infinitely blue. This world was suddenly all too big. He slumped to his knees, shivering as his shirt flapped around him, the wind from the lake on his body. He barely registered Karina running after him, calling a name that didn't belong to him now.

He had nothing. No self, no identity. No memories he could ever claim as his own. Christopher Winter had been a chain of lies, a life written by Malcolm Hands. Tobias Hart's memories belonged to someone who had worn his face and done terrible things, a long time ago. Both those men were strangers. Whoever he was, whatever he called himself, he was a blank. Hollow inside, Malykh had said. And that's what he was. He knew that now.

Karina's arms were around him.

He looked up at her, searching her face, his eyes lost.

'Just one memory,' he said, his words breaking as she cradled him. 'Just give me one bloody memory that's mine…'

She put her mouth to his and she kissed him. Her lips were like fruit.

She was warm and she was close and there was tamarind in her hair. He clung to her and willed the fear

and the horror away. The pain began to ebb.

They held each other in the church's shadow as the lake mist found them.

33

He had found the invitation the day he had placed lilies on Joyce's grave.

It had been tucked in front of her headstone, wedged in the damp, sweet-smelling earth. A corner of the card had been eaten by the rain but the words were still legible, even though the ink had run. Russian words, scrawled in Cyrillic script. He could just about translate them.

Come to tea, the invitation had read. *Don't be late.* There was a time and an address.

Pocketing the card he had put a hand to the freshly inscribed marble, wondering just who he was paying his respects to. The grave was probably empty, after all, more a memorial to Malcolm's subterfuge than the woman he had once loved. Whoever had played Joyce Winter had doubtlessly been laid to rest elsewhere, buried under her true name. The fiction of her death would have been immaculately constructed, naturally, the details of her demise neat and watertight. The service would have seen to that. Anything to keep the great machinery of shadows intact.

He had placed the flowers against the headstone and then he had walked away, past the stone cherubs and the mossy war graves and out through the gates of the sprawling Victorian cemetery by Mitcham Common.

Now, a fortnight later, he descended the stairs that led to a Westminster tea room, keeping the rendezvous arranged by the card. He felt intrigued and wary, not entirely sure what to expect from this encounter. Why had she summoned him? He hadn't seen her since the events in Bavaria. What did she want?

He entered the basement dining area, pushing through tall glass doors stencilled with roses. The walnut-panelled room smelt of tobacco, tea and sweet pastry and had the unmistakable hum of London money. People ate cake and made low-key conversation, barely louder than the chinking of their china.

She was waiting for him in the far corner.

'There you are,' said the Widow of Kursk.

The demon sat at the table, perfectly poised, black eyes bright behind the lace mesh of her veil. As ever a discreet malevolence surrounded her. She raised a gloved hand and indicated the vacant chair, beckoning him over. 'Do join me, Tobias.'

'I don't go by that name,' he told her, taking the seat. 'Not anymore.'

A smile rose on her bloodless lips. 'Really? So what do you call yourself, might I ask?'

'Christopher Winter. It's as good a name as any.'

'I don't think I'll ever get used to calling you that.'

It was Winter's turn to smile. His was tight and defensive. 'Well, that shouldn't be a problem. I'd like to believe this is the last time we see one another.'

'I'm sure you would.' She made a show of forming the next word. 'Christopher.'

Winter glanced at the sugar bowl, distracted by a glimpse of black among the glistening white. Looking closer he saw that there were three dead flies on the neatly piled cubes. Another fly was scaling the tongs, unsteady on the silver, its wings quivering.

'Such terribly small deaths,' said the Widow, observing them too. 'Not even their parasites mourn them. I certainly can't dine on their passing. Now a city the size of London, with one of those beautiful new bombs…'

She moved her eyes to him again. 'I'm surprised you came. You must know I could kill you.'

'Well, I can't imagine I'd receive a formal invitation to my own funeral.'

'A fair point. But I'd hate to be predictable.'

Winter leaned forward, determined to keep this conversation short. 'So why did you ask me here?'

She made a sympathetic pout beneath the lace. 'Concern. And curiosity. What do you intend to do with yourself?'

'I'm not entirely sure.'

'Are the SIS aware you're back in London?'

Winter grimaced. 'I've managed to evade them so far. Who knows how much luck I have left.'

'Will you return to the service? I imagine your

country still has a use for your talent.'

'Killing people isn't a talent.'

'A skill, then,' said the demon, sharply.

Winter shook his head. 'It was a job. It's not one I'd choose again.'

'Moral qualms? With your past? Pity. I was going to offer you a partnership.'

Winter shot her a look of genuine surprise, his eyebrows steepening. 'A partnership?'

The Widow nodded. 'Think of it. An assassin. And a creature who feeds on mourning. A perfect symbiosis, wouldn't you say?'

Winter snorted, his eyes on the other patrons, watching as a businessman charmed his mistress over a plate of scones. 'You could kill everyone in this room. You don't need me.'

She grinned, exposing a row of kitten teeth. 'I know. But I want you to be fulfilled too.'

Winter regarded her evenly. 'It's a kind offer. But I'm sure I'll get by. And besides, I don't need a parasite.'

There was amusement on the pale, ageless face behind the veil. 'Well, doubtlessly I shall be sated. I find myself in a time that slays a young president, after all. Poor Mr Kennedy. So much hope stolen from the world, so much to mourn. And these new weapons you men build. Such wicked and clever things. I imagine I won't run short of grief in the years ahead.'

Something very old and very dark moved in her eyes. 'The Greeks knew me as the Widow of Troy, the English

the Widow of Agincourt. In the revolution I was the Widow of Paris. History has rarely disappointed me.'

She rested a glove on Winter's hand. He could feel the chill of her ungodly flesh burning through the velvet.

'But listen,' she said. 'What will you do, really?'

Winter shrugged. 'To be honest I think I'll keep my head down for a while.'

The Widow mulled this. 'That may be very wise. You crossed a lot of people in your time. Made plenty of enemies in your youth. Some of them must still be out there. I doubt they've forgotten you. A baroness with a mahogany hand, for instance. What was her name?'

Winter averted his eyes. 'I wouldn't know.'

'Antonia,' said the demon, brightly, delighted to have recalled the name. 'Yes, that was it. The English girl. She turned somewhat bitter after what you did to her. And who can blame her? It's not easily forgiven. I'd certainly watch your back.'

'Consider me warned.'

Winter rose from the table, buttoning his coat. It was time to end this. She made his skin shiver, like the first shudder of autumn blown in by a summer wind, a promise of dead leaves.

'Tell me one thing,' he asked. 'Those creatures. The Almost. Are they still hunting me?'

The Widow paused, considering the question. 'I'm not sure. Possibly not. I imagine you might have confused them. There's probably no one else alive who's

willingly sent part of their soul to Hell. One thing I do know, though.'

Winter listened.

'When the day comes your death will taste delicious. A truly unique flavour. I look forward to feasting on the grief of someone who loves you.'

Winter peered into the Widow's veil, searching for the eyes. 'I do hope I don't disappoint you.'

He strode out of the tea room. As he approached the glass-panelled door he caught sight of the demon's reflection. A second later it had gone, replaced by a crack in the pane, newly splintered. Winter glanced back. The Widow's chair was empty.

Frost glistened on the clock face of Big Ben, catching the last light of the afternoon.

Winter stepped on to Westminster Bridge, hearing its iron span shudder as black cabs and Routemasters trundled across the river, carrying people home. There was an early moon in the London sky and the first stars hung above the spires of Parliament. A parade of gas lamps already burned along the length of the bridge.

A month ago a streak of silver, trailing fire, had torn through the heavens above the capital, crossing Highgate and Kensington and arcing over Mortlake, where John Dee's spirit-haunted warren of a house once stood. A dying satellite, people had guessed. Maybe a wounded Telstar, cast out of orbit. That night it had felt part of an

older, darker world, an age of comets and portents. It had fallen like a burning star.

This was only a respite, Winter knew, as the evening shadows collected. A chance to take a breath, nothing more. He could sense the war around them now, waiting at the edges of the light.

Ever since Bavaria he had known something else, too.

He tugged the lambskin glove from his left hand, feeling the wind on his skin. And then he trailed his fingers in the rain that had pooled on the cast-iron balustrade, his flesh tingling at the chill of the water, the nerves pulsing inside him. He wasn't hollow. He was alive, in this moment. And he wanted it. Fearlessly.

Karina smiled in the December dusk.

'Can you see the lights?' she asked.

She was waiting beneath one of the ornate triple-lantern gas lamps, dressed for the English weather in a Cossack hat and an olive trenchcoat. Behind her the horizon glowed, the streets lit by electric angels, reindeers and snowflakes. It would soon be Christmas.

'It's what we do, isn't it,' she said. 'Burn fires into the night.'

Winter considered the skyline. 'It's what we've always done. It's how we win.'

They began to walk, over the river and its bridge of lights, into the bright old city. A black fist of birds rose above the Thames. London shone against the gathering dark.

ACKNOWLEDGEMENTS

Kerensa Creswell-Bryant, who was there on Portobello Road, where it all began; Laura diZerega, for umlauts and architecture; Johnny King, for motorcycle know-how; Elena Smolina, for Russian assistance.

Neil Gaiman, Russell T Davies, Mark Millar and Steven Moffat, for encouragement and advice.

My agent, Julie Crisp, who lit the fuse in the first place; my editor Cat Camacho at Titan Books (thank you for believing in this tall tale); Titan's equally keen-eyed Joanna Harwood; Dana Spector at Paradigm.

Mum, my family and all my friends, especially Jordan Farley, Sally Browne, Louise Blain, Jacqueline Roach and Rob Power – trusted conspirators and keepers of secrets. And, of course, the brilliant team on *SFX*, the greatest magazine on this planet or any other.

And to you, unknown but splendid reader, wherever and whenever you are. You're the electricity that powers this ghost train ride. Thank you.

ABOUT THE AUTHOR

Nick Setchfield is a writer and features editor for *SFX*, Britain's best-selling magazine of genre entertainment in film, TV and books. A regular contributing writer to *Total Film*, he's also been a movie reviewer for the BBC and a scriptwriter for ITV's *Spitting Image*. *The War in the Dark* is his first novel. He lives in Bath.

STRANGE INK
Gary Kemble

When washed-up journalist Harry Hendrick wakes with a hangover and a strange symbol tattooed on his neck, he shrugs it off as a bad night out.

But soon more tattoos appear: grisly, violent images not his own which come accompanied by visions of war-torn Afghanistan, murder, bar fights and a mysterious woman – so he begins to dig a little deeper. His search leads him to the sinister disappearance of an SAS hero and his girlfriend, whose torment is reaching back from beyond the grave.

"*Skin Deep* is a fine debut for both Kemble and Echo Publishing, which offers more than a passing nod to John Birmingham and Stephen King" *Books + Publishing*

"The novel has the crucial ingredients of the best of the genre (cracking pace, intricate plotting, irresistible intrigue) while largely evading the cheesy, overblown language of its cheaper examples" *The Saturday Paper*

"It was hard not to like a book so well written and with such a great plot. It keeps you guessing until the end" *Weekly Times*

THE HOLLOW TREE

James Brogden

WHO DANCED WITH MARY BEFORE SHE DIED?

After her hand is amputated following a tragic accident, Rachel Cooper suffers vivid nightmares of a woman imprisoned in the trunk of a hollow tree, screaming for help. When she begins to experience phantom sensations of leaves and earth with her lost hand, Rachel is terrified she is going mad… but then another hand takes hers, and the trapped woman is pulled into our world. She has no idea who she is, but Rachel can't help but think of the mystery of Oak Mary, a female corpse found in a hollow tree, and who was never identified. Three urban legends have grown up around the case; was Mary a Nazi spy, a prostitute or a gypsy witch? Rachel is desperate to learn the truth, but darker forces are at work. For a rule has been broken, and Mary is in a world where she doesn't belong…

"Nicely done" *Daily Mail*

"Brogden keeps up a steady supply of shocks and chills"
SciFi Now

"Something special and unique" Risingshadow

THE SILENCE
Tim Lebbon

In the darkness of an underground cave system, blind creatures hunt by sound. Then there is light, there are voices, and they feed... Swarming from their prison, the creatures thrive and destroy. To scream, even to whisper, is to summon death. As the hordes lay waste to Europe, a girl watches to see if they will cross the sea. Deaf for many years, she knows how to live in silence; now, it is her family's only chance of survival. To leave their home, to shun others, to find a remote haven where they can sit out the plague. But will it ever end? And what kind of world will be left?

"A truly great novel with a fresh and original story" *Starburst*

"A chilling and heart-wrenching story" *Publishers Weekly*

"*The Silence* is a chilling story that grips you firmly by the throat" *SciFi Now*

ANNO DRACULA
Kim Newman

It is 1888 and Queen Victoria has remarried, taking
as her new consort the Wallachian Prince infamously known
as Count Dracula. His polluted bloodline spreads through
London as its citizens increasingly choose to
become vampires.

In the grim backstreets of Whitechapel, a killer known as
'Silver Knife' is cutting down vampire girls. The eternally
young vampire Genevieve Dieudonne and Charles
Beauregard of the Diogenes Club are drawn together as they
both hunt the sadistic killer, bringing them ever closer to
England's most bloodthirsty ruler yet.

"Compulsory reading... glorious" Neil Gaiman

"Essential for any fan of Gothic literature" *The Guardian*

"Up there with Bram Stoker's chilling original" *Daily Mail*

THE BOOK OF HIDDEN THINGS
Francesco Dimitri

Four old school friends have a pact: to meet up every year in the small town in Puglia they grew up in. Art, the charismatic leader of the group and creator of the pact, insists that the agreement must remain unshakable and enduring. But this year, he never shows up.

A visit to his house increases the friends' worry; Art is farming marijuana. In Southern Italy doing that kind of thing can be very dangerous. They can't go to the Carabinieri so must make enquiries of their own. This is how they come across the rumours about Art; bizarre and unbelievable rumours that he miraculously cured the local mafia boss's daughter of terminal leukaemia. And among the chaos of his house, they find a document written by Art, The Book of Hidden Things, which promises to reveal dark secrets and wonders beyond anything previously known.

"*The Book of Hidden Things* shows us that memories are stories that refuse to belong only to the past"
Aliya Whiteley, author of *The Beauty*

"If you loved the Neil Gaiman's *Ocean at the End of the Lane*, this book is for you" Helen Marshall, author of *Gifts for the One Who Comes After*

07/08/18

For more fantastic fiction, author events, competitions,
limited editions and more

VISIT OUR WEBSITE
titanbooks.com

LIKE US ON FACEBOOK
facebook.com/titanbooks

FOLLOW US ON TWITTER
@TitanBooks

EMAIL US
readerfeedback@titanemail.com